SAM WOOD

THE WAKARUSA WAR

BY

HENRY E. PEAVLER

"It is not enough to have a good mind. The main thing is to use it well."
Renes Descartes

This is a work of fiction. I created dialogues, personalities and actions; I condensed dates, arranged events in an order that helped the narrative, not necessarily the way they occurred. The historical figures, herein, are depicted in the same fictitious vein as all other characters.

All quotes and verses are in the public domain.

Living Springs
Publishers

WWW.LivingSpringsPublishers.com

Cover design by Jacqueline V. Peavler

Dedicated to **Dawn, Kelly, Miranda, Ashlee, Trey**
All my love.

Acknowledgements

To write is to expose oneself to the prejudices of others and, worse, the self-doubts inherent in the creative process. Writing reveals all the warts and wounds in the mind of the author, though that may not have been his intent. It takes a unique person to advise, suggest and have the knowledge required to do so. In that vein, many thanks to Living Springs Publishers and the one person who made it successful, Jacqueline V. Peavler. Thank you to the group of early readers who take the time to make suggestions and comments. Without you I would not have finished.

Author's Note

The Wakarusa War refers to incidents occurring in Territorial Kansas during the years 1855-1858; tumultuous years, prelude to a Civil War that would decide the future of the United States. The eyes of the Nation focused on a narrow wedge of prairie lying between the Wakarusa and Kansas Rivers on the western edge of civilized America. There, a small number of passionate men and women dedicated their lives to ensure that slavery would not blight the soil of Kansas. They paid a terrible price in death and suffering.

This book is second in a series of four. I intend that each volume will stand alone. There may be references to characters in this section that seem to appear out of the ether. Most likely they are carryovers from *Sam Wood Floods of Ungodly Men*. I believe that you will have enough information within these pages to overcome any feeling of inadequacy of understanding.

I have kept cultural dialogue to a minimum using it where absolutely essential and otherwise noting that the character described spoke with a slave dialect, or Irish brogue, or southern accent, whatever the case might be.

The events portrayed have had an impact on our country well beyond the dates they occurred, just as, I assume, the events of today will impact our great-great-grandchildren one hundred and eighty years hence. My hope is that it will be for the best and not the worst.

Henry E. Peavler
January 2021

Contents

Part One

"The louder she screamed, the harder he whipped; and where the blood ran fastest, there he whipped longest. He would whip her to make her scream and whip her to make her hush; and not until overcome by fatigue, would he cease to swing the blood-clotted cowskin. I remember the first time I ever witnessed this horrible exhibition. I was quite a child, but I well remember it. I never shall forget it whilst I remember anything. It was the first of a long series of outrages, of which I was doomed to be a witness and a participant. It struck me with awful force. It was the blood-stained gate, the entrance to the hell of slavery, through which I was about to pass."   Frederick Douglass

Leavenworth, Kansas Territory

One day in late April 1855 a young man sitting alone on the bank of the Missouri River near Leavenworth, Kansas, plucked a blade of buffalo grass to chew absently as he gazed at the rushing water; the Missouri at flood, the so-called April rise, was an awe-inspiring sight. An observer, had there been one, would have marked the serene countenance, the broad shoulders, an intelligent gleam in the eyes, firm-set muscles around his mouth. Little enough evidence to mark the unrest within his mind.

He tossed a small branch into the tumult, "You think that limb'll find its way home, Sulla? Back to Booneslick?" He turned to look at the object of his inquiry. Sulla twitched his large ears, acknowledged the attention, then resumed grazing. Eric chuckled at the indifference, "I should probably just go home," a slight Irish brogue more evident than usual, a sure sign of conflict. A big sigh led to rubbing his eyes, then holding his head in hand. "What to do?" The torment within boiling to the surface. "Time to make a decision, Sulla."

Something, what he first thought was a log, caught his attention, but was gone before he got a good look. He was certain that it was a dugout canoe. "I wonder how far that thing's come? Maybe all the way from Canada." That set him to thinking. He knew that Lewis and Clark had followed the Missouri to the Bitterroot Mountains, somewhere far to the north and west, "That canoe could have come two thousand miles, Sulla. I wonder what happened to the fella that owned it? I hope he didn't drown."

The young man, so deep in thought, was generally full of a youthful confidence, partly due to his strength, standing a bit over five feet ten inches with large forearms and shoulders, a result of his blacksmithing trade. More importantly, he was well educated, could read and cipher; particularly enjoyed Roman history. He read Shakespeare, the Greek philosophers; Plato was a favorite. What is truth? Are right and wrong absolute concepts? Most pertinent to the moment, how do you determine good and evil. Oh, young Eric, the educated blacksmith, was full of seething morality and anger over what was happening in Kansas Territory. The coming of the slaveholders and Border Ruffians intent on making Kansas a slave state, evil that they called good. He was going to do something about it, not ignore the problem and hope it would go away, not Eric McCrea.

But it would be easier if he weren't married. He didn't want to do anything to endanger Katie and little Tammy, "Blast it, Sulla, what's dangerous about going to a meeting? Everyone is making too much of it."

He tossed the blade of grass aside, pushed up, feeling older than his 21 years; brushed off his britches, stepped toward the river to see if the canoe was still in sight. A glance south, nothing but rushing water. Thoughts drifted back to that morning when he left home; mother and father Tanner advised against going to the meeting. Katie was torn between her parents and her husband; Eric loved Katie, he truly did, but he stormed out of the house, "I'm going and that's final." Katie sobbed, twisting a handkerchief, her cheeks red, "Eric, please," she pleaded.

Dad Tanner leaned against the wall of the stable, hatless, his huge arms crossed, watching Eric saddle Sulla. No recriminations, he'd already warned him not to go. He simply said, "Don't lose your temper, son, just listen, don't let them goad you into anything."

Eric led Sulla out, mounted, looked down at Riley Tanner, friend, business partner, father-in-law. "I'll be all right, Dad, but if I don't stand up to the slaveholders, how can I live with myself?" Riley didn't answer, just nodded his head.

Seventeen years earlier the McCrea's, Eric, his parents, and baby sister Tammy, fled Ireland, when their absentee English landlord raised the rent on the tenant farm. They had no choice but to leave. Eric had vague memories of the rough boat ride, the rancid septic smells in the hold, the gaunt look of the seasick farmers and shopkeepers, as the ship tossed on the rough sea; he was only four at the time.

New York was not the promised land they expected. The McCrea's were mocked for their Gaelic language and few words of English. They couldn't understand a word the New Yorkers mumbled, and they were speaking English; forget the German's, Italian's and other dialects they couldn't identify on a bet. The horrible noise seemed relentless in the run-down tenement where they settled. Wives doing laundry in the alleys, offal discharged in the streets, hollow eyed men with no place to go, no chance at honest work; a cesspool of walls towering over them. New York was almost more than Mother McCrea could bear, almost broke her, still weak from the birth of Tammy and the sea voyage.

"We should a' stayed in Ireland, Killian, at least we'd starve with people we know."

But Killian McCrea was a stubborn man. He was also an enterprising man, could do anything with his hands, blacksmithing, leather work, farming, anything that needed done he could do it, or 'damn well learn how'. Mrs. McCrea resigned herself to the new world; she took in laundry, cleaned houses for the rich, cooked for them, sewed. The family worked their way west finally arriving in St. Louis with prospects brightening, a few dollars in their pockets, a respectable home and food on the table. Then tragedy, Mrs. McCrea and Tammy felled by the cholera outbreak in 1848, followed closely by Killian McCrea as much from a broken heart as the illness.

Eric, now an orphan with no prospects, only 14, was apprenticed to Riley Tanner. He was a quick study, learned the business and art of blacksmithing so well that he was made a full partner even before marrying the boss's daughter. Eric enjoyed the work, loved it actually. One problem though, his in-laws treated him like he was still an apprenticed child. They treated his wife like a little girl even though she was 19, with a year-old daughter named after her husband's mourned little sister. They were well meaning, the Tanner's, good people. They were the only family he had.

Katie and Eric wanted a home of their own; solved the problem by deciding to move to Kansas territory, but darned if mom and pop didn't invite themselves along and Katie didn't have the heart to say no. Eric suspected that she encouraged them, and he didn't have the heart to say no to Katie. When she looked at him, innocent green eyes glistening impishly, whispered in his ear with just a hint of a Scottish brogue, inherited from her grandparents, he was putty in her hands.

They loaded up the anvils, the forge and bellows, the chisels, punches, and tongs; Mom Tanner's walnut dresser and table with six chairs. The two beds, all the kitchen utensils, stacked carefully for the 120-mile trip to a beautiful spot between Lawrence and Leavenworth. Eric drove one wagon pulled by the mules. Riley the other powered by the four-horse team; the ladies followed in the brougham, pulled by Sulla. Two claims were selected, side by side, with the help of Sam Wood, Douglas County Land Registrar. Good Kansas farmland with timber at the west end and a beautiful spring along the seasonal Buffalo Creek. A blacksmith shop was constructed near the house. Filing their claim in Lecompton, Eric and Dad Tanner conferred with the well-known abolitionist, Mr. Wood, who had a profound influence on the young, idealistic man. He invited them to attend Free State meetings in Lawrence and Topeka, an opportunity they gladly undertook. Life was looking good.

The afternoon blue sky carried a few cumulus clouds scudding east. Eric imagined those clouds could be seen in his old hometown of Boonville, where the Santa Fe Trail begins. At that very moment families were traveling west to Kansas Territory under the same clouds, coming for their 160 acres of land. Very few arrived like Eric, intent on denying slaveholders the right to own another human being. There were a few people in Lawrence, Sam and Margaret Wood, Judge Wakefield and Charlie Robinson.

Eric admired them, felt comfortable around them. He didn't like the pro-slavery men in Leavenworth, men like that self-righteous General Stringfellow, who owned the Leavenworth Herald, a newspaper that printed blatant lies about the situation in Kansas.

Today's meeting was called by the Delaware Squatters Association. Riley said at the breakfast table earlier in the week, "Son, there'll be nothing but trouble for you. They already announced their meeting is pro-slavery. Why aggravate them?"

"We're members of the Delaware Squatters Association just like the slaveholders. All of us are. We have an obligation to attend. The meeting is more than just slavery, we're talking about legal rights of claims on Delaware land. You should go with me."

"Please, Daddy, won't you go?" said Katie.

"I have to get Ralph's plow blade re-shaped and sharpened. Anyway, I don't want to go. Eric's a big boy, he can take care of himself."

Tammy began fussing, she wasn't the center of attention at the moment. Katie carried the baby to Eric, playfully put her in his lap. He laughed heartily at the obvious ploy by his wife, but it worked. Katie giggled, picked Tammy up, sat back down so Eric had both wife and daughter in his lap. She smoothed his red hair while the baby sucked on Eric's little finger. "You can make a difference by voting. You don't have to go to the meeting. Those awful Border Ruffians will be there. Maisey Epcot says we don't really understand how dangerous they are, being so new in the Territory and all."

Mother Tanner nodded vigorously as she poured coffee for Riley, "They are the vilest creatures I've ever seen, filthy, don't they ever take a bath." She offered a refill to Eric; he held his hand over the cup.

Katie lifted Tammy above her head causing a darling laugh that delighted them all. Katie agreed with her mother, "They look at me in the most disgusting way when I'm at the store. I'll be glad when the new mercantile is open in Lawrence, I don't want to go to Leavenworth anymore," Katie nuzzled the baby's neck.

"Stay away from those men. They're nothing but trouble. Don't make eye contact with them and never walk down the street by yourself," Riley said. "I don't trust them."

Eric nodded, "There aren't any Border Ruffians in Lawrence. As far as this meeting, don't worry Mother, nothing can make me do anything to risk Katie and Tammy."

A loud splash brought him back to the river. He took off the hat, tugged at his hair in frustration. Katie's gaze seemed to be everywhere, tormenting him. "Maybe I should just go home." He rubbed Sulla's muzzle; the big mule searched for a carrot that Eric didn't have. "I love this country. Free land just for the taking. Think of it, Sulla. We were forced out of Ireland because we didn't own our land. Never could buy it from the English bastards that did own it, now here, in Kansas, I own the land I live on. What a great country," Eric was wearing down, losing his resolve.

Voices interrupted from the direction of Three Mile Creek. He led Sulla that way, discovered a group of boys swimming naked in the calm of the elbow before the water gushed into the Missouri.

"Hello Eric," cried Ralphie Epcot whose parents owned the claim next to the Tanner's and McCrea's.

"Hey, Ralphie, that sure looks like fun."

"It is, come on and join us."

Eric gave it serious thought before making up his mind, "Can't right now."

Ralphie clambered up the grassy bank, "Sulla sure is big. Why do you ride a mule, Eric? Most people around here ride a horse."

"I got Sulla in payment for making a wagon frame for a fella and I just kind of took to him and him to me. A mule is smarter than a horse and a whole lot less trouble. King David and King Solomon rode mules. If they're good enough for a King, they're good enough for me. Besides, old Sulla understands everything I say to him."

"Really?" Ralphie arched his eyebrows, looked at Sulla in a different light. "What does Sulla mean, anyway?" He rubbed the mule's forehead; had to stretch to reach it.

"Ralphie, don't you know your ancient history? Sulla was a great Roman general and dictator." Eric patted the white and brown hide. Sulla knew they were talking about him.

"No, sir, I don't know any kind of history, can't even read, but I'm going to learn."

The other boys gathered around, shivering in the early spring coolness; soon lost interest in the mule lesson and commenced leaping and shouting back into the water. Eric was sorely tempted to join them but developed a new determination and began walking. It was about a quarter mile to the Leavenworth Herald office where the meeting was being held; he stopped, looked around cautiously, removed a pistol from the saddlebags and placed it under his shirt in the waistband of his pants.

Ralphie caught up, barefoot, hopping on one leg pulling up his britches, hair dripping wet, "What kind of pistol is that?"

"Colt 1851 Navy."

"You going hunting?"

"I'm going to the Squatter's meeting."

"Really, I thought you were against slavery. I know Katie is, she told my sister."

"I am against slavery. In fact, I'm an abolitionist, doesn't mean I can't go to the meeting."

Ralphie pondered this for a moment while putting on his shirt, "I think it's a pro-slavery meeting. My daddy isn't going, he doesn't agree with them, he says all they do is form committees and write resolutions, waste of time. See you later, Eric." He ran, shirt tail flapping, toward the saddle shop where his father was waiting. Eric could see Ralph Epcot standing by the wagon. He raised his hand. Eric waved back. Ralphie pointed excitedly explaining what Eric was doing. Big Ralph watched him enter the open door of the Herald office.

***

Malcolm Clark hauled his fat body up on the edge of the table facing the men crammed into the spacious meeting room. He wore a dark suit, the only man in the building so formally attired other than General Stringfellow who always dressed in a beige suit and vest, gold handled cane in hand. With his trademark yellow panama hat perched jauntily, he projected the image of a southern plantation owner, which he claimed to be. Windows along the right-hand wall and the open door allowed plenty of light. The stale smell of tobacco and sweat-soaked clothes permeated the rapidly filling room.

Clark's bulldog jowls and narrow beady eyes gave him a perpetually angry look. He had a temper to match; an easy man to annoy, especially if the antagonist happened to be an abolitionist. There weren't many expected at this meeting, for sure a couple of newspaper men, possibly Bill Speer and J.B. Kennedy from the

Lawrence Tribune, maybe someone from the new Herald of Freedom in Lawrence, probably Roscoe Smithson from the Topeka Gazette. Sam Wood was in Washington, meeting with the President, and good riddance as far as Malcolm Clark was concerned. President Pierce would make short work of the bothersome abolitionist. He did not like Sam Wood any more than Malcolm did.

Clark and General Stringfellow had prepared well. The agenda was set, and the resolutions already written. He chuckled, mentally patting himself on the back for the forethought. No need wasting time in committees when 95% of the attendees would be Blue Lodge members, as the slaveholders had been calling themselves.

Clark suddenly gritted his teeth, seemed to actually growl, causing some men in the front row to look at him.

"What's the matter, Malcolm?" General Stringfellow asked removing the hat to wipe his brow, the room was becoming a bit close, especially in the front.

Malcolm waved him off, recomposed himself. The cause of his anger was the sudden remembrance of what Governor Reeder had done, invalidating the March election, when a few Missouri citizens came into Kansas to vote for pro-slavery candidates. "What was wrong with that?" he thought to himself. They had as much right to vote as some abolitionist that had been in the Territory for a couple of days. The Governor claimed that 75% of the votes were cast by Missouri citizens, a crock of bull. Then he called for a new election.

Reeder had been given an ultimatum by General Stringfellow and Missouri Senator David Atchison, sign the election results into law or hang. He said he'd hang. The pro-slavery men had to back down. Malcolm looked at the reproductions of George Washington and Thomas

Jefferson on the wall. He made a mental note to get a portrait of Senator Atchison to hang between them.

"Malcolm, it's four o'clock. Let's get started," Dennis Johnson interrupted.

***

Back in the street Ralph Epcot sat motionless in the wagon holding the reins. Ralphie watched him curiously. "What's wrong, Pa? Aren't we going home?"

"Did Eric say if Mr. Tanner was going to the meeting with him?"

"No sir," Ralphie thought for a beat then added, "He has a gun under his shirt."

Ralph looked at his son, "He has a gun?"

"Yes sir, he put it under his shirt before he went into the meeting."

"Oh, that young fool."

Ralph handed the reins over, "Wait here, I'd better make sure Eric doesn't get himself into trouble. I'll be right back." He thought of Riley and Jane Tanner, good solid people and Eric's wife, Katie. "I guarantee they don't know anything about this." Forcing himself between some rough looking characters, he was able to find a spot along the back wall. Eric stood in the other corner trying to stay inconspicuous. The room was packed.

Clark rapped a large ceremonial gavel on the table, still sitting on the front edge, his leg hiked up nonchalantly. It was an affected gesture, making him seem one of the fellows, not lording over them from a position of authority. Malcolm was all about appearances.

"Gentlemen," he called for order then pointed to his left. "Oscar, open a couple of those windows. It's warming up in here."

While waiting, the buzz of conversation started again. Clark rapped his large gavel for order, "Anyone know a good joke while we're waiting for Oscar to finish?"

"I do," one of the nasty looking Border Ruffians at the door shouted, "What do you do when you see a Nigger flopping on the ground?" No solution was offered. "Stop laughing and reload."

Stringfellow found the joke extremely funny, laughed raucously, slapped his knee, pounded his cane on the floor, causing some of the others to laugh more at him than the story. Clark smiled appropriately, "Thank you Oscar, that clears the air a bit in here. Ok, I think we're ready to begin; Reverend Larson, please."

The Reverend pushed his way through the men standing in the back, past the rows of those seated on benches, "Let us bow our heads. Dear precious Lord, we ask that you bless this meeting and all those in attendance. Lead us, Lord, as we fight the abolitionists who come here to vilify us, harass us and to steal our Niggers, our personal property Lord, in direct violation of your holy laws and the laws of this great nation. We glorify in the knowledge that you, Oh Lord our God, have sanctified our way of life with your written word. I quote from Titus 2:9." Larson opened a small bible, glanced around piously then read, "'Bid slaves to be submissive to their masters and to give satisfaction in every respect; they are not to be refractory, nor to pilfer, but to show entire and true fidelity.' We abide by your word as law, precious Jesus, in your name we pray, Amen."

Amen echoed throughout the room. Clark and Stringfellow conferred as the men milled about whispering to each other. Ralph watched Eric who seemed troubled over something, most likely the distasteful joke. Eric scowled at the joke teller, who glared back, "What you lookin' at Bucco?" Eric started toward the Ruffian but was stopped by another man next to him who held his arm out barring the way, pointing toward the front where the meeting was starting.

Bill Speer turned and acknowledged Ralph from his chair near the table, a notebook in hand to record the meeting. Only a few Free State men were in attendance. Ralph recognized 'Tap' Tappan and Harold Barnett from Lawrence. The rest were pro-slavery, many of them from Weston in Missouri. He truly did not enjoy these meetings. They spent too much time talking, not enough time accomplishing things. Ralph didn't own slaves, was against the practice, but wasn't going to get involved except for voting; he believed there were enough Free State men to vote the slavery issue down, if they didn't get into a war over it first.

Clark banged the gavel on the table, "We'll have Niles Brooks from the resolutions' committee read the minutes of the meeting, then vote to approve the resolutions as written."

Brooks was a diminutive man who began in a halting voice, "The committee formulated these statements..."

"Speak up Niles, I can't hear you," someone shouted from the back.

He cleared his throat and began again, louder, "The committee has formulated these statements with the intention of presenting them to Governor Reeder, posting them to President Pierce and, of course, publishing them in all of the newspapers," he smiled at General Stringfellow, who nodded dismissively.

"First of all, be it resolved, that abolitionism has been rebuked and discomforted. Free-soilism has been crippled and overthrown. Kansas has declared loudly and decisively in favor of slavery. That Kansas is to become a slave State will admit of no doubt. The question has been decided. Her fate is sealed, and what has long since been the hope and prediction of the pro-

slavery party will soon be history. This was affirmed in the recent Territorial Elections, fraudulently challenged, without basis by Governor Reeder."

"Objection, Mr. Chairman," Eric shouted. All heads turned his way.

"Who is that?" General Stringfellow strained to see the offender.

"It's young McCrea, that new blacksmith," Clark patted the General on the shoulder calming him as if to say, 'moderator Clark has the meeting well in hand'.

"This is not a legal proceeding Mr. McCrea. Please keep your comments to yourself. Continue, Niles." Clark glared at Eric.

"But that statement isn't true, it's a damned lie. The Governor has called for new elections."

Stringfellow turned to Clark, "Throw that troublemaker out."

"You heard the General, now either leave or stay quiet. These matters don't concern you."

"There is no need for that kind of language in a public place, young man. It is beneath our dignity," Reverend Larson wagged the bible for emphasis.

"Beneath our dignity?" Eric sneered, "Keeping slaves in chains is beneath our dignity. I don't think a word carries a candle to that sin."

"I agree with Eric," Harold Barnett shouted.`

Reverend Larson was aghast at this afront. He prepared to launch into a sermon before Clark interrupted him, "Ignore them Brother Larson, we have other matters to attend. Niles, go on and don't stop this time."

Brooks seemed a bit rattled, applied his own handkerchief to brow before he could resume, *"Be it resolved, that we invite the inhabitants of every state, North, South, East and West, to come among us, and to cultivate the beautiful prairie lands of our Territory, but leave behind you the fanaticisms of higher law and all kindred doctrines; come only to maintain the slavery laws as they exist, and not to preach your higher duties of setting them at naught; for we warn you in advance, that our institutions are sacred to us, and must and shall be respected."*

He stopped reading, glanced toward the troublemaker, in violation of Clark's instructions. Eric stepped forward when the men around him moved aside, "How can you write resolutions when we haven't even had a dialogue about the issues? Even Sulla, a Roman Dictator, allowed discussion."

A ripple of laughter washed over the audience causing moderator Clark to snarl in anger. He slid off the table and pointed the gavel at Eric, "You keep your comments to yourself, boy. You're going to bite off more trouble than you can chew. Roman dictator," he mocked, "I've never heard such rot, you stay out of this, McCrea. One more word from you and there are men in here who will throw you from the room." Again, he rapped the heavy gavel on the table, causing the nervous Brooks to flinch. The jokester glowered at Eric, "He's talkin' about me, Bucco, name of Johnson. Another word and out you go."

"He's got a right to speak," Harold said, causing Clark to rap the gavel again. People were starting to mutter.

"Be it resolved," Brooks said quickly, glancing nervously in Eric's direction, then reading rapidly. *"That the institution of slavery is known and recognized in this Territory, that we repel the doctrine that it is a moral or political evil, and we hurl back with scorn upon its slanderous authors the charge of inhumanity, and we warn all persons not to come to our peaceful firesides to slander us and sow the seeds of discord between master and servant, for, much as we may*

deprecate the necessity to which we may be driven, we cannot be responsible for the consequences."

Bill Speer turned around, caught Ralph's eye and nodded toward Eric. Maybe Ralph could ward off trouble.

Eric shoved his way through the crowd, hand up to halt the proceedings, before Ralph could fight through the gawkers to stop him, "I protest this resolution. I want to include my comments in the report, a minority report. I know there are other Free State men here who support me. Mr. Speer, Mr. Epcot, Harold, Tap, I know you don't agree with these lies."

He pointed at each man as he approached the front, then turned to the audience, his back to Malcolm Clark who was seething with rage, face a furious crimson. Clark raised the gavel, "Out of order, out of order," he screamed, slamming the club down on Eric's head, a loud thud that caused those nearby to flinch. Stringfellow cried, "Oh Malcolm, no!"

Eric fell to the floor, badly stunned; Clark continued after him, swinging, angered beyond reason. Eric pulled the pistol, rolled over and fired, knocking Malcolm Clark back onto the table. Witnesses shocked, motionless; Eric scrambled to his feet, bumping men aside, stumbling, running. Arms reaching out, clutching at him, legs tripping, "Katie, Tammy," he cried.

***

Bill Phillips tented his hands, the two index fingers resting against his upper lip. He leaned back in the chair, eyes raised to the ceiling, "*My Dearest Mary,*" he dictated slowly, "*Words cannot adequately convey my love,* are you getting this Mrs. Bronson?"

"Yes Mr. Phillips, I am getting it, but thank you for speaking slowly?"

Good clerical help was difficult to find in Leavenworth, Kansas Territory. Mrs. Amy Bronson was the only remotely qualified candidate and while she had studied the fundamentals of Pitman's Shorthand, she was far from proficient.

"Where was I?"

"Cannot adequately."

"Oh yes," again, the tented hands, deep in thought, *"Shall I compare thee to a summer's day? Love is not love which alters when it alteration finds, or bends with the remover to remove. O no! it..."*

Amy put the pencil down, accompanied by an emotional sob, "Oh, Mr. Phillips, your words are so beautiful. Mary is the luckiest wife in the world," handkerchief raised to her eyes.

"Well, they're not really my words..."

She interrupted, still sobbing but with pencil poised, "I'm so sorry, please continue."

Bill smiled, "Let's take a break, Mrs. Bronson, we'll finish the letter later. We need to work on the Blankenship deed, anyway."

"When is Mrs. Phillips coming to join you?" she asked daubing at her eyes.

"Probably start this way next month, the house is almost finished."

Amy gazed at him fondly, secretly in love, forever to be unrequited; Bill was deeply devoted to his wife. Not that Amy would have been a temptation, in any regard, being twice his age at fifty-five; a widow with two grown spinster daughters living at home. Thin as a pole with a great beak of a nose, puckered lips that seldom smiled, Amy didn't attract much male attention.

Bill wasn't an overly handsome man, himself, but he exuded confidence with a relentless approach to life that made him seem commanding. His anti-slavery views were well known in Leavenworth causing immense unpopularity from a majority of citizens. He was not well liked, however, those with the same political views, while a minority, were finding their way to his office regularly. He would be better off, that is among people of like mind, in Lawrence or Topeka, but Sam Wood was in Lawrence and Cy Holliday in Topeka. They had a monopoly on the legal work in those areas.

The letter he was dictating to Mary would contain an all clear to begin the journey from Massachusetts with her brother as escort. Bill was appalled at the riffraff gathering along the Missouri border, but he didn't consider them a valid threat. So far all they had done was harass him verbally, no real danger to Mary.

One person he managed to offend was the owner of the Leavenworth Herald who, a few weeks earlier, sent an office clerk across the muddy street, offering a special rate on advertising in the paper. Bill scoffed, "I wouldn't be caught dead advertising in a pro-slavery rag, especially one that's got more misspellings than facts."

The clerk, a small round man with bald head framed by bushy hair above the ears and muttonchop beard, hustled back across the street, stepping gingerly, mud clinging to his shoes, straight to General Stringfellow. The comment was reported, word for word. Stringfellow made the poor man repeat the offensive statement twice before commenting, "He may get his wish."

Phillips found the whole thing funny, but insignificant. His clients felt just as he did about the matter. Then to spice up the whole affair, Bill's clientele doubled when his name, 'William A. Phillips, Esq. Attorney at Law', was on a list of businesses the newspaper published as being anti-slavery, therefore un-

American. Banner headlines shouted: AVOID THESE YANKEE BUSINESSES—TRAITORS ALL!!

Bill had a good laugh, circled the two exclamation points, underlined his name, then had Mrs. Bronson paste the article in the window for all to see. He commissioned a sign posted on the front of his office. William A. Phillips, Esq. YANKEE ATTORNEY AT LAW!!! And added three exclamation points for emphasis. The General said to his clerk, "That man needs to be run out of town on a rail."

"Mrs. Bronson, it's 4:30. Let's close early. Go on home to your family. We'll work on that deed tomorrow."

There would be no argument from the prim clerk, she refiled the Blankenship documents, began tidying the office. If nothing else, Amy was fastidious, an important qualification in Bill's decision to hire her.

"Shall I fill the water cask or wait until the morrow, Mr. Phillips?"

BOOM! A loud explosion, a gunshot, startled them, "That was across the street."

Amy ducked behind the filing cabinet as Bill cautiously peered out the window. Men were spilling from the Herald office, obviously in a panic. One man ran wildly, watching over his shoulder, a gun waving in the air, disappeared around the corner of Main and Leavenworth. A large white and brown mule carried the same man back into sight, turned south, disappeared in the distance. He opened the door, "Stay here, Mrs. Bronson." He ran across to the Herald office found Malcolm Clark, a local businessman, sprawled on the floor, Doctor Mills attending him. General Stringfellow glanced up, saw Bill in the doorway, pointed his cane and shouted, "Murderer."

Phillips looked around, the General was pointing at him.

***

Westport, Missouri
Ten Days Later

The Polar Star pushed off the docks at Lexington, Missouri early the morning of May 10, a Friday. With a hiss of steam, clank of the pistons, the side wheel slapped the Missouri River into a froth. Spring floods had receded enough to allow travel up the channel rather than seeking the calmer waters along the bank. Sam took the forward stairs to the bow, glanced up at the steam billowing from the twin stacks, smoke trailed behind as they passed the downstream flatboats, barges and paddle wheelers. He leaned against the Jack Staff, calculated their speed at about five miles an hour putting them into Westport Landing near ten AM. A pleasant breeze, plus no other passengers nearby, made it a good spot for deliberation. Out from his vest pocket came the Leavenworth Herald newspaper article to be read for the third time. The pro-slavery papers always exaggerated, but they usually contained a modicum of the truth. This news was staggering in its implications. The dock agent in St. Louis put a letter from Margaret at his disposal along with a letter from Bill Speer that held this newsclip.

A FOUL AND DIABOLICAL MURDER.
A USEFUL MAN HAS FALLEN BY THE HANDS OF A VILLAIN.

It becomes our sad and painful duty to record the death of one of our most respected citizens, Malcolm Clark, who was killed on Monday last by the vile and infamous scoundrel known as McCrea, the leader and mouthpiece of the Abolitionists. The facts of this fatal tragedy, as far as we have been able to learn them, are as follows: During a meeting held on Monday last, in pursuance to a call made through our columns, for the purpose of considering the propriety of extending the time to all squatters holding claims on Delaware lands, the order of the meeting was frequently disturbed and the speakers insulted and arrested in the course of their remarks by certain vulgar and impertinent outbursts from this same despicable villain, McCrea. For his obtrusion and ungentlemanly conduct at a meeting in which he was no way concerned, he was reprimanded, as he should have been, by Malcolm Clark, and respectfully requested either to leave the meeting or desist in his unjust interference with its proceedings. This he would not do, but continued in this same course, regardless of all advice and admonition, until a resolution had been declared carried (some fifteen minutes after the reprimand) by the vote of the meeting, which the perfidious villain pronounced to have been effected by gross fraud, although not affecting him or his interest. To this assertion, Malcolm gave the "d___d lie," which was followed up by McCrea in the most violent and abusive language. At this stage of the controversy, Malcolm Clark became exasperated, and offered to strike McCrea, when he received a fatal shot from the villainous hands of the dastardly Abolitionist. We were not present at the meeting, and consequently did not witness this sad and horrible occurrence, but when we heard the report of pistols and saw the rapid flight of the murderer, we hastened to the spot, and never shall we forget the scene there presented. Our very heart sickens, our very blood chills in our veins, when we recall the scene to our memory. We think we see before us the body of the dying man struggling and writhing in the agonies of death. We think we hear his dying cry ringing in our ears. We think we behold the ruthless monster McCrea standing up confronting us with that same hideous and malignant scowl which his countenance bore after the perpetration of this hellish deed. The murderer is now incarcerated at Fort Leavenworth, and God grant that the fiend whose murderous hands committed the foul and atrocious crime - the wretch whose hands are steeped in blood - be made to suffer condign retribution. The vile monster McCrea shall meet the just penalty of the law. He shall be hung by a rope of HEMP.

"Leader and mouthpiece of the abolitionists, despicable villain, vile monster?" is this the same young man I escorted around searching for a proper claim, along with his father-in-law, Riley Tanner? Whose beautiful young wife greeted me in their home with coffee and sweet bread, young daughter on her hip? No semblance of that idyllic scene echoed from these harsh, incriminatory words.

"I'm not even sure he was an abolitionist," Sam thought to himself, unaware that it was his own words that had motivated Eric. He glanced across the river, eyes vacant, fingers rubbing the article as if he could erase the incriminating words.

Other passengers began strolling about watching the solitary man ruminating in the morning shade of the wheelhouse. He was hatless, wearing a pale-yellow shirt stained with morning coffee from two days earlier, braces holding up brown woolen trousers. His boots were un-shined, common in his life when away from home. He was a little short of average, stocky and well formed, with large hands and legendary strength; considered a handsome man by most. Sam was robust of body and mind; but these malicious words caused him pain, a physical pain, making him sick to his stomach. He paced the foredeck, stopped at the rail, glanced down at the paper in his grasp. Eric McCrea was someone Sam knew; the thought that this could be the same young man he had met, grown fond of; this monster described in the paper was beyond comprehension.

He pulled another article, this one from the Lawrence Herald of Freedom.

UNFORTUNATE SITUATION IN LEAVENWORTH

We mentioned last week a shooting affair at Leavenworth, and that great excitement had grown out of the transaction. On the 30th ult., a dispute arose between Malcolm Clark and Mr. McCrea, during which the former felt himself insulted, when he assaulted the latter and gave him a severe blow over the head with a club. Mr. McCrea, feeling that his life was endangered, drew a revolver and shot Clark dead upon the spot. In a country where law and order predominate, no court or jury could be found which would not decide that it was a case of justifiable homicide, and McCrea would be liberated at once; but, as matters are in Kansas, we presume it will be magnified into a great outrage, and every means will be resorted to convict him of murder. A particularly odious description of the event was 'reported' in the Leavenworth Herald. It will thus be seen that readers on either side might find an account to suit their tastes.

The same facts and a young father, may hang because there are more who believe the worst, not based on evidence and a trial but on emotion and politics. What a crazy world, Sam shook his head in frustration. Guilt arbitrated by popular sentiment and not the facts. Letters from McCrea's father-in-law, Riley Tanner, were also in his possession; begging him to come back to Kansas and take over the defense for Eric. He knew he had to do something.

"Imagine a man standing in a pair of long boots, covered with dust and mud, drawn over his trousers, the latter made of coarse, fancy-colored cloth, well soiled, the handle of a large bowie-knife projecting from one or both boot-tops; a leathern belt buckled around his waist, on each side of which is fastened a large revolver; a red or blue shirt, with a heart, anchor, eagle, or some other favorite device braided on the breast and back, over which is swung a rifle or carbine, a sword dangling by his side; an old slouched hat; with a cockade or brass star on the front side, and a chicken, goose, or turkey feather sticking in the top; hair uncut and uncombed, covering his neck and shoulders; an unshaved face and unwashed hands. Imagine such a picture of humanity who can swear any given number of

oaths in any specified time, drink any quantity of bad whiskey without getting drunk, and boast of having stolen a half dozen horses and killed one or more abolitionists, and you will have a pretty fair conception of a border ruffian, as he appears in Missouri and in Kansas."
John H. Gihon, 'Geary and Kansas' (1857)

Elvira Brooks was enjoying the pleasant weather from the hurricane deck when she spotted her Lawrence neighbor, Sam Wood, gazing at the view. Elvira, a plump lady, short, with a perpetual smile sincere as the spring day, treated everyone with good cheer. She hurried down to the main deck to say good morning. The blue sky sparkled on the spring wildflowers bursting into color along the banks of the river as they glided toward the Kansas frontier. Such a marvelous day. She assumed that Sam was enjoying the same thoughts.

"Beautiful sky today, ain't it, Mr. Wood?"

Sam looked at her, confused for a moment because he had no idea of the condition of the day.

He glanced slowly around, folded the article back into his pocket, "Sorry, Elvira, I hadn't noticed, but now that you mention it, it is beautiful and those are pretty Indian paintbrush flowers," picking the only name of a flower he could vaguely remember.

Mrs. Brooks squinted at the near shore with no indication of the blooms named.

"Sam Wood, you just don't much care about nature do you? There ain't a Indian paintbrush one on that hill."

Sam gave Elvira the boyish grin, mischievous glint in his pale-blue eyes that made him look years younger than his age; eyes rimmed in dark blue that gleamed with delight or burned dark with rage, depending on his mood, "Guilty as charged, Elvira. Margaret has tried to teach me about the flowers and trees since we've been married. I'm a hopeless cause."

She plopped her plump body down on a barrel roped to the railing, smoothed her skirts, smiled at Sam, ready to visit, her favorite pastime and Sam's least. "I read in the paper about your meeting with President Pierce. I guess it didn't go as well as we'd hoped."

Sam sighed, resigned himself to the interruption, gave her his full attention, "No, it didn't. I'm afraid Pierce has already decided that Kansas will be a slave state. Clarke Pomeroy and I did our best to change his mind, but he's inflexible about it. The Southern States are putting a lot of pressure on him."

"That murder in Leavenworth sure isn't going to help matters," she said, grabbing at her bonnet threatened by a sudden gust of wind.

"Do you know the details of what happened?"

"Only what I read in the paper. Those awful pro-slavery papers never tell the truth. Did you see what the Leavenworth Herald wrote?" He pulled the article from his pocket, held it up in affirmation. She nodded, "I think that McCrea's wife came to Lawrence last week looking for you. Did you hear about what happened in Parkerville?"

Seeing that it would be a while, he sat down next to Elvira, crossed his legs and prepared for the news, "No, what happened in Parkerville?"

"Evidently they wrote an editorial agreeing with Governor Reeder voiding the March election."

"A Missouri paper complimenting Reeder? I'll bet that set the Border Ruffians off."

"You don't know the half of it, not just the Ruffians, everybody went crazy. First, they gave the owners, one of them is Mr. Parks, you might remember him, he's a cousin of Mr. Tappan's." She grabbed at her bonnet, finally taking it off as the breeze freshened, "Anyway, they gave the owners three days to get out of town or suffer the consequences." She inclined her head, giving him to understand that the consequences were ominous, whatever they might be. "Then they proceeded to tear apart the printing press, threw the whole thing, type and all, into the river. Then burned the building to the ground. Can you imagine? So much for freedom of the press," she finished with a flourish, her face flushed with exertion and proceeded to re-fit her bonnet, eyeing the trees to gauge the wind and snugged it tightly to prevent a re-occurrence.

Sam sat patiently waiting until it was apparent she was finished with the story.

"Did they?"

"Did they what?"

"Did the owners get out of town?"

"Oh my, yes! They skedaddled out of there faster than you can swat a fly; probably still running east. Those Border Ruffians mean business."

"Elvira, there is going to be a war. I feel it coming and I mean soon." He paced a trail in front of her. "We can't continue like this with a Free State Government writing laws and a pro-slavery government writing other laws, and nobody following any of the laws. People killing each other on a whim, just because they disagree, then no consequences for doing so. Anarchy, pure and simple."

"But we're the anarchists, Sam. We're breaking the laws."

He stopped pacing, scanned her face for a sign of sarcasm. Of course, she was right, in that sense. The laws of the land favored slavery.

"Maybe civil disobedience would be a better way to phrase it. Eh, Elvira?"

"What are we going to do Sam?"

He resumed pacing, "Continue what we're doing, I guess. Charlie is scheduling another Free State convention in Lawrence in June. The first thing I'm going to do is help Eric McCrea. He's a fine young man, I can't let him hang for murder if it was self-defense. Something provoked him. I plan on looking into the details when I get back to Lawrence."

Is Mrs. Wood meeting you in Westport?"

"No, I wish she were, I miss her terribly. I write every day when I'm gone, you know?"

"I know you do, Sam, you two lovebirds are the cutest couple I've ever met. You're welcome to ride to Lawrence with me and Mr. Brooks. Our wagon and team are at Littlejohn's stables."

"Thank you, Elvira, John T is supposed to meet me. I'm going to Bill Speer's house to pick up a few things we need at the Tribune office. Hello, look who's here. Paul, Jay, good morning."

"Have you two solved all the problems in the Territory?" Paul asked

"We're working on it, aren't we Elvira? Jay, it's good to see you. How long will you be with us in Lawrence?"

"I don't need to be in Athens until October, Mr. Wood. I want to he he..." his stutter got the best of him.

"Take your time, Jay," Paul put his hand protectively on his brother's shoulder.

Paul Brooks was more of a father than a brother to Jay. Their parents died some years before, leaving Paul as head of the family. Jay attended a boarding school in Cleveland prior to joining the Brooks in Lawrence to help Paul and Elvira start their new mercantile.

"Help fight the Border Ruffians," he stammered.

"We hope that won't be necessary, right Sam?"

"I was just telling Elvira that the President considers Kansas already a slave state. I'm afraid we're in for rough time trying to get a fair election. A letter from Charlie Robinson tells me we're going to convene a new Free State Legislature in June. The Pro-Slavery boys are meeting right now at Shawnee Mission and won't allow any of the Free State candidates who won their District a seat at the table. Then this murder in Leavenworth. I'm afraid we may be in for it."

"I, I, I'll do my part," Jay sputtered. A slight boy with wispy blonde hair and a lisp in addition to the stutter; Jay had a stubborn resolve in his eyes, serious about helping. No speech impediment was going to hinder him.

"We'll need every man we can get," Sam shook Jay's hand with enthusiasm.

"How's the new mercantile coming Paul? I'm glad to finally get a store in Lawrence. It'll be nice not to drive to Blue's or worse yet, to Westport, for supplies."

"It's going well, but I worry that our prices will be a lot higher than McCoy's, because of the transportation costs. That's why we were in St. Louis, working with the Graham Grocery Suppliers and Russell, Majors and Waddell Teamsters. We're finally getting some produce from local farms around Lawrence and Topeka. I think we'll be fine in the long run."

"Jay, what are you studying at the University."

"I'm gonna' study law and go into politics, m, m, m, maybe I'll be president someday and I'll end slavery b, b, b, by executive pro, pro, proclamation."

"That'll start a Civil War for sure, brother," Paul said.

"Jay graduated at the top of his class," Elvira said, grasping his hand in the same protective way Paul took with the boy. "Now going to the University, we're so proud of him."

The steam whistle screeched signifying their arrival at Westport Landing. Sam said goodbye to the Brooks family, promising to get together in Lawrence so Jay could meet the family.

"I think you'll enjoy meeting my family," Sam said, allowing Elvira to pass in front, "my sister is about your age, I think."

Elvira turned back, "Sam, Sarah is 21, Jay is only 17."

"I, I, I'm old for m, m, my age, a, a, almost 18." Jay corrected stuttering even more at the thought of meeting Sarah Wood.

"Well, Sarah's young for her age," Sam sighed, picturing his capricious sister.

"I can't argue with that," Elvira giggled, "but she is a sweet girl."

"The boys are always looking for new friends. Maybe you can help Margaret with their reading lessons."

The Wood boys were the feather in the hat for Margaret and Sam, not the glue; they would have been a contented couple even childless. The boys were as different as their mother and father, David, eight, short and stocky, like Sam; Lloyd, six, took after his mother physically, delicate features and slim. The differences were most evident in their personalities, David contemplative and cerebral, given to thinking things through, analyzing a situation. Lloyd more like Sam, barreling through life, reacting to situations as he confronted them, not worrying about the consequences. A more dedicated father would be tough to imagine, but like all busy men, it was hard to find quality time with his children.

The Wood family was comfortable in Lawrence; better off than most. Sam knew it. His income was substantially augmented by abolitionists in the East such as Amos Lawrence, namesake of the town. With more settlers arriving weekly, the legal work started to increase. They were not wealthy, but not destitute as many of the poor farmers. Those from Pennsylvania traveled over twelve hundred miles, dragging their farm equipment, household fixtures and families, expecting to arrive at the Garden of Eden on the Kansas prairie. Brutal reality slapped them in the face; harsh winters, thin soil, tornados; drought or flood drove many a dream-broken family back east or further west with hopes of striking it rich in the goldfields of California.

***

"That the Negroes were enslaved more than other races, and on a large scale, is evidently a result of their being, in contrast to other races, inferior in intelligence - which, however, does not justify such slavery"
Arthur Schopenhauer, On The Will In Nature 1788-1860 German Philosopher

Sam grabbed his luggage and his cane; jogged upstairs to the hurricane deck, said goodbye to Captain Morris Barker, "See you next trip, Mo."

"Sam, we're going to start a regular route into Lawrence next month. Part of the contract with Graham Suppliers to take shipments as far as Topeka."

"Paul Brooks was telling me about it. Come by the house when you dock. We always have room at the table."

Sam bade the officers goodbye then carefully examined the docks for any suspicious characters before disembarking. A necessary precaution as his reputation grew. He was vilified by the Border Ruffians, hated by the slaveholders, feted by the abolitionists, tolerated by his friends who found him difficult to work with and revered by those who recognized his passion. Sam made as many enemies as friends.

"Sam... Sam Wood, where you headed?" John McCoy shouted.

"Are you going back to Westport, John?" Sam asked, "Can I catch a ride with you? I don't see John T anywhere."

"Come on, my buckboard is across the street, I was just getting ready to leave. Paul, Elvira, hello. Are you coming by the warehouse?"

"Did our shipment arrive?"

"Yes."

"Then we'll be there in about an hour."

McCoy, an early settler in Westport, owned the largest mercantile and supply house in the area, in addition to the Westport Landing docks. He didn't look the part of a successful businessman, short with grey hair combed over his bald head, wearing ragged old clothes more suited to working on the docks than owning them. He was pro-slavery yet affable, not militant about his beliefs, which would not be good for business. McCoy liked Sam because there was nothing 'fake' in his personality. Sam wore his feelings on his sleeve, and everyone knew where they stood with him, just the kind of man John McCoy admired, regardless of his politics, and Sam felt the same about him. McCoy's horse and wagon sat in front of the Riverside Hotel, a shabby plank board building with a crudely painted sign announcing rooms by the night or week.

A middle-aged lady, years of hard life etched in lines around her eyes, sat nonchalantly smoking a thin cigar in a second-floor window watching the commerce below. She wore a red chemise with black thigh-length stockings.

An outraged mother shielded her son's eyes as they scurried past, "How can you allow that vulgar woman to display herself so improperly, Mr. McCoy?" She didn't await an answer, dragging the poor boy by the arm to a waiting brougham. He was struggling mightily to see what the fuss was about.

"I don't own that hotel," he answered, but she was too far away to hear. He glanced at Sam who just shrugged and placed his satchel on the ground prior to loading it into the wagon bed.

John Thompson appeared, seemingly out of nowhere, shouted, "Sam, get down."

He dove under the wagon and rolled to the other side as a shot rang out. Dust kicked up from the street where the bullet smacked into his satchel. Thompson barked, "upstairs window," pointing at the third story of the hotel. Sam glanced up, staring into the barrel of a Sharps rifle. He sprang to his feet and sprinted for the entrance to the hotel.

"I'll go upstairs," John T said, pulling a pistol. "Go around to the outside stairs."

Sam nodded, glanced up to check the window and ran toward the alley on the left side of the hotel. People were ducking in the street and along the jetties, taking cover where they could, some actually watching the drama unfold. A shot fired in the middle of the morning was unusual, even in the rough and tumble town on the frontier border.

John T reached the third floor, searched for the door to the room where the shot was fired. The back door was open, two men dashed down the outside stairs, four steps at a time. "Sam, watch out, they're coming down," he bellowed.

Sam rounded the corner as the men reached the ground. The first swung his rifle like a club. Sam ducked but took a glancing blow on the shoulder that sent him sprawling, a sharp pain numbed his arm; he tried to trip the second man who stumbled over the club; the man turned and fired a wild pistol shot splintering the corner of the hotel. Sam clambered up slowed by the numbing wound, gave chase running into bystanders trying to get out of the way.

"Stop those men," he shouted, grimacing with pain, holding his shoulder. John T was sprinting across the street to the docks, toward a bateau that was just pulling away, poled by two tough looking Border Ruffians, obviously waiting for the assassins. Leaping into the boat as it swung away from the docks, the men reloaded, spotted Sam, aimed and fired. Sam dove behind a cotton bale well before the shots rang out. "Get down," he yelled, "is anyone hit?"

"You stay down, Sam, they're shooting at you," Paul Brooks shouted.

McCoy came running up with a rifle, aimed at the boatmen who quickly ducked below the stern walls. He lowered the rifle without firing as the boat picked up speed in the current, two men at the oars, disappearing around a large steamboat.

"Did anyone recognize them?" McCoy asked.

"It lo, lo, looked like they were wa, wa, wa, waiting to ambush you, Mr. Wo, Wo, Wood."

"Yes, it did," John T agreed, "Welcome home, Sam," he put his arm on Sam's shoulder.

Sam pulled away, wincing, although the feeling was starting to return in his fingers, "Not the parade I was expecting."

"You need a doctor?"

He rotated his shoulder, "No, I'm fine. Just confused. Who knew I'd be here today?"

"We got a report that someone was going to try and get you," John T explained, "I've been waiting around to see if I could spot them. Let's find out who rented that room."

The hotel clerk was standing in the doorway watching the excitement; he readily opened the hotel registration book revealing that a Gary Blackwell had rented the room.

"I know who he is," McCoy said. "He just bought a large farm in Franklin. He's a slaveowner, got seven or eight slaves working on his place."

Sam said, "The excitement's over, gentlemen. Let's go about our business and we'll investigate this Blackwell when we get back to Lawrence. John T, I'll ride into Westport with Mr. McCoy. I need to stop by Speer's house and then I'll walk down to the store and meet you there."

Sam picked up his damaged bag, shook his head in frustration as the sweet smell of Lavender water seeped out of the battered luggage. The only casualty of the ambush being a bottle of perfume for Margaret. McCoy started the wagon rolling toward the hills. Westport was located about four miles from the river back into the woods, well above the floodplain. He asked, "Who is that boy with Paul Brooks?"

"That's Jay Brooks, Paul's brother. He's been at a boarding school; I think in Cleveland."

"What's the matter with him?"

"You mean the stutter?"

"Yeah, it's a chore listening to him."

"I don't know what causes it, John, but it doesn't affect his brain. According to Elvira he's a top student. Going to the University of Ohio in the fall."

"Well, the Brooks are good people. I hope they make a go of their store in Lawrence."

"Aren't they competition for you?"

"There are so blamed many people moving into Kansas that I can't keep em' all supplied. I'm opening another store in Kansas City, I ship goods over to Seth Hayes in Council Grove. Everything we get has to come from St. Louis. You wouldn't believe some of the stuff these eastern tenderfoots pack in their wagons to drag a thousand miles west. Most of it ends up dumped along the trail before they get 200 miles from here. I've written a little pamphlet detailing the dangers, describing what they need to take on the trip. And I built a warehouse to hold their furniture until they can afford to have it shipped to them."

"I've heard there are pianos and such scattered from Kansas to California."

"Oh, Hell, Sam, harps, expensive wood chifforobes, books and letters, tools. People don't have a clue about the terrible weather, lack of water. A lot of them die from snakebite. But they keep coming, just like they have for 30 years. The difference is, a lot of them are staying here, or in Kansas."

"Your docks seem to grow every time I come through."

"It's been a good investment, much better than I anticipated back when we bought this land from the Prudhomme estate."

"John, can I ask you a question?"

"About what?"

"About Gabe Prudhomme; who murdered him?"

"For Heaven's sake, that was over twenty years ago. My daddy got blamed for that murder. It wasn't true, but it hurt him that anyone would think he had something to do with it. Daddy was a preacher; did you know that?"

Sam shook his head no.

"Well, Francois was involved in that mess also, but…"

"Francois?"

"Chouteau"

"Pierre's brother?"

"Yes, you know Pierre, right?"

"I met him once. He spends most of his time at his trading post in the Dakota Territory, doesn't he?"

"No, actually, he lives mostly back at their place in St. Louis. Anyway, Pierre's brother Francois was one of the first settlers in Westport with my daddy, back in the 30's. In fact, his widow is Berenice."

"I know Berenice," Sam's eyes widened, "She runs a store over in Independence."

"Exactly, and she's involved in creating The City of Kansas with me and a few others, wants to call herself 'the mother of Kansas City'. But to get back to my story, Francois was a partner of Gabe's also, but no one ever accused him of anything evil," John looked at Sam.

"You suspect him of something?"

"I didn't say that. I'm just saying that something happened, and Daddy got blamed for it. He wrote a letter to the Prudhomme heirs, back east. I've still got a copy of that letter somewhere. You know how kids are when they get something for free. They couldn't wait to sell the land. Daddy told them they could probably get more if they hired an agent. I've still got the letter, Sam, if you want to read it."

"I believe you. I'm kind of a history buff, that's all. I was just curious; Prudhomme would have been rich since he owned all this land around here, just seems mighty suspicious that he wouldn't sell and then the next thing you know, he's dead."

"Things haven't changed much, have they? You almost got shot today and the same things' happening over in the Territory isn't it?"

"It is. I'm probably going to defend Eric McCrea on the murder charge in Leavenworth. We're doing everything we can to create a legitimate state legislature and enforce the law, but it's an uphill battle. These Border Ruffians are some mean SOB's."

"You know I'm more sympathetic to the slaveholder's, Sam, I don't give a damn about the Negroes, but I will agree that the Border Ruffian's need to be driven from this country; scares me every time one of em' comes in my store. Those men that shot at you are the meanest cusses I've ever seen."

"Why worry, John, you can always call on Sheriff Jones if there's a problem," Sam said with a wink.

"Hell, he's the worst of the lot," John laughed, "Sam, you've got to go a little slower on your Tribune editorials, the slaveholders are good American citizens and friends of mine. And anyway, there have been slaves all through history. The Romans had more slaves than citizens."

Yeah, and they threw their girl babies into the Tiber, you want to follow that custom too? I'll tell you the same thing I tell everyone. Just because some other culture practiced slavery doesn't make it right. They were just as wrong as America is."

John clucked at the horses urging them up a sharp rise, "Everyone knows the Negro race is inferior by nature, it's been proven time and again, scientifically. The Negro just doesn't have the same brain capacity as the white man. I've got some fine articles on the subject in my office if you want to read them. One is by a French fellow Arthur De something or other."

Sam shook his head, interrupted John's lecture, "Not everyone believes that John, I certainly don't, what about someone like John T? I know you like him."

McCoy sighed deeply and spoke as if he were addressing a child who couldn't understand his lessons, "You can train a dog to jump through a hoop or sit up and beg, and you can teach a Negro how to behave in public, that don't make them intelligent, they just repeating what they been taught, like a good dog. You take that fellow, Frederick Douglass, why everybody knows Lloyd Garrison feeds him every word he writes or says."

"No, he doesn't, I know both Garrison and Douglass very well, if anything, Fred Douglass is smarter than Lloyd. I had a meeting with them in Rochester, New York just two weeks ago, before I met with President Pierce."

"You seem to know everyone."

"You'd feel differently if you could meet Douglass. He's a brilliant man."

Sam picked up his satchel, rummaged through it.

"That smells like a St. Louis whore. What is that?"

"The shot broke Margaret's perfume bottle. Ah, this survived, my new pen. Look at that John, what do you say, pretty fancy, huh? Picked it up in Washington."

"You didn't have to go back east to get a new fountain pen, Sam. I have whole selection in the store."

"I'm sorry John, didn't know that."

The four-mile ride to Westport passed quickly with the conversation sociable, as was expected, no resolution and both men adamant in their position. Sam never missed a chance to try to change the minds of the pro-slavery advocates, if they were reasonable enough to listen. John McCoy was just such a man.

The wagon creaked to a halt in front of Bill Speer's home, situated on a slight incline above Main Street. John set the brake, turned to Sam, "Now let me ask you a question. Aren't you afraid of dying?"

Sam started to laugh but choked it off when he saw that McCoy was serious. "What do you mean?"

"You just got shot at, came within a few inches of being killed, yet you act like nothing happened. Aren't you afraid?"

He picked up his satchel, placed it on the bench, stepped down from the wagon before answering, "No, I'm really not. I guess I should be, but my wife tells me I'm going to live to a ripe old age, die in her arms. She's usually right about things like that. She's got some kind of direct line to the big guy." Sam pointed to the sky.

John chuckled while reaching for the brake handle, "Well, after today, I'm inclined to believe Margaret; either that or God's protecting you for some reason."

"Seemed more like John T was protecting me. Thanks for the ride and conversation, John."

Bill Speer's modest wood-framed home was whitewashed, the yard pleasant. Grass and potted flowers reflected the orderly personality of his wife, Linda, busy carrying buckets of water from the well to water the plants. Sam enjoyed the beautiful vista from the road before turning toward the house.

"Hello Sam," Linda smiled as he stepped away from the wagon. She waved at McCoy driving off.

"Mrs. Speer," he nodded affably, opened the gate and sat on a bench near the walkway. "Bill home?"

"He just walked down to the store," she pushed a lock of hair from her forehead. "He went to get some flour for supper. I hope you'll stay; I want to hear about the meeting with the President."

"I'd like to take you up on supper, Linda, but I'm riding back to Lawrence with John Thompson this morning. The article in the paper pretty much summed up the meeting with the President, except it wasn't mentioned that Jefferson Davis was there. Those men are not our friends. In fact, I'm afraid that they might be behind the Ruffians who just took a shot at me."

"Someone shot at you?"

"Sammmey," Speer shouted from the street, "My Prince of words, I heard that you just about met your demise at the hands of hired assassins?"

"Just did. If it wouldn't have been for Thompson..."

Speer held his hand up to interrupt, "I've already heard the story; John T is waiting for you at the mercantile. He's loading some supplies for your wife and some of the other ladies in Lawrence. You always stir up trouble, Sammy that's why I like partnering with you."

"I'm glad I'm of some service to you, Bill. Thought I'd stop by here to get the new plates for the printing press."

"Too late, I carried it to Lawrence last week. J.B. was getting impatient. I'll be in town Wednesday morning, and we'll finish the week's edition. You write up the assassination attempt. You think the President is behind it?"

"I sure hope not. My bet is Bogus Jones and David Atchison are behind it. What about this McCrea situation?"

Speer turned serious, handed the flour to his wife, sat down as did she, not wanting to miss any of the news, "Ralph Epcot tried to stop Eric, but he was too late. Eric was intent on having the Free State point of view included in the record; he wasn't belligerent or threatening, just forceful. Clark clubbed him on the head when Eric had his back turned. The shot was more a reflex than anything. Maybe he shouldn't have been carrying a gun, but no question it was self-defense. It was a terrible thing to see. We barely got Eric out of there without him getting strung up. He's being held at Leavenworth; we're waiting for you to enter a plea next week when the Judge holds court. But you haven't heard the latest."

Sam crossed his legs to be more comfortable, "What?"

"The mob in Leavenworth decided that a fellow by the name of William Phillips, a lawyer, do you know him?"

"No, what about him?"

Well, they decided that this fellow, Phillips, gave Eric the gun and the murder was premeditated. It's not true, but Clark's friends gave Phillips an ultimatum to get out of town by next week or they're going to lynch him."

"I hope he left," Sam said.

"I don't think so, he was pretty adamant that he is not guilty; leaving would imply guilt. Just arrived in the territory, I don't think he understands that being an abolitionist in Leavenworth is considered actus reus, guilty as charged."

Sam bade his goodbyes, strolled down the dusty street to meet John T at the mercantile. A new saloon caught his eye on the corner across from McCoy's, at what was, for all intents and purposes, the crossroads of the Oregon and Santa Fe Trails. John T was packing the wagon and said, when he spotted Sam approach, "Well, you're just in time, as usual. I already finished loading."

"Sam laughed, "Did you stay in Westport last night when I didn't show?"

"I stayed at Brother Robinson's over in Blue Valley, or as the white folk call it, Niggertown. I see where your meeting with President Pierce didn't go very well."

"They already consider Kansas a slave state. Clarke Pomeroy and I set them straight on the matter, but it didn't do much good. I think the only thing they'll understand are guns and bullets. I guess today kind of proves the point."

"Mr. Pomeroy is a good man," Thompson placed the last bolt of fabric in the wagon.

"He's a good spokesman for our side, well-respected in Washington. He was a Senator from Massachusetts you know, acquainted with everyone. He introduced me to Jeff Davis. There's a man I don't like much."

"Sam Wood," Harold Barnett shouted from the new saloon. "I saw you walk by, come on and visit a spell."

"I feel like a lemonade. What do you say, John?"

"Wait a minute, Sam, let's have one here at Mr. McCoy's, we've had enough trouble for one day. Harold can come over here."

Sam laughed as he started across the street, "But I haven't given my toast in there; we need to baptize it." John had no choice but follow; he somehow knew it would turn out badly.

Inside was crowded with men, some Border Ruffians, some pioneers on their way west, a few locals just trying out the new saloon. Sam walked straight to the bar, had the bartender pour three lemonades from the large jug sitting on the counter. He handed one to John T, one to Harold, then to the customers announced, "Gentlemen, I don't drink alcohol, but I'd be honored to buy a lemonade for anyone who'll drink with me, I'm Sam Wood, and these are my friends, John Thompson and Harold Barnett, a toast to the abolition of slavery in every state of the Union."

The bartender, Clarence, placed both hands palm down on the bar, "Mr. Wood, I don't want no trouble and we don't allow colored in here, your Nigger'll have to wait outside."

"He's not my Nigger, he's my friend."

"Sam, you fool," Harold laughed, "you're the only person I know crazy enough to pull this stunt. I'll join you, but I ain't drinkin' lemonade. I'll have a beer, Clarence." He turned to the crowd, "Come on boys, I know there are more Free State men in here, don't be shy, come on up and join us."

Several men rose and joined them at the bar, some drinking lemonade and some having whiskey or beer.

"What the hell is this, Clarence, you lettin' Niggers in here? And low-life, scum abolitionists spoutin' off about shit they don't understand. What the hell is this country comin' to?" one of the Border Ruffians said from the bar near where Sam stood. He was a large man with an unruly beard flowing down to a barrel chest with crisscrossed bandoliers and a brace of pistols; an imposing sight, the other men backed away slowly leaving John T, Harold and Sam alone at the bar.

"I just opened this place and I can't afford to have it busted up, ya'll go outside," Clarence begged.

"I've got no quarrel with this man... excuse me, these gentlemen," Sam added, as two more joined the first. "I doubt they even own any slaves, do you?" The men declined to answer. "That's what I thought. You're just stooges of the landowners who want free labor. Try thinking for yourselves, why don't you? How would you like to be chained up and beaten with a whip, worked like a mule, day and night? We've got to end slavery right now or we're gonna' have a war. Let's do it the easy way." Sam finished his lemonade, set a silver dollar on the bar. The Free State men cheered.

John T said, "Let's go back to Lawrence."

"Good idea, my friend, I've been gone for a month and I miss Margaret in the worst way. Harold," he said shaking hands with his friend, "I'll see you in Lawrence. When are you going back?"

"Right now, I'm leaving with you."

They stepped into the bright sunshine suddenly slammed with a discord of sights and sounds, of shop keepers, drunkards, Border Ruffians; of freight wagons, prairie schooners, a few Conestoga wagons lumbering by, horses, mules and oxen; pioneers stocking their wagons for the long journey west.

Sam loved being a part of it, knowing that his quest to end slavery was the most important mission in America, now or ever. He knew it with all his heart and believed, as Margaret guaranteed, he was destined to make it happen. Her premonitions were legend. Regardless of the outcome, the Woods were right in the middle of the battle; the meeting with the President assured that fact.

Just the thought of his beautiful wife stirred warm emotions in Sam, regardless of where he was. He pictured her smile, waiting on the porch in Lawrence, her arms around the two boys, auburn hair pulled back, a red ribbon gracefully tied, blue eyes radiant in the light. Sam was a happy man, very important when trying to solve the problems of an entire nation.

"Wood, you Nigger lovin' son-of-a-bitch. You insulted me and my friends, now you got to apologize."

Sam, startled out of his reverie, found the three seedy looking men facing him on the sidewalk.

"Oh hell," Harold said, preparing for battle.

"Gentlemen," Sam replied calmly, "I was just thinking about my beautiful wife. Please step aside, I'm anxious to get home. If I insulted you, then you have pretty thin skin."

"We fixin' to put a stop to you and your kind. You won't be so quick to insult if you're dead. Apologize or we gonna' finish what they started at the river, then kick the shit out of your Nigger."

Sam stood looking at the men, frustration growing by the second. "I've been shot at today, clubbed to the ground by a man who looked just like you, so this doesn't surprise me at all. As I said inside, John is my friend, he's a free man, not owned by anyone and he takes great umbrage at your insinuation he's a piece of property, isn't that right, John?"

"Ahhh, well... I," John stammered, honestly wishing to be left out of the equation, as did Harold. However, both men prepared to back Sam up; they were accustomed to his escapades.

"This is why we need to end slavery, so that you will treat this fine man with respect. He is NO ONE'S Nigger. And I'd like to see you whip him, yessir, I'd truly like to see that, because he could lick the likes of you and not even have to pack a lunch."

John glanced sideways to see if Harold had a response to that grossly overstated thought. He didn't seem to.

Stepping forward, crowding the goons, Sam warned, "Now step aside or face the consequences. It will be your fault because I'm a Quaker and don't condone violence."

The men looked at each other, astonished, not knowing whether to laugh or back down. When they confronted someone, the victim withdrew as fast as possible; this was not normal, what kind of a crazy man was this Sam Wood?

Finally, one swaggered, "Are you gonna' talk us to death or apologize like we said? You won't be so smart mouth when we wipe your kind out of Kansas. We're organized and you ain't. You're just a runty little ignorant son-of-a-bitch, and I don't like ya."

Sam removed his hat, handed it and the satchel to John, "It usually takes people a lot longer to decide they don't like me," he sneered, "but I don't have any more time to spend on garbage like you, you serve no purpose other than doing the bidding of the slaveholders. You are worthless trash and I don't like you either."

The deranged looking fellow with mangy hair sticking out of a soiled hat, pulled a knife from his boot and before he could get it waist high, Sam grabbed his wrist. With his free hand Sam clutched the man's shirt and set his powerful legs churning. Sam drove him over the hitching rail, held the screaming man's legs on one side of the rail, then using his cane, clubbed his ribs until he screamed in agony. The two friends started forward to intervene, John and Harold stepped between them. John merely shook his head no. Sam turned, threatening the remaining two with the cane. They backed away quickly.

"I hold you men responsible for this," Sam shepherded them up against the building. "Now I'm dirty and hot. I've a mind to whip the two of you just for good measure. You vermin have no right to be here, get a job or go back where you came from, whatever you do, stay away from me or by all that is Holy, I will kill you."

They stood with hands on pistols looking at each other. Sam stared them down not more than three feet apart. The wounded man lay moaning in the street with a large crowd gathered around. The Ruffians measured the odds; relaxed their hands, palms up in surrender. Sam backed away slowly and climbed into the wagon. They drove off, Harold riding alongside.

John McCoy watched the brawl from the store. As the wagon passed by McCoy smiled, pointed at the sky, then back at Sam, "Tell Margaret I want her to read my tea leaves," he shouted.

***

They exited the hills, rolled through the trees onto the prairie above the Kansas River; the wind picked up, the tall grass swayed, there was a slight chill in the air. Harold related his version of the Eric McCrea matter confirming Speer's narration, corroborating Sam's opinion that it was truly self-defense.

"What did that fellow mean, they are organized and we're not?" John asked.

"Oh, he was just spouting off," Sam dismissed it with a wave of his hand.

"I don't know about that, Sam. When I was in Leavenworth, there was some talk about Atchison and Stringfellow hiring the Ruffians, forming up a company of troops to attack Lawrence."

"Attack us for what?" John asked pulling the team around a big Conestoga wagon parked halfway in the road, California Here We Come written on the side, "You folks need some help?"

"We're just watering the animals," a lady poked her head out of the bonnet followed by two young girls. The father stepped around the oxen team with a bucket of water, "Thanks for asking, but we're fine."

John tipped his hat, urged the horses on, "That wagon is too big for where they're going."

"They'll break an axel before they get to Council Grove," Harold agreed.

"Why would they attack us, Harold?" John asked again.

"They hate Yankee Town. Think we're the cause of all the troubles in the Territory."

"They're pretty much right about that," Sam agreed.

"I don't think we can ignore the threat, those men are here for one reason, to make sure Kansas is a slave state. Whatever their motivation, they are dangerous. We need to expand Caleb's militia and what about James Lane? He seems like he might be a good commander."

Sam wasn't convinced, "Those Ruffians couldn't organize themselves into a card game. It would take someone like Atchison. He has the money to do it, but it's hard to believe a sitting United States Senator would do such a thing." Sam leaned back, put his satchel and cane into the wagon bed, almost falling off when they hit a deep rut. "You want me to drive, Mr. Thompson," he laughed "Did you hit the only rut in this road on purpose?"

John and Harold had a good chuckle while Sam rubbed his hip, "I'll have a bruise for sure."

"It'll match the one on your shoulder."

Sam returned to the subject, "Lane was organizing the Democrats when he came into the territory and now suddenly, he's an abolitionist. I don't buy it. I want to meet with him myself, get a feel for the man. You don't just change your stripes overnight. He's up to something."

"Charlie's saying the same thing, Sam, but we need to listen to Lane. He's got the experience. He's had a change of heart just like Governor Reeder did."

Harold Barnett exuded strength, well over six feet, broad of shoulder with a thick patch of blond hair. He was friendly to all, but quick to take exception over insults or slights of any kind. Harold was a modest dirt farmer with not much to show for it except a happy marriage to a devoted Shawnee Indian woman and five kids that he loved unconditionally. When strangers called his children half-breeds, he could no more turn the other cheek than he could not love them. The name caller lived to regret it. The Barnett family never missed church, much to the dismay of Reverend Lum. Harold was a devout man saddled with a never-ending litany of questions originating from his curious wife. She did not object going to the Christian church but insisted on understanding the inconsistencies. If God is all powerful, why doesn't he just make everyone good? How was Jesus able to rise up, if he was dead? Reverend Lum was a patient man but ducked around the corner when the Barnett family approached. The citizens of Lawrence considered Harold a good man to have on their side. John T and Sam counted him a valuable friend.

The conversation faded as they approached Lawrence; the only sounds were the wagon rattling and creaking of the harness as they reached Blue Jacket's Trading Post where Barnett peeled off, "I forgot flour and coffee beans in Westport. I sure hope Blue has some or I'll catch hell when I get home."

John made his goodbyes, drove steadily on for the short trip to Lawrence with time to think. He found himself doing that quite a bit as he grew older. Sam nodded off; the man could sleep anywhere, anytime. 'I love the guy, as much as any man can love another,' John thought to himself. He and Sally spoke of it often; their lives entwined with the Wood family. Sam's 'Nigger' was how the outside world saw it and even some of those in Yankee Town who mouthed abolitionism yet harbored the same deep-seated prejudice as the southerners. A good many people, while they didn't want slaves in chains, didn't want to live with them either; a fact of life, just have to deal with it. John knew this, as did every black man in America. Sam assured him that would change with time, but Sam didn't know, couldn't know, not being black. John held his chestnut hued arm out to contrast it with Sam's pale skin, glanced around furtively, surrounded only by the prairie, then had a good laugh at himself.

Life in Kansas was never dull for the Thompsons, the only colored family in the Territory when they arrived in the summer of '54', if you didn't count the Indians and most of them could pass for white. There were quite a few more black people now. Life was difficult, trying to survive on the frontier, more so for poor colored, free or slave. John was fortunate finding work in the village because of his carpenter skills. Sally worked all day keeping the household running. She was an excellent seamstress making all their clothes, including a lot of custom work for Lawrence families; those who could afford it. Skill with the needle kept her busy. The added income was nice. 'I forgot to ask Mr. McCoy about those new sewing machines I've heard about,' he thought to himself. Sally might even expand her dressmaking business if they could afford to get one.

She was writing a book at night. A journal of the slaves that escaped through Lawrence on the Underground Railroad. John was beyond angry over the horrible stories he heard from the brutalized fugitives who spoke in a numb monotone, as if they were reciting the details of a picnic rather than terror at the hands of a heartless owner. Sally was his rock, a former slave herself who was illiterate when they met, but she learned to read and write, leaving him behind in the knowledge department. He loved her with all his heart and truly didn't know what he would do if someone did her harm.

"What you thinking about so deep?" Sam stretched, rubbed his eyes and reached for the water bag.

"I thought you were asleep. I was just thinking about Sally, don't know how I'd manage without her."

Sam nodded "I know exactly what you mean," offered the water, taking the reins while John took a long drink, wiped his mouth, handed the bag back.

John said, "I've been thinking about getting Sally one of those new sewing machines."

"A sewing machine, what's that?"

John shook his head in amazement, "For someone who reads the paper as much as you do, how can you be so ignorant."

"You'll have to excuse me Mr. Thompson, sir, I've been busy trying to save the world, mostly, your people.

"My people?" John sneered, "Aren't they just people?"

Sam laughed, "Our people, then. I don't have a lot of time to keep up on all the modern inventions." Sam was oblivious to many things, forgetting birthdays and anniversaries. His mind focused on the task of making Kansas a free-state, fighting off the Border Ruffians, dodging assassination attempts, creating a legitimate Kansas legislature and keeping Missourians out of Kansas come voting time. He couldn't do it without John and Sally. They gave him the inroad he needed to the enslaved who would otherwise shun him like they did every white man. Plus, the Thompson's were the Woods best friends, not unheard of in America, but unusual.

David and Lloyd Wood, Caleb and Missy Thompson were playing in the street, when they spotted the wagon bringing their daddy's home. Both sets of youngsters ran lickety-split to rouse Margaret and Sally to the homecoming. Sam smiled at the sight of his wife and kids standing on the porch in the exact pose he envisioned in Westport.

"What?" John asked.

"Just glad to be home, my friend. Thanks for coming to fetch me. Oh, yes, and for saving my life."

"I came more for these supplies than for you," John kidded.

Sam ran to the porch scooped the boys up in an embrace then enfolded his wife into a family hug. The boys kissed him dutifully, started to run back to their friends, "You boys help John unload," Sam ordered.

"Yes, Pa," not with enthusiasm.

Margaret held him longer, an impish gleam in her ocean blue eyes, "I'll save my kisses for later when we're alone," she giggled.

"I missed you so," spinning her around like a feather, "I almost jumped off the boat and swam home when we got stuck an extra day in St. Louis.

Margaret wore her dark skirt, no bonnet, with a new red and white patterned apron made by Sally. Her auburn hair wrapped in a bun, cheeks with just a glint of color. Sam nuzzled against her neck, "Did you get my letters?"

"I cherished every word, missed you terribly, Sam. We've so much to tell you, but first, tell me about meeting with Franklin," arm in arm she guided him inside.

"Not much more to tell, the article in the paper was pretty accurate. He won't listen to reason when it comes to slavery..."

"No, silly, I know all that, I mean what is Jane like? Does she come out in public? I've heard that she had to go to an asylum after their son was killed in the train accident. Imagine what it must be like to lose a child."

"Meg, I didn't see the President's wife. I'm sure she's devastated over the death of her son, but we didn't discuss his personal life. Pierce looks terrible, I don't know if he was sick. He'd been drinking and we met in the morning. I was glad to get out of his office. Jeff Davis caught me in the hall and said that they would do everything they could to make Kansas a slave state. I believe he was trying to warn me of something, then someone took a shot at me in Westport."

"WHAT?" Tears welled in her eyes.

"The worst part is they broke the perfume bottle I bought for you," holding the satchel for her inspection. She started crying.

"It's alright, Meg, I'll get you another one."

She slapped his shoulder laughing, then crying at the same time, "Oh, you mean thing, you know that's not what I'm upset about. What would I do without you?"

The back door burst open. Sally and John rushed in, "My God, it's true isn't it. Someone tried to kill you?" Sally was crying as she went to hug both Sam and Margaret.

Then the front door opened with Sara and Charlie Robinson barging in, "We just heard the news. How bad were you hit?"

Sam looked as surprised as everyone. "I wasn't hit at all, Charlie. John T saved my bacon."

Sara took Margaret in an embrace, "Well, we need to get the word out because the story is that you got shot."

Sam and John spent the rest of the evening describing the assassination attempt to the neighbors. The Brooks family arrived for introductions of Jay, who was cornered by Sarah Wood, ushered outside then joined by all the children arriving with their parents. Sarah was horrified at the responsibility of supervising, when all she wanted was to talk with her new friend. Jay could barely get a word out in front of the beautiful girl, "Tha, Tha, Tharah," he lisped and stuttered, all to Sarah's delight. She had, and deserved, a reputation for immaturity, but, in truth, she was just burdened with a heavy emotional load of compassion. She cared deeply for everyone, especially those who were seen as different or odd. It was her duty, so she decided, to remedy the speech impediment of her brand-new friend, Jay Brooks. Sarah had a fresh purpose in life.

Tap and Marlee Tappan were the last to go, about eight that evening, leaving Sam and Margaret alone for the first time since his return. They lay in each other's arms past midnight, embracing, loving, sharing; Sam recounted the news from their family in Ohio; Margaret the happenings in Lawrence. She lightly caressed the bruise on his shoulder, "I'd better get to sleep; Sally and I are taking the kids on a picnic tomorrow. We're going to Mr. Branson's farm to pick some strawberries. Do you want to go with us?"

"I've got to finish writing the Shannon article before I meet with Bill and J.B. Say hello to Jacob and Chuck for me. Tell them I haven't forgotten them. I'll ride over there in the next few days."

***

Tap's wife, Marlee, was, in fact the first cousin of Mr. Park, the man run out of town in Parkerville. Marlee sent a letter home to her family in Illinois to find out his status. She was quite concerned because the news locally was that Mr. Park could not be located. Her letter provided a glimpse into life on the frontier as well as the inquiry as to her cousins' safety,

'...things are much better this spring but there are still men and boys who have no "woman cook." They live in tents or lean-

tos in the woods. We help as much as possible, especially with the children. Those who can afford it are buying beef of men who bring it in almost daily from the prairies in the vicinity; it is the best beef I ever found outside a city stall and has the advantage of being fed in the open air, with a wide range and plenty of water. Five dollars the hundred pounds, the whole creature, or five cents the fore, and six cents the hind quarter is the common price.

Three mail routes were established connecting Lawrence - a route from Westport to Whitfield passing through Lawrence and Osawatomie to Ft. Scott, and a third from Kansas City to Lawrence. Blanton & Litchfield also established a semi-weekly line of hacks between Lawrence and Kansas City. The frame hotel on Main street, which was commenced in the fall, was boarded and ready for customers; a clothing house was opened on Main street by Wright & Ballou, the "New Great Western Clothing House." a barber, Mr. Leis, came to town and saw a fine field for operations and concluded to stay; the first brick was made by Hammon & Page; and to supplement the labors of the barber a dentist is rumored to be looking at sharing space with him.

We are planning a wonderful celebration for the 4th of July. I'm sorry to report that the incident involving Cousin Jed is not isolated and there have been several murders as well as assaults on Free State men in all sections of the Territory. We never go anywhere outside of Lawrence without being with a group of friends.'

Marlee received word that Mr. Park was safe and sound back in Illinois. He would not be returning to Kansas.

***

Lawrence woke to a cool spring rain postponing the picnic plans for Margaret and Sally. Sam walked up the hill to the Tribune office shrouded by a canvas rain cover, documents shielded under his clothes. He rushed through the door spraying water everywhere, to the delight of Speer and J. B. Kennedy.

"You look like a drowned rat, Sammy."

Sam put the papers down freeing his hands to hang the wet cover on a hook behind the door. The office was cluttered with articles, research books, the printing press, shelves of type, all for what they called the 'library'. The center piece was a table with eight chairs used for town meetings, reporting the news, but most importantly for laying out the week's edition.

J.B. was a perfect fit for the Tribune, a correspondent not afraid to print the truth, passionately anti-slavery, motivated by Amos Lawrence and Eli Thayer of the New England Emigrant Aide Society to go west and help change the course of history. J. B.'s response was, "How can any newspaperman turn down an offer like that?"

Bill Speer looked the part of a newspaper editor wearing long sleeves, a green visor covered his bald head, ink from the roller stained his clothes. He continued sorting articles from various neighboring papers, carefully indexed for future use, "Woody, did you finish the story on our new czar, Governor Shannon?"

"I have finished that story, the story of the attempt on my life and written both my columns," Sam displayed the documents. "What have you two done to contribute to the cause?"

Speer and Kennedy talked over each other protesting the implication of being idle. Sam handed over the Shannon story; the two men sat side by side silently reading the article, more editorial than reporting, but that was Sam's way and it sold newspapers.

"WILSON SHANNON REPLACES ANDREW REEDER AS GOVERNOR"

By Samuel N. Wood
"President Pierce continues the Federal Government attempt to turn Kansas into a slave state by appointing Wilson

Shannon, former governor of Ohio, as the new Governor of Kansas Territory, replacing ousted Governor Andrew Reeder, who had the audacity to uphold the democratic ideal of fair and honest voting, in a place where the powers that be demand the vote shall be predetermined in favor of a Slave State. Shannon's primary claim to fame is that he has an older brother, George, who was a part of the 1804 Lewis and Clark expedition and poor George, God rest his soul, became lost and wandered aimlessly in the wilderness for weeks on end, not once, but twice, a condition that, I fear, will plague and define his younger brother, Wilson, our new Territorial Prince.

You will remember that Governor Reeder angered his friends in Washington by announcing that 70% of the votes in the March 1855 elections were fraudulent, made by Missouri citizens voting in Kansas. One precinct along the Kansas-Missouri border had 148 registered voters and reported a total of 620 votes. Our very own 'Tap' Tappan protested that he didn't mind a little graft and corruption but 'recording four and a half times more votes than there are voters was too much, even by Washington standards'.

So, what did our illustrious President, Franklin Pierce, do about this matter, did he invalidate the elections? NO! Did he chastise corrupt Senator David Atchison, the leader of the Border Ruffians? Again, NO! Did he congratulate Governor Reeder on a job well done? Again, and Again, NO! He fired Andy Reeder, unceremoniously, and set the Border Ruffians after him, forcing a frantic escape down the river to safety, I know, because I helped put him on the boat.

Are you listening Mr. President? You approved the Kansas-Nebraska Act, and in that document, it states that Kansas will be a Free State or Slave State based on a vote of its citizens, NOT the vote of the Border Ruffians, NOT the vote of the slaveholders from Missouri who flood into our communities like ants to a sugar cookie. Yet you have ratified the fraudulent March election and that illegal group of bogus legislators has convened in Shawnee Mission, a town hanging over the edge of Missouri, for God's sake. This is an outrage.

Be advised, Sir, just as Mr. Pomeroy and I told you at our meeting in May, we, the TRUE Citizens of Kansas, will not allow these illegal actions and will do whatever is necessary to ensure that only the votes of Kansas citizens will be counted.

"That'll get the riff-raff stirred up, Sammy," Speer said laughing. "I'll bet we get a visit from our friend, Bogus Jones, when this hits the eastern papers. By the way, did you read what that fool, Senator Atchison had to say about us?"

"Now what?"

"Where's that article, J. B., I just had it out a minute ago?"

"Right here. I still can't believe a United States Senator would say such things. I'll read it to you,

"...we can tell the impertinent scoundrals of the Tribune that they may exhaust an ocean of ink, Their Emigrant Aid Societies spend their millions and billions, their representatives in Congress spout their heretical theories till doomsday, and his Excellency appoint abolitionist after free-soiler as our Governor, yet we will continue to lynch and hang, tar and feather and drown, every white-livered abolitionist who dares to polute our soil." The Honorable David Rice Atchison United States Senator, Missouri

"Good Lord, lynch and hang... the frightening thing is he means every word of it. He probably hired those men who took a shot at me."

"Of course, he means it, Sam," Kennedy replied, "I'll guarantee you that Atchison was involved some way. I'll bet he had Bogus Jones arrange the whole thing. We're gonna' have to protect ourselves."

Sam knew he was right. The Territory was boiling with discontent and the abolitionists had no recourse, no one to maintain law and order, except themselves.

"Things are going to get ugly in Lawrence," Speer said.

Death is the most terrible of all
things, for it is the end, and nothing is
thought to be either good or bad for the
dead. Aristotle 384-322 BCE
"Nicomachean Ethics."

After escaping the mob, Eric rode Sulla hard all the way home, constantly checking the back trail; apparitions of a hard charging posse obscured his vision. Anguish contorted his face as images of Katie and Tammy flickered through his mind; self-recriminations of grief, each ending in a question of why? At one point, as he paralleled the Missouri, a fleeting thought of jumping in crossed his mind, let the water carry him away.

"Tammy, Katie," he cried again digging his heals into Sulla, frightening the animal who had never felt Eric's anger. Riding recklessly into the yard he launched out of the saddle, crumbled to the ground, crying out his guilt, too distraught to enter the house. Jane and Katie flew to him, panicked, fearing he was mortally wounded; seeing only that he was deranged. It took Katie and Jane together carrying him into the house before they could get the entire story. Katie raced to the blacksmith shop to fetch Riley, expecting a mob to show up at any moment. Finally, about ten that night they decided nothing would happen until morning. Riley resolved that Eric would turn himself in, there was no other recourse, "The Leavenworth jail is under construction, he'll have to go to the fort and surrender there. They can hold him until the trial."

Jane tiptoed around the matter, obviously not satisfied with that strategy. She was as distraught as the others, but always more levelheaded when a crisis was at hand and this was the worst crisis they ever faced, "I think we should consider another option."

Riley sat down expecting a strategy consistent with his plan. He was shocked at her suggestion. "Eric needs to run away. He should go back to Booneslick and stay until this blows over. There will be mobs looking to lynch him." She took the baby from her mother, "You'll have to go with him, Katie."

Eric sat motionless staring blankly at the table, devoid of emotion or energy.

Riley was adamant, "No running away, face it like a man. If he's innocent, as he says, then justice will be done. It has to be resolved legal or he'll be a wanted man the rest of his life."

No one slept that night.

Next morning, Jane prepared a large breakfast not knowing when Eric would get another good meal. The four of them sat silently picking at the food. Even the baby watched quietly in her grandmother's lap sensing something terribly wrong, "Tata, Tata," she begged Eric to pick her up; he did, but squeezed her so hard that she cried, as did her Tata.

The time came to leave. He held Tammy sobbing, refusing to let Mother Tanner take her. Katie tried to keep from crying. He stammered his apologies for the final time, begging their forgiveness. Not once did Dad Tanner say, 'I told you so'. Eric wished that he would.

They left for the 10-mile ride to the fort and another emotional parting. This time Eric clung to his wife until the escorting soldiers were forced to take him physically in hand. Then, when they applied the handcuffs, Katie began sobbing hysterically; tear-reddened eyes, wearing the long black dress normally reserved for church, she crumbled to the floor, her life ruined, her daughter fatherless. When the escort turned the corner, Eric glanced back one last time, his face a contorted veneer of pain.

Finally, Dad Tanner and the Lieutenant joined to lift Katie gently, helped her into the wagon for the trip back home. She leaned against Riley, riding in silence.

The village of Leavenworth was in an uproar. An informal hearing held by General Stringfellow found a witness claiming that William Phillips slipped the pistol to Eric McCrea on his way into the meeting. The witness, a fellow by the name of Johnson, who was stationed at the door as a bodyguard during the Delaware Squatters Association meeting, claimed to have a perfect view of the deadly transaction.

This new information, Stringfellow argued, meant the murder was pre-meditated and Phillips was just as guilty as McCrea. Stringfellow used the accusations as fuel for the fire, not just against the murderer and his accomplice, but against abolitionists in general. Abolitionists, the evil meddlers who wanted nothing more than to eradicate slavery. The mob was ready to lynch the murderer McCrea, but that would be difficult given his incarceration at the Fort. On the other hand, Phillips was roaming the streets a free man, stirring up citizens with denials of his involvement, even going so far as to claim that McCrea acted in self-defense. The citizens, all friends of the murdered Clark, worked themselves into a frenzy at these lies. A committee was appointed, resolutions and proclamations written, a delegation sent to Phillip's office. He was given 48 hours to clear out of Kansas Territory or prepare to suffer the consequences.

Bill Phillips sent Amy home with orders to lock the door, don't say anything to anyone, keep the girls away from the windows. Handkerchief clutched to tear stained cheeks, she rushed into the street, too frightened to look anyone in the face. Bill rode to Ft. Leavenworth, demanded to see the commanding officer.

"I'm innocent," Bill said. He was sitting in General Will Richardson's office. "Here is an affidavit from my clerk, Amy Bronson, attesting to the fact that she was with me in my office when we heard the shot fired. This is ridiculous, General."

Throwing his hands in the air, Richardson said, for the second time, more forcefully this time, "Mr. Phillips, I have no jurisdiction in this matter. I believe you, but what do you want me to do?"

"I want protection from those crazy Border Ruffians. And General Stringfellow, if he really is a General, which I doubt, and Dennis Johnson, the insane dentist, acting like judge, jury and now he wants to be the executioner. They're going to hang me."

Will sat back calmly, waited a moment while Phillips composed himself, then leaned forward, "In all earnestness, Mr. Phillips, I advise you to leave the Territory. Today, right now, go back home, go west to California, I don't care where, but go, I cannot protect you."

***

Margaret's father, Bill Lyon, Sam's brother, Stephan Wood and John Thompson built Sam and Margaret's home, the first wooden structure in Lawrence, about two blocks from the river on the east side of Massachusetts street. Located across from the Free State Hotel, which was under construction yet again after the original Hay Tent had burned down last February. John Thompson won the contract to excavate the basement. He employed several Negroes, mostly free men with the papers to prove it, but a few were fugitives. The Thompson home was well known, within the black community, as a safe refuge on the Underground Railroad.

Lawrence was growing despite the hardships. The tent city that typified the early beginnings gave way to new wood homes, even a few stone and concrete structures. The Brooks mercantile was a welcome addition, along with a barber and a dentist. The school district had recently been created; Tap Tappan taking on the administrative duties which included imposing a tariff on each household for books, supplies and desks.

Sam was involved in every committee, trial, town assembly meeting and some domestic disputes he probably should have avoided. He was founding member of the Atheneum Club, a sort of literary society that functioned more as a men's club than library. They met in the Hay Tent hotel until it burned down, then in Charlie Robinson's house, much to the chagrin of his wife, Sara, finally in the Tribune office.

Sam was a founder of the new Republican Party, replacing the Whigs, Free-Soilers and Liberty Party. He was a representative on the National committee planning the 1856 convention in Philadelphia; he was writing the town charter; corresponding with abolitionists all over the country; writing articles for the New York Tribune. He never traveled without pen and paper even roaming throughout the Territory. In the early days he was often forced to sleep out on the ground; now there were sufficient settlers throughout the region, he could always find a friendly table or a sheltered bed for the night if too far to make it home before dark.

The McCrea trial was the most significant task at the moment. Sam saw Eric's defense as a symbol of what was happening in the Territory, the fight for just and fair enforcement of laws, fair trials and fair elections. Events in Kansas Territory were a referendum on good and evil just as Eric had surmised. Sam felt the same, though not through the philosophical lens of Plato or Socrates, but in the real-life struggle between slaveholders and abolitionists. Sam and Margaret had long ago given up trying to understand the mentality of the slaveholders, how they could justify keeping their fellow man in chains. An evil so absolute that it was beyond reason, yet, the fact remained, they did keep them in chains. As far as Sam was concerned, that practice would never advance into Kansas Territory. In truth, he was going to ensure that slavery was eradicated throughout the United States or let there be war. He welcomed the commencement, it was inevitable, the sooner the better.

Eric languished in jail for three weeks before Riley Tanner and Katie McCrea could meet with Sam to plan the defense. Katie visited her husband three times a week which was all the military command would allow. Eric had regained his confidence, assuring his wife he would be acquitted. "It was self-defense, Katie," describing in detail the entire incident, "You know I would never shoot anyone unless I had to."

His newfound confidence was primarily due to the meetings he had with his attorney. "You're innocent, Eric, you've got to act that way," Sam explained. "Word gets around. If you behave as though you are guilty, then that is the perception the prospective jury will hear. Stand tall, man, shout your innocence. Tell the guards you regret it, but you had no choice."

Eric gazed through the barred windows into the courtyard of the military facility, "I can't get over the fact that I killed another man, Mr. Wood. It eats at me every night. His kids will grow up without a father. I think of my Tammy, how she would feel."

Sam listened quietly, understanding, as any father would, but reality had to be dealt with, not philosophical conjecture. "Eric now is not the time for this. You can worry about Malcolm Clark's immortal soul after the trial. I do want you to think of Tammy and Katie, but only because you have to prove your innocence and get back to them. Do you understand?"

A court date had not been set for the preliminary hearing, partly because Judge LeCompte was fearful of arraigning Eric anywhere a mob could get at him. Emotions were still at a fever pitch. LeCompte himself had been embroiled in the controversy when he attended a meeting in Leavenworth to protest Governor Reeder invalidating the March election. He was perceived to have taken the side of the pro-slavery faction. He was at the meeting to defuse the situation, by his own account, not speaking, just listening. The Leavenworth Herald reported that he was there to lend his support. The Missouri newspapers took that story and embellished it, making LeCompte seem like a leader of the pro-slavery group. By the time the story reached the New York Tribune, he was hailed as leader of the pro-slavery party in the Territory. To describe LeCompte as angry would be an injustice to the word, he was livid with rage. The judge was a pro-slavery man, but he was also a fair and honest legalist who believed the laws should be followed, and the Governor had the right to invalidate the election because of the Missourians voting in Kansas.

Riley and Katie arrived at the Wood home at noon. Margaret ushered them into the living room where Sam sat, paper, pen and inkwell close at hand. Their house was always bustling with relatives, settlers, anyone needing a bed for the night. Riley was forced to discuss the matter in the midst of the distractions. Children parading in and out, neighbors coming to visit, clients waiting their turn.

Sam thrived on it, not realizing, or maybe not caring that it was a disturbance to other people.

Sarah Wood came in from the yard where she was washing clothes, sat by Katie, wrapped a sympathetic arm around her but didn't say anything, just held the distraught woman, comforting her as best she could. Katie had been just fine until this kind gesture caused a loss of composure again, "Sarah, "I don't know what I'm going to do," she sobbed. "Tammy misses her daddy so much."

"I know, I know, Katie, I promise that Sam will take care of it. He always knows what to do."

Sam shuffled a few papers to buy time. He glanced at Sarah, a look that said, 'don't promise more than we can deliver,' but Sarah was oblivious to his message; she focused on counseling the distraught young mother.

Katie did need to remain calm for her daughter's sake, more importantly, for Eric's sake. A businesslike approach would be best, "I have here," Sam held up a sheaf of papers, "written depositions of six different people who witnessed the event, three pro and three anti-slavery. Each of them is willing to testify that Eric acted in self-defense."

Her face suddenly brightened, "Do you mean it, Mr. Wood? Eric told me what happened. It really was self-defense."

"I don't think there is any doubt of that. Mr. Epcot and Mr. Speer both affirm that Clark continued to swing the club at Eric even as he lay on the ground. Now, let me caution you, there is always a danger when dealing with the emotions that accompany a trial like this. Mr. Clark was well situated in Leavenworth. I'm going to ask for a change of venue and we have a good chance of having it granted. As long as Eric is in Ft. Leavenworth, he's safe. If he were in the town jail, I would be worried about his welfare. Right now, Eric is best left where he is.

A knock at the door and Tap walked in, "Interesting doings in Leavenworth."

"What," Riley said nervously.

"That attorney, Phillips, they accused of giving your son the gun, was taken across the river to Weston, by force. They shaved off half his hair, stripped him and covered him in tar and feathers. Then they sold him at auction to an old black man name of 'Nigger' Joe."

"Oh, my word." Margaret sat down next to Sam.

"But he didn't do anything. He's innocent. Eric doesn't even know him. We told the newspapers, Eric had never so much as met that man."

"I don't think the facts are of any interest to the Leavenworth mob," Sam lay the pen down and rubbed his eyes.

"What does it mean he was sold to an old black man?" Margaret asked, putting her hand on Sam's arm.

"I guess it was meant as a joke," Tap kneeled by the table, "Joe took Phillips to his house; he and his wife tried to scrape the mess off of him, give him some comfort. When the mob heard that, they got all riled up again and went looking for both Joe and Phillips. I left so I'm not sure what happened. We'll hear soon enough. Harold was still there. He'll let us know when he gets back."

Sam picked up the fountain pen, a blob of ink spread on his notes, leaking from the nib. "Oh, drat, my new fountain pen. Look at that Margaret." She quickly cleaned up the mess and handed him a pencil.

"I'll ride over to Leavenworth, meet with Eric, go over our strategy, then to Lecompton to visit with the Judge." Sam folded his notes in half to cover the ink, "what was the name of that boy who saw Eric take the pistol from his saddlebags?"

Katie answered, "Ralphie Epcot."

"Ralph's son?"

"Yes, the Epcot's have the claim next to us."

Sam made a note of the name, sat quietly for a moment. The other's waited patiently.

"Judge LeCompte doesn't want a big splashy trial any more than we do. He's President Pierce's man but he's also fair and square, just like Governor Reeder turned out to be. Maybe we can come up with a way to avoid a public trial. As time passes, the mob over in Leavenworth will run its course. The Border Ruffians are driving most of the emotion; the regular citizens have to go back to work, eventually."

They discussed the case until each was worn out. Then gathered the evidence as best they could. Sam informed them that he had to keep secret the names of the pro-slavery witnesses; they were afraid for their lives if word got out about testifying for the defense.

As the group stood outside saying their goodbyes, Harold Barnett rode down Massachusetts from the ferry.

Margaret spotted him, "My goodness Harold, you look so tired. Please get down, rest a while."

"I am tired Mrs. Wood, but you all need to know something. They hung Bill Phillips and Nigger Joe over in Weston."

May 27, 1855

The political climate in the Territory made life even more difficult than normal in a frontier community where the primary focus was on food supply, shelter from the harsh weather and basic needs. John Thompson continued to work on the construction of the Free State Hotel plus worked as a sub-contractor on Charlie Robinson's new barn. Sally, Margaret and the kids were going berry and mushroom gathering in Hickory Point, rescheduled from an earlier rain delay. John walked to the barn to take care of hitching the team for them, a chivalrous duty any husband would assume. Sally intercepted him, "Where you going, handsome?"

"To get the wagon ready for your trip," he recognized immediately the mistake, Sally was better with the livestock than most of the farmers in the area.

"What makes you think I need any help with hitching a couple of horses to the wagon, Mr. Thompson?"

"I didn't mean to imply anything, Sal, I just wanted to be, I mean I was trying to be, you know, helpful."

"Go on about your business and leave us be. We'll be back this afternoon with strawberry pie on the menu tonight," she started to walk away then turned back, "John," he waited while she put her arms around him for a tender hug.

He whistled, held her at arm's length, "Say, is that a new dress? Why you wearing a new dress to go berry picking? And it's a little short isn't it?"

"You like it," she said twirling around. "It's a new style, all the rage back east. See how the hem is above my ankles, won't drag in the dirt."

"You best be careful, girl, you'll have all the young bucks in the territory chasing you, showing off your legs like that." She shooed him away, he gave her a friendly pat.

The Belgian draft horses, named Thomas and Jefferson, came to Sally when they spotted her reaching for an apple. She had them hitched up in no time, drove around to Margaret's house where the children and Prince the setter pup, piled in for the ride to Hickory Point. Jacob Branson and Charles Dow farmed two claims side by side in excellent wild berry country about 6 miles south of Lawrence. Jacob's wife, Elenora, welcomed the Thompson and Wood families to her modest sod home, "I'd go with you, but I've got a rabbit stew boiling and dough risin', so I'd best stay here. Is Mr. Wood coming? We need to get this Frank Coleman mess straightened out."

"Sam mentioned that he needed to see Mr. Dow and Jacob about some claim problem. Is that what you mean, Elenora?"

"Yes, it is. Frank is about to drive me crazy. He's trying to claim some of Charles' land for his own. It ain't right what he's doing."

"Well, I'm sure Sam will straighten it out. Thanks for letting us pick berries on your land."

"There's enough berries out there to feed all of Lawrence. You remember how to get there, Sally?"

"I do, Mrs. Branson. Thank you."

Charles Dow lived with the Branson's while waiting to build a cabin on his own land. A thin man with stooped shoulders, always wearing a floppy leather hat, he was friendly to all, uneducated but full of good common sense. He rode into the yard to get a broad ax that he'd forgotten that morning, spotted the wagon, gave a yahoo, "Ya'll wait right there, I've got something for ya'."

"What's that all about?" Sally asked Elenora while Charles disappeared into the cabin.

"Oh, he's been making a surprise for the kids and he's ready to give em out now."

"A surprise," Caleb looked at his mom, who just shrugged.

Dow ran back to the group, greeted David, Lloyd, Caleb and Missy by name, petted Prince, then gave each of the kids a lucky rabbit's foot he had cured, dried and attached to a leather loop. "Now, these here'll keep off the hoo-doo, so's ya'll be protected from evil spirits n' such," he said proudly.

"What's the hoo-doo?" Caleb asked.

"I'm not rightly certain," Dow said scratching his head. "But a rabbit's foot'll keep ya safe from witches n' spirits when they out n' about, like good luck magic."

"Oh boy," Lloyd said, holding it for his mother to see, "Thank you, Mr. Dow, I'll always keep it with me."

"I don't think Quaker's need good luck magic." David said, as they drove off, but he carefully placed the rabbit's foot in his pocket, just in case.

Margaret looked at Sally, "Should we make them throw away? We really shouldn't be fostering these silly myths."

"I wouldn't! Don't make a big thing of it. Mr. Dow's a nice man and just wants to be friendly, lots of folks carry em'. Anyway, I'm not certain-positive that it don't work."

They drove up a hill through the untracked prairie, then down a swale to a copse of cottonwood and Osage orange trees, a small natural spring surrounded by wild strawberry and gooseberry bushes. They ate fried chicken and biscuits with a side of cheese, then began their chores.

The ladies used aprons to gather the fruit, depositing the bounty into a wooden box. The kids ate more than they gathered.

Missy and Lloyd strolled up the hill to get a better view of the countryside, started back when Margaret shouted, "Come on kids, we're ready to go home." She turned back to the wagon; suddenly, Prince charged past, barking furiously.

"Prince," Margaret laughed, clapping her hands at the exuberant canine.

Her heart froze at the buzz of an angry rattlesnake. She whirled around searching frantically at her feet, "snake," she shouted, then spotted it, her heart sinking; a grey-headed timber rattler coiled next to Lloyd and Missy, its head raised menacingly, rattles buzzing like a nest of bees. Prince sprang at the snake. Lloyd fell backward, scooted on all fours, jumped up and started running. Missy went the other way. Prince lunged at the snake, bounced back as the reptile struck at the beautiful Irish Setter, then coiled back, its tongue slithering out, a twisted warning, unheeded by the attacking dog.

David and Caleb were screaming, "Prince, here Prince."

"Did it bite Lloyd?" Margaret yelled.

Sally pulled at their clothes searching for fang marks. "I don't think so." She hugged them frantically.

"Mamma, you're hurting me," Missy struggled away.

Sally shouted at the older boys, "Back up; stay away from it."

Margaret grabbed a sturdy branch, started toward the snake, but it darted down a gopher hole before she could get close. Prince was barking and digging at the hole. Margaret pushed him away with the branch and shooed him toward the wagon. David and Caleb searched the dog for wounds. Prince was breathing heavy, his tongue lolling out. He trotted casually to the spring and drank; the boys looked at their mother, imploring. Margaret called Prince to the wagon, lifted his fur, groped through it, but couldn't find any bite marks. "It's a miracle that someone wasn't bitten. The snake must have struck Princes' long fur."

Lloyd explained, "Mr. Dow's rabbit's foot protected us, mama."

"Yes, I felt it," Missy agreed.

"Did it?" David asked, examining his for the first time.

"God sent Prince to save us." Margaret's red face and worried look caused Caleb to pat his pocket making certain the rabbit's foot was safely tucked away. "I'm not taking any chances," he whispered to David.

"Me neither," David caressed his own good luck charm as he looked back toward the gopher hole. Sally urged the horses on, the wagon lurched around and started up the hill. Lloyd and Missy sat with their arms around Prince, oblivious hero of the day.

***

"I can with truth and sincerity declare, that I have found amongst the negroes as great a variety of talents as amongst a like number of whites, and I am bold to assert, that the notion entertained by some, that the blacks are inferior in their capacities, is a vulgar prejudice, founded on the pride or ignorance of their lordly masters, who have kept their slaves at such a distance, as to be unable to form a right judgment of them." Anthony Benezet (1713-1784)

Gary Blackwell's farm lay east of Franklin a few miles. It didn't take Sam and John T long to find it. Several slaves, men, women and children were clearing, burning trees and digging stumps; they stopped to watch the strangers ride by. Blackwell, a thick faced, obese man with sparse hair slicked back with Rowland's Macassar Oil came out when he heard barking. He shouted at the slaves, "Get back to work ya' lazy bastards. I'll set the dogs on ya'." Then to Sam, "What can I do for you, sir?"

"Are you Mr. Blackwell?"

"I am."

"I'm Sam Wood."

Blackwell was shocked, but quickly recovered, "Ummmm... what can I do for you, Mr. Wood?"

John T said, "I think you know what this is about."

Blackwell slowly furrowed his brow; a stormy visage of rage overtook him. He snarled through clenched teeth, "Don't you never say nothin' to me, boy. I'll have you whipped till' you drop, you fuckin', Nigger; talkin' to me like you a white man." He started forward, shaking his fist, spittle spewing from his mouth, turned to Sam, "Your days are numbered Wood, you Nigger-luvin' bastard. You get off my property."

"Blackwell, I underestimated you, you're more ignorant than I thought. Next time you send someone to kill me, you'd best finish the job."

They turned and rode off. Blackwell stood watching; his fat body shaking with anger, "What the Hell you come here for, Wood?"

Sam stopped, turned Border Ruffian toward Blackwell, "So I can see what you look like. I want to know what kind of pathetic human being you are." Sam was also getting angry, "Backshoot a man, you dirty pig; but worse is what you do to them," nodding toward the slaves. "You're the one whose days are numbered, Blackwell." He turned back; they rode off.

"John let's go tell those slaves to come with us. We'll get them into Canada. This guy Blackwell is bad news."

"No, If Blackwell sees me talk to them, he'll send the overseer down, and they'll catch all kinds of grief over it. I'll get word to them. We'll get them out of here."

Sam nodded, turned in the saddle to see if Blackwell was still watching.

He was.

***

"Govern Kansas in 1855 and '56! You might as well attempt to govern the devil in hell."
Kansas Territorial Governor Wilson Shannon

Sam had no qualms about meeting with Territorial Judge LeCompte to discuss Eric's situation. He and the Judge had a cordial relationship from the start, each choosing not to discuss their political differences, instead focusing on solving the problems of creating a new state on the American frontier. The conundrum was that most issues they faced were encumbered by the slavery question. Dancing around the obvious disparities was a challenge but necessary to get anything accomplished. The ride from Leavenworth, after visiting with Eric, gave Sam time to think of his opening remarks to the Judge. Practicing on Border Ruffian much the same way Eric discussed matters with Sulla, "Judge, that young man is innocent. It was an act of self-defense, legal, moral, and otherwise... I think the best approach is the direct one. Straight to the point, don't you Ruff?" Border Ruffian didn't acknowledge the question with so much as a twitch of the ears, he was concentrating on the new Leavenworth Road which was still under construction and rough as a cob.

President Pierce appointed Samuel LeCompte chief justice of the Kansas Territorial Supreme Court; the understanding was that the Judge would help bring Kansas into the Union as a slave state. Pierce was sure of his man, sure that he would ignore the legal rights of the individual, in favor of the needs of the nation. And Pierce needed Kansas to be a Slave State to offset Nebraska being a Free State. He wasn't the first President to flout the laws of the land for his own personal good, nor would he be the last. LeCompte, on the surface appeared to fit the bill, but Sam had him judged as a man who would do what was right in the eyes of the law, regardless of what his boss wanted, even if the boss was the most powerful official in the land.

Constitution Hall was hot and humid when Sam arrived, escorted into the Judge's small office by the Secretary of the Territory, Daniel Woodson, a mousy, indecisive man that Sam was not fond of. The Judge was tall with thinning hair and a thick beard going grey. "Too many kids," he joked. "The hair they haven't torn out, I have; just trying to survive with four girls and boy, all at home, and the boy is the worst."

"I've got two boys of my own, so I know what you mean. Five kids are a handful. I don't envy you."

"Sam, do you know William?" The Judge indicated a stooped, old black man who shuffled in.

"I don't," Sam lied. "Pleased to meet you, William."

"William is our jack-of-all-trades around here. Don't know what we would do without him," the Judge bragged, "would you like a cup of coffee?"

"Just a glass of water if you don't mind."

LeCompte nodded to William. He returned a few minutes later with Sam's water and a cup of coffee for the judge. Waiting for the door to close behind him,

LeCompte said, "He can't read or write but he's smart as a whip. Can fix anything. Good man to have around and he doesn't cost the Territory much."

Truth of the matter, Sam knew William quite well. He was John Thompson's informant on all matters of interest in the Territory. John knew confidential political matters before they were even announced to the public. William had told John about the rumor of the assassination attempt on Sam in Westport.

"Well, what are we going to do about this unfortunate situation in Leavenworth City, Sam? I know that boy acted in self-defense. We need to diffuse this situation and get on with the business of the Territory."

Sam laughed realizing that all of his rehearsed speeches were rendered moot. "I agree with you Judge. What are we going to do?"

"I've been thinking about that since it happened. I wish that boy would have just left the territory until emotions simmered down, then he could have come back and nothing would have been done. The hanging of Phillips and the old Negro man were far worse than what McCrea did. But how do we hang a whole mob of people and the crime was in Missouri, not Kansas."

Sam finished off his water, looked for a place to set his glass. William suddenly appeared, "Would you like some more, sir?"

"No thank you." William glanced at LeCompte who put his hand over his coffee cup. He left again, closing the door.

"Now how did he know I was finished?" Sam asked.

LeCompte shook his head. "Don't know, maybe he's listening at the door, he kind of has a sixth sense about things like that."

Sam smiled, wondered if the Judge suspected anything, because the truth was that William could read and write like a teacher. The ignorant slave performance was just that, a ruse to allow him access to information he passed on to the black community and eventually, the abolitionists. He was invaluable in finding out what the pro-slavery Territorial public servants were up to.

"Sam, you might not like this solution, but I think it's for the best in the long run. You can win your case in court, and I know you relish the public stage to proclaim your views, but this isn't the time. I'm afraid that the same mob will grab McCrea and lynch him right in front of us."

Sam nodded without comment. If the Judge was going to solve the problem, then far be it from him to look a gift horse in the mouth.

"What we're going to do is concoct a scheme to get Eric outside the prison walls and then he's going to leave the Territory and not come back until it's safe."

Shock was probably insufficient a word to describe Sam's surprise. Judge LeCompte was known as a stickler for the law. This solution, while probably the most effective, didn't jibe with his pro-slavery reputation or his legal standing. But it made sense. The army was just holding Eric as a favor to the Judge because there was no jail in the village of Leavenworth; they wouldn't look for him if he didn't come back and there was no Leavenworth County Sheriff to worry about. In fact, it would probably be a relief to all parties if Eric disappeared.

"The only problem I see, Judge, is Eric's father-in-law. He wants Eric cleared so their family can get on with their lives without this matter hanging over their heads."

"I'm sure you'll figure something out, Sam," he said, rising to shake hands. "By the way, when we can find the time, I'd like to have a friendly chat about this new

Republican Party you're organizing. The article in the New York Tribune was interesting. I didn't realize how many influential people you've got on board. I know Bill Dayton very well, also Chuck Sumner. I understand you're going to nominate Salmon Chase for President. We don't see eye to eye on political matters but he's a fair and honest man."

"I'd love to discuss it with you, Judge. Maybe I'll convert you to our cause." The meeting ended cordially, even surprisingly, in Sam's mind, he gleaned a crack in LeCompte's slavery stance. Just maybe the good judge would be as big a disappointment to President Pierce as Governor Reeder had been.

"Wait, Sam," the Judge turned back to his desk, retrieved a sheet of paper, "take this with you." The document, on Kansas Territory letterhead, read as follows.

To: MAJ. GEN. WILLIAM P. RICHARDSON
Commander Ft. Leavenworth

Sir: You have been holding a county prisoner by the name of Eric McCrea, on my behalf. My instructions to you are to release the said prisoner, Eric McCrea, to the bearer of this letter, Samuel N. Wood whom you know as McCrea's attorney. I take full responsibility for the custody of the prisoner and hereby thank you and resolve you of any further obligation in this matter.

You may address any questions to me at my office in Lecompton or direct them to Mr. Wood who is authorized to respond on my behalf.

I remain respectfully yours,
Samuel Dexter LeCompte
Chief Justice
Kansas Territorial Supreme Court

Tired as he was, Sam resolved to ride the 15 miles back to Riley Tanners to discuss this latest development. The afternoon was hot and muggy, the air heavy with moisture. "I wonder if a storm is on the way, William," he asked looking at the sky. The abolitionist spy stood waiting with Border Ruffian saddled, "I gave him a good rubdown, Mr. Wood, and a bucket of oats. Ole Ruffian ready to go. You got yourself a fine piece of horseflesh there."

"Fastest in the territory," Sam agreed, checking to see if anyone was listening, "Why is LeCompte being so agreeable?" he whispered, pretending to tighten the flank cinch.

"He's mad at those Leavenworth people."

"For hanging Phillips?"

"Na, sir, for calling him a liar in the paper. Making him out to be dishonest. Plus, he don't think that boy can get a fair trial anywhere in Kansas or Missouri. I heard him talking to Judge Barrett about it. Whatever the reason, I hope this plan ya'll schemed out works for the McCrea boy."

"Is there anything you don't know about in this territory, William?"

"Nothing that's worth knowing, Mr. Sam." He smiled. "Say hello to John Thompson for me."

"I will. My regards to your family." Sam tipped his hat, rode downhill to the raft used as a ferry across the Kansas River, only to find Barry McGuire, the operator, taking a nap in the shade of a large Elm tree. Sam none to gently woke him, reminding the Territorial employ that he was on the public payroll. Barry grumbled all the way across complaining that 'some people got no manners.'

Under a spreading chestnut-tree
The village smithy stands;
The smith, a mighty man is he,
With large and sinewy hands;
And the muscles of his brawny arms
Are strong as iron bands.

His hair is crisp, and black, and long,
His face is like the tan;
His brow is wet with honest sweat,
He earns whate'er he can,
And looks the whole world in the face,
For he owes not any man.
The Village Blacksmith, Henry Wadsworth
Longfellow 1807-1882

The Leavenworth Road, commissioned by the army in the spring of 1854, was designed to facilitate troop movement between Fort Leavenworth and the new Fort Riley located just west of the village of Manhattan, about 120 miles distance between the two. The turnpike was still under construction as Sam made his way west back to the Tanner claim, located at the junction of the Leavenworth Road and Lawrence cutoff.

To placate the many new claimants in the area, the army agreed to engineer the Lawrence Road from the turnpike to the new ferry at the Kansas river just chartered in favor of John Baldwin. The entire stretch would be well constructed, peaked for drainage, macadamized and good solid stone and wood bridges constructed across the creeks. Traveling was getting to be much easier on both sides of the river. Before the Lawrence Ferry was constructed the only crossing for wagons and freight was the Pappan Brothers Ferry in Topeka, Lecompton Ferry or Chief Fish's Ferry at the Wakarusa River.

Sam reached the intersection about four that afternoon. The blacksmith shop was easily visible from the crossroads. Riley was still working when Sam reined Border Ruffian next to the iron ring set for hitching. A fancy wrought iron affair with a lion's head molded into the arch, deftly demonstrating the skill of the proprietor. Riley waved him in. Grimy with soot on his clothes, arms and face where he attempted to wipe away the sweat with his forearms; Riley was encumbered by a heavy leather apron scorched from sparks hammered like fireflies out of the metal he was working, "Hold on a minute, Sam. Grab a chair out front, it's too hot in here," he shouted above the roar of the bellows.

Hoops and bars of wrought iron, steel, other bundles of metal, all surrounded by tools of every description, cluttered the large building. "I'll bet he knows where everything is down to the last rivet," Sam thought. He turned to go back out, catching sight of a large blackboard next to the door, one word written on it, 'NAILS'. That's odd he chuckled. A beautiful new rocking chair on the flagstone veranda testified to the fact that both Riley and Eric were accomplished carpenters and furniture makers, as skilled in wood as in metal.

"You have news?" Riley appeared, wiping his hands on a rag as dirty as his clothes.

"We need to talk," Sam said, rising with his hand outstretched in greeting.

"Let me wash up, Sam, I don't want to get this grime all over you. Go on up to the house, I'll be there as soon as I tend the fire and wash my face and hands."

"Why do you have nails written on your board?"

"Just got a large contract to make as many nails as I can for Swede Johnson, the house builder in Kansas City."

"Mr. Wood," Katie greeted him. Jane held her granddaughter on hip while adding water to the coffee pot near the hearth. "We saw you ride up. I'm taking daddy this basin of water; he'll want to wash up. Sit down, make yourself comfortable."

What a shame this terrible event has disrupted such a contented family, he thought while waiting. Mrs. Tanner placed a cup of coffee in front of him. She looked harried. Sam would have preferred water or lemonade but didn't turn down the kind gesture. "I guess you have some news, Mr. Wood," she said, more as a statement than a question.

"Yes, Jane, I do. We have to talk," he set the cup back down quickly, the handle too hot to hold.

"It's hot, be careful," she looked out the open door as Riley entered, obviously a lot on her mind.

Sam didn't relish this conversation. He was almost sorry he'd agreed to the Judge's strategy; the case would be easy to win with an unbiased jury. The consultations with Eric had gone so well that the accused murderer now felt he was not only justified in what he had done, but he would be acquitted and promote his newfound abolitionist creed at the same time. On the other hand, Sam knew, if the mob got ahold of Eric before the trial could be completed, they would lynch him like they did the innocent William Phillips. He would leave it up to the family, not advocate either way. It truly was their decision, regardless of what the Judge said.

He gingerly touched the cup, picked it up, took a sip to wet his dry lips. The three of them sat watching silently, even little Tammy seemed intent on the news, whatever it might be. They assumed it was bad or he wouldn't have ridden back after having visited Eric early that morning.

"I've been to see Judge LeCompte. The good news is he thinks Eric is innocent, acted in self-defense and that's difficult for a judge to admit, probably unethical back east. Here in this lawless..." Sam caught himself before he got off subject into an emotional tirade that the Tanner's didn't need at that moment. "What I'm trying to say is that Judge LeCompte and I feel that it would be a mistake to go to trial."

They continued gazing at him, waiting, for further information. Riley looked at his wife, "So, what do we do instead of a trial? Let him rot in prison?"

"We think it would be a good idea for Eric to leave the Territory for a while, until the emotions die down. Something will happen, I don't know what, but something and people will forget about Eric."

"You mean send him to a prison somewhere else? Not have the trial now. I guess I don't understand, Mr. Wood." Riley was getting frustrated. The ladies sat quietly, listening but not contributing. Maybe they didn't understand what he meant, but Jane Tanner had a look in her eye as if she knew exactly where he was leading. Sam took note of her attention. She seemed to be contemplating an idea of her own.

"No, we're proposing that there won't be a trial. Eric will simply go away and come back when it's safe."

"Why that's a crazy idea, Sam. We raised that boy, he's our son as well as our son-in-law. We can't have little Tammy grow up to think her daddy is a murder. No sir, we have to clear his name in a court of law, legal." He stood, abruptly, went to the water pail, took a large gulp from the ladle, "No sir," he repeated firmly.

Jane watched Sam closely, Katie rested her forehead wearily in her hand, elbow on the table. She was exhausted, probably not sleeping at night, Sam thought.

"How would he get out of Ft. Leavenworth?" Jane asked.

"Jane, you're not seriously considering this?"

She didn't answer, just continued watching Sam.

"I have a simple solution, one that will be easy to implement. I, and a few other men from Lawrence, will go to the Fort with a letter from Judge LeCompte ordering Eric to be brought to Lecompton for arraignment. It will state that he'll be held in the Douglas County jail while there and don't expect him to return to Ft. Leavenworth. They'll be glad to be rid of him; they're just holding him as a courtesy. They have no jurisdiction over a civilian matter. There is no Leavenworth County law official at the present time. No one will look for him. He'll have to leave the Territory for a while. I propose that he and Katie go back to Columbia, Missouri. I understand you have family there."

"My parents," Jane answered. "You can stay with Mom and Dad," said the suddenly animated matron, turning to Katie, "they would love to have you, and we've already decided to quit going to Leavenworth. All of our business will be conducted in Lawrence."

"Jane, I forbid this kind of talk. Eric is going to have a trial and that's that. He's got to be cleared of this murder." Riley was as adamant as ever.

"NO!", she slapped the table, "He can't be cleared of this murder, Boo." He flinched at the use of her pet name for him. Never had she used it in front of a stranger. He slowly sank into the chair.

"Eric killed that man; all the rest is legal mumbo jumbo. In the eyes of God, he is guilty, has to live with that for the rest of his life. Let that be punishment enough, for him and for us." She tenderly placed her hand on Riley's shoulder, "This is what I wanted from the first day, when we heard those awful words from that poor tormented boy, what he had done. I will not sit by and let that filthy mob take him and they will if there's a trial. No, Riley, we're going to do exactly what Mr. Wood says."

They both turned to Sam, "Leave the details to me. Katie, you and Tammy need to be ready to go at my signal. You'll come to my house first, then we'll escort you to Westport, you'll catch the steamboat there," said with more confidence than he felt.

"How long do you think we'll have to be gone?"

"Until the next crisis. Maybe a week, maybe six months. I think we'll know when the time is right."

***

Cup of coffee in hand, Sam stood on the front porch, watching neighbors come and go, an occasional wave, the morning clear, another warm, breezy summer day in Kansas. Up the street, Elvira and Paul were unloading supplies, hauling them through the front door. He walked over to visit but quickly discovered that gossip would have to wait. The Brooks, including Jay, were busy as ants, checking off bills of laden and stocking shelves. Elvira waved, went back to work; Sam turned up the path to Charlie's house for a meeting with members of the interim city aldermen to discuss progress on the town charter, only to find the meeting had been postponed because Charlie was ill, and Judge Wakefield wasn't back from Topeka. He felt somewhat relieved since he hadn't finished the city charter promised at last week's meeting, this delay would give him time to create at least an outline. Caleb Pratt was coming up as Sam was going down Tenth street, "What's up? Aren't we meeting?"

"Charlie's indisposed, Wake's not back from Topeka, Tap, Dietzler and Pomeroy are visiting with Sara. I'm going back home to write the city charter."

"Oh, really, I thought that was already done," said Caleb dryly. Pratt, a young man, was handsome in a New England-pale sort of way, piercing dark eyes from some distant Mediterranean ancestor, his eyes full of energy. Sam proclaimed to everyone Lawrence's good luck in having Caleb Pratt on the side of the decent guys. He was founder of the Stubbs militia group, organized to protect the polls after the failed March 30 elections. The powers that be were considering Pratt for Douglas County Clerk, an important post in the upcoming elections; responsibility for validating voter registration would fall on him.

Sam didn't notice the sarcasm, "Don't worry, I'll have a rough draft by the time we meet. I'm sorry I haven't been to any of the Militia meetings. I've been busy."

"I know you have. Did you reschedule this meeting?"

"Charlie scheduled a meeting for June 8. Actually, I've got to write the resolutions for that meeting too, so I'll miss the Militia meeting again."

Margaret and Sarah were bustling around the kitchen when Sam returned, "Hi honey, why are you home so early? The meeting is not over already, is it?"

"No, Charlies' sick and Wake's still in Topeka."

Sarah took the opportunity to describe her success curing Jay's stuttering problem, "When he reads, he doesn't stutter," she proclaimed proudly, taking credit for a therapeutic remedy of major importance.

Her second goal was more ambitious, "I want to have a party and make it a part of the July 4th celebration. Please, Sam, just this once. We'll have a speech about how black people aren't free. Oh, drat, Sam, why can't we?"

"He didn't say you couldn't Sarah," Margaret scolded.

She loved her sister-in-law, but... "I wish she would find a man and get married," she confided to Sam.

Sam had other things on his mind, giving an answer not well thought out, "Sounds like a good idea, Pumpkin. Have at it."

Sarah stopped just short of the sob she was prepared to employ, eyes brightened, she gave Sam a big hug, "I've got to go tell Donna."

He took the opportunity to embrace his wife as she kneaded dough for the Dutch oven. She leaned back for a kiss, trying not to scatter flour; David came in, saw them, turned around and went back out to the porch. "He's been asking when you'd be home. He's got something he needs to talk about."

Sam gave her the kiss, daubed flour on her nose, dodged a friendly swat and left to see what was on David's mind. He found him on the front porch in the rocking chair, "Hey son, what's new?" he asked, sitting on the porch rail.

"I heard about you beating up those men in Westport."

"Really, that was quite a while ago. How did you hear about it?"

"Carol Barnett, I guess her dad must have told her. He was there right?"

"Yes, he was there, but there was only one man that threatened me with a knife, I had to stop him. Something about what Carol said that's bothering you Davey?"

"No, not something she said, it was Larry Tappan, he said that you're a bully and don't listen to anyone else and that our family are terrible Quakers, then he knocked me down," he started to cry silently with his head in the crook of his arm.

Sam knelt down as the boy sobbed. When David had gained his composure, Sam asked, "What happened then?"

"Caleb punched him in the nose. Then that new boy, Frankie, said that I was hiding behind my Nigger, cause Caleb and I walked away."

Sam turned away in frustration, "Oh, the sins of the fathers."

David talked on, not hearing, "I wanted to hit him in the face, but I didn't because Grandmother told me not to fight, it's against our religion, so I just walked away, and they laughed at me and called me a coward. Then Caleb got in trouble from his mom. But you don't have to follow the rules, and I want to be like you, helping people and being for what's right, but I don't want to make Grandmother mad."

Leaning back, Sam looked at the sky, not sure what to say. David always seemed so together, competent, Sam couldn't quite put his finger on what he was thinking. Finally, he said, "I apologize Davey."

"For what?" David asked, wiping his eyes.

"For not talking to you about the things I do. I'm always busy, aren't I?"

"What should I have done, Papa?

"That's a hard question. Larry is your friend; he was wrong to push you down. Frankie was wrong to call Caleb a name. I wouldn't have blamed you for hitting him, but your mother probably would," Sam hesitated to see if David was listening. "So, you have to make up your own mind about what's the right thing to do, and when you decide, then you have to live with the consequences. Larry called you a coward and you feel bad, but if you hit him, then your mother will be mad at you. Your decision, and there isn't always a right or wrong way. Whatever you decide you own up to the decision and accept the consequences. Does that make any sense?"

David contemplated the problem for a while, until Sam began to wonder if he was listening. Finally, he said, "I think next time I'll knock Larry down and go tell Mother what I did and face her consequences. That would make me feel better."

Sam smiled, "We just do the best we can and pray that God approves. Come on let's go get some of those fresh biscuits."

As they rose to go back inside, Larry Tappan, Jimmy Pratt and Caleb came charging up the road shouting that they were going fishing; David took off running for his cane pole. He and Prince tore up the road toward the river catching his friends at the crest of the rise; they put their arms around each other's shoulder, the dogs prancing alongside. Sam strolled into the house feeling plenty proud of the way he handled his fatherly duties, something that he often left for Margaret.

"What did you tell him to do?"

"I told him that the next time that happens, he should punch Larry right in the nose. See, like this, one, two, just like John Morrissey," he demonstrated a right and left punch at her nose, bobbing and weaving like a prize fighter.

"Sam," she scolded, eyes blazing, "You did not tell him such a horrible thing. That's no way to solve the problem. After all the work that I've put into teaching him the Christian way."

"I'm just joshing, Meg," exchanging the clenched fists for a warm embrace, "that isn't exactly what I said. I told him that I was sorry he had to deal with the situation because of my actions. He'll handle things a little differently next time."

Lloyd and Missy came in from playing in the back yard and they all sat down to a lunch of fresh bread, boiled beef and beans.

> *"He is not hers, although she bore*
> *For Him a mother's pains;*
> *He is not hers, although her blood*
> *Is coursing through his veins!*
> *He is not hers, for cruel hands*
> *May rudely tear apart*
> *The only wreath of household love*
> *That binds her breaking heart."*
> *Francis Harper from her poem, "The Slave Mother"*

"Goddammit, Sam, you are impossible to work with," Charlie Robinson pushed his chair back, knocking it over in anger. They were sitting around the table in the Tribune office making plans for the June 25th Free State convention and the July 4th celebration, both being held in Lawrence.

"Now Charlie, there's no need for blasphemy," Sam countered.

"Oh, grow up. This isn't Ohio high society, this is Kansas, for God's sake."

"All I'm saying Charlie, is that we should extend a formal invitation to them whether they come or not. It's symbolic. I don't know why that makes you mad."

"It's how you say it, you don't suggest, you order."

"Charlie, sit down," Judge Wakefield said. The judge was a corpulent man and found it difficult to follow Robinson's point of view as he paced around the table.

Harold Barnett got up and righted Charlies chair for him, "We invited the two Indian tribes, why you don't want to invite the Negroes, I'm not understanding."

"It's not that I don't want to invite them," Charlie sat back down with a meaningful glance at Sam, "they won't come even if we ask them. John T already made that clear. So, what are you trying to accomplish?"

"Everyone should be invited to the 4th of July celebration even those horrible Border Ruffians. This is a celebration of our declaration of independence. If they don't want to come that's up to them," Clarke Pomeroy said, always the politician, looking for common ground.

George Dietzler pulled himself erect with his usual pompous military bearing, after all, he was a retired Colonel, as he reminded them, constantly, "I have nothing against Negroes, you all know that. I am not a prejudiced man." Harold and Sam rolled their eyes at each other. Dietzler continued unfazed, "But... but," he shook his finger, "Why create a problem when the people under discussion don't want to come. There will be many citizens at the celebration, people from Leavenworth, Franklin, Hickory Point, I could go on and on, and not all of them are as compassionate as I am, after all I agreed to let those Indians come, even though I lost many good men in the battle of..."

Harold cut him off, "George, if you go off on that again, I swear I won't be responsible for my actions. I'm sick of hearing how many men you lost to those savages, as you call them. You went into their country looking for a fight, what did you expect them to do? I'm losing my patience with you. If you insult my wife and kids, I swear..."

"Please gentlemen, please, Harold, no one is insulting your lovely family," Wakefield gave the Colonel an evil eye. Harold crossed his arms, pursed his lips, narrowed his eyes, a sure sign not to anger him any further.

"Yes, Colonel Dietzler, thank you," Sam interrupted, "I appreciate your thoughts, but the fact is why should our black neighbors celebrate Independence Day when they are not free."

Charlie put his hand up, "But they are free, the Negroes living in Cherry Hollow aren't slaves."

"They aren't citizens," Harold steamed, "and a good many people around here treat them like slaves," he crossed his arms again, looking at Dietzler, who ignored him.

Colonel George Dietzler's views on race relations were well known. He wanted all the Indians herded onto reservations in the west and the blacks banned from the country; to Canada or back to Africa, he didn't care where as long as it was away from the United States. He was not alone, many people in the country shared those beliefs.

Reverend Lum, listened intently, hands folded together in prayer, thumbs resting against his nose. No one thought he was actually praying, this was just the repose he assumed when ready to make a comment, "I do not see what harm it would be to afford our black neighbors the courtesy of a formal invitation. If they chose not to come, at least they know we have extended the offer."

"But what if they do come?" Dietzler protested.

Tap stretched his long legs, raised his arms to ease the pain in his back, "Oh, for heaven's sake, George, they are our neighbors. No one will say a word about them being there. In fact, most people will be asking why they aren't if they don't come."

"Regardless, Sally made it clear to me and Louise last Sunday, 'until the slaves are free and we are granted citizenship, we won't be celebrating your Independence Day,'" Caleb Pratt said.

Dietzler rose out of his chair, pointed his finger, "Never," he shouted, "never will the Niggers be granted citizenship."

"Sit down, Colonel, that isn't the issue we're discussing," Sam gently pushed him back into the chair.

Silence hung over the meeting until Charlie broke the ice, "I move that we go ahead and make a formal invitation."

They all looked at Judge Wakefield, the chairman, "By a show of hands, all in favor of issuing the same invitation to the Negroes that was made to the Indians, raise your right hand."

All hands went up except George Dietzler.

"Motion carried," Wakefield made a note for the minutes, "I'll send the letter to John T. Let's get on to other business. Sam have you finished the resolutions for the convention?"

"I have, let me read the most important ones, it won't take but a minute. We need to go over the list of delegates. If each District sends five representatives, we'll have to meet in the Free State Hotel even if it isn't finished. There isn't enough room here."

Caleb said, "We could meet in Reverend Hutchison's new public hall, it should be finished by then."

"We'll decide that later, we also need to get letters out to each district chairman probably this week. Who is going to do that?" Dietzler asked.

"Let me read these. You need to approve them before we submit them to the assembly. Ok, here goes,

WHEREAS, certain persons from the neighboring State of Missouri have, from time to time, made irruptions into this Territory, and have through fraud and force driven from and overpowered our people at the ballot-box, and have forced upon us a Legislature which does not represent the opinions of the legal voters of this Territory, many of its members not being even residents of this Territory, by having their homes in the State of Missouri; and

WHEREAS, said persons have used violence toward the persons and property of the inhabitants of the Territory; therefore,

Resolved, that we are in favor of making Kansas a free Territory, and as a consequence, a free State.

Resolved, that we urge upon the people of Kansas to throw away all minor differences and issues and make the freedom of Kansas the only issue.

Resolved, that we look upon the conduct of a portion of the people of Missouri in the late Kansas election as a gross outrage on the elective franchise and our rights as freemen, and a violation, of the principles of popular sovereignty; and, inasmuch as many of the members of the present Legislature are men who owe their election to a combined system of force and fraud, we do not feel bound to obey any law of their enacting.

Resolved, That we, the citizens of Kansas will enact our own laws, elect our own representatives, and govern Kansas Territory and eventually the State of Kansas according to the laws and by the representatives elected in free and fair contests with the only votes counted being those cast by true Kansas citizens.

"That's it," Sam finished

"I like it," Charlie said, "Short and to the point."

"Shall we send it to the district chairmen along with the agenda letter?" Caleb asked.

"That makes sense to me," Harold answered.

"All in favor, raise your hand," Wakefield said. All hands raised. "I'll take responsibility for corresponding with the other districts. Tap, is the July 4th committee making headway on plans for the celebration?"

"We'll be ready. Mrs. Steele is in charge of the food committee, Mrs. Lyons in charge of decorations, Mrs. Robinson in charge of entertainment. Don't worry. Oh, yeah, Mrs. Hutchinson is in charge of invitations. We've heard from most of the communities around. They'll all be here, and Mrs. Wood is in charge of speeches."

Sam waited until the others left before sitting across from Speer, "What's up, Bill? Your mind isn't here today."

He handed Sam a note, "Your Nigger Luvin days is over. We know where you live."

"Where did you get that?"

"It was pinned to the door of our house in Westport."

"What are you going to do?"

"I guess move to Lawrence. Linda doesn't want to, but she agrees we have to do something."

"I think you need to make that move right away. Don't wait."

Bill nodded.

***

"This is the first I've seen it," Harold announced. The four men stood on the levee, still under construction, watching the rickety, flat bottomed ferry being pulled back from the north shore of the Kansas River. The new Baldwin Ferry had just been granted a charter by the Territorial Government to operate at the end of Massachusetts Street in Lawrence; the law governing ferries being one of the few that the Free State and Pro Slavery parties could agree upon.

"Gentlemen, good morning, where you headed so early?" Niles Baldwin approached Sam, Harold, Tap and John T as they waited their turn on the new conveyance.

"We've got a meeting in Leavenworth," Sam said in a matter-of-fact way, not wanting to give any additional information. Best keep the Eric McCrea strategy close to the vest. The fewer who knew about it the better.

"Niles, you should have built a bigger ferry. That thing doesn't look like it will hold a team and wagon?" Tap noted, red hair sticking out from under his old slouch hat, towering above those around him, taller even than Harold Barnett.

"Yeah, we have to unhitch the team, but they'll fit. If people don't like it, they can go on to the Pappan's or down to Fish's. Getting to be so damn many ferries on the river a man can't make no money."

"What are you charging, Niles?" John T asked.

"Well," Niles rubbed his scraggly beard, scratched under his sweat stained armpits, hiked up his filthy britches, "I'll give ya'll a special rate, four-bits for the lot of ya. That's half price."

Sam dug in his pocket for the fare, "Niles, that's pretty smart giving the locals a better rate. Looks to me like you've got more traffic than you can handle."

Wagons and teams, buggies, horse and rider, even people on foot who owned houses in North Lawrence commenced queuing on both sides of the river as the sun began to brighten the fine June morning. Indications were it would be hot by noon. The men manning the ropes and oars would be exhausted.

Once across, the four men rode to the Tanner house, four abreast on the newly improved road.

"Harold, you sure have a lot of time on your hands. That brood of yours must be doing all the work," Tap said.

"I do my share, but you're right about the kids doing most of the work. We've got four claims over there west of Hickory Point one for me, one for each of the boys. The two girls are hard workers; Autumn keeps the whole business running. I think they're better off without me around to confuse them."

"Is Autumn her real name," John asked.

"Nah, it's a Shawnee name, got a whole bunch of a's, ll's and u's in it; I can't pronounce it. It means Autumn though. She speaks English, Shawnee, Spanish, and some French. We been together 24 years, since we were both 17. She gets smarter every day and I get dumber."

"She must do some kind of work for Chief Fish. I see her at his place every now and then," Sam volunteered.

"She keeps accounts for him. They've been friends since she was a little girl."

"Oh, shoot," Sam said stopping in the middle of the road. "I forgot Judge LeCompte's letter. I've got to go back and get it."

"I've got it, Sam," John laughed.

"Why do you have it?"

"Margaret saw it laying on the table. Was on her way to take it up to the ferry. I was riding by when she came out of the house. I just forgot to tell you."

"Good, I don't relish waiting to cross the river."

Tap asked, "John T, did you talk to Sally about the 4th celebration? You guys going to attend? What about all your neighbors?"

"The kids want to go. You know Caleb and Missy don't really have any idea what being a slave is. They've never experienced it, been kind of sheltered. I guess some of Caleb's older friends have made ugly remarks to him. He's trying to deal with that."

"You ought to let them go," Harold counseled. "I guarantee my kids are going and if anyone says anything to them, they'll have to deal with me."

"No one's going to bother your family, Harold. Quit being so defensive," Tap laughed.

"Well, they better not," Harold sulked.

"I saw you talking to General Lane, Sam. What do you think about him?"

"Is he really a General?"

Tap answered, "Mexican American War. He's from Lawrenceburg; commanded the 5th Indiana Volunteers."

"He sure sounds like he's on our side. He's still a democrat, but he's against slavery. Margaret asked him to speak on the 4th about his thoughts on the militia. Seems like the kind of man we need."

"What's going to happen at the meeting next week," Tap asked putting his right leg over the saddle, stretching, attempting to get comfortable, his bad back was stiffening up on him.

"The usual resolutions, electing the officers, speeches, the same old thing. I'll send the convention minutes and constitution off to Washington for ratification and they'll deny it, probably won't even bring it up in the house or senate. Maybe, Lewis Cass can at least get it up for a vote, but it'll be denied, just like the last one."

They reached Riley's place to find the wagon loaded, hitched to a four-horse team. Jane hailed them from the door, "Get down, come in. I've got lemonade for you Mr. Wood."

The men removed their hats, dusted their britches, checked their shoes for mud and entered, nodding to Jane and Kate. Tammy was wobbly standing next to a chair for support.

"That girl's growing by the day," Sam laughed. "Don't let Margaret close to her, she'll snatch her home, she wants a little girl in the worst way."

"She's a handful," Riley said as he came down the stairs. "We're ready to go."

"What's going on?" Sam asked. "I thought it would be just the four of us and we'd take Eric back to my house. You all know Harold, John and Tap, don't you?"

Riley shook hands with each. "We've kind of had a change of heart," he said.

Sam's face reflected the concern he felt. This was no time to be changing the strategy. He looked at Jane.

"More a change of plans than a change of heart. Instead of you taking Eric back to your place and Katie meeting him there, we think it wiser to take Eric to the ferry at Delaware, just below Leavenworth. They can cross, take the new road out of Weston to Lexington, cross back over the river there and take the Santa Fe Trail to Columbia."

"We're not going to take the steamboat, Mr. Wood," Katie explained picking the baby up when she fell with a startled sob. "We're going to take the wagon with most of our things, since we don't know how long we'll be gone. Anyway, we don't want to take a chance of meeting someone we know on the river. Not as many people take the road these days."

Sam looked at John T, who shrugged his agreement.

"Sounds like a good plan to me," Tap added.

"Ok, the four of us will go get Eric. Where shall we meet you?"

"Meet us at the Franklin cutoff. You know that abandoned old sod house, the roof caved in, sits back off the road in the trees?"

"Sure, I know it. That's the old Barker place on the Sac and Fox land," Harold said.

"Right, meet us there."

Sulla was saddled and ready. John took the reins; Sulla trailed easily behind. The ride to Leavenworth was without much conversation as they contemplated the task at hand. The closer they got, the less confidence Sam had that the General would just turn the prisoner over to him based on a letter.

"I sure hope Judge LeCompte sent someone over to inform General Richardson that we're coming."

"You think he did?" Harold asked.

"Don't know."

The fort could be seen for quite a distance as they rode over the prairie, through the trees bordering Quarry

Creek. "The gates closed," Tap said. "They only close them at night or in an emergency."

They reined up in front of the main gate, a small door to the side opened; out stepped a smart looking Lieutenant.

"What's your business? Oh, hello Mr. Tappan, how are you? Can I help you gentlemen?"

Tap looked at Sam who gave him an eye signal to state the case. If the man knew him, he had a better chance of being successful. "We're here as a deputation from Supreme Court Judge LeCompte. You have a civilian prisoner here by the name of Eric McCrea. We've been deputized to escort him back to the judge in Lecompton."

Without hesitation the young officer said, "Wait here, I'll notify General Richardson."

The counterfeit deputies sat looking at each other. Total silence surrounding them, no insects buzzing, the horses standing quietly. Sam glanced up to find four rifles pointed down at them from the top of the wall. He looked to his right, nodded up at the guards, John took one look, his eyes grew wide as saucers. They held their breath, not daring to move.

A shout came from within, "At ease on the wall." The rifles disappeared; gate swung open. A different Lieutenant ordered, "Dismount and follow me."

They walked their horses to the hitching rail in front of the Commandants office,

"What's going on? Why the alert?" Sam asked.

No answer. They were taken to an anteroom without any explanation. Within minutes a Corporal entered, "Follow me please, gentlemen."

General Richardson, a middle-aged man, in excellent shape, with a very firm handshake greeted them personally as they filed in, "Mr. Wood, gentlemen, I've been expecting you."

"You have?" Sam said.

"Yes, I received word from Dexter LeCompte last week as to your plans." He smiled.

Sam handed him the letter. The General unfolded it, read dutifully, then placed it on the desk in front of him.

"Is the fort on some kind of alert?" Tap asked.

"We received word from the village that a Missouri mob is going to come demanding the very prisoner about which you speak. The fact of the matter is I will be happy to get rid of him. I can't imagine that even those crazy Border Ruffians would be foolish enough to make a frontal attack on the fort, but one should never underestimate their ignorance. I'm still quite unhappy about what happened to Bill Phillips. I personally warned him to get out of the Territory. It's my understanding that he had gone back to his office to get clothes and personal papers when the mob captured him."

"I tried to stop them," Harold said, "but there were too many."

The general merely nodded, "Well, I think your prisoner is waiting by the horses. I'm sure you want to get started on your way back..." he hesitated a moment for effect, "to Lecompton."

They didn't waste time on small talk, with Eric in the middle they rode out of the fort. Once underway Harold remarked, "You know, I don't think anyone would recognize you anyway, Eric. Not with that red beard."

"You do look a lot different than the last time I saw you running out of that meeting," Tap said.

"Thank you all for what you're doing," Eric had a hangdog, prison look about him, "when this is over and I can come back, I'll thank you properly. I'm so sorry for shooting that man."

Silence greeted his confession, not a denunciation of his actions, more an uncomfortable acknowledgement of the futility of the entire affair.

Katie waited on an old bench under an Osage Orange tree steadying little Tammy as she tried to stand alone. She didn't recognize daddy with the red beard. Eric scooped her up and squeezed until she squealed, "Tata, tata." She pulled at the beard.

Eric secured Sulla to the wagon on a lead rope. The deputies escorted the fugitives to the ferry, watched them board with promises of letters upon arrival in Columbia. At the last moment, Jane decided to ride with them. Interestingly enough, her bag was packed and part of the furnishings in the wagon.

Riding back to Lawrence, Tap said, "I guess the general was in on it from the start. You think there really was a rumor of the Border Ruffians attacking the fort?"

"It might have been an excuse for a drill of some kind," John T said, "I'm just glad it's over."

Hesitating for a moment, Sam added, "I don't think we've heard the last of Eric McCrea."

What, to the American slave, is your Fourth of July? I answer, a day that reveals to him, more than all other days in the year, the gross injustice and cruelty to which he is the constant victim. To him, your celebration is a sham; your boasted liberty, an unholy license; your national greatness, swelling vanity; your sounds of rejoicing are empty and heartless; your denunciations of tyrants, brass-fronted impudence; your shouts of liberty and equality, hollow mockery; your prayers and hymns, your sermons and thanksgivings, with all your religious parade and solemnity, are, to him, mere bombast, fraud, deception, impiety, and hypocrisy -- a thin veil to cover up crimes which would disgrace a nation of savages. There is not a nation on the earth guilty of practices more shocking and more bloody than are the people of the United States at this very hour. . . . Frederick Douglass, 1852 speech in Rochester, New York

July 4th, 1855 dawned to a fiesta of gunshots, bugles blowing, bells ringing, all heralding the day's celebrations. If any man, woman, or child remained abed as the sun rose on the first Independence Day celebration in Lawrence, they must have been ill or feeble. Even before the sun started its ascent, the procession of revelers began to arrive; wagonloads of Shawnee bedecked in colorful costumes; the Delaware in full ceremonial dress. There were squatters, farmers, ranchers on horseback; wagons loaded with dogs and kids hanging over the sides. Everyone carrying a jug of lemonade or spirits plus a dish for the potluck dinner. The Leavenworth delegation arrived in a huge, covered wagon, the stars and stripes flying proudly above. Children lined Massachusetts Street watching a seemingly endless caravan of wagons, horses, mules, oxen all ornamented in flowers with flags waving in the fresh summer breeze.

Prancing horses decorated with ribbons, colorful cloth and bright feathers, paraded across the prairie from Hickory Point, Blue Mound, Osawatomie and as far south as Emporia, ridden by ladies and gentlemen in their Sunday finest.

They poured in all morning from Manhattan, Topeka, Delaware, Lecompton. Three giant ox wagons hitched together drawn by eleven yokes of oxen lumbered in from Franklin, full of citizens of every political, religious and cultural affiliation. The exception being, no black families.

A gathering of this importance always carried with it an unwritten declaration of truce. There were abolitionists, slaveholders, free-state voters, pro-slavery voters, Border Ruffians and people with no affiliation one way or the other.

Baldwin's ferry was overwhelmed with traffic, those further back redirected west to the new Rosen brother's ferry near Lecompton or east to Paschal Fish's ferry at the mouth of the Wakarusa river. C.W. Babcock volunteered the pasture behind his house as the designated parking area; it filled rapidly, the overflow parked along the streets and vacant lots. A podium was erected for speeches and entertainment in the large field northeast of town by the Anderson grove. Tables were spread at the Pleasant Grove park on Mt. Oreod in preparation for the meal.

John and Sally left the Wood home at 7 AM, John to the stable to get Border Ruffian ready for the horseraces.

"I can send David to fetch him, John T, you don't have to do it."

"I'd feel better doing it myself. The boys are already out in the street watching the parade."

Margaret finally convinced Sally to say a few words about freedom, what it will mean to the slave.

"I know how you feel about Independence Day, Sally. Sam and I feel the same, but a few words from you will mean more than all the speakers put together. You're the only person here who can describe what it feels like to suffer at the hands of a cruel master," Margaret pleaded.

"Frederick Douglass would do it if he were here," Sam said.

Sally gave him a withering look, "Well, I ain't Frederick Douglass. That don't help, Sam. But I do agree with Margaret. I'll make a short speech. I've never given one before, I hope it doesn't cause more trouble than it's worth, some of those people out there are slaveholders and I saw some Border Ruffians camped over by the river. You've got to watch them, Sam."

Promptly at nine the band struck up 'Sweet Home' followed by 'Camp Town Races' and the day was officially started.

David, Caleb, Jimmy Pratt and Larry Tappan ran from Babcock's field where they helped direct traffic, to Barker Street for the horse races.

"I know Border Ruffian will win," David said.

Jimmy teased him, "My daddy said that Mr. Buckley is bringing a special racehorse from Westport. He's betting on it to win."

"That's cheating," Caleb announced.

"Why?"

"The horse has to be from Kansas, everybody knows that."

Jimmy looked at Larry, for conformation, it did seem plausible that such a rule existed. Larry merely shrugged.

Onlookers were lined up five-deep along the track. The boys crawled between spectator legs until they reached the road just as the starting gun sounded. The noise was deafening as the horses thundered down the street kicking dust and clods, obscuring the view, especially at ground level. They screamed for Border Ruffian; others cheered for their favorite. Many a dollar was riding on the winner. Even Sam placed a small wager, he considered it a sure thing, but forgot to mention it to Margaret in all the excitement.

The horses flew past, almost close enough to touch. Noise surged north with the passing, like an ocean wave rolling over the prairie. They could follow the progress with their ears as the contestants turned east on the Old Shawnee Road, then grew quieter and quieter as they charged past the Hanson place far across the fields and forest. Then the noise began to swell again as they turned back onto Barker; bearing down on the finish line about 20 yards south of where they crouched.

David clenched his hands in prayer, eyes tight shut.

"Open your eyes, Davey," Caleb shouted, "they're coming down the finish."

"We won," Jimmy screamed pounding David on the back; Sam charged across the line a full two lengths in front of the field, his arm flung high in victory. They jumped up and down hugging each other.

After receiving first place ribbon, Sam led Ruff back to the boys. They crowded around offering congratulations along with many friends and neighbors. The throng began to disperse. He held out the reins, "Take Ruff to the stables, rub him down good, water and feed, then turn him out in the corral. I've got a million things to do." The boys paraded Border Ruffian proudly amongst many offers of congratulations as they led the victor to the barn.

Chores completed, they hurried to the grove. Carol Barnett arrived at the same time, dressed in the youngest brother's hand-me-downs; woolen trousers, a cotton shirt her hair piled under a hat. Carol wanted desperately to be one of the guys, being nine, a bit older than Caleb and David, a bit younger than Jimmy and Larry. Joining the audience around the cannonball toss, they cheered Carol's daddy, Harold, locked in a battle with several others including two of his sons.

"My daddy will win," Carol assured them, as he easily tossed the 20-pound ball down the field.

"Your brother is big," Caleb said, "he might win."

"No, Bull is smart, even if he could beat daddy, he knows better than to do it," she laughed.

Competition over, Harold victorious, hugged his sons, accepted congratulations from the spectators. Carol and David ran to the podium where the band had struck up 'Row, Row, Row Your Boat'. All the children, many young adults and even some older married couples, plopped down in the grass, faced each other hand in hand and rowed their imaginary boat. Peals of laughter rang out for those mature participants who had difficulty getting back up. Sarah Wood hurried over to help Judge Wakefield's wife haul him back on his feet, "I've got to cut down on the apple pies."

The band immediately launched into 'Pop goes the Weasel'. Pretend 'weasels', squatted down and popped up at the appropriate time. The judge refused to participate no matter the good-natured teasing. Flags waved; fiddles played; a sea of bright colors, laughing voices celebrating the birth of the nation, of freedom from tyranny.

A lunch signal sounded. The crowd moved toward Pleasant Grove. Sarah, Donna, Maisey Epcot all helped serve the meal, locate lost children, shoo the dogs away. Whatever needed done they took it upon themselves to do. Sarah's party, the highlight of the fourth of July celebration, at least for the young ladies, was starting at six pm.

Carol found David and friends at a table near her parents, her best friend, Mary Dietzler with her, "Come on you guys we're all going to play hide and seek down by the river."

"We can play hide and seek anytime. I don't want to miss anything here."

Carol's sister Diane watched the conversation from the adjoining table. Diane loved to dress up frilly; this was the perfect occasion for it.

"She's an embarrassment to me Mother," Diane scolded Autumn.

"Who dear?"

"Carol, who else? Look at her, she's dressed worse than the boys. Her hair is ridiculous, and that hat. You can't even tell she's a girl. Why don't you make her at least dress decently? Her friend is presentable, although that smock is filthy."

Autumn loved her daughters with all her soul, but it would not have broken her heart had they been boys. Five boys would have meant two more land claims. Autumn was a businesswoman at heart, a mother of necessity.

"Diane, please stop worrying about Carol, she's only nine. Come on let's help Margaret and Sara set out the dessert."

Diane, 17, dressed in her Sunday finest, hair parted in the middle, bobbed up on the sides, was the embodiment of Kansas fashion. She had her eye on a promising young beau by the name of Jay Brooks; yes, the Ohio University stutterer sat squarely in her matrimonial sights, unbeknownst to, well, to everyone save Diane. Her knowledge of boys consisted of neighbor farmers, the image of her brothers, suitable enough in their own way, but not the type of romantic young man she dreamed of late at night. She first laid eyes on Jay when shopping in the Brook's Mercantile where he was leaning against the counter reading a poem to his sister-in-law, Elvira, remarkably without a stutter.

>*We were apart; yet, day by day,*
>*I bade my heart more constant be.*
>*I bade it keep the world away,*
>*And grow a home for only thee;*
>*Nor fear'd but thy love likewise grew,*
>*Like mine, each day, more tried, more true.*

Elvira, hand on heart, praised him, "Oh, Jay, you read so beautifully. Doesn't he Diane?"

Startled, unaware that they were mindful of her presence, she tried to make words form, but failed. Jay turned to look with a hint of a smile at the corner of his mouth. Out of the store she stumbled, breathlessly berating herself for such cowardice. Stalking behind the wagon, peering over the buckboards to see if he was looking, scolding herself for such childish behavior.

"Diane, what is the matter with you?" Autumn asked as she loaded a box of supplies.

"Nothing mother. Are you ready to go home?"

***

The meal over, everyone drifted toward the podium for the much-anticipated afternoon speeches. Chairs were erected for the ladies in the shade of the grove, umbrellas and a megaphone for the speakers. The crowd, at least two thousand, mainly Free-State adherents, some of the less antagonistic pro-slavery people and a few Border Ruffians already into their jugs.

"Why are they here?" Judge Wakefield wondered aloud to no one in particular. Harold, his three sons and several other Lawrence men were deputized to watch them and watch they did. "Bogus Jones sure won't do anything to control them," the Judge grumbled.

Sam spotted Jacob and Elenora Branson along with Chuck Dow, "Hey Chuck, Jacob," he hailed them. They waited while Sam jogged over, "Hello Mrs. Branson. Listen, I haven't forgotten you. I hope to get over to Hickory Point next week."

Chuck responded, "Thank you, Mr. Wood." He kicked the dirt, took off his hat. He had something on his mind, "This whole thing has me stumped. Frank Coleman and Harry Buckley, why are they pickin' a fight with me? I can't figure it out."

"I don't know either, Chuck, but we'll get to the bottom of it," Sam comforted him.

Elenora waved over a group, newly arrived as Sam turned to go. "Sam, wait a minute, have you met our neighbors, Mr. and Mrs. Barber?"

A young couple, along with two other men approached. Sam replied, "I know the name, but I believe Roger Kern registered your claim didn't he. I rewrote the legal description based on the survey that John Brown made. Over by Bloomington, right?"

"Yessir, Mr. Wood. It is a real pleasure. We were hoping to meet you. I'm Tom Barber, this is my wife, Marie, my brother Robert. That's my brother-in-law Tom Pierson and his wife Anne."

Hands were pressed all around.

Sam added, "I want to introduce you folks to my wife. I hope you'll stay for the festivities this evening."

Pierson was a bit older, took the initiative, "We're not only free-state men, but abolitionists, Mr. Wood. We came to Kansas to make sure it is a free state."

"We need all the good men we can get, and women," he added smiling at the ladies. "We're having a free-state convention in August. I'll make sure your names are on the list. Now don't forget about meeting Margaret tonight. She's got a couple of ladies groups that you need to know about."

Margaret signaled the band; they played a fanfare, and she climbed the stairs to the stage at precisely 1:30. "Welcome ladies and gentlemen to the very first fourth of July celebration in Kansas Territory. You've made it a memorable one just by being here and we aren't finished yet. Don't forget the fireworks on Massachusetts beginning at dusk. There are two parties tonight, one at the Pioneer house for the younger folks and one at the new Public House for the adults."

She thanked each of the members of the organization committee then finished with a fine speech about women on the frontier, concluding with these words,

"Woman's sphere is wherever there is a wrong to make right, a tear to wipe away, a good work to carry forward. And tis here to guard our beautiful State from the invasion of wrong, oppression, intemperance, and all that tends to debase and demoralize mankind. Yes, Kansas must and will feel that woman has an influence, and that influence on the side of God and truth."

The audience cheered heartily, threw hats in the air and even a few gunshots, which brought one of the deputies to discourage that behavior.

Charlie Robinson spoke next, white long-sleeved shirt, rolled at the sleeves, half untucked. Charlie projected the image of a working man's politician and proud of it. Let me roll up my sleeves, get right into whatever needs to be solved. As long as it didn't involve actual physical labor, Charlie was your man. He warmed them up with tales of arriving,

"almost one year ago to the coldest winter imaginable with no shelter, people living in tents, cooking in open air communal

kitchens, sharing food, clothes, fire, whatever it took to survive. We withstood these hardships for one reason," he shouted, index finger held high. *"Let every man stand in his place and acquit himself like a man who knows his rights, and knowing, dares maintain them. Let us repudiate all laws enacted by foreign legislative bodies, such as the one meeting, at this very moment, at Shawnee Mission in direct disobedience to Governor Reeder's orders."*

He shook his fist in defiance as the crowd screamed approval.

Several Border Ruffians began moving through the crowd possibly in a coordinated manner. Sam had his eye on them from a chair on the podium sitting behind Charlie, who continued,

"Tyrants are tyrants and tyranny is tyranny, whether under the garb of law or in opposition to it. So, thought and so acted our ancestors, and so let us think and act. We are not alone here in Kansas. The entire nation is agitated upon the question of our rights, the spirit of '76' is breathing upon our very souls. Every pulsation in Kansas vibrates to the remotest artery of the body politic, and I seem to hear the millions of free men, and the millions of slaves held in bondage in our land, the spirits of our Revolutionary heroes, and the voice of God, all saying to the people of Kansas, 'Do your duty.'" He pointed his finger at the crowd, repeating the punch line each time, *"Do your duty, Do your duty."*

The crowd went crazy cheering and stomping. A few guns discharged again, causing Sam to flinch. He was still watching the Border Ruffians when Margaret introduced him to respond to Charlies patriotic speech.

"Sam," she prompted, finally getting his attention.

He rose, walked to the megaphone, motioning to Harold about the threat.

"I see them," the deputy said.

"Ladies and gentlemen, you know me as a man of action. Those noble words so bravely spoken by Governor

Robinson," the crowd cheered again. "Yes, I call him Governor Robinson because in a free election with true Kansas voters that is what he would be as we stand here today."

"Now most of you," he pointed in a wide circle, *"are Free State men. But look about you and you'll see maybe a dozen Border Ruffians. Yes, gentlemen, I see you and I warn you with all my soul, if you disrupt these proceedings, I will bring down the wrath of God on your heads."* He brandished his cane, pointing at each one. The crowd grew quiet then a slow murmur started as they spotted the troublemakers. *"And don't make the mistake of thinking I'll have to do it alone. Look around you. There are men deputized to make certain my words are not idle threats."*

He stepped to the front of the podium. The crowed maintained the silence. He glared at a few of the Ruffians then turned back to the megaphone, *"Ladies and Gentlemen, let us rejoice in Governor Robinson's brilliant words, throwing down the gauntlet, drawing a line in the sand, stating clearly our resolve to make Kansas a free state and our nation a haven of free men of every color. NO more chains."* The crowd cheered again, and the mood could not be broken. *"Right now, the woods resound with our cheers. Two thousand voices screaming for a Free Kansas. Let us dream of that day, in the near future, that not only will Kansas be a free state, but four million slaves will pass through the Red Sea of Blood to a land of freedom. Whatever it takes, my friends, to make that happen."*

He stopped to let the cheers subside then held up a sheet of paper, "I have here a copy of the laws passed at Shawnee Mission last week; edicts that purport to be the laws of Kansas. Ladies and Gentlemen, they are the Laws of the State of Missouri. This law would have disgraced South Carolina in the palmy days of slavery. Let me read to you one of the articles,

'If any free person, by speaking or writing, assert or maintain that persons have not the right to hold slaves in this

Territory, they shall be deemed guilty of felony, and punished by imprisonment at hard labor for a term of not less than five years."

Boos and hisses echoed across the grove.

"Listen, listen, there's more,

'The enticing, decoying, or carrying out of the Territory a slave belonging to another person is punishable by DEATH.'" He paused to let that sink it. "I'll tell you true, neighbors, according to this new law passed by the bogus Kansas Legislature, I'm guilty of a felony by speaking to you here today and a crime punishable by death for actions I took over the weekend."

The crowd went wild cheering until they were hoarse. Margaret hugged her husband as he waved, shook hands with Charlie, held their hands together aloft.

Getting everyone's attention took a while before Margaret could introduce the next speaker, Mr. Cyrus Holiday from Topeka, who announced the construction of a new building, strongly hinting that it would serve beautifully as the capitol of the new State of Kansas. That, of course, brought another round of cheers.

Next, Mr. Babcock read the Declaration of Independence.

The town council monitored the Border Ruffian threat. "I don't think they're organized to cause trouble," Judge Wakefield assessed, standing behind the podium speaking to Sam and Harold. "Let's just keep watching them. Why the hell are they here anyway?"

"I think Atchison sent them to disrupt the party," Harold said, leaving to find his boys in the crowd. Sam climbed back on the podium to better watch the threat and enjoy Babcock's melodious, well-trained voice read the most important document in American History.

"We hold these truths to be self-evident, that all men are created equal, that they are endowed by their Creator with

certain unalienable Rights, that among these are Life, Liberty and the pursuit of Happiness."

Next, General James Lane made his address,

"If I believed a prayer from me would do any good, it would be that we be imbued with the wisdom of Solomon, the caution of Washington, and the justice of Franklin. As men born in a land of liberty, trained to precepts of freedom, and alive to those inspiring sentiments which have prompted in all ages heroic resistance to tyrants; as descendants of those who in 1776 braved the power of the mightiest monarchy on earth rather than submit to foreign thralldom, we repudiate this insolent attempt to impose upon us a government by foreign arms, and pledge to each other, as our fathers did of old, our lives, our fortunes, and our sacred honors, to a resistance of its authority. We have here today, on this fourth of July 1855, Whigs, Democrats, Free Soilers, and abolitionists, trying to unite and devise some means to rid ourselves of the oppressions of the Border Ruffian Legislature. May God grant us the strength to prevail."

"Where are they now, Bull?" Harold addressed his oldest son.

"They all wandered off together over by the corral in the southwest corner."

"Bull?" Tap said.

"Yeah, everybody calls me that cause I'm so big," he laughed showing his bicep.

"They call me Chief," the middle boy said, "because of my nose."

"That's a nose to be proud of," Sam laughed. "Shows you are your mother's son. What do you think, Harold, shall we go over there and tell them to leave?"

Jim Lane finished speaking, wandered over to the group and asked from the podium, "What's up fellas?"

"Can you see those Ruffians from there?" Tap asked

Lane turned back to the crowd, "Yes, I see them in the back corner, maybe nine or ten. Looks like they're standing around, probably drinking; their horses are saddled; maybe they're getting ready to leave."

Suddenly the crowd grew quiet as Colonel Dietzler began speaking with the obvious intention of introducing the two Indian speakers. "Ladies and Gentlemen, it gives me great pride..."

"Wait, why is George introducing the Chiefs?" Sam asked.

Harold growled, "He said he wanted to prove how compassionate he is."

Sam put his hands to his head, glanced up, saw Margaret, gestured to her, "What is going on?"

"He insisted," she mouthed the words to him.

The Colonel's voice boomed out, "...Our Aboriginal neighbors; peaceful Indians who have shown their ability to behave in a proper manner. Not savages like I fought in the Dakotas, but civilized men who value the freedoms that I and my ancestors won on the field of battle."

Sam moaned, "Oh Lord, will you listen to that. Chief Fish has every right to scalp him."

Dietzler continued, "...their presence and participation with us today is a mutual recognition of unity and goodwill. May we ever 'smoke the pipe of peace together.' Now let me introduce our friend and neighbor, Chief Paschal Fish of the Shawnee Nation."

Fish mounted the stage with his daughter Eudora and Autumn Barnett who were to act as interpreters. Fish, in spite of an excellent grasp of English, chose to speak in his native language. He spoke of gratitude that the war with the British was concluded favorably and his wish that the peoples of the United States would learn to live together in peace and harmony. Suddenly war woops and shouts could be heard in the distance.

"What in the world," Judge Wakefield said.

"Sam, come look," Margaret ordered.

He bounded up the stairs to a view of the Border Ruffians mocking the speaker, dropping their drawers, taunting Chief Fish, "Woo, woo, woo," pretend battle cries echoed across the field.

Sam bounded down the stairs, "Let's go," he ordered.

They skirted the crowd. Many of the audience looking back at the drunken louts, some in disgust, some laughing. "Here now, you clowns stop that," Sam shouted. Harold and his boys hunched up in front of the gang ready for anything.

"Oh, Hell, we was just funnin' with em'. Didn't mean nothing by it."

"I don't think it's funny," Judge Wakefield huffed and puffed arriving late to the confrontation, winded from the short run. "If you are going to act like animals go on and leave."

The Ruffians wandered back to their logs and stumps; additional jugs appeared out of the heavy packs.

"Judge, I'm supposed to respond to Chief Fish's speech and also the Delaware Chief Pechalka, but I'm going to stay here to watch these fools. Go make some comments will you please?" Sam asked. He moved a few feet away from the Ruffians along with Bull, Chief, Harold and Tap. Gradually their attention was drawn to the speaker.

After Wakefield's short speech thanking the Indian's for their contribution to the celebration, Margaret took the podium to announce the final speaker, "Ladies and gentlemen, a special guest, is with us today. Someone that best symbolizes all that the Declaration of Independence stands for, echoed in the words Mr. Babcock read to us just a short time ago, 'all men are created equal'. Please give a warm welcome to our neighbor and my friend, Mrs.

Sally Thompson. Polite applause from the audience and sounds of disbelief from the Ruffians even a few boos as Sally mounted the stage.

She took a deep breath hesitating on the top step, glanced back at John who gestured to continue and mouthed the words, 'go on'. A tension consumed the crowd and a hopeless sensation of defeat washed over Sally. Suddenly, Autumn Barnett began clapping. Others took up the welcome, sound grew, amplified, became a rousing cheer. Sally glanced at Margaret with a relieved smile, stepped to the megaphone,

"Thank you, friends, neighbors and all visitors to this celebration of the independence of our Nation. I am unable to participate fully because as a black woman, I am not considered a citizen. I am free legally, but not spiritually nor equally in the eyes of the nation. At any moment the Government might declare my presence intolerable and force me out of this country; the country in which I was born. My birthright is to be an American citizen, but I am not a citizen; I have no rights, no right to vote; no right to an education, to marry, to own property. Many states have already introduced laws to force the removal of all free black people from their boundaries, just as they did to the Indians. My brothers and sisters, most four million of them are held in bondage throughout the south and there are tyrants who want to bring the vile institution of slavery to our beautiful state. Just the mention of the word makes me shudder, causes me to cringe in fear of the whip.

A famous philosopher named Voltaire wrote, 'Anyone who has the power to make you believe absurdities has the power to make you commit injustices.' The south would have you believe that the slave is happy, contented, satisfied to be the property of his 'Massah'. Nay, desirous of being his property, singing in the fields, praising his master's kindness and generosity. Absurd! I scream. Absurd! Absurd to believe that any man or woman would be content fettered with chains, whipped for the slightest reason or no reason at all. Absurd to believe such lies, yet it happens every day in the south. Thank you, all of you, who see that injustice and stand ready to fight to end it...

A pistol shot rang out. Sally fell to the floor. John wailed a cry of anguish that could be heard at the river, "Noooo." He leapt onto the podium, cradled his wife's head as blood seeped into his hands.

Sam spun around looking for where the shot came from, spotted the Border Ruffians riding hard for Hickory Point Road. One was leading a horse, saddled but no rider; Sam took after him on foot. From the crowd emerged a Ruffian intent on intercepting the riderless horse; the shooter, Sam was certain. He jumped, grabbed the man by the nape of his neck as he climbed into the saddle. The other man, the one leading the horse, took one look and left at a gallop. The shooter kicked at Sam who pulled his hat off, looked him square in the face. It was the same man he had beaten in Westport the day of his return from the East.

With a swift kick between the legs he dislodged Sam who fell to the ground in considerable pain, yet more anguish in letting the man escape. He gingerly got to his feet watching the guilty man dash away. Turning back to the stage a large crowd of people were gathered around Sally. He slowly started walking that way, "My God, what have I done? It was my job to watch her," he said aloud.

Harold, Bull, Chief, Tap, Caleb Pratt, and a couple of others, charged by riding hard in pursuit of the murderers. Where'd they get the horses? Bull waved for him to come on. Sam watched for a moment, thought of following, turned sluggishly back to the stage. People were running here and there, others in the crowd stood dazed in small groups. David and Caleb came running up to him.

"Papa, are you ok? We saw you fall. Are you going after them? Mr. Barnett is already gone."

"I'm not hurt son. I know who did it. I'll follow later. I've got to check on Sally. Caleb, is your mother...? I don't know what I'll do..." Anger was surging through him. "I'll wipe out every Border Ruffian in Kansas."

"She's alive, Papa."

"She is?"

"Yes, but she's bleeding from her head," Caleb said, tears in his eyes. "A lot of blood." Sam kneeled down, gathering the boy in his arms.

"Wipe out every last one of them," he vowed to himself.

***

The posse took Hickory Point Road to the Turnpike then east toward Missouri, not knowing if the criminals veered off or not. A Shawnee family in a farm wagon turned into Blue's Trading post, startled by the strange group of angry men.

Tap shouted, "Did a mob of men go by here?"

"They turned down River Road to the ferry."

"If they get across, we'll never catch them," Caleb said, "They'll cut the raft loose."

On they rode, not sparing the horses for the short ride; horses they'd requisitioned from neighbors preparing to return home from the celebration.

Harold asked, "Has anyone got a rifle?"

"There's a Sharps in this scabbard," Caleb shouted.

Shawnee Road curved back to the east on the bluff before winding down to the ferry. The last load of six Ruffians reached the north bank of the river as the posse crested the butte.

"Take a shot, Caleb, the guy without the hat. He's the one Sam tried to tackle."

"I'll do it, Pa," Bull volunteered.

"No, I'll do it," Tap ordered, "I don't want you boys in trouble with the law. Anyway, I'm the best shot." He climbed down, took the Sharps rifle from Caleb, looked in the saddlebags for cartridges, calmly loaded and prepared to fire. Those six Ruffians already across pointed at the posse and road off at a gallop leaving their friends to cut the raft loose, not to mention face the superior angle of fire from the hill.

Tap braced the rifle on a low branch, took aim and fired.

"You hit him, Mr. Tappan," Chief shouted.

The criminals rode off, shooter slumped in the saddle supported by one of his friends. The raft drifted askew down the river chased by angry attendants.

"I hope Sally's not dead," Caleb said watching the Ruffians ride off. "If she is, there'll be hell to pay."

"Probably will be, regardless," Harold replied. "I agree with Sam, war is inevitable, and this is as good an excuse as any to start it."

The posse turned back to Lawrence.

"The only thing necessary for the triumph of evil is for good men to do nothing." Edmund Burke

The two weeks following the celebration witnessed accusations hurled back and forth through the newspapers. The Lawrence Tribune accused Atchison and his cronies of attempted murder. The Leavenworth Herald claimed that innocent Missouri citizens were assaulted, one wounded while returning home, by the 'Abolitionist Maniacs' in Lawrence. "Shot from ambush, for no apparent reason other than a disregard for law and order."

Sam was restrained from going to Westport by Sally's entreaties to please stay in Lawrence. "I don't want revenge and you might end up in jail or shot yourself. Please let it go, Sam," she pleaded. Sally's head was no longer wrapped in the white bandage that she had worn for a week after the shooting, in fact, the shaved wound above her ear was starting to show evidence of hair regrowth.

The house was full of people. Sam's brother, Stephan his wife Caroline visiting from Iowa; Sarah who spent the past two weeks as nursemaid to Sally, smothering the poor woman with kindness; and a settler family of five, from New York, by the name of Meyers. Like most newcomers, the Meyers were there for the 160 acres of land but uncertain they wanted to stay after witnessing the hardships of living on the frontier. Sam planned to take them on a tour of the area, point out some available land claims.

The children including the Meyers oldest son, Lance, came running into the house. David carried an object he displayed, "Look at this," he held up the round sphere.

"What is it," Margaret asked.

Lance proclaimed proudly, "It's a baseball. The best game you've ever played."

Mr. Meyer took the ball, held it up, "This is a game everyone in New York City is playing. They organize into teams and conduct baseball contests against each other. It's quite the rage. I'm sure Lance will have the boys around here playing it in no time."

"We used to play a game called 'town ball', remember Sam?" Stephan interjected.

"Yes, I do. Fun game, but it doesn't sound exactly like this New York game. We only had three posts, didn't we?"

Lance interjected, "We call them bases."

The boys ran back to the street to throw the ball back and forth to each other.

"Sam, I saw Mrs. Branson at Brook's today. She said that Mr. Coleman has threatened Chuck Dow over the claim dispute. Mr. Dow is such a nice man. I hate to see him suffer over this. Have you figured out a way to solve it yet?" Margaret asked.

"No, I have not. Coleman is really nothing more than a Border Ruffian. When the government surveyors redraw the lines, Coleman will have to accept it. I don't understand his reasoning, it's as though he wants to provoke Jacob and Chuck. It just doesn't make much sense."

"Maybe Coleman has some other reason, like he wants Mr. Dow's land for himself," John said handing a glass of water to Sally.

"Could be that, whatever it is, it'll be trouble in the end. I'll probably go over there next week and see what can be done. I'm trying to wean myself from the day-to-day work at the registrar office."

David poked his head out the back door, "Papa John, there's a man on the front porch asking for you."

"Who is it, Davey?"

"I don't know, I've never seen him before, he's a black man, I think a slave."

John got up with a glance at Sally to join him. They went outside leaving the rest of the party to wonder. In a few minutes, Sally came back, asked Sam to join the men on the front porch. Margaret raised an eyebrow questioning, but Sally was reluctant to say anything in front of the Meyers, not knowing their stance on slavery issues. She could easily put someone's life in danger, by revealing too much. She changed the subject, "Mrs. Meyers, what part of New York are you from?"

Sam found John speaking with a small, grey headed man who might be forty or might be sixty, it was hard to tell. He wore trademark slave rags of coarse cotton and had the hangdog look of a man accustomed to the whip.

"This is Sam Wood," John introduced him, "Sam this is, Jobah, his slave name is Martin Blackwell. I'll let him tell you the story."

"Mr. Wood," he began, his eyes fixed on the wooden planks of the porch as he crouched in the corner out of view from the street, "My Massah, Blackwell..."

"Go ahead, Jobah, we know how bad things are. You don't need to hide anything from Mr. Wood. He understands."

"I bin tole' ya'll kin help us," he broke down trying to continue. John placed his hand on the man's shoulder.

"Massah Blackwell, he most ungodly cruel n' heartless, Mr. Sam. I can't begins to share de depth o' evil in dat man. He done kill one of us since we bin here. Po' Silas, shot im' when Massah git almighty full o' likker.

Shot im' daid. He beat ma' sister mos' near to death las' week. He a wicked man. Kin ya help us, Mr. Thompson?"

"Sam, I'll take Jobah with me. You tell Sally to go on home and I'll be back shortly. Keep Caleb and Missy here with you tonight."

"Don't you want me to go with you?"

"No, there ain't going to be a trial, like in Ohio, this is gonna' be pack up and go, and when Blackwell comes around blaming you, I don't want you to know anything about what happens. Understand?"

Sam reached out to shake hands with Jobah, who pulled away in astonishment, then extended his hand, "I never shook hands with a white man, Mr. Sam."

Sam smiled, "Good luck to you. John T will see that you're safe," he went back inside to give Sally the news. As it turned, out the Meyers were loyal abolitionists, and the caution was not needed; but that didn't mitigate the danger. Even in Yankee Town, secrecy was paramount.

***

That same week, Sam, Charlie Robinson, Judge Wakefield and Tap Tappan sat on Sam's porch discussing the latest news from Atchison where a free-state man name of Butler was assaulted and beaten badly by a mob of Border Ruffians.

"It seems that no abolitionist is safe outside of Lawrence."

"I don't like it, Sam," Tap added, "Every time we make some progress, something like this happens. I hear Butler just arrived from Illinois and didn't realize the danger of provoking the Ruffians. Same thing that happened to Bill Phillips."

Robinson said, "I was at Blue's earlier having a cup of coffee, Coleman, Buckley and Hargis were drinking whiskey in there. I couldn't hear everything they said but

I caught enough to know that you need to watch yourself, Sam. These are dangerous men. We can't grow complacent."

"I wish they would try something, Charlie, give me a reason to teach them a lesson, I'm tired of talking to them."

It was a pleasant evening, several families were out for a stroll. George Dietzler and his wife, Rita, stopped, also Caleb and Louise Pratt. Sam took the ladies inside to visit with the other wives. He returned to the porch with another chair for Dietzler who was saying, "...We need to expand Caleb's militia and Jim Lane is just the man we need to command it. We best be prepared in case those Border Ruffians get organized, yet I don't want to alarm the newcomers."

"General Lane would be an excellent choice," Pratt said. "By the way, Tap, I heard that fellow you shot on the fourth is bragging in Westport about killing a Nigger in Lawrence. I assume he means Sally Thompson."

"Probably doesn't know she's still alive," Tap replied. "I've got a feeling we'd better hope for the best but plan for the worst. Sam, are you about finished with the incorporation papers? We could put out a call for every able-bodied man and make it from the Lawrence City Council or something like that."

"I'm close enough to being finished that we can start having elections."

The discussion grew heated as Judge Wakefield and Charlie Robinson insisted that they have a town meeting to handle these affairs because the town had grown enough that a few men couldn't make a decision for everyone. Sam argued that they made Lawrence what it was; they could form the first government and then hold elections in the spring. The situation demanded immediate action and an election would take weeks.

"Goddammit, Sam," Dr. Robinson said in a fit of anger, "This is why people are getting fed up with your tactics. You won't compromise. You need to listen to what other people are saying and not insist on your way all the time."

"There's no need for curses in my house, Charlie," Sam said.

Robinson muttered something incomprehensible and Sam accosted him, "What did you say, Robinson."

"I said that you are impossible to work with."

"Calm down, everyone," Dietzler said. "We don't need to be fighting each other. I'm more in line with what Sam is saying. I don't think we have time to hold elections."

"That's because you are ex-military," Wakefield said, "This isn't a military matter right now, we need to think in terms of the common good. Tap, what do you say?"

"I can see both sides, but we need to make decisions and not fight each other. Let's call a town meeting and get everyone over to the hotel and have a vote, militia first or finish the municipal charter, have elections, and then form the militia. What do you say?"

"That's fine with me," Sam agreed.

Charlie smiled, "Good idea, Tap."

That night David questioned his father about the disagreement with Robinson, an event that Sam downplayed as being of 'no consequence'. He wasn't really angry at Charlie. David wasn't having that explanation.

"But Daddy, Jimmy Pratt said that Mr. Robinson told his daddy that he put you in your place. What does that mean?"

"He said what?" Sam shouted. "I'll go over there right now. Who does he think he is?"

"Sam, come on now, I doubt Charlie said any such thing. You know how young boys are, and remember your advice to David," she cautioned with a stern look. By the time Margaret got him calmed down it was eleven. They lay quietly in the dark, with no lamp, the window open for the breeze, a sliver of moon obscured by low hanging clouds. Margaret sighed deeply.

"Ok, Meg, let's have it. I know you're mad at me. I didn't handle it well, did I?"

"You didn't. I know you can't change who you are, nor am I asking you to, but the Robinsons are our friends. Sara is one of my best friends... you have to be more patient when you're working with someone who's on your side. Save your anger for our enemies."

"I guess I'll have to go apologize. Right?"

"Don't you want to?"

"Not really, he should apologize to me."

"Well, I think you should. It doesn't matter who's right or wrong. We need Charlie and Sara. We can't build this town while the two leading citizens are fighting each other.

"All right, I'll do it. I'll bet he holds a grudge over it anyway."

"It's not Charlie I'm worried about holding a grudge, Sam."

He kissed her, snuggled down with his face cuddled against her arm. He fell asleep in minutes. Margaret got up to close the window, then lay silently, listening to Sam's heavy breathing and the patter of rain against the windowpane.

Part Two

"But Lawd! I've seen such brutish doin's---runnin' niggers with hounds and whippin' them till they was bloody. They used to put 'em in stocks. When they didn't put 'em in stocks, used to be two people would whip 'em---the overseer and the driver. The overseer would be a man named Elijah at our house. He was just a poor white man. He had a whip they called the BLACK SNAKE...."The first overseer I remember was named Kurt Johnson. The next was named Mack McKenzie. The next one was named Pink Womack. And the next was named Tom Phipps. Mean! Liked meanness! Mean a man as he could be. I've seen him take down and whip em till the blood run out of em.

LUCRETIA ALEXANDER, AGE 89 LITTLE ROCK, ARKANSAS: FEDERAL WRITERS: SLAVE NARRATIVE PROJECT

It was in the spring of 1854 when Sam issued a promise to emigrate to Kansas, fight the forces of slavery and make Kansas a free state. His pledge was a spur of the moment comment at a time no one believed the Kansas-Nebraska Act would be ratified. It was a decision that he second-guessed often, yet admitted his misgivings to no one, except Margaret. What would their lives be like had they stayed in Ohio? Sam anticipated the monumental task of keeping Kansas free, but he underestimated the challenges of living on the frontier with no shelter, no ready source of food. Had he been alone it would have been easier. With Margaret and the boys, it became a matter of life and death. Fortunately, he had his in-laws, Bill and Elizabeth Lyons, his brother Stephan, the Thompsons and, most importantly, Margaret who took over all of the household management. Sam's entire focus was on making Kansas a free state.

He regularly corresponded with the organizers of the new Republican Party. Monthly letters to Salmon Chase, Zachariah Chandler, Bill Dayton, Abraham Lincoln and Charles Sumner, all former Whigs or Free-Soil Party members who dissolved their party affiliation to form the Republican Party in 1854 at the Little White School House in Ripon, Wisconsin. Not all of them abolitionists, but all opposed to slavery in Kansas. The slaveholders were chomping at the bit to establish slavery North of the 36 30' parallel in the western territories, which was allowed by repeal of the Missouri compromise and passage of the Kansas-Nebraska Act. The only obstacle was Popular Sovereignty, the Stephen Douglas-Henry Clay compromise that allowed the citizens of the territory to determine their destiny, Free or Slave?

Sam still considered himself a Quaker in the mold of his grandfather, Asa Mosher, an adherent of the Hicksites. Margaret believed in an all-powerful God guiding them in their noble quest; Sam felt that God was inside of him. On solitary rides through the Territory, he often thought of his friend Felix Francis, who was as spiritual as any man but didn't believe in a supreme deity other than the forces of nature. Truth was, Sam didn't put much thought into the why, he was more focused on action. Leave the reasons why to the philosophers.

One quiet evening that week he shared with his family a story from childhood. Sam didn't often reminisce. The children listened engrossed with the story. The Thompsons were there, and this particular story was prompted by a sad tale Sally told about a runaway slave who passed through Lawrence that Spring.

Sam listened quietly as Sally finished then, after a lengthy pause of reflection, "I remember traveling with my father. I was ten, maybe eleven years old. We were in Lexington, Kentucky. I believe your uncle Stephan was there and probably Toby," he looked at the boys. "There were a few of us. None of my sisters. Father wanted us to see a slave auction. I'll never forget it as long as I have a memory. White men, women, even children dressed in bright clothes like a circus; the slaves in chains... most naked, maybe a modesty cover." Sam bowed his head, eyes closed as if that horrible scene were before him at that moment. "The fear on their faces... no, it wasn't fear, more a look of defiance almost pride, you might say, like we couldn't strip their pride no matter the treatment. One young man caught my eye. A ring of iron encircled his neck, shackles on his hands and feet, a chain from the iron ring around his neck down through his handcuffs on down to the manacles on his ankles as if he had been born with them. The man, maybe 17, 18, looked at me. I cowered behind father, he pushed me back out, made me look; 'don't ever forget the sin thou has witnessed here today, Samuel. It's the disgrace of mankind, nothing less. No greater shame than this exists.' That proud slave made me feel like I was on display. Stared into my soul, 'look at what you've done' he seemed to say."

"I've witnessed them, Sam. To see the white people treat the slaves like cattle, so...what's the word, Sal?"

"Nonchalant."

"Yes, nonchalant. Like examining the teeth of a horse."

Exactly, but that wasn't the worst," he reached for Margaret's hand. "We turned to leave. I heard a scream, smelled flesh burning, 'What is that Father?' I asked him. He had tears in his eyes. I'd never seen my father cry."

"Why was he crying?" David asked.

Sam looked at the innocent children listening so carefully. Finally, he said, "My father told me, "the new owners are branding their slaves."

"What does that mean?" Missy asked.

Sam looked to John, sorry that he'd broached such an unpleasant subject.

"It's alright, Sam, they need to know. The white men took a hot iron and burned their initials into the flesh of the slave so that everyone would know who owns them."

***

"So, we passed, handcuffed and in silence, through the streets of Washington, through the Capital of a nation, whose theory of government, we are told, rests on the foundation of man's inalienable right to life, LIBERTY, and the pursuit of happiness! Hail! Columbia, happy land, indeed!" Solomon Northup, Twelve Years a Slave

Sam received regular correspondence from prominent abolitionists, including Harriet Tubman, Frederick Douglass, Sojourner Truth, William Still, Lucretia Mott, William Lloyd Garrison. They were actively working with the Republican Party organizing abolitionist conventions throughout the north.

Writing for the Tribune became cumbersome; he left most of the day to day reporting to J.B. Sam held meetings for the Actual Settler's Association and drafted legislation for the Free State convention. He planned to return east for the 1856 Republican Convention in Philadelphia, where he was slated to nominate Salmon Chase as the Republican nominee for President. Sam traveled to Washington three months earlier to participate in the gathering of Republican dignitaries who planned the '56' convention and wrote a platform including the words:

'There should be neither slavery nor involuntary servitude, except for the punishment of crime, in any of the Territories of the United States."

He was stirring the slavery pot and it was coming to a boil faster than he could imagine.

On Tuesday, August 28, 1855, Sam, John T, Caleb and David, were in the land registry office located in the basement of the Territorial Capital Building, called Constitution Hall, on Main Street in Lecompton. They helped Sam copy deeds and affidavits, run errands, doing whatever needed done. He was no longer the official registrar but functioned as the legal advisor to the new registrar, Roger Kern, who was away on business. Sam was filling in for him plus managing the legal work that had accumulated while he had been working on the resolutions for the Free State Convention planned for October in Topeka.

Registering claims was the most important part of creating a fair and just system of land ownership; claimants rode into Lecompton from as far as Atchison, Emporia and west to the Saline River. Entire families would come for this momentous event in their lives, acquiring 160 acres of 'Gods good earth', as one young wife expressed it. They lined up in an orderly fashion and waited their turn, supplied with coffee or lemonade, the men smoking, the women knitting. Sam had taken on the job out of necessity. Both pro-slavery and free-state settlers had confidence in the service he provided because he handled each claim according to the established procedure and guidelines of the law, leaving politics out of the equation.

Sam took the settlers written and oral oath verifying their right to a claim, then wrote the property description which, in the furthest reaches of the Territory, might be no more complex than from the big rock on the northwest corner to a tree marked with an X on the northeast and so on around the boundary of a new homestead; at least until they could get a professional surveyor out to the property. People took the process seriously and any threat to their precious land was seen as an assault on their very existence.

"I need to go over to Hickory Point with Chuck and Jacob and see if I can settle this argument once and for all. They've been fighting with Frank Coleman for five months," Sam said.

"Papa, you want us to go with you?" David asked, pointing to Caleb. The boys loved traveling to the claims and were beginning to know the Territory as well as anyone.

"Not this trip, son."

David glanced at John T who acknowledged his concern. There must be more to it than a simple claim dispute. Dad expected trouble or he would have taken the boys.

Sam was well aware of the issues involving Branson, Dow and a Missouri fellow by the name of Franklin Coleman concerning their land claims eight miles south of Lawrence. A big part of the problem was that Branson and Dow were abolitionists and Coleman a pro-slavery man. Missouri settlers who staked claims prior to the Shawnee Reservation government survey wanted their claims to stand as originally drawn, while the government wanted the lines to be referenced from the Shawnee survey. The dispute concerned about 250 yards of a timber claim between Dow and Coleman. Branson's line was pushed either way depending on which line was accepted. All claim disputes were packed with emotion, sometimes ugly, but this one was a powder keg. The group, already mentioned, was joined by a couple of Missouri thugs by the name of Hargis and Buckley. Sam didn't like the way it was shaping up, and he wasn't in the mood for trouble.

"Gentlemen, I'm here to settle a legal problem concerning a claim. I don't believe we need any of you that aren't party to this matter." He pulled his cane from its scabbard and felt under his shirt to make certain his pistol was at hand.

Harry Buckley defiantly got off his horse, "We got every right to be here, Wood. It's still a free country, far as I know, and I'm damned tired of you tellin' me what I can and can't do."

"Harry, you don't even have a claim here. You live in Missouri."

"By God, I'm fixin' to move here and that son-of-a-bitch," he said, pointing at Jacob Branson, "told me he was gonna' steal my Niggers when I do."

"Never said no such a thang," Branson drawled. "I said, if'n you brang em' here, they'll be free men and ain't nothing you kin do to keep em' from leavin'. Ain't that right, Mr. Wood?"

"Yes, it is, Jacob, but that has no bearing on the matter at hand," Sam was getting angrier by the second, "you don't even have any slaves, Buckley."

"By God, I might get me some, if'n I want too."

Sam barked, "I'm here in an official capacity to settle a land claim dispute between Chuck Dow, Frank Coleman and Jacob Branson. We are not here to discuss the slavery issue and if we were you would be at a terrible disadvantage, Buckley, because that would require an intelligence you don't possess. Now, stay out of this, I mean it," He used his club to emphasize the point.

"Someday, someone's gonna' shove that thing right up your ass."

"Or shoot him," snarled Josiah Hargis.

"It isn't going to be either of you two. Go on about your business and leave this to the parties involved. I mean it, go on now!"

Buckley and Hargis mounted their horses; but the contemptuous scowls revealed everything that needed to be said about their intentions.

"All right let's get to it," Sam said. "I'd like to get home before supper."

They checked the common corners of each 160-acre tract, all of which had been professionally surveyed. Coleman's survey was the oldest and did not reference the Shawnee Reservation government survey. That was the problem and for some reason, Coleman refused to wait until the formal US Government survey, scheduled to begin 'soon'. Coleman was belligerent, argumentative and disrespectful; manners that sorely tried Sam's patience. They stood at the southwest corner of Coleman's claim, "Frank, you'll get 160 acres of land whichever line becomes the official boundary. From where I'm standing, I see no difference between this strip of land and that one. What exactly are you asking for?"

"I want the land I claimed, legitimate, when I got here. I damn sure don't want to share it with those two," he drawled, pointing at Chuck and Jacob.

"You jumped that claim and drove off the man who owned it. What do you mean legitimate? You even tried to burn down my house and steal my claim," Jacob shouted.

"I don't understand why yer so agin' me, Frank? I'm willin' to work this out, but I don't know wut ya want," Chuck said. He pulled off his hat, extended his hand in friendship only to have Coleman brush him off. Chuck shook his head.

Coleman stomped off, mad that his compatriots had been dismissed, nothing was resolved, the problem not even defined. Sam rode the short distance to Jacob's home. Elenora Branson poured coffee while the men discussed the unreasonableness of the entire situation.

"I don't know what more I can do," Sam said, "You may have to take him to court if he keeps arguing after the government survey."

"I sure can't figure it out," Chuck shook his head.

"He's a dangerous man, Mr. Wood. I'm afraid he's gonna' do somthin' bad," Elenora sat down with the men, "he's pro-slavery. You can't predict what those fools will do or why they do it, other than they want Kansas to be a slave state. And that doesn't make a lick of sense. Not a one of them has a slave."

Tom and Robert Barber rode up to the house as Sam stood outside saying his goodbyes.

"Tom, Robert, I'll bet you came to borrow that cross-cut saw, didn't you?" Dow said.

"Yep, thank you, Chuck, we really appreciate it," Robert answered.

"Hello Mr. Wood," Tom got off his horse to shake hands, "Marie sure enjoyed that bible study class your wife invited her to."

"As did mine."

"We're mighty glad to have you folks in the Territory," Sam answered tipping his hat before riding off.

He rode across the prairie past the stand of trees where strawberries flourished, now and forever called Rattlesnake Spring, onward to the Barnett farm about three miles north.

Autumn greeted Sam from the door of her well-constructed, very neat sod home with extensions on each side to accommodate the children. The interior was cozy attesting to the workmanship of the Barnett family.

"Mr. Wood, did Davey and Caleb come with you?" Carol asked.

"No, they wanted to, but I had some business to take care of. Definitely next time." Autumn sent Carol off to find Harold. Sam accepted a cup of cool water, "You folks have really built yourselves a comfortable place, Mrs. Barnett."

"Thank you. Harold is a farmer by trade, but he can do most anything, and he makes sure the boys learn all the skills he has from carpenter to plowing."

Harold arrived along with Bull, "You'll stay for supper, Sam?"

He accepted graciously; Autumn, Carol and Diane hurried about preparing a meal. Sam took the opportunity to describe the events concerning the Dow-Coleman dispute.

"That fellow Coleman is bad news," Harold replied.

"And all of his friends," Bull added. "Mr. Buckley already threatened to kill Chuck, claimed that he and Jacob were plotting to steal Coleman's land."

"That's a new accusation, I haven't heard that one. But it's not true, any more than Jacob threatening to steal their slaves. Those men are just making up excuses as they go along," Sam said.

"How's Sarah today, Sam?" Bull asked. "Tell her I said hello, will you please."

"Fine as far as I know, Bull, I'll tell her you asked about her." The question didn't trigger any curiosity in Sam's mind; as a result, Sarah didn't receive the message.

"I saw the Barber's over at Jacob's house, they are neighbors of yours, aren't they?"

"Fine people," Bull said.

"They help us with plowing or calving, and we do the same for them. We're blessed with good neighbors all around. Same goes for Jacob and Chuck," Harold added, "except for Coleman."

The ride home was mostly in the dark, but with a good moon. Border Ruffian knew the way blindfolded. Something was troubling Sam, but he couldn't quite put it all together. Harold's fear that Atchison was up to something; the ruffian in Westport saying they were better organized; Coleman being unreasonable over a simple matter. It added up to something, but what? "I need to discuss it with Judge LeCompte," he advised Ruff, who was preoccupied with getting home.

> *"And oft the blessed time foretells*
> *When all men shall be free;*
> *And musical, as silver bells,*
> *Their falling chains shall be."*
> **Henry Wadsworth Longfellow, Poems on Slavery.**

The Fourth of July party was postponed because of the attempted murder of Sally Thompson. As it turned out, most people couldn't have come that evening anyway. The new date at the end of August proved to be a better choice after a late summer rainstorm cleared the air and the recently completed Public Meeting House proved ideal for the big soiree. Sarah, Donna Steele, Maisey Epcot and Diane Barnett, invited 150 people. A potluck dinner was organized, musicians summoned with fiddles, a flute, guitars and a piano. Sarah and Margaret were in charge of decorations; flowers, flags, wreaths and paintings hung about the hall. Any excuse for a party was welcome in Lawrence.

That summer, when Jay wasn't working at the store, he followed Sarah around like a puppy. More often than not she had other projects to work on, but that didn't discourage the love-struck young college student. When Sally got shot, Sarah spent two weeks helping the 'wounded warrior' as Margaret had labeled her. Everyone claimed that her speech was the talk of the July 4th celebration and the attempted murder created a martyr in the eyes of the abolitionists.

Sally wasn't buying it. She knew that the attempted murder was just the extreme expression of what many white folks felt; a slave, former or not, had no right to be speaking. It was obvious in their expressions when they looked away quickly as she walked into the store. Maybe back in Massachusetts or Pennsylvania, but not on the Kansas frontier, even in Yankee Town. We don't want you in chains, but we don't want you for a neighbor either, was the subliminal message. The Robinsons, Woods, Barnetts and Tappans the obvious exception and their opinions ruled in Lawrence. Elsewhere, Sally and John knew to maintain their humble, subservient attitude, walk softly, blend into the background or risk the wrath of the Border Ruffians.

Sarah felt that she was making good progress in 'curing' Jay's stutter. What she didn't notice was that he just quit talking around her. She discovered he didn't stutter when he read, so they took to reading poetry to each other, as part of the 'therapy' she was practicing. Sarah was 'in love' with her childhood friend Jimmy Kendrick although she hadn't seen him in four years. Jay, on the other hand, was smitten with the beautiful Sarah, planned to ask for her hand in marriage with a whirlwind honeymoon to school in Ohio. He lived in his daydreams, felt that it was all a logical progression of their friendship because he loved her, not imagining that she didn't feel the same.

Diane Barnett was perceptive enough to realize that Jay had strong feelings for Sarah, even if the object of his affections was oblivious to the situation. Diane was at a disadvantage, not being able to visit as often as the girls who lived in town. It was a five-mile ride from the Barnett farm. She got into town two or three times during the week and every weekend for church. Last Sunday she finally worked up enough courage to speak to Jay

"I loved listening to you read poetry that time, Jay. Did you write it?"

He seemed to look at Diane for the first time, a look that she hadn't seen before, "Really? I, I, I thought you must have ha, ha, hated it, the way you ran out of th, th, the store."

"No, it was so beautiful, I didn't know what to say."

"Well, I didn't write that poem. Matthew Arnold did," he stammered. "I would be honored to read some to you, if you're really interested."

"How about this afternoon? How about right now while we're waiting for church to be over?"

They sat under the large elm that Reverend Lum called the prayer tree in the side yard of the church. Jay read,

> But our love it was stronger by far than the love
> Of those who were older than we—
> Of many far wiser than we—
> And neither the angels in Heaven above
> Nor the demons down under the sea
> Can ever dissever my soul from the soul
> Of the beautiful Annabel Lee;

"That was wonderful, Jay. Who wrote it?"

"Edgar Allen Poe. I didn't know you like poetry, Diane. Why haven't you mentioned it before?"

"I don't get much of a chance to talk about it at home and you are always busy with Sarah."

She wanted to continue the conversation, as did he, but the demands of the day intervened, "Diane. Come on, daddy is ready to leave," Carol shouted from the corner of the church, uncomfortable in her Sunday dress, anxious to get home to change. "Hello Jay."

Jay smiled, closed the book; they walked to the street, the spell broken. That evening, Jay decided to confide to his brother and sister-in-law of his secret plans to ask Sarah to marry. If he noticed the look of horror that passed between Paul and Elvira, he must have misinterpreted it as approval.

Paul finally found his voice, "But what about your plans to go to college?"

"Sh, Sh, She'll go wi, wi, with me," he answered.

"But, But," Elvira suddenly developed her own stutter, "But have you spoken to Sarah about these plans? Has she agreed to this?"

"Why no, but why wouldn't she agree? We've spent almost every day together since I arrived."

Elvira looked at Paul, the expression conveyed her feelings; poor Jay was delusional.

Paul said firmly, "Jay, you talk to Sarah first then we'll discuss the matter further."

Later that night, after turning out the bedroom lamp, Paul whispered to his wife, "That boy is about to get his heart broken." She nodded in agreement, but it was too dark to see. The answer was obvious and didn't need vocal affirmation.

All week Diane looked forward to the party. She'd been to the mercantile on Wednesday, said to Elvira, "Hello Mrs. Brooks, is Jay in?"

"Diane, how wonderful to see you." Elvira stepped down from the ladder where she was stocking canned goods on an upper shelf. "Jay just carried a few things over to Mrs. Rasmussen. He'll be back shortly. Please sit and wait for him."

"Oh, my no, Mrs. Brooks, I don't want to interrupt his work. Tell him that I stopped by. Daddy's at Mr. McCrea's new blacksmith shop leaving something to be fixed. He'll want to leave, shortly."

"Diane, wait for him," she pleaded, surprising the lovestruck girl with the passion of her offer.

"Well, I suppose Daddy will come get me when he's ready. He knows where I am."

"Yes, yes, of course, Dear. Isn't it wonderful that Mr. McCrea decided to move his shop to Lawrence? Riley and Jane are counting the days until Eric and Katie return with their granddaughter." She leaned in close, "I heard that they are thinking of coming back in a few weeks, but that's all very hush hush," finger to lips, eyes wide to convey the importance of the information.

Diane listened politely. She knew the general details but wasn't acquainted with Eric or Katie. Harold stuck his head in the door, "Come on princess, let's go."

"Goodbye, Mrs. Brooks, be sure to say hello to Jay for me. I'll see him Friday night."

"Yes, I will, Diane. Good luck," she called, wringing her hands, "Oh my," she thought to herself. "What a situation. The poor boy."

"What did she mean, 'good luck'," Harold asked.

"I'm not sure. She was acting quite strange."

Margaret stopped the Barnett's as they rode out of town, "Tell Autumn that the Ladies Bible Study is meeting Thursday night instead of Wednesday. You come too, Diane. Sarah will be there."

"I'll tell mother, Mrs. Wood, thank you."

"And the Barber's."

Harold tipped his hat, took the reins, "Gee up there, Solomon, Lizzie."

Margaret shouted, "The topic of discussion is Proverbs 31:30."

Diane waved that she heard.

Margaret watched the wagon rattle down the street, ran into the store, "Elvira, what did she say?"

"Oh Margaret, what should I do? I wish Jay would never have said anything about his plans to ask Sarah to marry him. She'll break his heart, if he would switch his affection to Diane it would be such a relief."

"We'll have to hope that Diane wins him over first. Do you want me to talk to Sarah about it before the party?"

"I don't know what to do. He asked me last night if he should go ask Sam for her hand in marriage."

"Oh my," Margaret stifled a laugh. "What did you say?"

"I said no, talk to Sarah first. That boy has an abundance of intelligence but very little in the way of smarts. Sarah has helped him overcome his shyness, but she may have created a monster."

"Sarah will have to deal with it in her own way. She created the monster, let her tame it."

***

The new Hutchinson Public House served the perfect venue for the party. Dancers swirled around the large first floor room, children scurried about, the men discussed business, the ladies gossiped, adolescent boys stood along one wall, girls along the other eyeing each other warily.

Sarah and Jay were lost in their own world, a make-believe world that Jay created when he told Sarah his plan to marry her. "But Jay, I didn't know you felt that way about me. We're just friends. I am flattered, but you're little more than a child. I'm a grown woman," Sarah spoke before thinking, obviously shocked by his proposal.

His mouth dropped open; eyes stunned by this duplicity. "Surely you could tell that I was growing to love you," he spluttered.

"I've told you that my heart belongs to another," she sighed, looking to the ceiling as if her childhood love sat in the rafters. "Jimmy and I promised each other we would be married someday." She was secretly thrilled at the attention, didn't want to embarrass Jay, but he was far from her idea of a suitable marriage partner.

"That was when you were 13," he was growing angry, "we all say things like that as children. Now we're adults."

"Jay, You're not yet 18."

"Tho what!" he lisped, stuttered and stammered, "You ha, ha, haven't even th, theen him in f, f, five years." The entire summer of therapy seemed to come unraveled.

Diane eyed them from the refreshment table where she ladled punch. Her biggest challenge was to keep young men from spiking it with alcohol. She spent an inordinate amount of time wiping up spills after pouring over hands instead of the cup, her attention engaged on the drama in the corner.

Margaret caught Sam's arm as he walked by with a jug of lemonade, "Do you know what they are talking about?"

He took a good look, "Don't have a clue. But Jay doesn't look very happy."

"Put the lemonade down and dance with me. You men do nothing but talk politics, tonight we're going to relax."

He gladly followed instructions, took her in his arms while waiting for the music to start again, "Is that a new dress?"

"I wondered if you would notice," she twirled causing the skirt to flare, "See how wide the pleats are? Sally made it for me. Do you like the color, Sam? It's not too much is it?"

The music began, a slow waltz, the floor quickly filled with dancers. "I think it's beautiful, Meg, but you make anything you wear beautiful." They danced, cheek to cheek, alone in the embrace of the music; even at music's end they swayed silently, just the two of them.

While waiting for the next dance she asked a question that she already knew the answer to. Sam was oblivious to personal matters outside his own, "Did you know that Jay asked Sarah to marry him?"

"No, what did she say?"

"Look at them and you'll know."

Jay appeared on the verge of tears as Sarah tried to comfort him, her arm draped over his back patting his shoulder.

"Should I go over there?" Sam asked.

"No, Sarah needs to deal with it, herself."

Tap walked briskly toward them, "that guy Blackwell is out front with Bogus Jones. I don't know what they want, but it looks like trouble. I'll get Harold."

"What is it, Sam?"

He kissed her, "Not sure, I better go find out. The pistol was in the house; too late for that; he grabbed his club from behind the band.

"What's going on, Sam?" Sara Robinson asked.

"I'm not sure, on my way to find out."

Charlie Robinson and Judge Wakefield were talking with Jones and Gary Blackwell, who was furious, his face flushed with anger.

"What proof do you have?" Wakefield said calmly as Sam stepped outside, glanced at the clear sky, a warm evening with plenty of light left in the summer's day, "What's up?"

"You know very well 'what's up' you thievin' son-of-a-bitch," Blackwell shouted.

"Some of Mr. Blackwell's slaves have gone missing," Charlie explained.

Jones interrupted, "You stole them. That's a felony; you need to come with me. You're under arrest, Wood."

Sam scoffed, "First of all, I don't know what you are talking about, and second, there are no slaves in Kansas. If you brought enslaved people into the Territory, they became free the second they crossed the border." He turned to walk back inside.

Jones shouted, "Hold on there, Wood, I'm not finished with you."

Sam spun back, poked his club in Jones' chest prodding him back a step. "I told you to stay away from me. I don't recognize you as sheriff in Douglas County and I don't recognize the bogus legislature that created your laws. Don't make me angry, Jones. I don't know where your slaves are. If I did know I wouldn't tell you."

"Your Nigger stole' em'. He was seen at my place talkin' to em'."

"Who stole them?" Judge Wakefield asked.

"His Nigger," Blackwell pointed at Sam.

"He's not my... Oh for God's sake. He means John Thompson. Go get him Tap, please?"

Blackwell, not accustomed to being around abolitionists, stomped around getting madder by the second, "You people are destroyin' America. What the hell's the matter with ya'? Nigger's got no sense; they won't last a week without a white man tellin' em' what to do."

"Well sir, that is a matter of opinion and we disagree with you on that point," Wakefield argued. The judge loved a good argument, but Jones interrupted him.

"Gary, it don't do no good talkin' to these people bout that. They breakin' the law that's all that we got to tell em'."

Thompson appeared at the door, "John T, you remember Mr. Blackwell? He wants to know; did you steal his slaves?"

"No, the only thing I know about this man is he hired some assassins to try and kill you."

Blackwell pulled his pistol, "That does it you black bastard, I'm gonna' kill you."

Sam snatched the weapon out of his hand, poked him in the chest with the club. Blackwell stumbled backward, fell down; he cried out, "What the hell kind of place is this, lettin' Niggers talk to a white man like that?"

Sam pointed the club, "You two get out of here; stay out of Lawrence." He removed the cartridges from the gun and put it into Blackwell's saddlebags.

Blackwell tried to get up but couldn't haul his fat carcass off the ground; finally, Jones reached down to assist him. "Arrest Sam Wood, sheriff, you saw him assault me. You should'a shot him for that."

Jones glanced at the abolitionists gathered around, glared at Sam, then helped Blackwell on his horse. Jones turned back, "You get hung for stealing slaves. This ain't over Wood. Not by a long shot."

As they rode off, Judge Wakefield turned to John, "Did you help his slaves escape?"

"I heard there was five or six colored folk traveled through here a few days ago. Rumor was they were headed to Canada. I didn't see em' though."

Wakefield laughed, "Yeah, I'll bet you didn't."

Back inside, Margaret waited nervously for Sam to return. A sigh of relief greeted his tap on her shoulder, "Sam, is that the man who tried to shoot you? Sally says it is."

"I'm pretty sure he hired the shooters. I think Atchison put him up to it. I can't prove any of it and no one would do anything about it anyway... how's the party going, beautiful? You still owe me a dance." He hugged her and tried for a kiss.

"Well, let's see, Sarah went home mad, Jay is dancing with Donna; Diane went to comfort Sarah; David has a big bump on his head where he got hit with that ball; Lloyd and Missy took Rita Dietzler's apple pie and carried it over to Cherry Hollow so the black neighbors would feel like they were part of the party. Colonel Dietzler is quite angry. Elvira Brooks claims she got sick from Rachel Tappan's baked bean casserole. Bull Barnett is looking for Sarah; she's got more boyfriends than she knows what to do with. Here he comes now."

Bull tapped Sam on the shoulder, "Hello Mrs. Wood, Sam. I was hoping to have a dance with Sarah, but I don't see her."

Sam left the response to Margaret, "She's over at our house. Why don't you go and see if you can get her to come back to the party?"

Bull, not shy in any situation, crossed Massachusetts street, intercepted Sarah and Diane coming out the front door of the Wood home. She ran to her brother, hugged him, "Hi Bull, what are you doing?"

"Hello little sister. I just got here, had to clean up after work. I came to see Sarah. Will you dance with me?"

Sarah looked from Diane back to Bull. He had never so much as spoken to her prior to this very moment. Diane shrugged, as surprised as Sarah, not knowing anything about her brother's intimate thoughts; didn't think of him as having intimate thoughts. He was her brother and that was the only role she could imagine for him. The idea that he had romantic feelings for Sarah, or anyone for that matter, was inconceivable. As for Sarah, she had never thought of Bull in any way other than a neighbor, Diane's older brother.

Seldom at a loss for words, Sarah stood speechless. Bull waited quietly, no hint of apprehension, just an expectation of her acceptance. She ultimately found her voice, blurted out, "What's your real name?"

"Harold, Junior."

"I'll call you Hal. Bull sounds like the name of a big dog, not a man."

"That's fine with me," he offered his right arm, Diane his left. They marched together back to the festivities. Diane veered off when she spotted Donna waving her over frantically, demanding to know what was going on. Hal took Sarah firmly by the waist and they twirled around the floor.

Sarah caught a glimpse of Margaret out of the corner of her eye, raised her eyebrows and shoulders questioningly. Margaret smiled approvingly.

"You're a good dancer, Sarah, able to follow a big, clumsy lug like me."

Being four or five inches shorter, Sarah had to look up to see if he was joking, found herself looking into his gleaming brown eyes with no hint of sarcasm. She noticed for the first time the handsome tilt of his nose, the firm jaw, a bright smile that took her breath. Sarah felt her heart melting. A sensation so sudden, so unfamiliar that she had to look away to keep from stumbling.

Donna and Diane whispered together about all that was happening; the details differed in exactitude but not in drama. They watched Sarah and Hal looking fondly at each other, saw Jay walking toward them. "This is the best party ever," Donna closed her eyes and squealed with delight. They would have giggled together all night, but Jay interrupted to ask Diane for a dance. Donna pushed her forward not wanting to be the reason she declined. Chief Barnett materialized next to Donna his hand extended and the evening was destined for a rousing success.

Music filled the hall, couples danced, punch consumed, food eaten. Doing their best to escape the strain of everyday life, lovers whispered words of endearment, children played, hearts were broken; new friendships sowed, and troubles forgotten in the gaiety of the moment. The hardworking people of Lawrence spent these few hours away from the toil and hardship in joyous celebration while the eyes of the nation were focused on the outcome of their struggle against the pro-slavery forces circling unseen on the borders of their lives.

***

September 1, 1855
TOWN MEETING

"Quiet, everyone! Quiet, please," Charlie tried to call the meeting to order. It seemed that every able-bodied man and half the women in town were crammed into the Free State Hotel. Finally, Sam cracked his club on a table and shouted, "Quiet!"

The din subsided. Charlie in his trademark rumpled outfit, ornamented with a black cutaway coat certainly outstripped the farmers and tradespeople making up the majority of the audience. He initiated the meeting with a few announcements.

"The delegate meeting in Big Springs will commence next week. Those of you who are voting delegates MUST be there. The Free State Convention will be held the second Tuesday of October in Topeka. I don't need to emphasize the importance of that meeting, do I?"

The audience cheered at this timely news. The sham pro-slavery legislature continued to meet in Shawnee Mission denying admittance to the legally elected Free State delegates. As the cheers died down, Sam added, "I remind you that no one is to acknowledge the laws enacted by the bogus legislature in Shawnee Mission.

Don't file a suit in their courts and don't call their law enforcement to settle disputes. We'll handle our own courts and enforcement."

Charlie echoed those sentiments then added, "Lastly, Ladies and Gentlemen, I don't know where rumors come from or how they get started, but Sam Wood and I are not having a quarrel. I consider Sam one of my best friends and the greatest ally the Free State movement has. We would not be here today without Sam Wood." He reached out to shake Sam's hand who performed that ceremony with relish then held Charlie's hand in the air, "Governor Robinson, Ladies and Gentlemen." The crowd cheered with gusto.

Reverend Lum recited a prayer, wearing his characteristic black suit, holding a wide-brimmed black felt hat, speaking without notes, "Lord, we are your humble servants doing your bidding without complaint, an island of morality in a stormy sea of sin and degradation. We ask you to watch over us as we wage a holy battle for the bodies and souls of our black neighbors, held in bondage by the slaveholding forces of the south. As you say in the book of Galatians, 'There is neither Jew nor Greek, there is neither slave nor free, there is no male and female, for you are all one in Christ Jesus'. Especially give us the strength to ward off the foul breath of the Border Ruffians and their leader, the devil disguised as a man, Senator David Atchison, who has sworn to lynch and hang us, and... and..."

"...tar and feather us," Tap prompted.

"And tar and feather us AND drown us, thank you Brother Tappan, simply because we cherish the life and dignity of all human beings. Be with us, O' Lord. All these things we ask most humbly in your name. Amen."

Amen echoed throughout the crowded hall.

Sam spent the best part of the past week lobbying his neighbors to organize the militia prior to formulating the city government. The hard work paid off when the vote was counted, overwhelmingly in favor of the formation of a Safety Committee to oversee the militia. But not before several citizens voiced their concern that 'certain' town leaders were making decisions, inappropriately, for the community as a whole. However widespread and who was indicted by the comments was lost in the excitement of formulating the new militia to defend their city.

Colonel George Dietzler took the floor with details of the plan for a city militia commanded by General James Lane and a Safety Committee chaired by Charlie Robinson.

"Won't the Territorial Government and the Army protect us?" Mrs. Meyers asked. She and her husband had filed a claim across the river, north of Lawrence and quickly immersed themselves in the activities of the community.

"I'm more afraid of them than the Border Ruffians," Tap said, causing everyone to laugh.

Colonel Dietzler added, "The army is supposed to remain neutral but they're under the control of the President and he wants Kansas to be a Slave State. We have to be able to protect ourselves."

Tom Barber asked, "Do we have to provide our own weapons?"

Several voices echoed the sentiment. They felt at a disadvantage with no weaponry beyond the pistols, rifles and swords that they had brought from the east.

Harold said, "I heard that Atchison requisitioned Sharps rifles from the war department and Jefferson Davis provided them; and they have a cannon."

Tap said, "They'll be well provisioned with guns."

Sam offered some comfort, "Folks, I received a letter from John Brown, and he will be here, when we need him, with Sharps rifles and just as important, reinforcements to back us up in any way we need. Owen and John Brown, Junior are already here as you know. John Senior is in Osawatomie. And I'm not going to go into details, but I have an excellent source for weapons within the week. Don't despair over these rumors, we'll be much better organized and just as well armed."

Charles Dow asked, "Mr. Wood, kin I be in the Militia, if'n I'm from Hickory Point?"

"Chuck, there are a lot of folk here from Hickory Point, of course you can?"

"Well, I'm only asking cause I ain't got no weaponry at all," he drawled.

Judge Wakefield said, "You mean to say you came to Kansas Territory without a weapon of any kind?"

"I did have me an old Colt-Patterson 5 shooter, but it fell off'n the steamboat and into the Mississippi River and drownded, I reckon." That brought a roar of laughter surprising the shy man, but he continued the best he could under the circumstances, "And now I ain't got the money to buy no more weaponry, as ya'll call it, but I still want to be in the Militia."

"George, what arrangements can we make to provide Mr. Dow with a rifle?"

Dietzler said, "I will make it my personal obligation to see that every man here has a good rifle or pistol, and we will figure out some way to pay for them. Now, let's get down to the business of getting organized."

James Lane began by offending the entire Brown clan; he wasn't in agreement with having John Brown come into the territory and cause more trouble than he was worth. Several people disagreed with him, most vociferous being John Brown, Jr. and his brother, Owen. They began a shouting match before Sam called for order again, "General Lane, we certainly value your military experience and leadership. But keep in mind the purpose of the meeting, which is to save Lawrence from the Border Ruffians. Rather than argue over the makeup of the troops, please address your plan for the militia."

Lane grimly stepped to the front, produced a document and began reading the list of officers for the new regiment of Kansas Jayhawkers, "I've already spoken with all the officers and I've drafted commission letters to deliver to Governor Shannon which establishes each one of you as an officer in the Kansas Free Settlers Militia. We're gonna call ourselves Jayhawkers and when we start training you need to come up with a blue shirt. Like Colonel Dietzler said, we will have weaponry," he smiled at Dow. "George Dietzler is a Colonel as are Sam Wood, Clarke Pomeroy and Caleb Pratt. The rest of you sign up here at the table and list your military experience. I'll assign you to a company and give you a preliminary rank based on your service record. Sam, who's going to record the names of the troops?"

"J.C. said he would, Archibald are you here?" he shouted. "Owen Brown and who was the other one that volunteered?"

"Judge Wakefield did, but he had to go home, another stomachache," Lettie Steele answered to a groan from the crowd. I'll do it if no one else will," she volunteered.

"All right, Mrs. Steele, there's pen, ink and paper next to Mr. Archibald. Now, could I speak to the company commanders." Sam, George, Clarke Pomeroy and Caleb Pratt walked outside with Lane where they ran into

General Nathanial Lyon, commander of Ft. Riley, starting to enter the building.

"Well hello Nathan," Sam reached for a handshake. Lyon's troops remained in their saddles while the commander addressed the Lawrence officers. "Congratulations, on your promotions, Colonel Wood, George and Caleb. A field promotion, so to speak, wouldn't you say, General Lane?"

"You two know each other," Dietzler asked?

"Yes, General Lane and I served together in the Mexican War. We've discussed the makeup of the militia and agree that you four are the best choices for company commanders. Charlie Robinson will maintain his civilian status and act as liaison with the government. You fellows know that I can't be involved in the local politics, but I can make certain there's fair play in the matter."

"What brings you to Lawrence?" Sam asked.

"Someone broke into the arsenal in Liberty, stole some rifles and a cannon. We have troops from Ft. Riley and Ft. Leavenworth fanned out across the territory."

"You'd be better off looking in Missouri," Pratt said. General Lane nodded in agreement.

The setting sun framed the troops in a startling light causing them to turn away from the sudden glare, their swords and insignias gleamed bright for a moment until the rays sank below the horizon. The horses snorted and blew, restless as the evening cooled. Sam recognized one of the troopers, left the officers and extended his hand to Jimmy Kendrick. "Hello Mr. Wood," Jimmy said.

"Jimmy Kendrick, I didn't know you were in Kansas. Does Sarah know that you're here?"

"I wrote her a letter, but I never did hear back. My ma'll let me know if we hear from her. I'm not even sure where she is."

"Why, she's right across the street at my house," Sam exclaimed.

The boy almost fell off his horse in surprise, "I thought she was in Iowa with Stephan."

Sam said, "Hold on, I'll see if General Lyon will let me take you over to see her."

Up the street strolled Sarah and Donna curious about the commotion, "Why are the soldiers here?" Donna asked.

Sarah watched Sam speaking to one of the troopers, suddenly realized who it was. She charged up the street shouting, "Jimmy, Jimmy". She leapt up, grabbed him around the waist trying to haul herself onto the horse. The troops struggled to control their mounts as the young girl created a disturbance among the soldiers who looked at her and Donna with more than a casual interest. They didn't often get to see girls their age. General Lane turned to see what the ruckus might be.

"Oh, my God," Sam muttered when he realized what his impetuous sister was doing. General Lane looked to his aide and said, "Lieutenant," with a stern look.

Sarah kept saying "Jimmy," as he tried to maintain control of his mount and keep her from falling. His mates were laughing hysterically.

"Private, put that woman down, this is the United States Army, not a dance hall. I mean right now," Lieutenant Rodgers shouted as he turned his horse around to deal with the impropriety.

"Sarah, let go, I'll get in trouble."

"Jimmy, I've missed you so much," she hooked her leg around his stirrup, wearing a smile as bright as the sunshine. The other soldiers were laughing so hard they could barely control their own horses. General Lane looked at Sam for explanation, "My sister. That's her old childhood friend."

Lane shook his head, laughed. "I've seen everything now, Sam."

He mounted, ordered the troops to follow him, by twos.

Jimmy said, "I'll see you when I get a pass, Sarah."

She jumped off and waved as the soldiers filed by, each tipping their hat to the beautiful girls.

"Damn Kendrick, didn't know you were such a lady's man."

"You been holdin' out on us, Jimmy."

"Why don't you share? There's two of em'."

"Quiet in the ranks," the Lieutenant shouted pulling back to review the excited troopers. He glared at Jimmy as they filed by then fell in behind the last pair, but not before glancing at the girls with a bright smile and a tip of his own hat.

"What about Hal?" Donna asked as the troopers rode off.

"I don't really know."

Sam joined the others on the steps of the hotel, "How in the world did Harold know they had a cannon if it just got stolen?"

"James went back inside to ask him," Pratt answered.

Lane returned shaking his head. He stood watching the troops as they rode down toward the turnpike. "I believe that I'd better ride after them and let General Lyon know who the men were that stole the rifles from the munitions dump."

"Who was it," Dietzler asked?

"Those two men that Bogus Jones calls his deputies were with them. Harold heard them talking at a saloon in Westport. I don't recall those boys' names."

"I know who they are," Sam said. "John T and I had a run in with them a year ago. The big one is Bill, they call him 'Big Bill' and the little one is Lester. I don't know their last names. But I can tell you this, they're dumber than a box of rocks, they make Bogus look like a college professor."

***

The worst thing in this world, next to anarchy, is government.   Henry Ward Beecher

Lawrence, Kansas
September 10, 1855

It was almost two weeks before Jimmy received a pass. Two weeks during which Sarah spent most weekend evenings and Sunday afternoon with Hal. Afternoons which included Diane and Jay, along with Donna and Chief. No mention of Jimmy's pending visit during their time together and Sarah fell more and more under the spell of Hal's obvious intentions. She enjoyed everything about being with him. He was attentive but not pushy, allowing for her exuberant personality but demanding in his quiet way a serious respect for each other.

Jimmy was knocking on the Wood door at ten o'clock after an early morning trip down the river. Sarah came charging down the stairs when he was announced and jumped into his embarrassed arms.

"My goodness, Sarah, you look so different."

"Well, I hope so, I'm 21 years old now, not a little girl like the last time I saw you. Jimmy, you looked so handsome in your uniform. Have you had breakfast yet, how does it feel to be in the army?" Sarah rattled off questions not giving Jimmy a chance to speak. Lucky for him Margaret came down the stairs; he stood to greet her, "Hello Mrs. Wood, so nice to see you again."

"Why Jimmy, you've grown two feet. But, call me Margaret, I haven't changed that much and when you say, 'Mrs. Wood', it makes me look around for my mother-in-law. I'll bet you're hungry, aren't you? Sarah come help me get something for Jimmy to eat."

David and Caleb came charging in from the back yard and stopped in their tracks when they saw Jimmy standing in the living room. "Who are you?" they said in unison.

"I'm Jimmy Kendrick, who are you?"

"I'm Caleb Thompson."

"And I'm David Wood, did you come to arrest some Border Ruffians?"

"No, not really. I don't even know any of them. I've just heard about them."

"Don't mess with em', they are really mean," David said as he and Caleb charged out the front door spotting Jimmy Pratt and Larry Tappan through the window.

Kendrick laughed as he watched the boys disappear up the trail toward the top of Mt. Oreod. He thought about his home in Ohio and the special times he'd spent with Sarah and Caroline Lyon at church and school. He missed those days. He missed his mother and father, but he was a soldier now and had a duty to perform. He was clear about his obligation, though many of the men were not, and some even planned on deserting. Jimmy couldn't stomach that kind of talk and felt like reporting them to his company commander, Lt. Rodgers, but he never did.

"Jimmy are you daydreaming," Sarah asked him. "Sit down and eat. Margaret and I make the best ham and eggs in the world, don't we Margaret?"

Margaret continued with her household chores, ignoring the silly girl, awestruck to find Jimmy back in her life. "Jimmy, why did you just up and leave? What happened? Did something bad happen to make you run off like that?"

"Sarah!" Margaret said emphatically. "Let that boy eat his breakfast. You haven't given him a chance to inhale let alone talk." Margaret sat with them, watching Jimmy eat with the gusto of a young man away from his mother's home cooking.

"Sarah and Mrs. Wood," she glanced at him, "I mean Margaret, this is wonderful. I haven't eaten this well since I left home. You know I can't get over that you have children and are married to Sam Wood. It doesn't seem real from when we were in Ohio. Remember that play we had about Benjamin Lay? That was so much fun wasn't it Sarah?"

"It was. I miss those days, sometimes. We didn't know how good we had it, did we?"

Sam came hurrying in stripping his coat and moving close to the fire, "Jimmy, where's your horse? How did you get here?"

"Sam, your shoes," Margaret scolded as he hurried back to the porch and took off his mud caked shoes. Sarah grabbed a mop and broom and cleaned up after her brother shaking her head at him the whole time.

"By the river. I caught a ride from some fur traders heading to Missouri. They didn't even charge me because I helped pole in the shallows."

"I have to go that way on Monday. I'll take you back to the Fort. We have a Free State meeting scheduled in Topeka, Tuesday evening. What have you heard about the break-in at the Liberty arsenal? Any scuttlebutt at the Fort?"

"That's above my pay grade, Mr. Wood, but I did hear one of the southern boys say that he hoped we never did find that cannon and when the time came to use it on the abolitionists, he would light the fuse."

"My goodness," Margaret said. "What kind of troops do they have over there at the fort?"

"They're about even divided, Margaret. About the same number of southern boys as northern boys. Same with the officers, but General Lyon, he's different, everyone knows that he's against slavery and the southern boys keep their opinions to themselves when he's around."

John and Sally Thompson came in the back door in their stocking feet. "Jimmy Kendrick, is that you?"

"Yes, ma'am, Miss Sally and how are you," he stood, shook hands with her and John? Sarah put her cleaning supplies away as the conversation continued. She gave Margaret a look of concern as it became apparent that Sam and John were going to spirit Jimmy off on some errand they were planning.

"Jimmy and I were about to go for a walk, I want to introduce him to Donna and Jay," she protested.

The men ignored her, went right on with their plans. "We've got to pick up the crates today," John said.

"I know it, we can't leave them in the warehouse any longer. I'm afraid that someone is going to discover what's in those crates, and we'll be in big trouble," Sam said.

"What?" Sarah's faced flushed with anger, "If you're going to Westport, that will take you all day and all night," she said glaring at Sam. The three men watched her warily for a moment, John turned to Sam, "Shall we take the boys?"

"Let's do," Sam said. "Jimmy, are you ready?"

He looked for help from Sarah who glared at him with her arms crossed, "Ready as I'll ever be."

"Good, go find Caleb and David, they're down by the river, we'll get the buckboard. Meet us here in 10 minutes. Meg will you pack some food?" Sam turned to Sarah, "You want to go with us pumpkin?"

She erupted into a smile, "Ok, I will."

John said, "Best get your horse ready, Sarah, and one for Jimmy. Sam and I'll get the Belgians hitched to the wagon."

"I'll help," Sally said.

Tap pulled up in front of the Wood's house with his wagon and four large draft horses just as Jimmy and the boys returned. "We're going with you Daddy," Larry shouted as he ran inside with David and Caleb. Jimmy introduced himself to Mr. Tappan as Sally drove the buckboard up behind Tap's rig. "I'm going too," she said.

"We've got more people than freight," Tap laughed. Margaret struggled down the walk with a large basket of food. Lloyd and Missy clambered into the wagon then stormed back into the house crying when told they couldn't go. Sarah arrived on her horse leading a roan-colored gelding for Jimmy; they started off down Massachusetts Street toward the Santa Fe Trail.

"Where are we going, Sarah?" Jimmy asked.

"To Westport to get some guns; Sharps rifles and some kind of pistols, all sent to us by Reverend Beecher."

"Henry Ward Beecher?" Jimmy marveled. "He's about the most famous man around these days. Does everyone know about this? Have you ever met him?"

"Uunh huh, never met him, but Sam knows him; Sam knows everyone. No one is supposed to know about it, but now we need those rifles because General Lane has formed a militia. I think there's going to be trouble. Do you think the army will help us if there is?"

"I don't know, but Lt. Rodgers always says we have to stay out of the politics."

Sarah shivered in the cool air, "Jimmy, my coat's in the wagon, under the seat. Would you get it for me?" He rode alongside, had David hand the coat over, then dropped back and waited while Sarah put it on. They rode behind the wagons for a while then got in and rode in the back with the horses tied to the buckboard for the rest of the trip to Westport. Laughing, oblivious of the others, they reminisced about their lives in Ohio, shared thoughts on the challenges of life on the frontier. Jimmy reminded her that he once thought of being a preacher.

He was happy in the presence of the beautiful young girl that had been such an important part of his childhood, vowed, in his loneliness, to never let her out of his life again. Sarah had a nervous feeling in the pit of her stomach. When she looked at Jimmy, she saw her old childhood friend, nothing else. It suddenly dawned on her that she was falling in love with Harold Barnett, Junior.

It was dusk as they drove through Westport with nary a second look from anyone as Conestoga and freight wagons, buggies and carts navigated the streets of the bustling village. When they reached the warehouses above the river, it was starting to get dark; the offices were closed for the evening.

"What shall we do," Sarah asked?

"I brought blankets and we have food, we could sleep here," Sam said.

"I've slept in worse places," Sally said.

Tap looked through a darkened window, bars covering the opening, "Do you know who owns this warehouse?"

"I don't," Sam answered.

"There's a lamp on in that house down the road there," John T said, "we should at least check with them to see if they know."

Sam and Jimmy grabbed a lantern, walked the hundred yards to the house. David, Larry and Caleb set off exploring down by the docks, seemingly oblivious to the cold breeze off the river. The others sat watching for movement from the messengers. Sarah and Sally huddled together under a blanket as the wind picked up making a cold night even colder. "You boys stay within hollerin' range," John yelled after the explorers. Lights began dancing around the house; before long three men and two lanterns appeared.

"This is the manager of the warehouse and he's agreed to let us get our crates," Sam announced.

"Normally I wouldn't but seein' as how it's the Lord's work you're doin', I'll make an exception. What're ya gonna' do with all them bibles anyways?"

Tap climbed onto the wagon, "We're going to see that every God-fearing man and woman in the territory get one." Sally and Sarah giggled under their blanket while Sam hurried the warehouse manager over to open the doors; they backed Tap's wagon inside.

"Someone owes me for three days storage."

"The bill of lading says we've got three days storage coming with the shipment," Sam protested.

"Yessir, that may be, but they've been here for 6 days."

"Never mind, I'll pay it. Sarah, where are the boys? They can help with the smaller boxes."

"They went down by the river; I'll go get them."

"I'll go with you," Sally said. "Wait, we better take a lantern."

"You should have brought some more of your Niggers, friend. I can go get some if you want me to."

"I believe we can handle this. You go on into your office and I'll call you when we're done."

"Oh, no sir, I can't do that, I have to account for every crate."

The boys came running up from the river, followed by the ladies. All hands joined in loading rifles, pistols, shot and powder, all in crates marked, 'Bibles'. The rifles were the bulkiest with ten rifles to a crate. They put them in each of the wagons and filled in around with the smaller boxes, leaving enough room to make sleeping pallets for those not driving. They tied the powder behind the seat of Sam's wagon. Dave and Caleb lifted a small box, the bottom fell out; Colt Dragoon Pistols, wrapped in burlap, tumbled all over the dirt floor of the warehouse.

The manager picked one up, unwrapped it, "That don't look like any kind of bible I've ever seen. What the hell's going on here?"

"Nothing illegal or immoral," Sam said. "We'll gather these up and be on our way. I thank you for opening up after hours. Here's the fee for the three-day storage and a little extra for your trouble. We'll be off now."

"I think I should report this to someone."

"Report what? That a shipment of bibles was picked up from your warehouse. We had one box of pistols for our personal use." Tap explained.

The manager stood, holding the lantern reflecting a look on his face that could only be described as suspicious.

"I don't like the way he watched us while we was leaving," John T said to Tap as they rode in the second wagon following Sam.

"I don't either, John, we'd best git while the gittin's good, it's a cold night, maybe he won't feel like rousting his horse out to find the sheriff."

Sarah and Jimmy rode in front with lanterns to guide the way. Sam worried that the warehouse manager would raise an alarm yet hoped the cold night and late hour would cause him to wait until morning. With the heavy freight they could only load one wagon at a time on the ferry crossing the Kansas River at Tiblow. While they waited for Tappan's wagon Sam said to, Sarah, "It's late Pumpkin, why don't you and Sally and the boys stay at Jim McDaniel's tonight. The light's still on, I'll go over and see if Lauren has some beds for you. I think it's going to start raining and it's too cold for you to be out here"

"No, Sam, I haven't had any time to visit with Jimmy. The boys are fine and can sleep on the wagon and I guarantee you that Sally won't agree."

Sam said no more but thought he would broach the idea with John when they got across. Suddenly the sound of gunshots shattered the cool night air. They could make out lanterns on the far side of the river. The ferry was about halfway across. The shouting was indistinct, but Sam could tell it was trouble. It took another 10 minutes to reach the south shore; John T shouted, "It's Bogus Jones, that manager must have alerted him after all. They wanted Riley to take us back, but he wouldn't do it."

"Did anybody get hit," Sarah yelled.

"No, they were just shooting into the air to get our attention, but it scared the bejesus out of me," Sally hugged Sarah, turned to Sam, "What are we going to do now?"

"I got no use for that bastard Jones, excuse my language, ma'am. I'll just lag here for a while and let you git on down the road," the Ferry Master said.

"Riley," Tappan said, "we'll need about an hour head start to be able to beat them home."

"Well, it's going to be at least that long time I get me some supper and have a drink over to the boss's place. So ya'll just mosey on and leave this here to me."

"We owe you one, Riley," John said.

"We African's got to stick together don't we, John T?"

Sam didn't bother with suggesting the women and children stay; he pointed the teams west, pushed them hard as he dare under the circumstances. The lanterns ran out of kerosene about two miles from Chief Fish's and the horses limped in at four in the morning. They asked leave to feed and water the animals and buy some kerosene for the short trip to Lawrence. The boys were fast asleep on blankets piled on the crates. Sarah and Jimmy had been riding for quite some time leading with the lamps. They were all exhausted. Chief Fish rousted two of his boys, sent them back down the road to scout for signs of the posse.

They reached Lawrence just before sunup, backed the wagons into Charlie Robinson's new barn. "We'll unload later," Tap said, "I'm flat out beat. I'm going to bed."

Sam took the boys home, put them to bed, returned to the stables to help Jimmy, Sarah, and John rub down the horses, make certain they were well fed and watered. Margaret greeted them with coffee, bread and fresh churned butter, a treat any day. It tasted especially sweet on this one. They sat on the front porch, under a fine wooden awning constructed by Stephan Wood last month while visiting from his home in Tabor, Iowa. The travelers shared the tale with Margaret from start to finish. Sally yawned, stretched, gave John a let's go home look, then stood to hug Margaret goodbye. Sam got up to get more coffee, he was not tired.

Chief Fish and his two boys came charging into the yard, "They're coming Sam, about five minutes behind us."

"How many, Pash?"

"Jones and three rough looking men. Big Bill is one of them."

"Jimmy, get a rifle and position yourself over there by the hotel. John T go roust out Charlie and Tap. Tell them to bring weapons but stay hidden until we see if I can sweet talk them into leaving. Everyone else sit tight. Let's act like nothing is amiss."

Sam sat back down to wait. Paschal took Sam's pistol, leaned against the porch beam. His youngest son, Owen, pulled him down to his level, whispered in his ear, "How do you sweet talk someone, Papa?"

"Not sure, let's listen and learn from the master."

The posse rode straight to Sam's house as if expecting him to be waiting for them. Prince leapt up from his repose on the porch, began barking at the intruders, neighbor dogs joined the chorus. The horses shook their heads, snorted, winded from the hard ride. Jones failed to engage in any pleasantries, "We came for them guns, Wood. Where are they?"

Sam got up slowly, calmed Prince, walked to the edge of the porch hooked his fingers in his suspenders, thought for a moment, "Bogus, I don't know what you're talking about. Would you care to lite a spell and have a cup of cof..."

He was interrupted rudely and abruptly by Big Bill who shouted for the whole town to hear, "No more of your bullshit, you son-of-a-bitch, now where the fuck are them guns? We gonna…"

He continued talking, but Sam was already charging down the wooden plank walkway, before the deputy could even figure out what was happening; a roar of anger scared the posse, "NO SIR! I won't have it," Sam screamed waving his arms like a madman, spooking the horses. "Blasphemy in front of my children, I won't have it you fat tub of rat guts." He grabbed the horse's mane and Bill's arm, drug them sideways causing the horse to bolt and Bill to crash to the ground. Sam directed two massive blows to his chin, barely dodging the flailing hooves of the horse.

Meanwhile, when he pulled Bill's horse over, it caused Jones' horse to bolt off up the road before he could get it under control. The other deputies watched gap-mouthed looking at each other. Sam reached down, grabbed Bill's pistol and fired over their heads. Jones finally regained his saddle only to face several Lawrence citizens pointing guns at him. He turned tail and ran chasing his deputies.

While Sam was pummeling Big Bill, John T grabbed the reins of his horse before it ran off with the others. They loaded the stunned deputy into the saddle, pointed the horse south, slapped it on the rump and watched as Big Bill struggled to hold on racing after his friends.

Sam breathing hard, tried to gain his composure, "John T, what kind of a man would come into my house and curse like that right front of all these women and children?"

"An evil one?"

"I hope to tell you. Those are not good men right there and we will have trouble with them before this is over."

"Well, this seemed like trouble enough, but if there's more to be had, we best get organized."

By then half the town was out in the drizzle and cold trying to make sense of the situation. Small groups were scattered all over the street, with those who knew what happened sharing the story with those who didn't. The best part was letting the citizens of Lawrence know that they had rifles and pistols. They would not be without weaponry.

Pash and the boys mounted their horses for the ride home, "Sam, we'll ride down a way to make certain they left for good. If we see anything, one of the boys will come back and let you know." They rode down Massachusetts turning up the collars of their coats.

"That was fun wasn't it, Papa," Billy Fish said.

"I guess it was entertaining, but I'm glad no one got hurt. I don't know boys, maybe we ought to move down south to Oklahoma. These white people are gonna' have a war sure enough. I feel it coming."

"We don't really want to go, do we Owen?" Billy said.

"Not really!" Owen replied, deep in thought about something troubling him, "Papa, what was the sweet-talking part. I still can't figure it out."

Paschal laughed, spurred his horse the boys whooping and hollering after him.

***

Jones called a halt at Blue's trading post to let the horses catch their breath. He leapt out of the saddle, dropped the reins, began stomping and hollering; he kicked one of Blue Jackets chickens across the yard, squawking, flapping its wings in a shower of feathers.

"Son-of-a-bitching Wood, I'll never run off from that bastard again. I'm sending a letter to Atchison. I'll take an army back over there, wipe out Yankee Town." He stood looking back towards Lawrence. Blue stood on his porch watching the posse. "Goddammit," Jones screamed.

"What about Big Bill, Boss?"

"Lester, ride back there and see if you can spot that fool, he's more worthless than you turds, Jesus Christ, I need a damn army. We're gonna' burn every house and kill every man. Mark my words, boys, Atchison'll authorize it, I guarantee."

"Hey, here comes Bill."

The deputy rode up angry, "Thanks a lot, you sons-a-bitches, I had to fight off seven or eight of em' just to get outta there. No thanks to you. I think my nose is busted," he moaned.

"Oh, shut up Bill," Jones said spurring his horse. They didn't look back or they'd have seen Paschal turn into his brother's yard and watch them ride back toward Missouri.

"Treat us like men, and there is no danger, but we will all live in peace and happiness together. For we are not like you, hard hearted, unmerciful, and unforgiving. What a happy country this will be, if the Whites will listen."
David Walker 1785-1830

The September delegate convention in Big Springs and the subsequent October constitutional convention required a great deal of planning. The sixteen districts would each send three to five delegates. Jim Lane was appointed to act as president of the assembly; a gesture made to demonstrate to the Border Ruffians that the convention would be backed by the might of the Kansas Free State militia. In August and early September, meetings were held regularly in communities throughout the Territory with most conducted in Lawrence. On a day in early September several men gathered in the Tribune office to go over the resolutions and the first draft of the constitution itself.

Most of the writing fell to Sam, S. M. Goodkin from Osowatamie, and J. S. Emery from Topeka. Of course, they followed the pattern of the northern state's constitutions with an executive officer, a senate and house of representatives, and the requisite state officers. A good deal of the language was boiler plate with a few exceptions. And those exceptions created the most controversy.

"This language will not pass muster. Why even submit it for vote?" Charlie was growing frustrated with Sam.

"We have to include the language that all men and women, white, black or Indian, shall have the right to vote in Kansas, even if it is voted out of the final document," Sam insisted. "It may be a symbolic gesture but a very important one for our cause. Let the rest of the country see that we mean business."

Colonel Dietzler stated, or more accurately lectured, "Sam, this smacks of something your wife would insist on adding to the constitution. Frankly, I can tell you for a fact, NEVER will Indians, Niggers or women be allowed to vote in these United States," he smacked the table with the flat of his hand, "never, sir, do you understand that?"

"Calm down, George," Tap mediated. "Maybe not in our lifetime but it will happen someday. Regardless, I agree with Sam, why not include it, let the delegates vote on that language. The newspapers will report that we included it. Great publicity for us."

Dietzler stood, glared at the assembly with his most regal military bearing, "Not only will they never be granted the right to vote, all Indians and Niggers shall be removed from our great state forthwith, and I don't care where you send them."

"You want to ban the women too, George?" Sam rubbed his eyes, tired but mostly frustrated; George failed to grasp the irony. Dietzler was sincere in his rhetoric, plus had the backing of many influential men in the north and south. If it were left up to these men, the United States would consist of only white people of European decent. Dietzler was tolerated by the Free State movement because he was one hundred percent behind the abolition of slavery. The reason was obvious to those involved; it would be easier to banish the blacks once they were free. Their owners would have no recourse against the government and would, in fact, support the idea.

Goodkin, a burly man with thick brown hair and round glasses, gestured with his hands, "Look, we are going to be in session a couple of weeks. If we can iron out the language now it will save us time come the convention itself."

"I'll agree to the wording that Mr. Goodkin and Mr. Emery propose as long as we add my language to the freedom of religion section," Sam said. He was realist enough to know that the majority of delegates would never agree to grant voting rights to blacks or women under any circumstances. But he made his point, and it would be broadcast throughout the Union.

The only language rejected by the assembly was in Article II where Sam proposed that the vote would be extended to all black citizens who otherwise met the citizenship qualifications for voting. The final wording of that section was a compromise between the liberal progressive Free-Soilers, read abolitionists, and the more conservative faction who did not want slavery in Kansas but refused to interfere in the rights of other states to ban the practice. Everyone in Lawrence who bothered to read the document recognized Colonel Dietzler's contribution.

Elective Franchise Article II

Sec. 2. Every white male person, and every civilized male Indian who has adopted the habits of the white man, of the age of twenty-one years and upward, who shall be at the time of offering to vote a citizen of the United States; who shall have resided, and had his habitation, domicile, home, and place of permanent abode in the State of Kansas for six months next preceding the election at which he offers his vote; who, at such time, and for thirty days immediately preceding such time, shall have had his actual habitation, domicile, home, and place of abode in the county in which he offers to vote...;

The fundamental difference in the Topeka Constitution and the Shawnee Mission Pro-Slavery

Constitution was in the Preamble and Article I, Sections 6 and 7.

Preamble.

We, the people of the Territory of Kansas, by our delegates in Convention assembled at Topeka, on the 23d day of October, A.D. 1855, and of the Independence of the United States the eightieth year, having the right of admission into the Union as one of the United States of America, consistent with the Federal Constitution, and by virtue of the treaty of cession by France to the United States of the Province of Louisiana, in order to secure to ourselves and our posterity the enjoyment of all the rights of life, liberty and property, and the free pursuit of happiness, do mutually agree with each other to form ourselves into a free and independent State, by the name and style of the State of Kansas,

Article I
Sec. 6. There shall be no slavery in this state, nor involuntary servitude, unless for the punishment of crime.

Sec. 7. All men have a natural and indefeasible right to worship Almighty God according to the dictates of their own conscience. No person shall be compelled to attend, erect or support any place of worship, or maintain any form of worship, against his consent; and no preference shall be given by law to any religious society; nor shall any interference with the rights of conscience be permitted.

Sam's influence was keenly felt in Section 7 where the words 'nor shall any interference with the rights of conscience be permitted', reflected the Quaker Exposition of Sentiments, a kind of statement of rights, that he helped draft at the Pennsylvania Yearly meeting of Progressive Friends in 1853.

Ex-Governor Reeder, now a staunch abolitionist, returned to Kansas in triumph and was elected as delegate to the United States Congress. He was admitted as a non-voting member, so the gesture was mainly symbolic, but the real and perceived rebuff to President Pierce was obvious.

The convention lasted sixteen days. The date for ratification of the Topeka Constitution was set for the first week in December.

"There are thousands who are in opinion opposed to slavery and to the war, who yet in effect do nothing to put an end to them; who, esteeming themselves children of Washington and Franklin, sit down with their hands in their pockets, and say that they know not what to do, and do nothing...." Henry David Thoreau, Civil Disobedience and Other Essays

Sunday, November 4, 1855

November arrived warm and comfortable, a nice respite from the previous year. Those who remembered that cold winter knew not to let their guard down. They worked feverishly preparing for the harsh weather ahead, putting up hay, chopping wood, building barns and outhouses. Most territorial citizens, including the Barnett's and the Barber's heeded the Lord's decree to rest on Sunday.

This particular day of worship Reverend Lum chose to preach about the joys of thanksgiving, "'Let them give thanks to the Lord for his unfailing love and his wonderful deeds for mankind, for he satisfies the thirsty and fills the hungry with good things', that is from Psalms 107:8-9," piously looking over his flock of Quakers, Methodists, Lutherans, Protestants, a few Indians, several Black families in the back thanks to Margaret Woods insistence.

Sam had not been listening to the sermon but, for some reason, he caught this last bible verse and made an involuntary 'scoff' of derision, which in turn caused Reverend Lum to stop. All eyes turned to Sam, including a scornful look from his embarrassed wife, "Sam," she whispered firmly. He mouthed, "Sorry," but the damage was done.

Harold knew what Sam was thinking, because Autumn had already made a note to discuss this matter with Lum; she displayed her question for Harold, 'is the Lord filling the hungry bellies of the Indians and slaves since church began?' Harold did not envy the good Reverend knowing what awaited him after the service.

"Mother, please!" Diane whispered.

"What?" Autumn was not one to shy from an inconsistency. "I have a right to question him," she whispered. In the pew behind, Hal and Sarah sat side by side giggling at the entire affair. Sarah had grown to admire Autumn. She was the financial force behind the family's success constantly looking to acquire more land around their growing farm.

Diane wished for the service to end. She so looked forward to the Sunday afternoon visit with Jay under the prayer tree, reading poetry together. Jay was leaving in a few weeks and had not mentioned anything about taking Diane with him. Even if he did ask her to marry, she was afraid Harold and Autumn would refuse, probably raise a fuss about her being too young, even though Autumn was only 17 when she married. "I'll be a prisoner on the farm forever," she sobbed to herself. Autumn put a hand on Diane' knee thinking she was still angry about the bible controversy. But to the romantic young girl, being stuck on the farm was a fate worse than marriage to the stuttering Ohio college student.

David and Lloyd were whispering to each other, planning an afternoon picnic. Margaret elbowed David, shushing him, while looking to Sam for help. Sam was, in his mind, composing the 'About Town' column, due the next morning. "About Town" was the most popular article, mostly gossip, entertaining a much greater readership than Sam's political column, 'Wood's Wisdom'. Actually, people did read Wood's Wisdom, but mocked his opinions more than anything. Sam advocated women's suffrage, women's equality, emancipation and reparations for the slaves, end corruption in government, universal suffrage for every man and woman regardless of color or property ownership. He was derided in public, in private, even to his face and, of course, in editorials throughout the Union. A cartoon in the St. Louis Republican parodied Sam in a dress at the stove while Margaret wore trousers reading the paper. Bill Speer enjoyed the publicity. The paper was doing well financially. Colonel Dietzler wrote copious letters to the editor demanding that Sam's opinions be censured. Speer offered to give him equal space on the editorial page. Somehow, they all remained friends outside the political arena, recognizing that a common goal of eliminating slavery was more important than personal rancor.

"Daddy, Mama's talking to you," Lloyd pulled Sam's sleeve.

"Sam let's go home, the service is over," she gathered her bible and hymn book.

"Daddy, can we go have a picnic, it's warm enough?"

"Ask your mother," he replied, wondering if he would be able to remember all the details of the sermon. Actually, he might even write Wood's Wisdom about the hypocrisy inherent in the bible verse that Reverend Lum used. He thought about an opening line, 'Where are these good things the Lord is providing for the thirsty and hungry slaves, or are we only talking about God's white children?' That would get the Reverend riled up.

Sam hitched one of the horses to the buggy and they plodded down Massachusetts toward the Wakarusa. The weather was excellent for a November afternoon. Margaret spread a blanket in the sun near a large Elm. Sam leaned back on his elbow while she removed her bonnet and shook her hair down.

"What?" she said laughing. Sam continued to stare at her.

"I'm looking at the prettiest girl in Kansas Territory, that's what."

"Just in the territory?" she teased.

David and Caleb charged up with two good sized bass and a small catfish.

"Go clean them boys; put them in the burlap, it's there in the river. We'll eat them tonight."

They hurried off leaving Sam and Margaret alone again. She looked at him with a mischievous smile.

"Now what's on your mind?" he asked.

"I wish the children weren't here with us," she tossed her hair seductively.

Sam laughed, rose to hands and knees, kissed his wife gently. She put her arms around his neck, pressed her face to his and they held each other tenderly; but the moment ended as Lloyd and Missy came charging into camp and jumped on Sam's back. "Ohhhh, you're kissing," Missy screamed. Lloyd put his arms around Daddy's neck, pulled him over and tried to tickle him. Sam gathered both of them into a bear hug, tickled until they screamed for mercy. Lloyd shouted, "Missy, your bloomers are showing," laughed so hard he had to go pee.

"I don't want to wear a dress, why do I have to?"

"Because you're a little girl and you went to church today. Why didn't you change before we came on the picnic?" Margaret asked hugging her.

"I didn't have any long pants at your house, and we didn't go home to get some. Why didn't Mommy and Daddy come on the picnic with us?"

"They had other things to do," Margaret looked into the face of the dark child whose eyes, inherited from her white grandfather, sparkled paler than an ocean wave.

She was two shades lighter than her mother, with John's curly black hair. Caleb, on the other hand, was two shades darker than Sally with brown eyes and brown hair. Margaret loved them both as much as her own sons.

Sam lay on his back, one arm over his eyes.

"You two go play while it's still warm enough," Margaret hurried them off, snuggled into the crook of his free arm. "Sam, I want to have another baby. A little girl," she craned her head to look, but Sam really was asleep, so she tried to sleep too.

She was somewhere between life and death, between a nightmare and a daydream, she floated above everything; heard a twig snap, people shouting and screaming. Where are they, the Border Ruffians, why couldn't she see them? It was an ambush; they are in the trees. She tried to shout for Sam. David was shaking her awake; Sam was gone. She looked at her son, his eyes wild with fright, clothes soaked and water dripping from his hair.

"Get in the buggy, Mother, we have to take her to the doctor, fast."

"Who, Davey?"

"Missy," he shouted running toward the cart.

Margaret jumped up, grabbed the blanket, threw it to Caleb sitting in the back as Sam ran past, cradling the child carefully, "What happened, Sam?"

"Get in, you'll have to hold her."

Margaret crawled into the front seat; Sam carefully placed the child, dripping wet, on her lap. Margaret put her right hand to her mouth, taking a deep breath trying to hold back the bilious surge in her stomach at the sight of Missy's left leg bent just above the ankle. Quickly she put her hand under the child's leg and ordered Sam to wait. She had Caleb bring the blanket and place it under the broken leg for support. They started off at a canter, Sam pushed the horse as fast as he could safely go.

"What happened?" she asked.

"She was just playing by the shore and her leg slipped down in the crack between two rocks. She fell over and it, it sounded like a gunshot. I can't believe you didn't hear it. The boys started screaming. Scared me, Margaret. For a few seconds I thought that we'd lost her. She fell face first in the water; David jumped in and held her head out so she could breathe. She's unconscious from the pain, I hope she doesn't wake up until we get to Charlie's."

"The Robinson's are in Topeka today, remember? We'll have to go to the new Doctor. Go straight there."

"I heard that he's a little strange."

"Sam, we have no choice."

As they turned on New Hampshire Street, Missy began sobbing and moaning. Margaret pinned her arms and legs to keep her from thrashing. David leapt from the moving buggy, charged up the lane, calling for the doctor. Mrs. Thomas ran out the door, a woman of about 40 with the manner of someone who knows what she's doing; took one look, ordered David to run to the Scranton's new house, "The doctor's over there checking on Grandmother Scranton, just past Delaware Street. Hurry child."

"Mr. Wood, come around here and take the girl, blanket and all, I'll walk alongside to support that leg, it's ok, darling, be brave, we'll get that pain stopped real soon." By the time they reached the office and had her lying on the fancy new examining table, Doctor Frank Thomas was rushing up from the street, a small, rotund, bald man of about 50 with a fringe of white hair. Dora was already cutting away Missy's wet clothes.

"What in the world have we got here, nurse? Broken leg, huh? Aye, broke leg!" He suddenly looked up to find the Wood family hovering over the examining table, their faces etched with worry.

"Too many hands in the sick bay, nurse," he ordered.

Lloyd shrunk away from the strange man, "Can I stay with her, Doctor? She's my best friend in the whole world. Is she going to die?"

Frank scoffed, "Not on my watch, Jack, now clear the deck, sailor, or I'll call the Marines. Nurse, send for the next of kin, I don't believe these folks are it."

Sam and Margaret looked at each other ready to snatch Missy away from the insane man; Dora grabbed Sam's arm, ushered him outside with the other's following. "Don't mind Frank, he's a bit eccentric, but he's a fine doctor. Retired Naval officer, you know. Why don't you go get the girl's mother, Sally, isn't it?"

"I'll go get her and John T, right now," Sam ran toward Cherry Hollow glad for an excuse to leave, wishing that Charlie Robinson was home; he forgot the buggy, his wife and children.

***

Thursday November 15, 1855
Free State Hotel Lawrence Kansas

Dr. Thomas didn't have any trouble setting Missy's leg, but Sam asked Charlie Robinson to have a look at it just as a precaution.

"To tell you the truth, that's a better job than I could have done, Sam. He's an excellent doctor. We're lucky to have him."

The patient tried to follow doctors' orders but got restless after a week. She and Lloyd got around town in a small cart hitched to the back of Caleb's pony. They stopped at the hotel where John was finishing excavation of the new well.

"Papa, we're going to ride to the river and watch the ferry for a while," Missy yelled at John. He waved, unsure why they bothered. Normally they wandered the area at will, after all, they knew everybody.

The Pioneer Boarding House hotel, the old Hay Tent, was never more than a stop-gap effort to accommodate the influx of eastern folks moving west. The sod floor and prairie grass thatched side walls were gabled at both ends. Sod was used to support the doors and windows. It burned to the ground in September 1854 and a new one erected with not many improvements.

The New England Emigrant Aid Society knew that it would not meet the coming demand. The Society wanted to build hotels in all of the Free State towns, Lawrence, Topeka, and Manhattan. The biggest problem was, of course, money, there was never enough, plus quality lumber was scarce and what was available was sold at a premium. Most milled lumber had to be shipped from St. Louis; delivery was often two months after the order. The mill owner required cash on the barrel head. It didn't help that clashes between Yankee Town and the Border Ruffians were frequent and many people injured on both sides of the fight. Most of the deaths during 1854 and 55 were attributed to conflicts over land disputes, but in every instance one of the combatants was pro-slavery and the other an abolitionist.

The Aid Society representatives, Clarke Pomeroy, Charlie Robinson and Charles Branscombe had orders to get the new hotel built as soon as possible and to the highest standards. It was to be the finest hotel between St. Louis and Denver. Sam had his suspicions that the three agents were spending more time on their own land speculation than the business of the Society. Bill Speer expressed that opinion in the Tribune. This notion was reinforced when the Society revoked the privileges of Pomeroy and Branscombe to conduct business outside of the affairs of the Emigrant Aide Society job parameters. Charlie Robinson was not happy about 'meddling' in the Society's business.

Pomeroy hired Hiram Stenjham, to construct the building. He was a big blonde Swede, with excellent recommendations as a general contractor, just arrived from New York State. He, in turn, hired John Thompson, and his crew of former slaves, to finish the basement and dig a 60-foot-deep well adjacent to the hotel. John and his men had been at the job all that spring and summer of 1855 and contractors began laying the stone walls in April. The plan had been to use wood framing for the upper walls, but Robinson decided to construct the entire building out of concrete and stone because of the lack of lumber.

On June 20, 1855 a steamboat, the Lizzie, arrived with the tongue and groove hardwood flooring plus the doors and windows. By August 5 the roof was in place and the first and second stories completed, the new Free State hotel had become a reality.

Sam's regiment, the Kansas Rifles Number 1, held a military ball on November 15, complete with fancy invitations all elaborately planned. The tables were covered with wild game, fresh vegetables, newly baked pies and plenty of lemonade and tea. Over 200 people attended. It was by all accounts the grandest party in the history of the territory and was attended by people of every political persuasion, all calling a truce for the evening; but the comradery would be short-lived. All hell was about to break loose in Kansas territory and the Free State Hotel would suffer the brunt of the carnage.

"It is much to be wished that slavery may be abolished. The honor of the States as well as justice and humanity, in my opinion, loudly call upon them to emancipate these unhappy people. To contend for our own liberty, and to deny that blessing to others, involves an inconsistency not to be excused."

John Jay, founding father, first Chief Justice of the Supreme Court, abolitionist, in a letter to R. Lushington, March 15, 1786

Tuesday, November 20, 1855

Ten AM, the Tribune office was full of townsmen, loitering, gossiping, some just getting warm; Charlie, Judge Wakefield, Tap and Caleb Pratt were playing dominoes and drinking coffee by the wood stove. The morning had dawned grey, misty and cold.

"How's the little girl, John T?" Wakefield asked when John entered, stamping his feet, seeking the warmth of the stove.

"She's home today since it's so cold, thanks for asking, Judge."

"What did you think of Charlie's new doctorin' competition?" Caleb Pratt joked.

Charlie laughed, "He's a darn good doctor in spite of that sailor act, we'll need him as fast as people are moving in… hey Chuck, Jacob, what brings you fellas up from Hickory Point on a cold morning?"

"Hello, Doctor Robinson," Chuck Dow said, nodding to everyone, "John T, is Mr. Wood around?"

"I saw him headed this way; I'm surprised you didn't pass him."

Sam walked in, "Chuck, what brings you up here so early in the morning, and Jacob along with you?" Sam had a bad feeling he already knew the answer.

Chuck kicked at the floor, "That darn Frank Coleman again, Mr. Wood. He's back on my land and this time he's burning lime, he even built a kiln. What am I gonna' do? They're all riled up agin' me down there; Harrison Buckley told Frank he'd take care of shootin' me. I don't know why they're all set agin' me like they are."

"And Buckley said he's gonna' kill me, Sam," Jacob Branson added. "This time I got a feeling he means it, he keeps sayin' I'm the one stole Blackwell's slaves. I've never even met Gary Blackwell. I think they plannin' to kill both of us."

"Those are serious allegations, gentlemen," Judge Wakefield said.

"I thought this was just a simple claim dispute, Sam," John T said.

Chuck turned and put his hand on John's shoulder, "How's little Missy? I got this piece of peppermint sugar candy for her when I was in Westport yesterday. You'll give it to her for me, won't ya and tell her Chuck Dow said, 'hey'?"

"I'll sure do it Chuck. I know she'll appreciate it and tell you in person next time she sees you."

Lloyd came charging into the office up to John T, "You're supposed to come home. There's a man looking for you. He wants you to help him build something."

John laughed, "I can always use some work, Lloyd."

"Hello Mr. Dow, I've still got my rabbit's foot." He took it from his pocket and displayed it proudly.

"Lloyd, I just gave John T a piece of sugar candy for Missy, but it's big enough for both of ya, if she'll share with ye'." Lloyd's eyes grew wide, he charged out after John to a chorus of laughter.

"It don't take make much to make that boy happy does it, Sam."

Sam took off his coat, "I'm getting fed up with Frank Coleman's antics."

"Sam, did you know that those men, pretty much all of them, jumped their claims in the last year, year and a half?"

"Wake, that whole section is the blamedest mess you can imagine. It originally belonged to a fellow named Farley, he had four claims, one for him, one for his brother, one for his father, and one for a brother-in-law. Am I saying that right Jacob?"

"Yessir, Farley and his people, were Free State men, just like me. We were about the onliest ones back then."

Sam continued, "Then along comes the Missourians looking for timber claims and they just jumped Farley's land basically driving him and his family away, then burned his cabin. That was the Morrison's from Westport plus Hargis and Coleman. Jacob held on to his claim but had to fight them off just to keep from burning down his house, with him and Elenora inside."

"It was my wife took a shot at them. I think that's what made them leave us alone. They figured if she was that set on stayin' they best find some other land."

Sam added, "Then Chuck Dow comes along last year and takes the claim between Branson and Coleman. Everything would be fine except Coleman insists on using the original Farley survey and everyone else's is based off the Shawnee Reservation survey. There's about 250 yards affected and all of that will get straightened out when the new surveys are completed by the government. Why Coleman can't wait..."

"When will the new surveys be finished?"

"Who knows, it's the government."

Wakefield shook his head in frustration, "Sam and I'll ride over there tomorrow and talk some sense to those men. At least find out what it is they are really up to."

"As my German grandmother would say, they are nothing but bummler's," Caleb said.

"What's that mean?"

"A loafer, do nothing."

Jacob nodded, "All those Border Ruffians are bummler's. They ain't worth a wooden nickel."

"Those are the men we'll be fighting when the war starts," Sam walked Jacob and Chuck to the door.

"Maybe if we keep slavery out of Kansas, we can avoid war," Robinson said.

Wakefield slammed his domino down, "Hell, Charlie, that's what's going to start the war. See you tomorrow, Chuck."

"Be faithful, be vigilant, be untiring in your efforts to break every yoke, and let the oppressed go free. Come what may - cost what it may - inscribe on the banner which you unfurl to the breeze, as your religious and political motto - "NO COMPROMISE WITH SLAVERY! NO UNION WITH SLAVEHOLDERS"
William Lloyd Garrison, Narrative of the Life of Frederick Douglass

Wednesday, November 21, 1855

Margaret lay quietly listening to the rain. It was 4:30 in the morning; she had a bad feeling about the day. Word had spread of Dow and Branson's visit to the claim office and dire warnings of violence in Hickory Point. The rain stopped about 5:30, much to Sam's relief, because he, John and the boys were planning a wood cutting expedition. Margaret and Sally prepared a food basket; the men drove to Lecompton where Sam stopped to see if Governor Shannon was available, but he was at Shawnee Mission. Sam found Judge LeCompte and brought him up to speed on the Coleman-Dow dispute.

"Sam, what do you want me to do? I don't really know any of the parties involved. You've handled the land registry so well I haven't had much to do with it."

"To tell you the truth, Judge, I don't know what to do. I guess just wait until the government survey is finished and hope nothing comes of it before then."

Sam walked to the door of LeCompte's office, stopped to let William in, nodded a greeting and turned to leave.

"Have you heard from the McCrea boy?" LeCompte asked.

"Just that they arrived in Missouri, waiting for the right time to return. His in-laws moved into Lawrence, so they won't have much to do with Leavenworth when he does come back."

The judge nodded, "That was a wise move."

Sam walked east two miles to a bend in the river where there was still a good bit of firewood to be found. By the time he arrived the wagon was about half loaded. He grabbed an ax and began chopping logs John T had reduced to a manageable size with the cross-cut saw. The boys carried and stacked the kindling.

They started back to Lawrence, but because of the deeply rutted trail after the recent rain, the loaded wagon made slow progress. The big draft horses strained under the weight, mud up to the axles in some places and up to the boy's knees in others. It was close to four in the afternoon before they reached home, backed the wagon into John's yard to unload his half of the firewood.

Judge Wakefield watched them pull through Lawrence, his horse saddled and ready. He started toward John T's house thinking that he and Sam were scheduled to go to Hickory Point to resolve the Coleman-Dow claim dispute. Sam noticed the judge following and jumped off the wagon to wait for him. David called out, "Daddy, you haven't done any of the work yet." Sam laughed, waved them on.

Suddenly, with an unforgiving blast, a gunshot shattered the relative calm that had been the state of affairs in Lawrence for the past year and a half.

Just like that the good days were over for decades to come.

Hickory Point
November 21, 1855

The village of Hickory Point lies some seven miles south of Lawrence on one of the many roads that branch off the Santa Fe Trail in the area between the Wakarusa and Kansas Rivers. These roads had names like California Trace and Old Oregon Road. Early settlers believed that the region would someday be a hot bed of commerce because of the heavy traffic bound for new settlements in the west. Traffic had increased exponentially with the 1848 news of Gold in California. Travelers had been using the main turnpikes for twenty-five years, but none of them could possibly foresee what impact the railroads would have on the area when they finally reached that part of the frontier. Still, land was plentiful, and claims could be had for the asking, if you were strong enough to fight off the claim jumpers and the Border Ruffians.

Jacob and Chuck weren't expecting Sam, they had forgotten about the possible meeting in Hickory Point. They were busy burning lime on Jacob's land a good mile from where Frank Coleman had been trespassing the previous day and didn't know if he was there or not. At nine that morning, Chuck left to take a wagon-skein and lynchpin to Poole's blacksmith shop for repairs. He arrived back at Jacob's claim about 11 and he was fit to be tied, "He's still over there Jacob. He's a cutting timber fast as lightning, I ain't a gonna' have a tree one left on my place."

"Dammit, Chuck, lets settle this once for all."

They walked to Branson's house about a quarter mile north where Chuck was rooming with Jacob and his wife until he could build a home of his own. Mrs. Branson was not pleased with what she witnessed of her husband,

"Jacob Branson, what are you doing with that shotgun, where are you going?"

"We're gonna settle this thing for it goes any further. Chuck, get yourself armed, man."

"No, Jacob, I ain't a gonna do it. If'n I take a gun, I'm liable to shoot somebody and this ain't worth it."

"Ain't worth it? If fightin' for your land ain't worth it, nothing is. Suit yourself, but I'm a goin' armed."

They walked to where Frank Coleman was working on Chuck's claim. He had another man helping him; when Coleman saw Chuck and Jacob approaching, he jumped on his horse and rode to Hickory Point, a half mile west. Jacob stopped to talk to Harvey Moody who was burning lime on Dow's land. Chuck listened for a minute then continued on the half-mile the blacksmith shop to get his repaired equipment.

"Harvey, you know this is Chuck's land. Why you doin' this?"

"Mr. Branson, I'm just tryin to earn a honest dollar. I got no dog in this hunt. I'll leave right now if'n you want me to."

"I want you to, and I don't want Frank Coleman on this land neither."

Chuck reached the blacksmith shop, paid for his equipment and was ready to leave when Harry Buckley walked in with a shotgun, "Dow, you Nigger loving son-of-a-bitch; I'm gonna shoot your ass right here. You threatened me for the last time."

"Mr. Buckley, I ain't never threatened you bout' nuthin'. I don't understand what this is all about," he pleaded, the shotgun pointed at his chest.

Daniel Poole was a big man, as blacksmiths tended to be. He put his hammer down on the anvil, stepped up to Buckley and ordered him out of the shop; his thick

Scandinavian drawl making the point emphatically, "I won't have those words spoke in my establishment, Mr. Buckley. Now you get out of here before I get angry with you. I don't understand, either, why you're picking on this poor man."

At that moment, Salem Gleason, a farrier, stepped into the shop, heard the exchange but was not sure why Poole had ordered Buckley out. Gleason said, when he spotted the shotgun, "Ahhh now, Harry, put that gun away, you hear me, put it away, you won't do your wife and kids any good being in prison." Buckley pointed the shotgun down. Chuck was visibly shaken as he nodded thanks to Poole and Gleason walked around Buckley into the cold.

The blustery north wind freshened, seeming to bleed through his clothes absent the warm forge of the blacksmith shop; he glanced back to be certain Buckley wasn't following. Desolate gusts howled between the buildings, chasing most people indoors, a door banged back and forth on an old shed behind the blacksmith shop. Chuck shivered thinking he would rather have a coat than a gun, right then. He walked back toward Jacob's house, trying to understand the hatred toward him and Branson; there were other free-state men in Hickory Point, and they weren't harassed like he was. Other claim disputes were worked out between the settlers, but try as he might, Dow could not make any sense of this matter. He half decided to let Coleman have his way, just to make peace; bringing shotguns to the argument changed the entire complexion of the problem.

He passed Rodger McKinney's house, saw Coleman talking to McKinney on the front porch. Chuck pulled his shirt collar tighter to ward off the cold damp air.

McKinney was always friendly toward him, a nice guy. He wondered what they were talking about.

He paused, thinking, trying to decide what to do, then impulsively shouted, "You win Frank, I'll tell Mr. Wood to change the boundary lines. I don't wanna' fight no more." McKinney and Coleman stood staring at him. He started back to Jacob's house; a weight lifted from his shoulders. He knew Jacob would be mad, but at least they wouldn't have to fight with Coleman and his friends anymore. Chuck was feeling good for the first time in months.

The wagon skein and lynchpin were cold in his ungloved hands; he began to wrap them in his shirt to avoid contact with the cold of the metal. He passed Frank's house, saw Mrs. Coleman entering the front door, he heard Rodger McKinney shout, "No Frank," suddenly a loud explosion sounded directly behind him. He flinched and turned to find Coleman aiming a shotgun at him from about six feet away. Stunned, he didn't understand what happened, "Did you just try to shoot me in the back, you coward? Didn't you hear me say you could have the land?"

Coleman didn't answer. He was busy replacing the cap that failed to discharge the bullets. He raised the gun again. Dow started toward him his right palm outstretched, as if to say 'halt'; the wagon skein in his left, "I'm unarmed Frank, why…"

Franklin Coleman pulled the trigger, pellets blasted Chuck in the chest and neck, a blow that knocked him over backward and burned through his flesh like an artillery round. He clutched at his throat, made an attempt to rise, saw Mrs. Coleman at the door to her house, hands to her mouth, shock in her eyes; he heard that same lonesome gate banging in the wind. He reached out to Mrs. Coleman, with blood-stained hands from the hole in his neck, a gesture for help. She turned away in horror; he sank back in the dirt, blood pouring from his wounds, until he bled to death.

The murderer walked into his house, "He threatened me, everyone saw him walking toward me with a gun in his hand." Coleman was beginning to shake, and his eyes were wild with the realization of what he'd done. By this time McKinney and Buckley arrived followed by Moody and Hargis. "He didn't have a gun, Frank, quit saying that," McKinney cautioned. Then Gleason arrived giving support to what McKinney said.

"I thought he did," Coleman lied, with his hands to his face. His wife looked on in disbelief glancing from McKinney to her husband. She knew the truth because she had heard and seen the entire cold-blooded murder, but her loyalty was with her husband. "You've got to go turn yourself in to Sheriff Jones, right now, this afternoon before Dow's friends find out."

"He's still layin' out there Rodger, shouldn't we bring him in out off the street," Gleason held the curtain aside.

"Leave the Nigger-lover lay," Buckley answered. "Serve as a warning for the rest of these Goddamned abolitionists. Quit carryin' on so, Franky, you only did what we agreed to do."

"You watch your language in my house," Mrs. Coleman said. She was getting angry, tears formed in her eyes. "Take Frank to Westport and find the sheriff, tell him it was self-defense. Go on, get some horses and go before they come looking for you. Jones will protect you. I'm going to my sister's house." She was not a part of the conspiracy, but she could manage the aftermath better than the shaken men.

"There is no law, no restraint in this seething cauldron of vice and depravity."
The New York Tribune describing Kansas.

Lawrence 4:30 PM
November 21, 1855

Three shots, in succession, had the men and women of Lawrence ducking for cover until they realized that it was a signal to convene at the Free State Hotel. Sam felt sure that something bad had happened, this was the first time the signal had been employed. Wakefield rode back at a gallop while Sam ran the three hundred yards to town. A large group of Lawrence citizens gathered around two riders that Sam couldn't make out until he got closer. Harold Barnett and Thomas Barber were shouting when they saw him, "They murdered Chuck Dow and Jacob Branson."

Sam stopped in his tracks, shocked beyond belief, "My God, it's my fault," he sank to one knee, looked at Wakefield stunned, about to fall out of the saddle. They locked eyes for a horrible moment, guilt and dread reflected on their faces. Sam felt sick to his stomach, "I'll get my horse and cane. Do you men have rifles? Go over to Dr. Robinson's and tell him what happened. Get some Sharp's rifles. I'll meet you back here in 15 minutes."

"I'm going too," Tappan yelled.

John T found Sam in the barn, asked if he wanted company; Sam preferred John stay and help with any defenses that the Safety Committees might determine proper. "I hope this is just a misunderstanding, John T, you know how rumors are around here." John was not in the least optimistic.

For some reason Charlie Robinson had a premonition that this was the beginning of something disastrous. He unlocked his barn, distributed two of the Sharpe's along with ammunition. The men hurried back to where Sam was waiting.

"Sam, this is not a Lawrence problem, this problem needs to stay in Hickory Point, don't you agree?" Robinson held his arm, kept him from mounting.

"What do you mean, Charlie? Friends of ours have been murdered. We have to get justice for them, defend ourselves; we knew this was coming."

"All I'm saying is try to keep the problem down there. Let the Hickory Point people resolve it, I don't want Jones and his Ruffians anywhere near Lawrence."

Sam shook his head in frustration as he, Tap, Harold and Tom Barber started for Hickory Point. The thought that he might be responsible raced through his mind as they followed the road over the treeless plain toward the Wakarusa and Jacob Branson's house. "How do you know what happened, Harold?" Sam asked.

"We ran into Rodger Mckinney at the Lecompton Road; he was riding to tell the Judge about it. It sounds like a real mess over there in Hickory Point. They sent for Jones so no telling what we're gonna find when we get there."

Several horses, a couple of wagons surrounded Branson's rough looking cabin when they arrived. "Looks like we came to the right place," Tappan said.

The front door opened, two rifles appeared, "Who's out there?" Phil Hutchinson called. Smoke and sparks poured from the chimney, lamps lit the windows as Barnett shouted, "Friends of yours. Colonel Wood is with us."

The rifles dropped, several men advanced shouting greetings of relief that someone was coming to take charge. The men might not have been so confident had they been able to read Sam's mind, share the feeling of guilt that he was somehow the cause; yet his instinct for command took over. Sam dismounted asked for a report before they even reached the warmth of the cabin. Chuck Dow was lying on the table under a sheet. The newcomers removed their hats, bowed their heads as they were shown the body. "Where's Jacob?" Sam asked Mrs. Branson.

"He's gone to Hickory to make sure the law arrests that man who did this," she sobbed. Sam turned to Harold for an explanation. He expected to find the body of Branson next to Dow's corpse.

"We thought he was dead too," Tappan answered.

"He's with Philip and Miner Hupp, they went to swear out a warrant against Coleman. They should be back by now," Phil Hutchinson said. He was a Captain in the Territorial Guard under the command of James Lane. Sam was surprised to see him in the cabin knowing that Lane would not want his troops, volunteer or not, involved in this incident. Several other men lounged about supplied with hot coffee. Sam knew most and introduced himself to the few that he didn't, including Elmore Allen, a sharp-faced, middle-aged man from Mississippi, who surprised Sam with the depth of his hatred for pro-slavery men. Allen spoke with a distinct southern accent, carried an old shotgun and a small broad sword. Most of the men were armed with pistols or just knives. Sam and Tappan were the only ones with Sharp's Rifles. The Curless brothers, Edmund and Lafayette, carried nothing but hand carved clubs. Sam examined them with envy.

Horses were heard outside as the door flew open to Branson, the Hupp's, Major Abbott and J. B. Kennedy.

"What in the world are you doing here, Sam?" Kennedy exclaimed.

"I could ask the same of you, J. B.," Sam replied.

"Well, you told me to report the news and this is about the biggest news I can imagine. Did you know that Jones was behind all of this? Their goal is to raise an army and wipe out every, man, woman, and child, in Lawrence."

The men were shocked into silence. The fire crackled, Jacob's old dog stood up from his place on the hearth, scratched himself and strolled to the door. Hutchinson allowed him out; a blast of cold air refreshed the conversation.

"What, in God's name, have the people of Lawrence got to do with this?" Tappan asked.

Kennedy and the others waited for Major Abbott, who was removing his coat and hat, "It was all organized at a meeting in Westport a few months ago. They planned to goad Jacob and Chuck in hopes one of them would do something to start a fight then blame it on the abolitionists in Lawrence, they're looking for an excuse to clean out the town. They grew tired of waiting so they just up and killed Mr. Dow. Buckley tried to do it earlier in the day and was scared off by Poole and Gleason. Coleman finished the job, shot him in the back."

Sam was looking at the body, confused, because the wounds were in the front. Gleason, who was a witness, explained how Coleman fired the first shot at Dow's back, reloaded and fired again when Chuck turned in self-defense. Gleason, a Free State man had avoided the issue of abolitionism until now. He felt that he could no longer ignore the atrocities of the Border Ruffians; Dow had been a good friend.

"Where are Coleman and Buckley?" Tappan asked.

"We just don't know. I rode over to Westport looking for answers. The only thing we can say for certain is that Jones is hiding them and possibly Governor Shannon is complicit in this. I honestly believe that the man giving orders is Senator Atchison," said Abbott.

A string of oaths came from Collins Holloway and a few of the other rough farmers in the room. Sam cautioned them in strong terms that there was a lady present. Mrs. Branson sat at the table near Dow's body obviously fatigued.

Sam said, "Gentlemen, it's late, and I fail to see any further action that will benefit us tonight. I suggest we all go home and reconvene at Major Abbott's at a convenient time tomorrow and make our plans."

"We could burn Coleman and Buckley's houses. It would serve them right," Holloway said.

"No, we won't," Sam said quickly.

"I agree," Major Abbott added. "Let's not sink to their level. We need to find the men who did this and bring them to justice. If Shannon is involved, we'll have to appeal to Washington. Meanwhile, we're on our own, we are the law."

Sam and Tappan left together for the lonely ride home. The night sky was filled with spotty clouds and the waning crescent of a moon. The north wind was steady; they pulled their hats down, scarves tight around their throats. Sam seldom wore gloves, but he pulled a pair from his saddle pack. They spoke of their humble friend, Chuck Dow, who did not deserve such a fate; a pawn in an ill-devised scheme by men who used him for motives beyond Dow's simple understanding. Sam and Tappan vowed to see that justice was done.

"I've seen my fair share of death, Sam, but this beats all for senselessness. I guess we understand now why

Chuck was so confused. He was doomed from the start. Nothing or nobody could have prevented this."

Sam shook his head, "I should have figured it out, Tap. We knew there was something besides the boundary dispute, I just couldn't make sense of it. Yet it all falls into place now that the truth comes out. I worry that Coleman will escape before we can bring him to justice, but someone else planned this thing.

"Strange isn't it, Sam, the biggest criminal in the territory has the backing of the law and the politicians. We've got our work cut out for us. I fear the job may be bigger than the resources we've got to deal with it. When you're fighting the President, a Senator and a Governor, the deck is stacked against you."

"Tap, we will win. I don't know how exactly, but we will win."

Despite the late hour, Margaret had a welcoming lamp lit in the window facing Massachusetts Street. There were still men at the Free-State Hotel discussing the news, so Sam briefed them about the happenings in Hickory Point. Word came from Lecompton that Frank Coleman had turned himself into Judge LeCompte who, in turn, sent him to Westport and the protection of Sheriff Jones.

"We have to call up the Safety Committee patrols," General Lane said. They were organized into groups of 15 to 20 men. Dietzler and Lane engineered plans to construct redoubts along Massachusetts Street at strategic intersections. Lane proposed they execute those plans and begin constructing the defenses. Material still needed to be gathered, dirt hauled to reinforce the barricades; it would be too late if Jones did bring a large contingent of Missourians in the next few days. Charlie Robinson agreed for a change and the plans were finalized about midnight. They would begin the next day.

Sam took Border Ruffian to the barn, wiped him down with a saddle blanket then turned him into the corral with fresh hay and oats. "We're going to have a civil war, Ruff, it's just a matter of time." He nuzzled against the warmth, gathering comfort from the contact. Sam was bone weary with a fatigue that went beyond physical exertion, he was worn out with worry about his family, about his cause and the coming battle he knew would tax all of them beyond endurance.

Margaret had warm milk ready for him when he finally opened the back door. He hugged her until she asked, "Is it that bad, Sam?"

"Maybe worse, Meg. I think this is the beginning of the big war; I don't see any compromise. They've threatened to wipe us out; we have to defend ourselves. I should have seen what was happening, but I was too wrapped up in other matters to reason it out and now a good friend is dead." Margaret sat with him, holding his hand in her lap, she let him talk until he was left with nothing more to say.

"I have some water heated, Sam, let me help you wash and let's go to bed. You've been going since five yesterday morning, we can discuss this after we're rested. The Good Lord is watching over us. We've been chosen to help free the slaves. We both knew there would be bloodshed."

Sam exhausted, more mentally than physically, stroked her cheek, "Doesn't make it any easier, does it?"

She helped strip off his dirty clothes, her tender caresses washed away the dregs of the day. They held hands and mounted the steps to bed.

***

On Saturday, they buried Chuck beneath a large elm tree near the western boundary of his land, within sight of the Branson home. The poor, unassuming man finally found peace, in death. The children he loved so dearly gathered around the simple wooden coffin as Reverend Richard Mendenhall gave the eulogy. Missy Thompson asked, "Mama, is Mr. Dow in that box?"

Sally nodded yes, her eyes red from crying.

"Remember when we put Mr. Francis in a box like that one? He was my friend, too." Then quietly to herself, "Why do all my friends die?"

Elenora Branson, wearing a long black dress with a somber dark hat and veil, rested her hand on Missy's shoulder, "I hope that folks remember he was a fine man." Jacob stood next to his wife, slightly behind her, face stamped with anger; an anger that would not diminish until the man responsible for the murder of his best friend was brought to justice.

Hal Barnett draped his coat over Sarah shivering beside him in the chill November air. Harold and Autumn, the Barber family, the Tappan's', thirty or so people from the Hickory Point area all listened in silence. As the ceremony ended Sam and Major Abbott circulated among the crowd reminding them of the rally being held on Main Street in Hickory Point come Monday. John T gathered up the four kids, put Missy on his shoulder. Margaret left with Sally and the other ladies for the Branson's house where a small reception was planned.

A few of the local men began to fill the grave. Reaching the edge of the clearing, Lloyd stopped, ran back to the gravesite, paused a moment, peered over the edge at the still visible coffin; the men with shovels hesitated while the boy paid his last respects. Chief Barnett leaned against his shovel, "He was a good man wasn't he little Mr. Wood?"

Lloyd glanced up at the handsome young man, nodded, "He was my good friend. He gave me this," reaching in his pocket he pulled out the good luck charm given to him by Chuck that summer.

"Rabbits' foot," Chief said.

Lloyd turned to look at the others, waiting for him, curiosity on their faces. He held up his beloved rabbits' foot then dropped it into the hole.

"He'll appreciate that," Chief said quietly.

***

November 24, Monday turned cold but dry, a day well suited for the angry mood of the citizens of Hickory Point. Free State men and women gathered to protest in front of Franklin Coleman's vacant house at the spot of the murder. Reverend Mendenhall opened with a long prayer echoing his call to arms against the forces of evil that he vowed to take the year before at the funeral of his friend, Felix Francis.

"Those responsible for this shameful act will be held accountable, relegated to the gates of hell, no doubt. But before their everlasting punishment commences, they will be brought to justice here on earth. I fear that government officials are behind this fiendish murder. The very men charged with protecting the citizens of our territory have the blood of this innocent man on their hands. They will face earthly judgment, as God is my witness."

Sam challenged the crowd of about 200 with an inspiring call to take up arms against the Border Ruffians, "Ride to Lecompton, confront Governor Shannon, ask him point blank was he involved in this monstrous act? We already know that Atchison and Jones had a hand in it."

A Committee of Justice was organized, resolutions drafted condemning the murderous act, offering condolences to the victims and issuing a call for the arrest of Franklin Coleman and Harrison Buckley. Major Abbott took command; the men were divided into groups of four, each with a quadrant of the area to search. There is no doubt that had Coleman been found he would have faced the death penalty imposed by the self-formed Committee of Justice in Hickory Point; but his whereabouts remained secret. Jacob Branson denounced Coleman and Buckley in the most vivid of terms assuring one and all that both men would be dispatched forthwith if he could find them, "Chuck Dow was my best friend. A simple soul who never wronged man nor beast on this earth. He loved the children, treated them as part of his own family. He was murdered by a cowardly monster who should face a firing squad and I'll pull the trigger."

Branson was also a simple man with a modest manner of speech; but he made himself understood in front of the cheering throng of anti-slavery men and women, many of whom sat on the fence not wanting to become involved. The death of their friend Dow was the catalyst. It was time for action.

That evening, Sam sat sipping cool water provided by Major Abbott's wife, Abigale, in their comfortable home on the Wakarusa not far from the road to Lecompton. The day had been gratifying, not in the fact of finding Coleman or Buckley, but in the number of abolitionists who rallied to the cause.

Abbott removed his pistol, put it in a cupboard, "I'll bet we had over 200 people there during the early part of the afternoon."

"I'm surprised we couldn't find those two criminals with all that manpower. They must be in Independence or maybe even Atchison. Jones isn't going to show his face or take a chance on us finding them," Sam held the glass while Abigale filled it again.

"Not with the angry state of mind of the neighbors," Abbott agreed. "Sam, I truly appreciate you staying to see this out. I'm surprised there weren't more people from Lawrence here today."

"Robinson has a tight rein on them. He wants to keep the hostilities away from town."

Abbott sneered, "That ain't going to happen. They want to wipe us out and Lawrence is where they'll start, that's what this is all about. We need to make Robinson understand, if they can eliminate Lawrence, they'll have free reign to elect their pro-slavery agenda. All we've worked for will be lost."

A loud knock at the front door roused them to their guns before Captain Hutchison and the Hupps were ushered in by Abigale Abbott.

"You ain't gonna' believe this," Philip Hupp announced without formality.

"What?" Major Abbott asked impatiently.

"You know Squire Cameron over on Smithson Road?"

"I don't know him," Sam answered.

"I know who he is," Abbott said pensively, "He's one of the Missouri boys who jumped a claim over that way about six months ago. He belongs with Jones and his crew."

"Exactly," said Captain Hutchison. "And bogus Jones appointed him Justice of the Peace this morning."

Sam and the Major looked at each other, burst out laughing. "He's got no right to appoint anyone anything," Abbott said.

"Be that as it may, but he sure did it. This afternoon Harrison Buckley went to Cameron's house and swore out a warrant against Jacob Branson for threatening his life at the rally."

This news so shocked Sam he could not think of anything to say. What did it all mean? Buckley was the criminal, a co-conspirator with Coleman and Jones to murder Mr. Dow. Yet they were turning the story inside out and making the innocent Branson the criminal and Buckley the victim.

"Why this whole thing is crazy," Abigale Abbott said, "Buckley's the guilty one, not Jacob."

"Surely nothing will come of it," her husband assured her.

Philip and his son Miner Hupp stood listening quietly by the door. They accepted coffee from Mrs. Abbott, placed their rifles in the corner before sitting near the hearth. They were big men, tall and broad of shoulder, Phillip was 55 and Miner 35, they came from Massachusetts to start a new life on the frontier. They were anti-slavery but had become devoted abolitionists after witnessing the mistreatment of slaves.

"I wouldn't put it past Jones to do something terrible like murder Jacob and then say he had to shoot him in self-defense," Philip said.

"If he does, Pa, then we'll have the right to shoot Jones," Miner answered.

Sam paced in front of the hearth, "This is a situation that requires some serious thought. We have no one to turn to for help, at least as far as the law is concerned. The official law, in this case, is in the hands of the criminals. We're on our own trying to stay within the confines of justice. We'll have to make it up and trust to providence that we do the right thing. Has someone warned Jacob about all of this?"

"Miner ride over to Jacob's house and let him know what's happening. He might want to get out of town for a while," Philip ordered. Miner left in a rush.

"We never did hang the wrong one but once or twice, and them fellers needed to be hung anyhow jes' on general principles." **A** judge on the frontier.

J B Kennedy arrived at Abbott's house about six that evening bringing more rumors of bad news. "Report is that Jones has rallied about 2,500 Missouri Ruffians under the command of his friend, Colonel Boone from Westport."

"I know Boone, He's a stooge of Atchison," Abbott scowled. "the man is a loose cannon, dangerous, no telling what he might do. If that's true, we'd better warn General Lane and have him get his militia armed and ready."

"You haven't been to Lawrence in a couple of days," Kennedy continued. "Lane and Robinson have redoubts in the streets and armed guards around the perimeter, not letting anyone in unless we know them. Companies of men are arriving from all the surrounding towns."

As if reading Sam's mind, Kennedy added, "I saw Margaret this morning Sam, she said they're fine and not to worry. One of the biggest barricades is in the street in front of your house across from the hotel. It's full of armed men."

Suddenly the door burst open, Miner Hupp stumbled in wild-eyed out of breath, "Jones arrested Jacob, hauled him off in chains, he may already be hung."

Abbott leapt to his feet, "My God, has Jones gone mad. If he harms Jacob, we won't be able to restrain the men in Lawrence. This will turn into outright war."

Sam slammed his fist on the table, "This proves they're trying to provoke us. Major, we've got to locate Jacob right now. We can't waste any time. Phillip, Miner would you mind rallying some of our forces, men who aren't afraid of a fight? Hupp, how many men did Jones bring to arrest Jacob?"

"Maybe 14 or 15. Mrs. Branson didn't think to count em', but Harrison Buckley was one of them and she cussed him up and down according to my mother, who's over there with her. I wish I could have heard it."

"We need to send some men to guard them in case Jones decides to burn Branson's home," Phillip said.

"We need at least 15 men and two or three to guard the Branson house," Abbott ordered.

"Get Harold Barnett and his boys," Sam yelled out the door. Then as an afterthought, "and Tom and Robert Barber."

The Hupp's left on the run. Kennedy and Captain Hutchinson were dispatched to watch the Lecompton Road, the most likely route the Jones gang would be taking. Major Abbott rode northeast toward Franklin to see if he could find any news or if anyone had seen anything. Sam stayed to organize the men. By eleven that night there were twelve men at Abbotts home and three more guarding Jacob Branson's house. Abbott returned with no further word or idea where Jacob was.

"Major, I wonder if we shouldn't send scouts out, two riders each way so one can bring word if Jones is spotted," said Sam.

"We need to do something besides just sit here," Harold agreed.

"If he's taking Branson to Lecompton they've got to go by here. They don't want to ride up through Lawrence," Tom Barber said.

"I'm afraid they've already hung him," Miner Hupp said, "How can this be happening," he shouted angrily.

A commotion outside caused all heads to turn. J. B. Kennedy screamed from the porch, "They're coming up the road, almost past Blanton's Bridge, come a runnin'."

The men grabbed what weapons they had, the Hupps their rifles, a few had pistols, but most carried only broad swords or knives. They charged out of the house around the corner to where Captain Hutchison was holding a lantern standing in the middle of the road. Sam ran to Hutchinson's side, cane in hand; the rest of the party fanned out along the road with the Hupps in the forefront.

"You men halt there, who is that?" Sam called as the dark riders rode up and reined in their horses.

"What's up here?" shouted one of Jones gang.

"That's what we want to know," Major Abbott ordered, "What's your business here?"

"I'm taking a prisoner to Lecompton where he'll stand trial," Jones said.

"Jacob Branson are you with them," Sam shouted squinting into the meagre light cast by the one lantern.

"I'm here, a prisoner," Branson answered.

"Come over here with us," Phillip Hupp shouted followed by a chorus of agreement from the rescuers.

"They say they'll shoot me if I leave," Branson said.

"Come ahead, Jacob, they'll all die here tonight if they fire a shot," Sam answered, and the rescuers sighted in on the Jones posse with more speed than thought possible, before the gang could think to draw their guns.

"I'm coming if they shoot me or not," Jacob cried and kicked the mule he was riding. The man holding the reins let them slip through his hands without protest.

Sam caught the mule, "Is this your mule Jacob?"

"No," he jumped off, disappeared into Major Abbott's house as quickly as he could go. Sam turned the mule around, slapped it on the rear sending it back to the Ruffians.

"You men are interfering in a lawful arrest. I've got a warrant issued by a legal representative; there will be hell to pay for this. You must be feeling pretty damn brave tonight, Sam Wood, do you want a war, is that what you want?" Jones said.

"Shoot that son-of-a-bitch, Sheriff," Gary Blackwell shouted.

I've never backed down from a fight, especially from the likes of you," Sam yelled, "and now you've murdered a good friend of mine, Jones..."

"I never murd..."

"You hired him," Sam shouted. "Don't lie, you coward, you make me sick to my stomach, you worthless pile of rat dung."

"Shoot him, Goddamnit," Blackwell yelled again.

"Anyone draws a gun I'll blow em' out of the saddle," Harold held a shotgun to his shoulder. Hutchinson cast the lamp Harold's way to prove his point.

Harrison Buckley bellowed, "We've got 3,000 men ready to ride on Lawrence and we will wipe you out."

Jones started forward as if to push through the line, Harold pulled him up right quick with the cocked gun pointed at his head.

"Don't shoot," Jones cried. "There's no need for bloodshed in this matter."

"You're a coward, Jones," Sam stepped up next to him, "I've always known you're a coward. Get down off that horse and let's settle this between us, otherwise, you take these men back to Missouri and stay out of Kansas."

"I'm the by-God sheriff. You're in treason against the government."

Harold shouted, "Where is Frank Coleman? He has to stand trial for this murder."

"He acted in self-defense," Buckley screamed.

Sam grabbed the reins of Jones horse, "You arrested Jacob Branson, an innocent man, there sits one just as guilty as Coleman. Harrison Buckley get down off that horse, you're going to jail for attempted murder. You're under arrest."

"Damn you Wood, I've got a warrant for Old Man Branson's arrest, stand down or I'll arrest you for interfering in a lawful detention."

"I'm Jacob Branson's attorney, let me see this warrant and we'll take it under advisement, but I'll tell all of you," he shouted at the rest of the posse pointing with his cane, "You are falsely representing peace officers in Kansas. You're all from Missouri."

"By God, you son-of-a-bitch, I told you before, I don't have to show you anything. I'm the legal Sheriff of Douglas County, Kansas Territory. You better give Branson back…"

Sam cut him off with a whack of his cane against a nearby tree, "We don't know any sheriff named Jones in Kansas, do we boys? I heard of a postmaster in Missouri name of Jones and you bear a strong resemblance to him. Get out of here or let the shooting begin."

The ruffian next to Jones pulled his gun intent on shooting Phillip Hupp. Sam, already in motion, clubbed the gun hand knocking the pistol to the ground where it discharged harmlessly, startling the posse. They wheeled their horses around and bolted off.

Raucous cheers went up from the motley rescue party. "We've got to go to Lawrence and tell them what happened," Abbott shouted.

It was almost dawn by the time the liberators of Jacob Branson arrived in Lawrence led by Major Abbott beating a drum, the others shouting and cheering, with Branson himself cheering the loudest. They stopped at Charlie Robinson's house, who was not happy, urged them to get out of town and not bring trouble into Lawrence.

The rescuers trooped to the Free State Hotel where a large crowd gathered, cheered lustily for the successful rescue, not worried about Charlie Robinson and his fears of retribution. Sam explained in vivid and eloquent detail all of the facts from the day of the murder, the burial of Chuck, to the false warrant for arrest and then the details of the rescue. The citizens of Lawrence were wild with enthusiasm for successfully saving one of their own.

Finally, Jacob spoke and in his humble way told of the threats against his life and how his wife was at home not knowing if he was dead or alive. His unpretentious feelings were shown through the passion in his halting voice and the tears that flowed down his cheeks, "I don't want to bring no trouble on the people of Lawrence so I will get out of here now and go back home," he cried, breaking down with emotion from being a prisoner and the joy of being rescued.

The euphoria of the moment began to wane as the morning advanced; the Hickory Point men returned to their families. Sam trudged to his own house and a bed that he hadn't seen in 48 hours.

***

Douglas County Sheriff Sam Jones was madder than he had ever been in his life. Not only had he lost his prisoner, but he was humiliated in the process by a man that he hated with all of his soul. No doubt the angry men blamed him for the failure of their mission, but the furious look on the sheriff's face kept the men silent on the matter.

Jones knew he had no choice; he resolved to show the people of Yankee Town how powerful he had become. The disgraced posse rode to Franklin where they stopped at Gary Blackwell's house. Gary was not impressed with the way he, meaning Jones, had let the prisoner slip through their fingers. Blackwell was wealthy, with farms in Missouri and Georgia, in addition to the property in Franklin. He came to Kansas Territory to ensure that it entered the Union as a slave state, having been urged on that mission by his friends, David Atchison, John Gordon, the Governor of Georgia and Jefferson Davis, who was a cousin of Blackwell's wife.

"What are you gonna do Sheriff?" Blackwell took of his coat, threw a log on the fire, "that little scuffle was not well handled. You should have shot that bastard. I won't have a Nigger left, if I stay in Kansas, the way it's goin' right now."

"These Goddamned abolitionists are going to learn their lesson before the week is out. I'll tell you what I'm about to do, Mr. Blackwell, I'm sending for Colonel Boone to bring his troops up here to Franklin, so we'll be ready to march on Lawrence within the week. Bring me a pen and paper, Lester, get ready to ride."

Jones scribbled a letter to Boone ordering him to make haste in bringing as many men as he could muster, men prepared to march on Yankee Town with guns blazing. Lester was deputized to carry this message post haste and return with Boone's estimated time of arrival. The soldiers commanded by Colonel Boone were all Missouri men, a good many of them Border Ruffians who were being compensated by David Atchison and slaveholders, like Blackwell. They had money stockpiled for this very event. Jones expected 2,500 men, heavily armed.

Blackwell, a corpulent man with a great overhang of a belly, was father to four sons who managed his farm holdings and acted as overseers of his slaves. They were as cruel and hardhearted as their father. He opened the kitchen door, bellowed, "Get Elijah out here, I need a horse saddled."

To Jones he said, "I'll have a fresh horse made ready for the messenger." Jones merely nodded. From the kitchen a matronly voice was heard to say, "He asleep."

The look on Blackwell's face would have frightened the Sphinx had it been witness. The enslaver grabbed a short-handled whip hanging behind the kitchen door; wails of pain were heard as he shouted, "I didn't ask you where he was you ignorant bitch, I said to get him and you'd best move your fat black ass to get it done or you'll wish to God you'd never heard my name." Lester took the opportunity to sneak a peek into the kitchen; it was clear from the look on the woman's face that she wished for that very thing.

A sleep-dazed black man of about 65 stumbled from the kitchen, out into the night to do his master's bidding without so much as a coat to ward off the night chill, which was considerable. It was obvious to all present that the man didn't own such an object of commonplace necessity, nor did they think it unusual that he didn't have one.

Blackwell placed the whip back on the hook, "Jones, I don't mind Missouri men coming in here to fight, but for this you need to notify Governor Shannon, have him put the Kansas Militia in play. The right thing to do is tell Shannon that Lawrence is in full rebellion, led by Sam Wood, and he needs to send troops to quell the uprising. They'll be commanded by Missouri men anyway."

"Someone needs to shoot that Sam Wood," Big Bill grunted

General agreement was nodded all around. It was late but the men were abuzz with excitement about the nights skirmish no matter its outcome. The strategy involved was beyond their comprehension and they were just waiting for further orders which, they assumed meant an attack on Lawrence.

Jones wrote another letter, which echoed the communiqué sent to Colonel Boone:

"DOUGLAS COUNTY, K. T., November 27, 1855.

To His Excellency, WILSON SHANNON, Governor of Kansas Territory.

SIR - Last night I, with a posse of ten men, arrested one Jacob Branson, by virtue of a peace warrant, regularly issued, who, on our return, was rescued by a party of forty armed men, who rushed upon us suddenly from behind a house by the roadside, all armed to the teeth with Sharpe's rifles.

You may consider an open rebellion as having already commenced; and I call upon you for THREE THOUSAND men to carry out the laws. Mr. Hargus (the bearer of this letter) will give you more particularly the circumstances.

Most respectfully, SAMUEL J. JONES, Sheriff of Douglas County."

The letter was carried by Josiah Hargis, spelled Hargus in the document, who was a friend and neighbor of Coleman and Buckley. Hargis put on his warm sheepskin coat, "Boy, fetch me another hoss and best be quick, or your massah put the whip to you like he done the Nigger bitch inside." The 'boy' did as he was told, kept his mouth shut at the insults.

Jones slept peacefully the rest of the night knowing that he would have his revenge in short order; Sam Wood was to die early because he had been a thorn in his side since both arrived in the Territory. Jones was not a man given to a great deal of thought to what he did. His office had been handed to him after a raid on a free state voting box which he stole and carried back to Missouri causing Atchison to believe that Jones had been the instigator of the voting theft. Jones was nothing more than a follower, a hanger-on, but he accepted the honor gladly.

From that point forward, his life had been a whirlwind of success, he was advanced to Postmaster in Westport, then Sheriff of Douglas County, Kansas Territory, a job for which he was singularly unqualified, lacking in even the basics of experience. But he was loyal and dedicated, if he was anything; orders from Senator Atchison were like commandments from God Almighty, himself, as far as Jones was concerned. He took literally the idea of killing all the citizens of Lawrence not imagining that this was murder. He gave no thought to the moral right or wrong of the matter and the action could not begin soon enough as far as he was concerned. The fact that it had been a months old conspiracy was kept as a secret between Atchison, Jones and the men who carried out the murders, Franklin Coleman and Harrison Buckley. Jacob Branson was supposed to have died the same day.

***

General Stringfellow of 'The Leavenworth Herald sent the following message to all of the Missouri border newspapers:

"TO ARMS! TO ARMS!!
It is expected that every lover of Law and Order will rally at Leavenworth, on Saturday, December 1, 1855, prepared to march at once to the scene of the rebellion, to put down the

outlaws of Douglas County, who are committing depredations upon persons and property, burning down houses and declaring open hostility to the laws, and have forcibly rescued a prisoner from the Sheriff. Come one, come all! The laws must be executed. The outlaws, it is said, are armed to the teeth, and number 1,000 men. Every man should bring his rifle and ammunition, and it would be well to bring two or three days' provisions. Every man to his post and do his duty."

Bill Speer and J. B. Kennedy published the true account of Dow's murder and Branson's rescue in the Tribune. Anti-slavery men poured into Lawrence, expecting to fight, but found the situation nothing like they anticipated. The town was fortified with barricades in the streets and guards at the city limits. Throughout the Union word spread that the citizens of Lawrence were in full rebellion against the Territorial Government. Nothing was further from the truth. Charlie Robinson was simply preparing for the possibility of hostilities from the Missouri Ruffians, which most Lawrence citizens didn't expect to happen. How could it? The very thought was beyond human reason; the residents of Lawrence had done nothing. The murder occurred several miles from the village and the only citizen of Lawrence who was involved in the rescue of Jacob was Sam Wood. Everyone, on both sides, knew that he fought 'on his own hook' taking responsibility for his actions and backing down from no one. How could anyone blame the people of Lawrence in this matter?

Of course, the citizens failed to grasp the villainy of the parties involved, especially Missouri Senator Atchison, surrogate of President Pierce and the Washington cartel. Lawrence residents attributed honorable qualities of reason, law and order to slaveholders who damned sure didn't have any qualms about wiping Lawrence off the face of the earth; men, women and children included. Atchison had given fair warning in a newspaper article carried throughout the nation. Yet there were still citizens who refused to believe that a Senator and the President of the United States would resort to violence, voter fraud and even murder to force slavery into Kansas Territory.

"My creed on the subject of slavery is short. Slavery per se is not sin. It is a social condition ordained from the beginning of the world for the wisest purposes, benevolent and disciplinary, by Divine Wisdom."

Samuel Morse. In favor of slavery (b. 1791--d. 1872) Artist and inventor.

Sam woke early the next morning to the sound of voices downstairs in the living room. He was tempted to pull the covers up, snuggle back down and go to sleep, but it was way too early for good news, "I hope it's not another murder."

"Sam, we have visitors," Sarah's worried tone confirmed the expectation.

"Couldn't have been more than three hours sleep," he mumbled, thinking himself alone. Lloyd and Missy were fast asleep on a pallet next to the bed; "must have had a houseful last night," half stumbling, he managed to pull on a pair of pants, negotiated the stairs. A delegation awaited, Charlie Robinson, General Lane, Judge Wakefield and George Dietzler, all eyes followed his sluggish progress to join them.

"Long night, Sam?"

"It's been a long few nights, seems like months. You fellows too, I suppose."

"We've been busy," Lane nodded toward the street.

"It looks good, Jim. I hope it proves overcautious, at least we're ready if something does happen."

Wakefield handed him a sheet of paper, "Read this."

"We, the citizens of Kansas Territory, find ourselves in a condition of confusion and defenselessness so great, that open outrage and mid-day murders are becoming the rule, and quiet and security the exception. And, whereas, the law, the only authoritative engine to correct and regulate the excesses and wrongs of society, has never yet been extended to our Territory

- thus leaving us with no fixed or definite rules of action, or source of redress - we are reduced to the necessity of organizing ourselves together on the basis of first principles, and providing for the common defense and general security. And here we pledge ourselves to the resistance of lawlessness and outrage at all times, when required by the officers who may from time to time be chosen to superintend the movements of the organization."

Signed by officers of the Lawrence, K.T. Committee of Free Safety, December 2, 1855

"We sent that by messenger to the Governor in Shawnee Mission," Lane said, "Speer is printing it in today's Tribune."

"You've already sent it? I would have been more to the point. You've stated the general situation adequately. Without spelling out the specific crimes committed, and the measures taken to defend the city; Atchison and Shannon will ignore this completely."

Margaret bustled about providing coffee, leftover bread and butter, then retreated to the kitchen but close enough to overhear the conversation. "Please join us, Margaret, this concerns you too. Sam, you've got to get out of town," Wakefield said without preamble.

He wouldn't have been more surprised if one of them had whacked him with his own cane, standing in the corner next to the back door. Sam glanced that way.

"Now Sam, I know what you're going to say, we're not suggesting you run and hide. This is for the good of Lawrence, it has nothing to do with your bravery. Just the part you played in the rescue of Branson," General Lane implored.

Robinson didn't give Sam time to respond, "We've already been told that Jones is gathering a larger posse to find and arrest you just to prove his point that the people of Lawrence were behind this thing. If you're not here, there's nothing he can do."

The group glanced at each other while Sam pondered the situation. None of them relished the job of communicating the Safety Committee's recommendation.

He reached for Margaret's hand, she did not want Sam away from the house any more than necessary, but she was a realist, "Charlie, you know that Sam won't go into hiding because of Bogus Jones. On the other hand, if there is something needed of him, say in Topeka or Manhattan, then that would be a different matter."

Sarah interrupted the somber atmosphere, brought a washbasin to the kitchen, "Sorry everyone, but Sam will be in a much better mood if he wipes the sleep out of his eyes."

Charlie had a good laugh, Sam chuckled, kissed Sarah on the cheek, proceeded to his ablutions, in the kitchen, in full sight of the prominent visitors.

She produced a towel; he formulated a response while standing, "They were wrong arresting Jacob on that trumped up charge, no other conditions should be contemplated in the matter. They haven't even acknowledged Chuck's murder. We spent all day yesterday trying to determine if they arrested Coleman. They have not. Coleman was allowed to leave the territory and, I promise you, if we wouldn't have rescued Jacob, he never would have reached Lecompton alive. It was all part of the plot. I fully expect them to carry out their threats against us. We cannot legitimize the fraudulent government in Kansas, we just can't."

A shuffling was heard from the back porch. Wakefield, naturally skittish, jumped up shouting 'Who's there?' he imagined Border Ruffians in every shadow and gust of wind.

"It's just John and Sally come over for coffee," Margaret smiled. Cool air accompanied the Thompsons, surprised to see such distinguished guests so early in the morning, "Oh, pardon us, Judge, Dr. Robinson, General Lane, Colonel," John T greeted each man in order, trying his best to be cordial to Dietzler. The man's racial views were well known in 'Niggertown' as the Colonel referred to Cherry Hollow, "We didn't mean to interrupt, we can come back later, Margaret."

Sam insisted the Thompsons sit, "These gentlemen have advised me to get out of town."

All four protested, "Now, Sam, please be reasonable about this matter. I'm thinking of the common good," Robinson turned to the Thompsons, "John T, I can't tell you how much we appreciate the work by the Negro community in building the barricades and blockading the roads."

John nodded, "Proud to do it, Charlie, it's our town too. We'll do our part."

Dietzler added pompously, "Just to be clear, there is no money to pay you. You did it as volunteers."

Sally's mouth dropped open; John T. grabbed her arm to prevent an outburst, which would not have been pleasant. Fortunately, loud knocks at the door interrupted the conversation. All eyes turned that way. Margaret put a hand on Wakefield's shoulder, pushed him back in the chair, went to open the door.

"We're surrounded," Tap stumbled in, his face pale, a look of fear obvious to all.

"What do you mean?" Dietzler asked.

He supported himself against John T's chair, raised his voice, "I mean Lawrence is surrounded, even across the river. Thousands of soldiers or Border Ruffians or someone. They're going to attack, about a mile out of town; won't let anyone leave or come in. I was driving to Hickory Point and they wouldn't let me through. We're in trouble."

General Lane pushed his chair back, searched for words but couldn't find them. He ran from the house shouting for his junior officers; they rode the perimeter of Lawrence, discovered it was all true, if not worse. Lane called the company commanders together in the Free State Hotel; Lyman Allen commander of the Lawrence Stubbs; Samuel Walker, in command of the company from Bloomington; Major Abbott, the Wakarusa company and the Pottawatomie company under the command of John Brown, who arrived with four of his sons, men, arms and ammunition.

Sam introduced John Brown to General Lane. "I hear you ain't so happy to see me here," Brown said, without bitterness.

"Given the circumstances, Mr. Brown, I welcome you with open arms."

"We're in a bit of a fix gentlemen," Charlie Robinson admitted. "You need to station your men in defensive positions throughout the village and wait for further developments."

"Well, sir, that's all well and good," John Brown commanded the room. He was not a tall man; thin with angular features, thick brown hair belying his age and difficult life. He was father of 21 children, many having died in early childhood, yet no sign of rancor. A man of God, his absolute commitment to the abolition of slavery was already legend in the north. Kansas was about to grasp the full force of the unmitigated resolve he brought to the fight, "I suggest we consider another strategy and that is attack this no-good slaveholding filth and drive them back to Missouri. My boys and I have scouted this situation thoroughly; there are about 1,700 men stationed south and east of town under Colonel Boone. Colonel Kearny, out of Independence, has about 800 men scattered north and east of us, stationed near Lecompton. There is a group of Missouri Dragoon's across the river. We total about 1,000 well-armed men here in Lawrence, wouldn't you agree, General Lane?" The General nodded. "Well, the Missouri boys are scattered pretty thin and a quick attack would take them by surprise; straighten things out right quick. Not only that, but most of em' are drinkin' more whiskey than water. They are a miserable specimen of human beings," Brown concluded.

There was much in the way of a shuffling, uncomfortable pause when Brown finished his speech.

"My first reaction is to agree with John," Sam stood looking out the window at the soldiers behind the barricades below. Everyone turned toward him.

Sam Walker introduced himself, shook Brown's hand, "John, I'm very happy you are here. Your reputation proceeds you, believe me. I want to consider all options, but right now I think Charlie Robinson's advice is the best. I know for a fact that Governor Shannon believes we are the party on the attack. Shannon actually thinks those are Kansas boys out there surrounding us."

Robinson agreed, "Shannon ordered Jones to call out the Kansas Militia, but Jones got Boone and Kearny out of Missouri to bring their troops. The Kansas Militia is here in Lawrence under the command of General Lane. We have to act prudently and not give them a reason to attack us."

"We need to give serious thought to what John is proposing. This mess is all part of the conspiracy that was hatched months ago," Sam turned from the window, stood by Brown, "all of those men are acting on orders from Senator Atchison. Charlie, I'll take you up on that offer to get out of town. I'll go to Lecompton and roust Shannon out of his rocking chair and drag him over here by the nape of his neck, show him what's really happening."

Captain Allen gave General Lane a serious look of doubt, "I find all of that damned hard to believe. I know Atchison is pro-slavery, but to accuse him of deliberately planning the murder of American citizens, I have to protest, it can't be true."

Several voices chimed in at once to set the record straight; finally, Major Abbott was able to convince the doubters of the veracity of the report. Beyond the question of who was behind the situation there was no doubting the serious trouble that Lawrence found itself on December 3, 1855. The meeting adjourned with orders for the commanders to return to their troops, advise them of the situation and deploy them in a defensive manner throughout the city. Sam, Wakefield, Robinson and Tappan retired to Sam's house to discuss the plan of how to best advise the Governor of the situation.

"Gentlemen," Sam announced, "I'm perfectly willing to let myself be arrested and test this matter in the courts. It would bring us sympathy and focus the rest of the Union on the atrocities being committed here."

"I'm against that, Sam," Robinson said, "I'm worried that you wouldn't make it to trial. This man Jones is liable to murder you just like they did Dow."

"I agree with Charlie," Tap nodded.

"Let's sit tight until tomorrow, see what happens," Wakefield said.

***

Sam sat at the table editing the final draft of the Topeka Constitution. Margaret and Sarah bustled about the kitchen attending various chores including a washtub full of warm water with the weekly wash inside. This domestic scene was disturbed when John T rushed into the house, handed Sam a copy of a message from Governor Shannon to General Richardson.

"I assume William got this to you somehow," Sam said.

John nodded. Sam read it out loud so that Margaret could hear,

HEADQUATERS, SHAWNEE MISSION, K.T., NOVEMBER 27, 1855.

To: MAJ. GEN WILLIAM P. RICHARDSON:

From: TERRITORIAL GOVERNOR WILSON SHANNON:

Sir - Reliable information has reached me that an armed military force is now in Lawrence and that vicinity, in open rebellion against the laws of this Territory, and that they have determined that no process in the hands of the Sheriff of that county shall be executed. I have received a letter from S. J. Jones, Sheriff of Douglas County, informing me that he had arrested a man under a warrant placed in his hands, and, while conveying him to Lecompton, he was met by an armed force of some forty men, and that the prisoner was taken out of his custody, and defiance bid to the laws. I am also duly advised that an armed band of men have burnt a number of houses, destroyed personal property, and turned whole families out of doors in Douglas County. Warrants will be issued against those men and placed in the hands of the Sheriff of Douglas County for execution. He has written to me, demanding three thousand men to aid him in the execution of the process of law.

You are, therefore, hereby ordered to collect together as large a force as you can in your division, and repair without delay to Lecompton, and report yourself to S. J. Jones, Sheriff of Douglas County, together with the number of your forces, and render him all the aid and assistance in your power in the execution of any legal process in his hands. The forces under your command are to be used for the sole purpose of aiding the Sheriff in executing the law, and for no other purpose.

"This proves that Shannon is getting false information. Come on, John, let's get this over to Charlie."

"Just don't let him know where you got it," John cautioned.

The 'army' surrounding Lawrence was composed of coarse men, most of them drunk, not inspired by ideology just looking for spoils of war. Many of them were young southerners with no more motivation than the pleasure of hunting down an 'armed force of some 40 odd abolitionists', a force that Sheriff Jones convinced Governor Shannon existed. The Border Ruffians who answered the call to put down the 'rebel abolitionists' expected to be paid by the Federal Government, as promised by Senator Atchison; and to profit from plundering the houses and businesses of Lawrence. It was a motley, dangerous army that encircled the innocent citizens of Lawrence, Kansas Territory.

They had no one to call for help; stranded as they were on the western frontier with little in the way of resources, but much in the way of resolve. The townspeople were joined by Free State men from the surrounding communities and small farmers with land claims in the area, but, unlike the invaders, they were drilled expertly into a well-disciplined unit by General Lane and his officers. The Free State men came prepared to fight and were surprised to find the city in a lockdown with no plans for attacking the besieging marauders, but they, for the most part, understood the wait and see strategy. The exceptions being John Brown and Sam who both advocated a quick surprise attack. General Lane was adamant in maintaining a defensive strategy.

That evening, a delegation of Shawnee led by Chief Fish slipped through the Ruffian's lines to volunteer with the abolitionists. They met with the Safety Committee who, after much deliberation, decided that their involvement would put the tribe in great danger. Many thanks were given, a resolution of gratitude written with a promise to call them if the situation deteriorated.

***

Lane assigned a detail of men to make the distinctive cone-shaped bullets for the new Sharps Rifles from molds and bars of lead included with the shipment from New England in the boxes marked "Bibles"; the so-called Beecher's Bibles paid for by Reverend Henry Ward Beecher.

The wives and daughters of Lawrence gathered at the Wood home to turn the bullets into cartridges. Once the initial shock of the invasion wore off, the citizens of Lawrence went about their business calmly, but always alert for any sounds that might indicate the battle had begun. Guards were posted on the perimeter. Every private residence, public meeting hall and the Free State hotel was full of the volunteers, and, in some cases, their families, all prepared to fight to the death to keep Kansas a free state.

Margaret Wood and Sally Thompson were joined every evening by other ladies, both black and white, sometimes as many as 15, with almost as many children, in and around the Wood home keeping themselves occupied while their mothers produced cartridges. The process was simple, a sheet of 2 x 3 inch paper was rolled into a cylinder and glued to hold its shape; then the bullet was inserted into the cartridge, dipped in paraffin to hold it in place and an inch and a half of powder poured into the cylinder which was folded over to hold the powder. When the Sharp's Rifle lever action was engaged, it sheared off the excess paper and the powder was ignited by the percussion of the hammer. It was mindless work that allowed the ladies plenty of time to visit.

The afternoon of December 4, 1855, Harriet Brown was describing the matrimonial bliss she shared with her husband, Ralph. Margaret chanced a quick glance at Sara Robinson because they shared knowledge of a different nature. In fact, Sam had seen Ralph leaving a house of ill repute in Independence when Sam was in the area on newspaper business. He told Margaret the story, first receiving her assurance that she would keep the news secret, which she did, in a way, telling only Sara, her best friend, and of course Sally Thompson and then Sara told her husband Charlie who confirmed the account since Sam had already told him about the incident the day it occurred. As far as anyone knew, that news had not reached the ears of Ralph's wife, Harriet.

"Ralph is forever bringing some little trinket or gadget as a token of his love for me, which, of course, I don't really need because he tells me every day how much I mean to him. You know, there was a vicious rumor, when we left Providence that Ralph was involved..." she paused and gave the ladies a knowing glance, "...involved with the wife of our preacher. Can you imagine?" said with a strong emphasis on the last word, causing several of the ladies to nod in understanding.

Harriet continued, "Isn't it disgusting the lengths some people go just because of jealousy? I swear, nothing but lies." She paused waiting for the agreement expected in this type of generalized comment and it was forthcoming in sighs and nods of the head, although Margaret certainly had different thoughts concerning the philandering Ralph.

"I hate to speak out of turn," Lettie Steele said, "But if I were you, I would watch out for that floozy, Gertrude Hoffmann, in Bloomington…"

"Oh, I know who you mean, Lettie," Cora Doy interrupted, "Big blonde woman, always bounces around to show off what God gave her and that fake smile with the so sweet German accent, oh please. We saw her at the post office, and it was all I could do to drag John back to the wagon. She pinched Donny's cheek and that boy followed her around like a bull in heat. I didn't say a word to either one of them all the way home."

"Oh, Cora, how could you say such a thing," said Linda Pomeroy, who had to hide a grin behind the cartridge she was forming.

"She better keep away from my husband if she knows…," Sara was saying as the door opened; General Lane and Sam walked in.

"Jim is something wrong," Laura asked nervously. Margaret gave Sam a look that said, 'What's going on?'

"Nothing yet, ladies," General Lane sighed, he was tired, "We're just taking an inventory of our powder. How much do you have and how many cartridges have you made so far?"

"We don't have much powder," Margaret said. "Sara and I were about to go over to her house and get another keg."

"Don't bother, we gave the last of the powder stores to the men with mussel loaders. With the Sharp's Rifles that Brown brought we have about 400 men armed, they'll each need, what Jim, 10 cartridges per man?"

"I'd like each of them to have 20. So, we need between 5,000 and 10,000 rounds. How many do we have now, Ladies?"

"Only about 3,000," Lettie answered. A quiet reflection came over the group as they contemplated the problem. Finally, Harriet Brown spoke up, "My father has a keg of powder at our farm south of Hickory Point."

"That would be a big help, plus Major Abbott has some powder at his house, but how do we get it?" Sam asked.

"Someone could sneak through their lines," Sara said, "They're pretty thin over around the river. It would be a long way around, but it could be done."

"That would take too long," Jim said after some consideration of the scheme.

Sam and General Lane left the women to their contemplation of the problem leading Harriet Brown to say, "I'll bet those mean old men would let a woman through if they thought she needed medicine for a sick child."

"Or if she was expecting," Lettie said.

"Or both," Cora added. "What are you thinking Harriet?"

"Well… we could say that Randy's medicine is at Pa's farm and we need milk for somebody's baby here in town."

"That part might be true," Laura added.

"I think it's worth a try," Margaret said, "maybe even take Sally along as a maid. Those slaveholders would think that pretty normal. I'll get Sam and Jim. We'll see what they think about it."

Jim, it turns out, thought the idea had merit but was reluctant to let Laura go on such a dangerous mission. The Ruffians were known to molest women when on a rampage, and this was a tense and unsafe situation under the best of circumstances; being a professional soldier, he knew the dangers associated with men and guns in a skirmish, especially after drinking whiskey all day.

Sam, on the other hand, thought the idea was of tremendous value both to the cause and to Margaret. He had absolute confidence in her judgement and ability. Everyone knew that Margaret was an equal with Sam in all respects, not just the household matters but in every aspect of their lives.

The ladies discussed among themselves who would go, including taking children feigning illness, but that idea was discarded for safety reasons. Lettie volunteered to go, yet too many ladies leaving would be suspicious; the decision was made for Harriet, Margaret and Sally to take a wagon with Sally sitting in the back as norms dictated. They would place a pillow under Margaret's gown and let the Ruffians assume that she was in need of some medication or comfort from the Brown farm; the men would not want any details of a lady's predicament.

Harriet assured everyone that her husband would protest this idea of putting his beloved in danger; however, upon hearing the news, Ralph replied, to other gentlemen in attendance, that he 'wouldn't give a damn if she stayed in the country and the Ruffians would come out the worse if they tried to stop her'.

"Dear General Easton: The governor has called out the militia, and you will hereby organize your division and proceed forthwith to Lecompton. As the governor has no power, you may call out the Platte (Missouri) Rifle Company. They are always ready to help us. Do not implicate the governor, whatever you do."

Secretary of Kansas Territory, Daniel Woodson

Apparently forged letter circulated through all Missouri border counties at the instigation of General Stringfellow.

Free State men frantically finished the defenses in the streets. Lane doubled the guards posted around the perimeter of Lawrence; every house sheltered volunteers who had came defense of the abolitionist ideals. The Free State hotel was full of militia, tents were raised in vacant lots, communal tables for eating built under shelters. The ladies of Lawrence made certain no one went hungry.

The issues were simple, no confusion on either side, the Federal Government wanted slavery in Kansas, the abolitionists said, "No! Slavery Stops Here". From the slaveholding south point of view, Lawrence had to be eliminated and the Boarder Ruffians just wanted to kill some abolitionists and steal their property.

It is true that a grudge existed between Sam and bogus sheriff Samuel Jones, but that was an effect, not a cause, of the situation. Nonetheless, more than a few abolitionists blamed Sam for the troubles, still believing that the matter could have been resolved without violence. Sam knew better, he knew that it didn't matter what the citizens of Lawrence did to alleviate the situation, the only way the Border Ruffians would call off the invasion was if all the abolitionists agreed to leave the Territory.

One reason Sam approved the dangerous mission to procure more powder was because he knew those kinds of sacrifices would have to be made. "This is war, gentlemen. We are fighting for our lives," he told the Safety Committee that afternoon in the meeting where the final decision was made. The vote was far from unanimous on even allowing the ladies to leave.

Harriet took the reins when John T brought the wagon around, "You think I should go with you," he asked casting a worried look at Sally.

"No, too many of them know you're a friend of Sam's. Don't worry, we'll be fine," Sally assured him.

John T protested to Sam about Sally going.

"Don't complain to me, my friend, talk to your wife about it. She's pretty headstrong, if you haven't noticed."

"Well, I don't think that she or Margaret should be going," John T said, but he let the matter drop because Sally was headstrong, would not appreciate his interference. He prayed for her safe journey and while he was at it, offered another prayer for Sam who seemed to be backsliding more and more in his faith. "How did we get ourselves into this mess," John T thought to himself, watching the wagon roll out of town.

Mrs. Brown drove around the barricades accompanied by cheers of the troops shouting wishes of good luck as they passed. It was a dull grey day, a sheen of moisture in the air, cold and damp, not a day to be out; yet the prairie was beautiful in its own stark way, beige-brown with dormant grass and a few barren trees along the road. The ladies rode silently thinking about the task ahead. It seemed more of a lark in the safety of the house, but on the open prairie under a vast sky of grey the reality slowly sank in with the chill of the wind.

"We'll be fine," Sally said, as much for her benefit as theirs. She sat behind the driver bench on a cushion provided by John. They could see camps of men along the near horizon on both sides of the road; a group on horseback blocked their way as they approached the turnpike. Margaret's heart beat fast; she offered a silent prayer. Harriet pulled the team to a stop.

"We've got orders not to let anybody in or out of Yankee Town. Where ya'all going?" a middle-aged man, heavily bearded asked. Two of the men were obviously Border Ruffians, wearing tattered buffalo coats that smelled to high heaven. They were seriously armed with rifles, pistols and swords. Margaret didn't recognize any of them.

"We're going to my Pa's farm over south of Hickory Point. I've got to get some medicine for my son, Randy, and some herbs and other items for Margaret's condition," she said nodding toward Margaret's belly.

"Are ya'all comin back this away," he said.

"Yes, we won't be gone long," Margaret answered.

"Orders are to stop any men, Orville," his companion said.

"Well, that's the truth, he didn't say nothin bout women, Ya'll go on and be careful."

"Thank you," Harriet said not waiting for any further discussion.

It took another hour to reach the Ralston farm where Harriet's mother and father implored them to stay and not go back. The parents were aghast at the fact they had come.

"No Pa, we've got to go back, they're needing this keg of powder; if we don't go back Ralph will have a heart attack worrying about me."

"Hummph, Mrs. Ralston sneered, "I'd sooner believe he's the one that sent you."

"Mama, please, don't be that way. Help us get this powder into bags so we can tie it around Margaret's waist, those guards think she's expecting."

Bottles were filled with milk, the powder safely wrapped around her waist. Harriet and Sarah had to help Margaret into the wagon, trying to stifle a laugh at the poor woman weighted down with explosives. Margaret was breathing hard, giggling herself, much to the merriment of mother and father Ralston; disregarding the danger of riding shrouded in a potential detonation that would destroy the entire wagon.

They borrowed two books of medicine one written by John Hughes Bennett and the other Elizabeth Blackwell, as further proof of the veracity of their deception. Although Harriet wanted to leave immediately, her father would not allow it until the horses had been rested, fed and watered. They didn't depart the Ralston farm until almost four in the afternoon.

The stop at the Abbott home was quick with Abigale thankful for news from a reliable source. She'd heard ugly rumors about battles and skirmishes, unable to verify anything because no mail was allowed in or out of Lawrence.

"The Major sends his love and promises you that we're fine," Margaret comforted, as they placed a keg of powder under the wagon seat behind the cushion. Sally made certain that her long dress concealed any evidence and was assured that she looked exactly as she did before. The wagon pulled away from the Abbott home, not far from where Chuck Dow was murdered and the scene of the Branson rescue just a few days earlier. It seemed an eternity ago.

Margaret leaned upon her faith for the strength needed to get through difficult times. Thoughts of Sam and the children flooded over her as they approached the check point looming ahead. This time they were guilty of the very crimes the enemy suspected of them and if caught would suffer the consequences; although she couldn't imagine what that might be. Sally put her hand on Margaret's shoulder because she was experiencing the same dreadful thoughts; she wished for John's quiet strength to help guide them safely home. Margaret grasped Sally's hand and they rode united toward whatever fate awaited them.

***

DECEMBER 4, 1855
FROM: DOUGLAS COUNTY SHERRIF SAM JONES
TO: HIS EXCELLENCY, GOV. WILSON SHANNON
Sir - In reply to your communication of yesterday, I have to inform you that the volunteer forces now at (Franklin) and Lecompton, are getting weary of inaction. They will not, I presume, remain but a short time longer, unless a demand for the prisoner is made. I think I shall have a sufficient force to protect me by to-morrow morning. The force at Lawrence is not half so strong as reported. I have this from a reliable source. If I am to wait for Government troops, more than two-thirds of the men now here will go away very much dissatisfied They are leaving hourly as it is. I do not, by any means, wish to violate your orders, but I really believe that if I have a sufficient force; it would be better to make the demand.

It is reported that the people of Lawrence have run off those offenders from that town, and, indeed, it is said they are now all out of the way. I have writs for sixteen persons who were with the party that rescued my prisoner. S. N. Wood, P. R. Brooks and Samuel Tappan are of Lawrence, the balance from the country around. Warrants will be placed in my hands to-day for the arrest of G. W. Brown, and probably others in Lecompton.

They say that they are willing to obey the laws, but no confidence can be place in any statements they may make.

No evidence sufficient to cause a warrant to be issued has, as yet, been brought against those lawless men who fired the houses. I would give you the names of the defendants, but the writs are in my office at Lecompton.
Most respectfully yours,
SAMUEL J. JONES,
Sheriff of Douglas County.

Late the night of the third, a solitary figure slipped into the Kansas River upstream from the ferry, swam across, then crept silently within hailing distance of the sentry.

"Pssst, can you hear me?"

"What the... who is that?"

"I'm a friend. I need to talk to Sam Wood."

"Come out here where I can see you," the guard backed out of the light cast by a weak flame from the lantern and crouched behind a tree. "I'm fixin to raise the alarm if you don't identify yourself."

"I'm Eric McCrea. I'm an abolitionist like you. I've got some men with me on the other side of the river with a cannon that we need to bring over here. Go get Colonel Wood; tell him, 'Eric McCrea is at the river', he'll understand."

"Hold on," the guard rousted his counterpart, asleep in a tent nearby. The groggy man stumbled out, took the sentry's rifle, pointed it in the general direction of the voice in the dark, "Don't move till Morgan gets back. I don't trust you."

"I'm sitting here waiting, pardner. Don't worry, I won't do anything. What company you with?"

"We're with Major Abbott out of Hickory Point, and I'd sure like to go back home. All we've been doing is marching back and forth, drilling every day for the last week. Shooting at targets in the dirt. I don't think them Missourians are gonna' do anything but sit out there and drink whiskey. All we get is one ration every other day. Don't even wet your whistle."

"Well, I'm coming home. That's why I'm here. We brought a cannon up from Kansas City. Need to get it across the river though. Where's the ferry operator?"

"No one can use the ferry. General Lane's orders."

A rustling behind them startled the guard, "Halt and identify yourself."

"It's me, Morgan. I brought Colonel Wood."

"Eric is that really you?"

"Yes, it is."

"What's your wife's name?"

"Katie."

"Your son?"

"My daughter's name is Tammy."

"Come into the light."

They greeted each other with hearty handshakes all around. Eric explained how he came to be with three other men bringing a cannon up from Kansas City; a cannon donated by abolitionists in the east, including Senator Sumner and Thomas Bickerton. David Buffam brought the cannon by wagon, stopped in Columbia, put up at the home of an abolitionist who knew Eric's story. Eric was introduced and agreed to act as guide.

"I think the time is right for me to come back, don't you, Sam?" he grinned.

"About as good as it's going to get. This fight is all anyone will remember for years. Morgan, do you know where Niles Baldwin lives?"

"No sir."

"You men stay here while I go get Niles and we'll take the ferry across to get the cannon."

The smuggling operation took the rest of the night. General Lane was rousted out of bed to the joyous news of a piece of artillery, a welcome addition to the free-state defense. He ordered the cannon placed on the redoubt on Henry street near the intersection with Massachusetts. Bastions were designed and constructed to brace the cannon. Work began before daylight, was finished before noon.

Sam took Eric to the new blacksmith shop where Riley and Jane were staying during the siege. The wayward son returned to tears, hugs and plans to bring Tammy and Katie when safe.

****

Even Ralph Brown grew concerned as the hours passed and no sign of the explosive smuggling ladies. The Safety Committee began making plans for an inquiry, the main question being how many men to send out to negotiate for their release. John Brown was beyond angry and began rallying his men to march on the Border Ruffians as he first advocated. Other's among the commanders began to grow restless, their men bored from inaction; maybe Brown's strategy should be reconsidered. Sam Walker joined forces with Brown. A mutiny was brewing.

General Lane ordered them all to stand down until a reasonable decision could be made; a company of men charging out of Lawrence was certain to bring violent retaliation from every side. Finally, Lane and Robinson agreed, Colonel Pratt would take a squad of men under a white flag to ask for information about the ladies. Brown did not take the news well. He vowed to withdraw his men if a plan of attack was not devised immediately.

In the Free State Hotel, Charlie Robinson presided over a meeting of the Safety Committee debating the issue of sending an emissary to Governor Shannon with the truth of the situation. Despite the cool day outside, the atmosphere inside was warm from the closeness of the men, smoke in the air and emotions boiling over. Most of them, just a few months earlier, had been farmers, merchants and tradesmen in their home states; got the itch to move to the frontier, make a difference and just like the ladies in the wagon, the romantic ideal faded the closer to the moment of danger.

"Shannon is the Governor of Kansas Territory, but he's got Missouri men surrounding us in an armed blockade," Walter Babcock said, "he should be protecting us not attacking us."

"He doesn't know the situation, Walt, we've got to get someone over there he respects; that might be you. The only news he's getting is from Atchison and Jones and they accuse us of being an armed rebellion against the government. I've seen a copy of a letter verifying that. They have convinced the rest of the country that we are in open rebellion against the United States. All lies, but perception is more powerful than truth in the political world."

"Well, it damn sure can't be Wood, he's the one that started this mess," Floyd McDaniel groused.

"McDaniel, if you keep that up, I'm gonna get angry and you don't want to see me get mad."

"All I know is that you, Tappan and Brooks where the only Lawrence citizens involved. Why is he punishing us for something that you did?"

"That's already been discussed, we've got to quit arguing about what happened and focus on what to do. Jones would have found another excuse to bring in the Ruffians," Tap said.

McDaniel continued his tirade, standing with his hands on the table glowering down at Sam, "I'm just as much against slavery as you are Wood, but it isn't worth getting killed over."

"Then you aren't against it as much as I am, McDaniel."

Ignoring the implied threat, Sam addressed Charlie, "I think the only course of action is to send two or three men to Lecompton. We'll have to walk…"

Sam you can't go, Shannon would arrest you on sight, in fact, I want you out of town along with anyone else even remotely connected to the Hickory Point rescue." Robinson added as an afterthought, "That includes Tap, Harold and Tom Barber."

"That's what I'm getting at Charlie, I can guide the men there. I've walked to Lecompton, Topeka and even Manhattan, several times, we can get there faster than riding around on the roads and have less chance of being stopped; but I or John T have to go, we can't tell you how to do it. I promise not to venture near His Highness, even though I know for a fact the Judge told him about the threats against Dow."

"That makes sense to me," Tap said, "The question is who goes with Sam?"

Shannon looked at Babcock who nodded with a grin, "Well, I know the Governor pretty well. I think he'd listen to me, but he knows George Lowery better. I'll go see George right now, I'm pretty sure he would do anything to end this mess."

"I know George," Sam got up to go with him, "but is he capable of making the trip?"

"Let's go talk to him. He's with Colonel Wakefield over on the Henry Street redoubt."

They walked out as Clarke Pomeroy came in, wearing a preacher's frock and round felt hat. Sam shook hands and wished him luck. Pomeroy planned to carry letters, Lawrence newspaper articles and official accounts of the situation to Washington; a tactical attempt to enlist the aid of Congress.

"How do you plan to get through the enemy lines?" Sam asked.

"I'm an ordained minister so I'll promise to bless them and pray for their success against you evil abolitionists," Pomeroy joked. A former educator in Massachusetts, he was the chief financial officer of the New England Emigrant Aid Society. His hair, abundant on the sides and back diminished from a very high forehead giving him the appearance of a religious monk.

"Clarke, I've got a letter for Horace Greeley I want you to take. I'll send David back with it."

"Have him hurry, Sam, I'm about ready to leave."

Sam and Babcock walked across the street, found David, sent him back with the letter. They perused the fortifications along Massachusetts street, admiring the embankments, "This is amazing," Walter commented.

"Jim Lane and I've had our differences," Sam said, "but you have to give him credit, he's created a disciplined army of men in a short time."

"They're well drilled, and the fortifications are first rate. Those idiots surrounding us are drunk most of the time. I heard they've been looting houses and stores and molesting the women in Franklin. I'm scared to death that they'll just form up and charge despite orders from their leaders. My God, what kind of men has Shannon loosed on us?"

"It would be a terrible tragedy if they do that, Walt. General Lanes' men will cut them to pieces, remember they think we're a bunch of abolitionists without any defenses. I hope that doesn't happen," Sam waved when he spotted Judge Wakefield drilling the men on the use of the cannon.

***

The ladies approached the checkpoint north of the Wakarusa River after crossing Barber's Bridge. The scene was not promising as a dozen mounted men blocked the road while others on foot, rifles drawn, watched them advance.

Harriet pulled back on the reins, "Oh dear, there are a bunch more men than when we came through. Be brave ladies."

"These are completely different men," Sally spread her skirts then gripped the back of the seat to steady her nerves.

Two grubby Ruffians rode alongside as Harriet pulled the team to a stop; others on foot gathered around the wagon. Their leader was a thin faced, beady-eyed man with one arm and a pistol in hand, "What's the meaning of this ladies? We have a military blockade going on here. You'd best turn around and go back home."

"Our home is in Lawrence. We just drove through here a few hours ago and told them we would be back, why are you detaining us?" Margaret asked.

"Ma'am we ain't detain' nobody yet, but we got a right to know what yo're carryin," said a younger man, obviously from the deep south.

"Young man, you are drunk, we don't have any spirits. We have the items we went to get, these medical books, some milk and some herbs for Margaret, can't you see that she's expecting."

"We explained all of this to the other gentleman that was here when we passed through," Margaret added.

"That air gentleman, ain't here now, we are. What fer you got a Nigger? I thought you was agin' havin' a slave," said while eyeing Sally coarsely.

"I'm a free woman," Sally answered, her head held high, "slave to no one."

"I don't give a damn if you're free or not," the man with the pistol said. "You best not be talking to your betters in that tone or I'll slap some respect into you."

"Hell, Martin, she's a good lookin woman. These folks is up to sometin', I'll bet she got sometin' hid up under them skirts, stand up and lift up yo're dress so's we can see what you got."

"What?" Harriet shrieked. The man stepped back in surprise. She handed the reins to Margaret, grabbed her umbrella, chased him several feet whacking him on the back, "Shame on you, animal." She picked up a rock and threw it at him, then another.

"Stop a'chuckin rocks at me ma'am," the Ruffian cried.

His cohorts were laughing wildly enjoying the show, urging Harriet to throw another. She climbed into the wagon as fast as she could, screamed, "Why are you bothering us? Go home you animals. I pity your wives and mothers." She grabbed the reins from Margaret, whipped the horses into a fast trot jerking Margaret and Sally backward.

"What is the matter with men?" Harriet sobbed, urging the horses faster.

Margaret put her arm on Harriet's shoulder, "Slow down Harriet. Sally are they following us?"

"Some of the men on horseback are starting this way."

"Look ahead," Margaret said, as riders approached. They recognized Caleb Pratt leading a squad of his men.

"Hello ladies, we were beginning to wonder about you. Everyone will sure be happy to see you."

The enemy patrol fell back seeing the troops from Lawrence intercept the lady smugglers. Hurrahs chorused up as they passed the first redoubt. When Sam heard the cheering, he knew immediately what it was, ran down the hill to find two men trying to lift his wife out of the wagon.

"Meg," Sam laughed, "What have you been eating, darling, you look like you gained 50 pounds."

Ralph hurried to his wife's side, she looked at him with a question in her eyes, he wrapped her in his arms, whispered, "I'm so glad you're back." She dissolved against him, tears overflowed to her cheeks. They were all exhausted from the trip but comforted by the glorious reception, triumphant in their safe return.

"Caution, Sir! I am eternally tired of hearing that word caution. It is nothing but the word of cowardice!" John Brown

Charlie, Judge Wakefield and Sam spent the afternoon writing the following message for Babcock and Lowery to carry to Governor Shannon:

TO HIS EXCELLENCY, WILSON SHANNON
GOVERNOR OF KANSAS TERRITORY:

"Sir - As citizens of Kansas Territory, we desire to call your attention to the fact that a large force of armed men from a foreign State have assembled in the vicinity of Lawrence, are now committing depredations upon our citizens, stopping wagons, opening and appropriating their loading, arresting, detaining and threatening travelers upon the public road, and that they claim to do this by your authority. We desire to know if they do appear by your authority, and if you will secure the peace and quiet of the community by ordering their instant removal or compel us to resort to some other means and to higher authority."

Signed by Officers of the Lawrence Safety Committee

Walt Babcock, George Lowery, 'Tap' Tappan, John Thompson and Sam Wood trekked west out of Lawrence, hugging the Kansas River, not venturing from the cover of the trees. A decision was made to cross to the north side after sighting several Ruffian patrols. The crossing was made and progress better with fewer encounters but still hindered by reluctance to light a lamp. They whispered to each other when resting, which wasn't often. Emotions were high, they were tired, but primarily concerned over their loved ones in Lawrence; apprehension about finding Governor Shannon grew the closer they got to Lecompton.

"Sam, I know Governor Shannon very well. He's just misinformed about the situation. He's been listening to

Jones and Atchison instead of riding over to see for himself. He'll do what I ask," George Lowery said.

Sam was in the greatest danger, being the sworn enemy of the bogus sheriff, certain never to reach a jail if caught. Tap considered himself an unfortunate bystander because he had not returned to Hickory Point after the night Dow was murdered, yet the rumor was Jones had writs and warrants with his name on them; although no one had ever seen these phantom warrants.

When they arrived at the river crossing in Lecompton, Lowery and Babcock continued on to Constitution Hall while Sam, Tap and John T waited by the river for word of their progress. It wasn't long in coming. A light was seen advancing toward the river; the men quickly ducked behind a deserted wooden barn.

"Mr. Wood, sir, are you there? "A voice asked.

"William, is that you?" John asked.

"Who else it be, John T? Come on out'n them bushes actin like field Niggers, following the star, You gentlmens got quite a ruckus goin over to Lawrence. I got news for ya."

"Hello William," Sam said shaking his hand. "This is Mr. Tappan..."

"Yessir, I figured as much. His name's on Mr. Jones list."

John explained to Tap that William was a handyman in Constitution Hall.

"Yassir," He chuckled, "I keeps my flock aware o what the white folk up to in the Territory. Here's what happinin'; the guvnor's in Shawnee Mission, but half the escort is here fixin' to head that way. They takin' them two gentlmens ridin' with them. Was I you, I'd get back to Lawrence, them Ruffians fixin' to attack."

This was a long speech by William, more than he was used to sharing. John and Sam had known him since moving to the Territory. If the truth were known that he aided abolitionists, he would not only lose his job, but his life would be in danger.

"I best get back. God bless ya'all."

"William, we can't thank you enough," Sam shook his hand again.

"Jes be careful, them Ruffians lookin' fer you. They are very bad men."

William nodded at John T and Tap, walked back to Lecompton while they tried to decide what course of action was best; continue to Topeka or go back to Lawrence. None of them liked the idea of leaving their wives and families in the midst of danger while they hid; but to go back would violate the Safety Committee's edict that no one associated with the Branson rescue should stay in Lawrence. General Lane had already conducted Sheriff Jones and his deputies through town to convince him that all men he claimed to have warrants against had left, whereabouts unknown.

"William knows what goes on in this Territory. If he says they're gonna' do something tonight or tomorrow, I think we should be there. I know a place to hide where no one will find us."

"Where?" Tap asked.

"I'll show you if we go back. Make that decision first."

"You sure we'll be safe there, John T," Sam said.

"Safe as a bear in a cave. The owner doesn't even know about it."

"Come on John, fess up, where is this hideout?"

"In Charlie Robinson's barn. I built a little room along the south side where we pile the straw bundles. You can't see it from inside or out. You and Tap can stay there, no one is after me; I'll bring water and food, inform the wives of what's happening. Then if they do start something, we can be there to help."

They turned back toward Lawrence.

HEADQURTERS FIRST CALVARY }
FORT LEAVENWORTH, DECEMBER 1, 1855 }
GOVERNOR - I have just received your letter of this day. I do not feel that it would be right in me to act in this important matter until orders are received from the Government. I shall be ready to move instantly when I receive them. I would respectfully suggest that you make your application extensively known at once, and I would countermand any orders that may have been given for the movement of the militia until you receive the answer. With much respect, your obedient servant,
E. V. SUMNER, Colonel First Cavalry.

Walt Babcock was a little taller than Sam but thin in body. He sported muttonchop sideburns and was considered handsome by the ladies, especially his wife and their three children. Mr. Lowery was a tall man, slightly stooped, clean shaven with an old slouch hat, but his bright eyes and forthright gaze projected a sense of great control and intelligence. He was acquainted with the Governor through a territorial committee on legislative issues and while they were diametrically opposed on the issue of slavery, they found common ground for respect on other issues. The Governor trusted him.

Walt and George walked with confidence to the large wooden building in the center of Lecompton, bustling with activity even at this late hour. They approached the door and were halted by armed guards questioning their purpose.

"We're emissaries sent by the Lawrence Safety Committee with a dispatch for the Governor. I'm Water Babcock and this is George Lowery."

"Wait here," he said, curtly, nodded at the other guard, soon returned with Secretary of the Territory, Daniel Woodson.

"George Lowery," Woodson exclaimed. "Do you bring news from Lawrence? We don't know what's going on over there. Come inside."

"Hello Daniel," George answered. "We've come to give the governor a report on the situation, we feel he's been misled in the matter. We have a letter for him."

Woodson read the letter, "You've got to get this to the governor, but he's at Shawnee Mission. You're in luck because part of his escort is here and riding that way... William," Woodson called. "Pick out two good horses for these men and prepare them for the ride to Shawnee Mission with the Governor's escort."

Lowery turned to Babcock with a look that said, this is the man. "I'll go with you, I like to get a look at the horse flesh myself, if you don't mind."

William answered, "Yassuh, joins me please."

When they reached the corral, it was full of horses used by the Territorial Government to send messengers and dispatches wherever needed. William picked two good ones and Walt agreed immediately. As they were saddling, Walt whispered "Do you know John Thompson and Sam Wood?"

William hesitated, took a long distrustful look at this white man questioning him, "I cain't recollect. Maybe if'n I seed em', I might member em'," spoken in his best slave dialect.

"They're waiting down by the river for word of what happened to us."

William said no more as they finished saddling. He handed over two full canteens and the reins to both horses, "Yu kin fetch some biscuits n' hard tack in de kitchen. God Bless!"

Walt considered saying more but changed his mind as William took a lantern and turned back toward the river. Babcock and Lowery joined the patrol. The commander rode up to them, "I understand you want to get to Shawnee Mission as soon as possible. So do we, we'll push the horses. We'll be stopped by that mob at the Wakarusa guarding the Lawrence Road, but they won't be a problem. I don't know what's going on any more than anyone else, but that rabble needs to be dispersed, and pronto."

They rode out at a fast trot, columns of two.

MAJ. GEN. WILLIAM P. RICHARDSON
Ft. Leavenworth
Sir - I have reason to believe, from rumors in camp, that before tomorrow morning the black flag will be hoisted, when nine out of ten will rally around it, and march without orders upon Lawrence. The forces at Lecompton camp fully understand the plot and will fight under the same banner...

...I fear a collision between the United States soldiers and the volunteers, which would be dreadful. Speedy measures should be taken. Let me know at once - to-night - and I fear that it will then be too late to stay the rashness of our people.

J. C. ANDERSON. A member of the Pro-Slavery Territorial Legislature and a camp follower of the events in Lawrence, by letter, after realizing the tide was turning against the Border Ruffians and they were going to attack Lawrence without orders.

The three men backtracked until they reached the low water crossing, only this time they spotted lights on the south side of the Kansas River; it was very doubtful they would be friendly. A quick conference resulted in a plan to cross and if accosted say they were pro-slavery looking to join the invaders. John T was to play a slave in this charade.

"What if they ask why we don't have horses?" John asked.

Sam gave it some thought, "Well, maybe they won't ask and if they do, I'll think of something, you know, sweet talk them."

"Oh, Lord Massar Tappan, We bees in trouble now," John said, only half joking.

Sam ignored them, walked into the river, marched toward the light that flickered in the trees about 100 yards ahead, "Hello the camp," he hollered.

"Who the hell's out there?"

"Friends! We looking to join the fight. You're with General Easton ain't ya?" Sam answered.

There was silence in the camp, finally a voice, "Come on in with your hands where we can see em'."

Two men greeted them; rifles raised.

"No need for that gentlemen," Tappan said, "We're on your side."

"Why'd you bring a Nigger?"

"To make my dinner. He does what I tell him. If I tell him to shoot an abolitionist, he'll do it, ain't that right, John?"

"Mose definit, Massar, I'z' a good Nigger."

"Hell, Ned, we should'a had everybody bring their Niggers, we could drink whiskey and leave the killin' to them."

Sam ambled up with his right hand outstretched for a handshake, cane in his left; a third man stepped from the shadows directly behind his compatriots with rifle raised, "You fuckin' idjuts, that's Sam Wood."

No hesitation on Sam's part, he saw the glint of the lantern on the barrel as the Ruffian swung out from behind the tree. He grabbed the man who was reaching to shake hands, pushed him backward into the rifle causing it to twist out of the gunman's hands with the leverage of a tree trunk. Sam smacked him on the side of the head, at the ear, just enough to disable him. John moved quickly to snatch the gun from the third man who seemed shocked at what was happening.

"Where'd you get that Sharp's Rifle?" Sam asked the man on the ground, but he wasn't recovered from his beating, then looked to the man whose shirt and gun he held.

"They was givin em' out at camp one night and he got one of em'. We figured they was stole, prolly from the armory in Liberty. You really Sam Wood?"

"You know he is. We should a' known from that cane he carries. There's gonna be hell to pay for this."

"No need to get yourselves in trouble over this, boys," Sam said. Here's what I'm going do for you. Leave all your weapons here. Tap, Tappan, you with us?"

Tap shook his head, "I never would have believed it. All those stories about you are true."

"And the legend still grows," John moaned.

"Tap, get their pistols."

Once the weapons were secure, Sam ordered, "Pick up your wounded man; start back up this road with lantern held high so we can see all three of you. After you've gone about a quarter mile sit down and decide what you want to do, go on to camp, report this and catch all kinds of grief or come back here and get your guns; pretend this never happened. Your choice, I don't care either way, now start walking."

With the wounded man supported between them, they struggled up the road, the lantern swinging, easily visible until they disappeared into the trees.

"What do we do now?" Tap asked.

Sam picked up one of the rifles, "Evidence," he explained. "John T what shall we do?"

"Put your arm on my shoulder and Tap put your arm on Sam's. I know where we are, and they can't follow us. I just have to find the trail. We should have kept the lantern."

Two miles seemed like ten in the dark, but John knew the trail well; the waning moon, when visible through the trees, provided some light from the western sky. They arrived exhausted but safe at four in the morning.

The secure room was triangular from three feet at the entrance to over six feet wide at the apex. John and Sally made the cabin cozy with two cots, a chair, a cask for water and a chamber pot. "I've had several fugitive slaves in here before moving them on to the north," John said, "No one ever suspected, least of all Mr. Robinson."

"So, this is your secret place. Probably best not to tell Charlie about it," Sam said laying down on a bunk, falling asleep immediately.

Tap laughed, "Damn, John, I thought that was all bullshit about clubbing and manhandling people. It's hard to believe a man of that size is so strong."

"I give him a hard time about it, but don't ever underestimate him, physical or mental, that's the mistake most of his enemies make. I'll be back with food and water later. Don't talk too loud or bang against the walls, you'll be fine in here."

***

The Governor's escort, along with Lowery and Babcock, reached Shawnee Mission just before six am. Lights glowed in several of the windows and the Governor was already at work in his office. He greeted the men with honest sincerity mixed with curiosity and, after reading the letter sent by the Safety Committee, an angry red to his face.

"What in the hell is going on here?" the document still held in his hands.

"We believe you haven't heard the true story, Governor. We want you to come to Lawrence and listen to our side."

Shannon issued orders immediately and they were off. In the coach he questioned them about the events from their point of view, "Were either of you at Hickory Point during all of this mess?"

Lowery answered, "No Governor, everything we heard was second hand."

"Sam Wood was there wasn't he?"

Both men sat silently until finally the Governor said in a melancholy voice, "You know Sam and I aren't so different. I understand the man better than most, we're both from Ohio, I knew his daddy, David. Sam and I have had many a conversation and what he did to straighten out the Land Registry Office was nothing short of a miracle. If I'm going to get the honest story it's gonna have to come from the horse's mouth so to speak. You think I can get an audience with Mr. Wood after all of this?"

"Don't know if you can or not," George said, "I'm not even sure where he is."

They reached the Wakarusa about one that afternoon to find the commanding officers for the invaders already gathered, following orders from dispatches sent by messenger ahead of the coach. Shannon quickly took charge, explained to the officers that he was going into Lawrence to determine the situation for himself.

Jones said, "I advise against that Governor. We have no way of protecting you in there."

Shannon glanced contemptuously at the sheriff, "If I find that any of you have misled me intentionally in this matter..." He let the comment drop, turned to General Easton, "You hold your men in their current positions until I return. There's an escort coming from Lawrence to meet me and I'll take my personal escort as well."

Shannon arrived at the Free State Hotel at two PM on December 6, 1855 with the threat of Civil War strong on the minds of everyone, not just in Kansas, but throughout the Nation. People were holding their breath waiting for intelligence from the Territory, fully expecting news of a massacre in Lawrence because the Pro-Slavery newspapers were the only papers getting published; a virtual lockdown of Lawrence had prevented any accurate news from reaching the general public. That afternoon, unknown to the Safety Committee, Clarke Pomeroy, had been captured by the Ruffians carrying letters, dispatches and copies of the Tribune to Washington to try and get help. He was under lock and key at 2:30 as Governor Shannon entered the Free State Hotel to cheers from the Citizens of Lawrence. Coffee and food were organized for the visiting troops by the ladies, including Sally and several of her Cherry Hollow neighbors. One young trooper looked at her and said, "I thought they didn't believe in no slaves in Lawrence."

"We are not slaves. Not all black people are held in bondage."

He shook his head, confused as were many others in that place including His Honor, Governor Wilson Shannon. He sat listening to General Lane and Charlie Robinson as they explained the situation, emphasizing that if the rabble did attack, the citizens of Lawrence would show them no mercy.

"Everything I understand about this situation has come from Sheriff Jones and Senator Atchison. Is there no one here who was eyewitness to these events, besides Sam Wood, that can tell me what he saw, someone I can trust? I understand Roger McKinney rode to Lecompton after the Coleman-Dow affair, but I never received a report from him. Is Roger in town?"

"If he is, I doubt he will be forthcoming. He's protecting his family right now."

Shannon rose and walked to the window gazed out at the darkening sky as a storm approached, both natural and man-made.

"Gentlemen, I need to speak to Sam Wood. Do you know where he is?"

Charlie shook his head no, "I don't, Governor. All the men who were in Hickory Point have left."

"Do you know someone who might know where to find him?"

Charlie thought for a few seconds, "Let me see what I can do."

In the hallway the Safety Committee and other men of prominence were gathered, "Harold, can you go find John T and bring him here, please?" Robinson said.

When John appeared, Shannon was surprised to see a negro standing in the doorway, but he quickly gained his composure, "Thompson, I need to speak to Sam Wood, as soon as possible, do you know where to find him?"

John did not like this situation at all. Were they setting a trap for Sam? Using him as a scapegoat to appease both sides, John glanced at Charlie, "Dr. Robinson, this is an awkward position for me, Sam is my friend?"

"I think the Governor will state in writing a personal guarantee of Sam's safety."

John thought a moment and said, "Governor, I believe you and I'm sure Sam would take your word for it himself, was he here; but just to be clear on the matter, I think it would be best if I could carry a sentence to that effect on a sheet of paper signed by you. Don't you agree?"

"Yes, Mr. Thompson, I do agree with you." He took paper and pen and wrote the guarantee.

John said to Lane and Robinson, "Make sure no one follows me, if I suspect I'm being followed it will take a lot longer to get him back here." They both nodded in agreement.

The Governor, Lane and Robinson tried to write a memorandum of understanding, a Peace Treaty that would appease both sides; but the matter looked unpromising. Shannon knew that anything less than full surrender by the abolitionists would be seen by the Border Ruffians as a defeat and accuse Shannon of collaboration with the enemy. Shannon was smart enough to understand that the situation was just the opposite of what he expected; Missouri Militiamen had taken control of a Kansas Territorial City.

A loud cheer interrupted their discussions, "Sam must be coming," Jim Lane grinned.

The door opened; several men spilled into the room forming a phalanx around the conquering hero returning to help vanquish the beast before them.

"Governor, good to see you."

Shannon asked the other men, "May we have the room to ourselves... thank you," as they filed out. "Jim, you and Charlie stay please."

Sam sat next to Shannon, Lane and Charlie across the table. The Governor gazed on Sam, "This is an unfortunate situation, Mr. Wood. You told me this was coming months ago, didn't you?"

"Will, I can't take credit for being a fortune teller, but I do know that Civil War is inevitable, it cannot be avoided. I believe this is the beginning. I think we're certainly better prepared than the enemy, you've seen what Charlie and Jim have done with the real Kansas Militia and if those Ruffians attack tomorrow, a whole lot of Missouri mothers and wives will be in mourning come the next day."

Shannon appeared to agree with him after witnessing firsthand the defensive preparations, "Sam tell me what happened at Hickory Point."

"Starting when?"

"At the beginning."

"Well, it goes back to a claim dispute between Frank Coleman and Chuck Dow, one that I could not understand and just didn't make sense..."

Sam spoke for 30 minutes explaining detail after detail of the events leading to Dow's murder, not leaving out his own fear that he might have contributed by missing a meeting in Hickory Point that afternoon.

"But Dow's wounds were in his chest."

Sam explained the circumstances, he had not seen the murder but heard first-hand accounts from Roger McKinney and Salem Gleason; Dow was unarmed and the first shot, a misfire at his back.

He continued with the events leading to the arrest of Jacob Branson, from a warrant sworn out by a hastily appointed bogus Justice of the Peace based on a claim by Harrison Buckley who had attempted murder on Dow the day of the killing.

"You were at the Wakarusa for the rescue of Branson?"

"I was."

"One question, Sam, how many men did you have in your rescue party?"

"We had a total of 15, under the command of Major Abbott, but we sent three men to guard Branson's cabin to keep the Ruffians from burning it. The group that stopped Jones was 12."

"Did you all have Sharp's rifles?"

Sam laughed, "Are you kidding Governor, we were the worst armed rescue party in the history of the world.

Me and two other men had clubs, Harold had a California Gold Rush Percussion, the Hupps had model 1841 Mississippi's, some of the men grabbed branches to make it looked like they had rifles and Major Abbott had a large stone that he was gonna' chunk at Jones."

Shannon sat with his hands covering his eyes, obviously exhausted, "So Jones just let Branson ride over to your side without a challenge?"

"That about sums it up. He said something like 'there's no need for bloodshed in this matter'. He's a big man out there with 2,000 Border Ruffians, but he'll be standing way behind those men if there is an attack."

"You probably don't know this Sam, but Jones came in here with six or seven men yesterday demanding us to give you up. He walked up on your porch; Margaret stopped him at the front door."

"What happened?"

"He said he had an arrest warrant and was going to search the house. Pretty good crowd had gathered by then and Margaret told him to let her read the warrant. You know Jones, I doubt there is a real warrant, so he says, I don't need to show you no warrant, I'm sheriff of Douglas County and if I tell you I'm gonna' search this house then I'm gonna' do it. Margaret sees Judge Wakefield in the crowd, tells Jones that he is her attorney and if he'll go get his written warrant and put it in the Judge's hand and if it says that he can search her house, she will allow it. Jones looked around once or twice, the crowd's gathering in close and they didn't act real friendly; he just turned and got on his horse and rode away."

"I didn't know that," Shannon said.

"He's free to come in here any time but he won't get any cooperation from the citizens of Lawrence." Lane said.

"Sam, we need to finish this memorandum so I can go back and negotiate with the Missourians. My advice to you is avoid Jones at all costs. Aren't you going back east for the Republican Convention? Maybe you could go early."

"I'm going to Philadelphia for organizational meetings next month. Don't worry, I'll avoid him but if he molests me or mine..." he left the consequences to the imagination. With a smile and a nod to the others, he began to leave, stopped and walked back to shake Shannon's hand, "Governor, if you pull this peace treaty together, you'll be legend in Kansas Territory. Good luck, and Godspeed."

***

"Sam, what's going on in there?"

"They're writing a peace treaty," shaking his head. "It'll be about as valid as Penn's Treaty."

Harold smiled, "If Shannon believes those Missourians will agree to any terms, he's delusional."

Jim Lane stuck his head out the door, "Is the Judge out here? And Dietzler?"

They both answered in the affirmative.

"We need you to help draft some language. Sam, do you want to help us?"

"No, you go ahead. I've got some other business to attend."

Harold took him by the arm, "Come on, everybody's waiting over at your house."

He wasn't exaggerating, the house was full; women hurrying about preparing food, cleaning, chastising children being children. Sam loved it. Just his kind of homecoming. Margaret didn't allow smoking in the house, so the back yard was full of men sitting on chairs, logs, large rocks, and some standing. Appropriate greetings were offered, hugs to his family, a kiss to his wife and Sam joined the throng outside; Tap, in the center of attention, was acting out the story of their hike from Lecompton in the middle of the night.

"...so, Sam's got this big fella by the throat, just kind of holding him up against the tree, cracks the other fella on the side of his head, smack on his ear, and says to him, now get this, he says, just as nice as you please," Tap exaggerates Sam's Ohio twang, "'where'd you get this Sharps rifle?' like they were old hunting buddies or something."

John T stood off to the side, caught Sam's eye, "the legend grows," he mouthed. Sam shook his head, what could he do?

Harold brought the group up to speed on the events across the street. As the evening progressed, Governor Shannon left with Jim and Charlie to negotiate the Peace Treaty; the party began to disperse.

"Eric, do you know Tom Barber?" Sam called the two together.

"We met yesterday; Tom is having some horses shod at the shop. We actually have some friends in common in Columbia. Tom's aunt..."

"Actually, my wife's aunt."

"His wife's aunt knows my in-laws. It's a small world isn't it?"

"When are you bringing Katie and Tammy back?" Sam asked.

"As soon as the Missourians leave. Probably next week. We'll live on the farm and Mom and Dad Tanner will move into a house here in town."

Tom Barber asked, "Do you think I need to bring my wife into town? No one has bothered the women so far, but I worry about those Ruffians when they start to leave. They're going to be angry."

Margaret overheard, "Bring her here, Tom. Have Mr. Pierson and Robert bring their wives. They're welcome to stay with us."

"I will if she'll come. We're going to ride back to Bloomington right now. It sounds like the Governor is going to make the Missourians disband," Tom answered.

"Autumn and the girls too, Harold," Margaret added.

"I doubt Autumn will leave the farm. Where's Bull? I haven't seen him all afternoon."

"Probably with Sarah," Robert Barber answered grinning.

"When did that romance take place?" Eric asked.

"You missed the big party back in August. They've been like two peas in a pod since."

Bull chose to stay with the Wood's while Harold rode home to see if the rest of the family wanted to return to Lawrence, "If you're staying here, I'll probably stay at the farm," he told his son. "But you need to come home tomorrow we're way behind on the farm work."

Bull may have been a grown man, but he was still his father's son. The crops had been adequate that summer; but with winter well upon them, a great deal of work remained undone. The Barber's and Barnett's pooled their labor, helped construct barns and shelters, fed the animals, put in and harvested the crops. The farmers of Douglas County Kansas looked out for each other.

Sam and Tap wandered back to the hotel. Most of the Safety Committee and all of the company commanders waited for the negotiating team to return. Small groups whispered together; tension was as thick as the smoke clouding the large room on the first floor. No word had been received from the summit meeting and no reports of any troop movements by General Lane's sentries.

"Wake, what kind of document did you write? I hope you held those men accountable for any damage they inflict."

"There's a copy in the 'war room', come on, you can read it."

"Have the other's read it?"

"No, just Charlie and Jim."

"We better have a look. I hope they haven't given away the farm."

"Mr. Babcock, come in here and read this peace treaty to us," Judge Wakefield shouted.

Babcock leaned against the table, glanced over the document, began reading in his sonorous baritone to a group of fifty or sixty of the leading Lawrence defenders.

TREATY OF PEACE.

WHEREAS, There is a MISUNDERSTANDING between the people of Kansas, or a portion of them, and the Governor thereof, arising out of the rescue at Hickory Point of a citizen under arrest and other matters; and,

WHEREAS, A strong apprehension exists that said misunderstanding may lead to civil strife and bloodshed; and,

WHEREAS, As it is desired by both Gov. Shannon and the citizens of Lawrence and its vicinity to avoid a calamity so disastrous to the interests of the Territory and the Union, and to place all parties in a correct position before the world; now, therefore, it is agreed by the said Gov. Shannon and the undersigned citizens of the Territory in Lawrence now assembled, that the matter is settled as follows, to wit:

We, the said citizens of said Territory, protest that the said rescue was made without our knowledge or consent, but that if any of our citizens were engaged in said rescue, we pledge ourselves to aid in the execution of any legal process against them; that we have no knowledge of the previous, present or prospective existence of any organization in the said Territory for the resistance of the laws; and we have not designed, and do not design, to resist the execution of any legal service of any criminal process therein, but pledge ourselves to aid in the execution of the laws when called upon by the proper authority in the town of Lawrence..."

"What," Sam shouted, cracking his cane on the table. He slammed it a second time, stormed out the door then back again, "that's...bull," he shouted, too angry to think.

"Who approved that language?" Tap barked.

"They should be shot," Owen Brown threatened.

"Let me finish," Babcock interrupted holding up the document,

...and that we will use our influence in preserving order therein, and declare that we are now, as we have ever been, ready to aid the Governor in securing a posse in the execution of such a process, provided, that any person thus arrested in Lawrence and vicinity while a foreign foe shall remain in the Territory, shall be examined only before a District Judge of said Territory in said town, and admitted to bail; and provided further, that all persons arrested without legal process shall be set at liberty; and provided further, that Gov. Shannon agrees to use his influence to secure the citizens of Kansas Territory remuneration for any damage suffered in any unlawful depredations, if any such have been committed by the Sheriff's posse in Douglas County; and further, Gov. Shannon states that he has not called upon persons, residents of any other States, to aid in the execution of the laws, that such as are here, are here of their own choice, and that he does not consider that he has any authority to do so, and that he will not call upon any citizen of any other State who may be here.

We wish it understood that we do not herein express any opinion as to the validity of the enactments of the Territorial Legislature.

WILSON SHANNON,
CHARLES ROBINSON,

J. H. LANE.   *Done in Lawrence, K. T., December 7, 1855.*

"That is unacceptable," Tap said in the silence that greeted the last words.

"They'll play the devil trying to arrest me. I guarantee that," Sam calmed down a bit, "Wake, how could you agree to this language? We can't give any legitimacy to the bogus legislature or to Jones."

"I didn't think of it in that light, Sam. We were just trying to word it in a way that the Missourians would agree to it and leave. No one is going to turn you in."

"We should have run those troublemakers out of the Territory," John Brown said, entering the room for the first time. "I just heard what you agreed to. Come on, Owen. We're going to make certain those sinners leave." The Browns stormed out of the hall, no one tried to stop them.

Caleb Pratt put his hand on Sam's shoulder, "Don't worry, my friend, no one in Kansas Territory will allow you to be arrested by Jones, or anyone else for that matter."

Sam accepted the assurance at face value, shook hands with Caleb. He added, as everyone listened, "Gentlemen, the most vital business before us right now is, we have to ratify the Topeka Constitution this month. Realistically in the next week to ten days. Once it's ratified, we have to get it to Washington for approval. I'll take it myself and get Senator Cass to have it brought before Congress. If those Ruffians don't disperse, we'll have to take John Brown's advice and run them off. Time is of the essence."

Suddenly Owen Brown charged into the room, his face contorted in anger, tears in his eyes, "Come quick, there's been a murder."

***

When the peace treaty was signed by all parties, Jim Lane and Charlie Robinson rode slowly back to Lawrence. "Sam isn't going to like this, Jim."

"I know it, but they wouldn't have agreed to anything less. The most important thing now is to free Lawrence from the threat of invasion and make those men go back to Missouri."

Governor Shannon spent a few extra minutes after signing the document conferring with the Missouri Commanders, "Gentlemen, I realize that this won't meet with complete approval of your men, but you have to see to it that they withdraw peacefully. If they don't, I will authorize troops from Ft. Leavenworth and Ft. Riley to intervene."

As he walked back to the coach for the trip into Lawrence, Sheriff Jones gave him such a look of derision that Shannon almost fired him on the spot. He gave Jones the same look right back before he climbed aboard.

As they neared the Free State Hotel, Lieutenant Clark rode alongside the coach, "It looks like some kind of trouble ahead, Governor. I'm going to ride into town and see what the problem is. He ordered the coach to wait. Shannon got out, climbed ponderously to the driver's seat to watch.

Had the governor looked the other way he would have observed several horses running hard toward the command tent. The riders were whooping and hollering causing Jones, General Easton and Colonel Boone to interrupt orders to break camp.

"What's going on, men?" Boone asked.

"We sent a couple of those damned abolitionists to their winter quarters."

"What?" Easton demanded, "who did?"

"I did, George Clark, I'm the Pottawattamie Indian Agent. We were guarding the Lecompton-Bloomington road and four men came riding out of Lawrence. We ordered them to halt. They kept going so we opened fire."

"I killed that first one, George," James Burnes said with a menacing look.

"You idiots, we just signed a peace treaty. This skirmish is over. You'd best get out of the territory or you'll be charged with murder," Easton ordered.

"Bullshit," Jones shouted. "This skirmish isn't over, General. You may be leaving but me and Senator Atchison are going to wipe out Yankee Town with or without you," he turned to the jubilant murderer, "You won't be charged with anything George. You and Colonel Burnes go on back to your homes for now. I'll be in touch. We've still got to arrest Sam Wood and I guarantee you that son-of-a-bitch won't never live to see the inside of a courthouse."

"I'm going to ignore the fact you said that sheriff. My men and I are going back to Missouri. You've managed to make a mess of this wretched affair; you lied about the whole thing. Don't involve me in whatever you are planning," General Easton said.

"Nor me, Samuel." echoed Colonel Boone. "If you try to implicate me in this fiasco, I'll deny everything."

In Lawrence, Lieutenant Clark rode back to the coach at a gallop, "There's been a murder, Governor. You'd better come see for yourself."

Shannon stepped from his fancy coach expecting a hero's welcome, instead found the citizens of Lawrence in shock, crying, gathered around a wagon parked in front of the hotel.

"What is it, General Lane?"

"Those bastards murdered a young farmer on his way home to see his wife."

"Who is it?"

"Thomas Barber."

The governor walked to the wagon. The crowd parted. He could hear the wailing of the man's wife as she sat in the wagon, Tom's head in her lap. Shannon tried to offer condolences; she ignored him, not aware of anything, hysterical in the realization that her husband was truly dead. The mood of the crowd subdued any thoughts the governor had of further jubilation at the end of the battle.

"Where's Sam Wood?" Shannon asked looking around.

"He gathered a posse to look for the murderer."

"He needs to leave that to the sheriff."

Jim Lane scoffed, gave him a withering look that didn't require an answer.

The Governor turned back to the coach, "Straight home to Shawnee Mission, Lieutenant. Don't stop." A wave of despondency washed over him, crushing his already exhausted body. He stared blankly out the window as the dry, cold Kansas prairie rolled past.

Sarah Wood climbed into the wagon, gathered Marie Barber into her arms finally convincing her to come in out of the cold so they could prepare the body.

That the State whose walls we lay,
In our blood and tears, to-day,
Shall be free from bonds of shame,
And our goodly land untrod
By the feet of Slavery, shod
With cursing as with flame!

Plant the Buckeye on his grave,
For the hunter of the slave
In its shadow cannot rest;
And let martyr mound and tree
Be our pledge and guaranty
Of the freedom of the West!
FROM THE POEM, "BURIAL OF BARBER",
JOHN GREENLEAF WHITTIER, 1856

Mourners streamed out of the Lutheran Church, marched up the hill to Pioneer Cemetery and a grave dug not 50 feet from the resting place of Felix Francis. Such was the emotion generated by the death of Tom Barber that the procession stretched from the village church clear to the top of Mt. Oreod. More than 300 people gathered to see Tom laid to rest in the beautiful setting surrounded by the ugliness of the conflict that took his life. The weather turned considerably colder causing the breath of the procession to fog the pathway ascending the mount. A cold rain began to spatter the bereaved before the eulogy was complete; no one left.

John lifted Missy to his shoulders before beginning the long trudge up the hill.

"Daddy, is Mr. Tom in that box?"

John nodded, "Yes, he is."

She began squirming, "I want down, Daddy. I don't want to go. All my friends are getting dead. Please don't make me go."

John looked helplessly at Sally. Before she could say anything, Sarah volunteered, "Here, give her to me. I'll stay home with her."

"I'll stay too," Lloyd said. "I don't want to see anymore funerals either."

"Hal, carry her back to our house for me. Then you can catch up with everybody."

"No, Sal, I'll stay with you."

"Tom was your best friend, go on. We'll wait at home for you."

Sarah, Lloyd and Missy sat in the Wood kitchen waiting for the funeral to end. She warmed cups of water, stirred in some tea leaves to sip while they waited.

"Did Papa, kill the man who murdered Mr. Tom?" Lloyd asked.

"They can't find him. But they know who it is."

"Just like they can't find the man who killed Mr. Dow, right?" Missy asked.

"Right. Sometimes life isn't fair. I wish it was. You children shouldn't have to see such things at your young age; but we have to make the slaves free," she added more in the way of convincing herself than them. Sarah thought the best of everyone; was at a loss over the actions of the Border Ruffians. Confidence in her fellow man was shaken to her Quaker roots. Visiting with the children seemed a breath of fresh air.

"Some people call me a slave. Don't they, Punch."

"Yep! But I make them stop."

"Why did you call him, Punch, Missy?" Sarah laughed, but Missy was serious.

"That's his new nickname because he told Rollo Meyers that he would punch him if he calls me names again AND if he makes fun of my broken leg."

"Well, Punch is a good nickname."

"Aunt Sarah, do you love Mr. Hal?"

"Well," she lengthened the word formulating her response, "I'm very fond of him. I think maybe I am in love with him."

"He's really strong," Lloyd added, giving his approval based on that quality alone.

"And very handsome. My Momma said so, too. But what about Mr. Jimmy, remember how you used to love him?"

Sarah sighed; Missy had stumbled onto the major problem in her life. She did feel strongly for Jimmy but in a different way from her feelings for Hal. A way she couldn't even explain to herself. The problem had been somewhat resolved; Jimmy was transferred west to Ft. Massachusetts in New Mexico Territory, the San Luis Valley. A letter from him lay unopened on the hutch in the kitchen. She meant to read it, picked it up every evening to do just that, but decided to wait until the latest troubles died down so she could give her response adequate consideration.

She ended the reminiscence, found the two children waiting patiently for an answer, "I love Jimmy in a different way, kind of like a brother."

"That's how I love Punch, don't I," she said, expecting Punch to agree. He gave it a bit more thought before responding, "We're best friends, Missy. I don't think best friends love each other. I'll think about it."

Sally had a good laugh. She needed it, couldn't wait to share the story with Hal.

***

The threatening storm broke the morning of the 18th. Cold weather and snow did more to drive the marauders away from Lawrence than the Peace Treaty. In spite of the wintery weather and the Missouri Commanders ordering them to stand down, rogue bands of Border Ruffians roamed the prairie and river bottom around Lawrence. For several days. General Lane sent patrols into the countryside daily and posted guards night and day inside the city. John Brown's squad of troops, including his five sons, chased the remaining ruffians out of the Territory by the end of that week. The Safety Committee was fearful that Brown would do something to ignite trouble before the free state delegates could get the Kansas Constitution ratified.

Plans were being made for a New Year's Day fete, everyone invited, a truce declared for the festivities, with Governor Shannon as guest of honor and all military commanders invited regardless of affiliation or place of residence. John Brown was furious at the disrespect of allowing slaveholders into the Free State Hotel and at a meeting on the 20th, he let everyone know it in no uncertain terms, "You're all cowards! We should have driven that riffraff out of the Territory the day I arrived. You've kowtowed to them, coddled them, let this bogus sheriff run roughshod over you, this is war gentlemen and you're cavorting with the enemy."

"Mr. Brown, I appreciate your zealous attitude," General Lane replied, "But we have women and children here, this was not the time or place to start a battle. Governor Shannon may be pro-slavery, but he performed admirably and took our side. This has caused him a great deal of grief from Senator Atchison and President Pierce, not to mention Jones and the Border Ruffians. It's water under the bridge, let's move on."

Brown would not let the matter lie and trouble would come, but for today, he merely replied, "Sam Wood has more guts than all of you combined," then stormed out of the meeting leaving John Brown, Junior as the only representative of the Brown family trying to be reasonable.

That night Sam, Margaret, John and Sally sat around the oak dining table discussing plans for returning to Ohio and a speaking tour that Sam would embark on prior to the Republican National Convention in Philadelphia. Arrangements were being handled by members of Horace Greeley's staff; stops were planned from St. Louis to New York.

"Sam," Margaret grabbed his club, pretended to take a swipe at a phantom Ruffian, "You know these people are expecting a giant of a man, a club in each hand, with tales of cracking heads and taking no prisoners."

"They want the brutal details," John T agreed.

"My goal is to get more people to move to Kansas and vote. Making her a free state is more important than any contribution I've made," he took the club before she hurt someone.

On January tenth a meeting of delegates finalized the wording for the constitution, resolutions and memorandum being prepared for Senator Cass who would present the Bill in Congress for ratification. The legislators hired transcribers to copy the documents, the originals signed by Governor Robinson and the Secretary of State. Sarah Wood helped with the drafting, spending two days in Topeka finalizing the documents.

On the twelfth the delegates met in caucus to authorize submittal of the documents to the United States Congress for ratification. Prayers were made, speeches given, congratulations issued all around. Sam kept his thoughts to himself, but he had little confidence anything would come of the entire process other than keeping the issue alive in Washington.

The work of the free state legislature was complete, the Topeka Constitution finalized amidst the most trying of circumstances. Sam stood amongst a group speaking with Cy Holiday and others from Topeka when a commotion was heard outside. Phillip Hupp burst through the door, "Sam, It's Jones, right behind us. He's coming for you."

Before the words were out of his mouth, Sam was out the back door and astride Border Ruffian, secure in the knowledge that he could outdistance any horse in the west. Ruffian was not only fast but possessed extreme endurance, much like Sam himself. He galloped hard all the way from Topeka to Lawrence, not even bothering to look back. He put Ruffian into the barn with food and water, wiped him down and strolled across to the Brooks home where he watched Jones searching the streets. Margaret allowed the sheriff to walk through the house to verify that Sam wasn't there. Jones left frustrated again after a crowd began to gather asking him what he wanted. David came and fetched Sam home for supper when it was obvious that Jones had given up and gone back to Lecompton.

"Papa, why do you hide from Bogus Jones? Why don't you just whack him with your club and get it over with."

"I will Davey if he catches me, but I'm following the rules of the Safety Committee and Governor Shannon. I'm staying away from him. When I go back east, we won't have to worry about him for a while."

"The day he was to sell the children from their mother he would tell that mother to go to some other place to do some work and in their absence, he would sell the children. It was the same when he would sell a man's wife, he also sent him to another job and when he returned his wife would be gone. The master only said, "don't worry you can get another one"."

Born In Slavery: Slave Narratives from The Federal Writers Project

Life in Lawrence was frantic for everyone, more so for those under indictment, including Sam, Judge Wakefield, Tap and Charlie. Sam always had one eye looking over his shoulder, the other on the road ahead. The Border Ruffians and Missouri 'militia' were nothing more than gangs looking for easy plunder, still making forays into Kansas then skedaddling back to Missouri to count their booty. He had to dodge them as well as Sheriff Jones.

Finally, in late January, Sam, Sarah, Margaret and the boys enjoyed a meal together for the first time since the murder of their friend Chuck Dow.

"Missy and I ate the sugar candy he brought us. I miss Mr. Dow, Mama," Punch said. The entire family adopted Lloyd's new nickname.

"He was a good man," Margaret answered.

"Coleman still hasn't been brought to trial. We don't even know where he is," Sam reached for a piece of bread.

"I hope he left forever," David grabbed the container, held it close to Sam. He wasn't supposed to reach across the table.

"Charlie and Jim Lane will be here this evening to speak with you," Margaret smiled at David for his good manners.

"How long will you be gone, Papa?"

"I have a lot of things to do, Davey, so probably two months. Mr. Greeley is setting up a speaking tour for me. I'll start in St. Louis and end in New York City, but it'll be fun. I expect to recruit a lot of abolitionists to come to the Territory."

"Can me and Caleb go with you?"

"No, I need you to stay here and protect your Mother."

"Ok, we will; can I have your old club?"

"Welllll..." Sam hesitated.

"Daddy, I don't mean to whack somebody with it. I want to use it as a bat."

"A what?" Sarah asked.

"A bat, that's what we call the stick we hit the ball with. Baseball is really fun."

"I guess so. But don't let me hear about you hitting anyone with it. Anyway, how can you play ball in the snow?"

Sarah helped Margaret wash the dishes while Sam supervised the boys washing up before going off to bed.

Later when the others were busy elsewhere, Sam and Margaret sat by the fire, holding hands quietly, "I've been thinking that we should have another baby, a girl this time. What do you say to that, Sam?"

"I say that sounds wonderful, Meg, but we can't just pick and choose. What makes you think that it will be a girl. You're not expecting, are you?" a hint of alarm in his voice. "If you are, I won't leave."

"I would have told you if I was, but when the time comes, I know it will be a girl."

He held his tongue knowing Margaret too well to argue, her sixth sense about these matters was uncanny. He wanted a little girl as much as she did, but he would love another son just the same.

A knock at the door, Charlie and Sara entered, "hello everyone," Sara said cheerfully.

"Where's the Judge?" Sam asked

"Stomach problems again," Sara answered.

"I'm worried about him," Margaret lamented.

Jim Lane joined them. They drank coffee, ate cake, shared news of family and friends back east; discussed the latest rumors and happenings on the frontier. Finally, Jim said, "Sam, the mail isn't getting through. We've sent letters and dispatches, had no answer, no indication that Washington has received our messages. All we can figure is that it's being held in Westport or Independence. The new telegraph lines from here to Kansas City are down more often than not."

"You know what's happening, Jones and Atchison are behind it, reading our mail and cutting the lines."

"You'll have to hand carry the constitution and articles of statehood to Washington yourself."

"I can't think of a safer method to get the documents back there. Do you feel confident that you can get past the Ruffians, Sam?" General Lane asked.

"It won't be difficult, I plan on going south of Kansas City, circle down to Osawatomie, visit John Brown, if he's there; eventually end up in Lexington. I'll catch a packet, go on to St. Louis. Where's the mail pouch?"

"We'll have it ready tomorrow morning."

Sam woke early, kissed his wife and family and climbed into the buggy for the 50-mile ride to Osawatomie with Tap, who agreed to bring the buggy back. In Osawatomie they stopped for a quick visit at the home of Reverend Adair, whose wife, Florella, was John Brown's sister. The Adair's were struggling in the freezing weather, their small cabin packed with family all sick with ague, aggravated by lack of good food and too small a congregation to support the Reverend. Most of the church members were in worse shape than Adair. Sam helped with a little money, the best he could do.

The tiny village was in danger, sitting precariously between communities of pro-slavery forces who were normally at each other's throats. The cold, snowy winter kept all of them busy trying to survive; too busy to worry about harassing each other. The peaceful interlude ended with the arrival of warm weather and John Brown who would not avoid conflict with the slaveholders, in fact, welcomed it.

Sam contracted a hack to take him on to Lexington, Missouri where he would board a steamboat for St. Louis.

Part Three

A sense of relief flooded through Lawrence as the Border Ruffians slowly vacated the area, leaving the countryside littered with waste, denuded of firewood, trashed with empty whiskey bottles and the detritus of their camps. A post debacle tension remained behind, a reminder for the citizens not to lower their guard. So many senseless deaths left a residue of bitterness that would not be easily dissipated, neither with the passage of time nor the burial of the dead. The battle would rage on in the meeting rooms of the free-state delegates in Topeka and the pro-slavery men in Shawnee Mission. Sam knew that the pen and ink battle, while necessary, would pale against the bullets and blood conflict that was coming.

In Lawrence, Eric and Katie McCrea moved into a new home on New Hampshire street, again with Riley and Jane Tanner. Eric seemed content with the arrangement. The farmland between Lawrence and Leavenworth was leased to Ralph Epcot. Eric and Riley reformed their partnership, and the Tanner-McCrea Blacksmith and Carpentry Company added another business name to the slowly growing village.

Sarah and Hal spent more and more time together. The heavy snow actually gave them increased opportunity as Sarah would stay in the country or Hal in town when travel was inadvisable or, in some cases, impossible.

Sam was off to the east for a multi-city speaking tour asking families to join him in Kansas to stop the spread of slavery. He beat the snowstorm out of Osawatomie and arrived in Lexington in threatening but passable weather. The wharves along the Missouri River were busier even than those in Kansas City and Independence. The city was full of men when Sam arrived making him apprehensive, a feeling confirmed when he questioned the hotel manager about who they were.

"Pro-slavery men returning from the Territory. They voted in the elections over in Kansas," he answered in a matter-of-fact tone, not taking the time to glance up at the questioner; wouldn't have recognized him if he did. He added, "Big celebration because Kansas is a slave state now."

Sam was so shaken he forgot what name he used to register, hoping that it was his usual alias of Richard Smith from Louisville, Kentucky. He retired early preferring to wait in his room until it might be safe to venture downstairs for supper. The view out the window of the bustling city found hundreds of freight wagons rolling up and down the wide street below; most bearing the initials, RMW for Russell, Majors and Waddell, the largest trading firm in the west based out of Lexington. RMW had wagons carrying goods from Missouri to Denver, even as far west as Sacramento; they stopped at Paul Brooks mercantile in Lawrence every week.

Sam moseyed cautiously down to the lobby at nine, detoured by the registration desk to glance at the register to see what name he used. A heavyset fellow was looking through the book, so he went into the lobby jammed with noisy men, a few women, lots of smoke and the clinking of glasses. A female piano player pounded away on an out of tune piano singing the new Stephen Foster song, "My Old Kentucky Home, Good Night"; she was joined by several men gathered around the piano hoisting glasses, smoking big cigars.

"The sun shines bright in the old Kentucky Home,
Tis Summer, the darkies are gay,

The corn tops ripe and the meadows in the bloom,
While the birds make music all the day
The young folks roll on the little cabin floor,
All merry, all happy and bright,
By'n by Hard Times come a knocking at the door,
Then my Old Kentucky Home, Good Night.
"Weep no more my lady, oh! weep no more today!
We will sing one song for the old Kentucky home
For the old Kentucky home far away

Several slaves waited tables, emptied spittoons, cleared tableware; in general, fetched whatever the white folk wanted. He watched them closely, not one reacted to the words of the song. He didn't really expect them to. Sam glanced suspiciously from face to face, took a table in a back corner to avoid notice, but it didn't work. His suspicions confirmed; a stout fellow, red of face from the free-flowing liquor, the same fellow checking the guest register, watched Sam until he sat down.

"Hello neighbor, I know you from somewhere," he sat without being asked. "I never forget a face and I know you're someone, come on now, where was it? Atchison, Leavenworth, Shawnee Mission? I'm Kingston Northbert and I know we've met." Kingston waited for Sam to introduce himself and clear up the mystery. Sam couldn't for the life of himself remember what name he had used to register.

He wagged his finger at the man, "Yessir, Mr. Northbert, I remember you, it was in Lecompton when we all rallied around Sheriff Jones and the fine boys getting ready to wipe out Lawrence."

"That's where it was," Kingston agreed, slapped his knee, drained his glass, "and we would have done it if Shannon hadn't double crossed us."

"Exactly right. I'm on my way to Washington with a petition demanding the President recall Shannon; install someone who understands the situation."

Northbert nodded enthusiastically, hesitated while ordering another drink, "By God, I want to sign that petition. My name will carry some weight with Pierce, if I do say so myself."

Sam wanted to kick himself for such a rash statement, recovered as best he could, "And you shall do it, first thing in the morning. Where can I find you?"

"Room 204. If I'm not in there, come down here, I may stay up all night listening to that pretty lady sing, drinking their good whiskey." He laughed a drunken roar heard by everyone; fortunately for Sam, one of Northbert's friends grabbed him by the arm. They stumbled together to the piano for another Foster song,

"The Camptown ladies sing this song,
Doo-da, Doo-da
The Camptown racetrack's five miles long
Oh, de doo-da day

"Goin' to run all night
Goin' to run all day
I bet my money on a bob-tailed nag
Somebody bet on the gray.

Sam bolted for his room without eating. He paused on the stairs to gaze out on the raucous lobby as the white men and women partied, waited on by black men and women, most of them dressed in the finest servant's livery of swallow-tailed coats and white vests. He turned to go but recognized one black face turned toward him from the scene below, a young man of handsome features, smiled and nodded, he knew who Sam was. He waggled his head toward the entrance of the kitchen. Sam followed.

"Hello Mr. Wood."

"I'm afraid I don't recall your name."

"Joseph Fedder, my mother is Mary. You would probably recognize the scars on my back."

An image of a young boy, his back crisscrossed with the welts of a master's whip, flashed before Sam's eyes. This was one of Mary Fedder's boys. Two years earlier, Sam had convinced an Ohio jury that she was freeborn and had been captured into slavery, "Oh, my goodness, you've grown into quite a young man, what's it been, two years at least. How are your parents?"

"Very well, thank you, Mr. Wood. We've followed your troubles in Kansas. Always hoping for the best."

"What are you doing here" You're not back into slavery are you?"

"No, sir, I'm a free man, Working my way west. I want to go to California, get rich like everyone else."

"Well, I don't think everyone is getting rich in California, but some are. We're in Lawrence, Kansas. Stop there on your way. John and Sally will be disappointed if you don't. Please pass my regards to your mother and father." They shook hands, Sam glanced toward the lobby, turned the other way, ran up the servant's stairs to his room.

He wrote letters until midnight, some addressed to the correct address, some using an alias as the sender; the letters to Margaret were sent to the Brook's house next door bearing the name of Richard Smith from Louisville, Kentucky. He addressed one letter to Margaret under his signature, containing a deception devised by Wakefield and Tappan. Sam made an appointment to meet the Safety Committee at Major Abbott's at a certain time. Wakefield would bring a Federal Postal Inspector and see who might show up. Probably nothing would come of it, but it was worth the try. Sam wished he could be there, especially if Jones did come to arrest him after illegally reading the mail.

He slept well, woke at six, rushed downstairs where the slaves were clearing the mess from the night's festivities preparing for breakfast. There were few other patrons that early. Sam ate quickly, hurried to get safely aboard before Northbert was up and around. He booked a cabin on the Emma Lee to St. Louis where he would meet the coordinator for his speaking engagements. The boat left without incident.

Once underway, Sam relaxed, took a stroll, explored the Hurricane Deck, introduced himself to the captain; strolled down to the Boiler Deck, finally to the Main Deck. A familiar voice hailed him. "Mr. Sam, it's me, May Bixby, from the Sam Cloon."

Sam was face to face with an old friend. During the Wood family's first trip to the Kansas frontier May and her sister had provided invaluable assistance in battling a cholera outbreak on the steamboat from St. Louis to Independence.

He grabbed May's hand, greeted her affectionately, "My goodness what a pleasant surprise, is Violet here too, what's it been, two years? Where are you going?"

"Oh, it's a long story, Mr. Sam, and yes, Violet here too."

"I've got nothing but time, sit down here, tell me all about it. Are the Bixby's on board?"

"Mr. and Mrs. Bixby done passed on, Mr. Sam, from the dysentery, and I don't expect to see em' in heaven when I get there, neither. Not to be disrespectful, but good riddance," she began to laugh before she could finish, "and now, we's, de property of little Miss Mary Bixby, all of 13-year-old and she wants to go back home to Virginia, ain't life grand?"

"Let me make arrangements for you to escape to Canada. It wouldn't be hard," Sam said quietly.

"Lord no, why me n' Violet, we rule the roost. That chile do anything we say. We gonna' make some changes and they gonna' be for the best. The Negroes on the Bixby plantation gonna' be the best fed slaves in the land."

"May, me and Lilly are hungry, what shall we do?" a blond-haired adolescent face peered over the railing from above. May looked at Sam, they both burst out laughing.

"Just sit tight, Mary. I'll be right there. I'm hungry too."

Sam walked with her to the forward stairs, "What about when those girls grow up and get married? their husbands won't be so naïve."

"We'll worry bout it when the time come, Mr. Sam. The only thing those two got going for em' is a whole parcel of land in Charlotte. I suppose some fellow, got gold in his eyes, would overlook their shortcomings," she laughed, "might be someday we'll take you up on that Canada offer."

He made certain they knew how to reach him in Lawrence.

"To all intents and purposes Roxy was as white as anybody, but the one sixteenth of her which was black outvoted the other fifteen parts and made her a Negro. She was a slave, and salable as such."
Mark Twain, Pudd'nhead Wilson

St. Louis was humming with activity. Over 100,000 people, many of them Irish and German immigrants swelled the population of the city, creating both economic growth and challenges. Slaves were beginning to clamber for their freedom, escaping into Illinois, stowing away on riverboats going west into Kansas then Nebraska or Iowa. Lawsuits by female slaves petitioning for their freedom, were not uncommon, freedom suits that Sam advised on periodically. It was a vibrant, racially mixed city with several newspapers fueling a desire for news from Kansas. The news was accurate based on the political persuasion of the writer.

Sam was met at the wharf by a very large, blonde, blue-eyed gentleman that he took to be a Swedish fellow. "I'm Gabriel Pennington, Mr. Wood. Please call me Gabe," he shook hands eagerly; possessed of a huge booming voice and a personality to match. He grabbed Sam's bags, guided him to a waiting brougham and off they went. Gabe briefed him on the next day's schedule; breakfast with a group of black abolitionists and businessmen, then the rally being held at the Old Cathedral, "Then to the steamboat. We'll have to sleep on board. The meeting in Louisville is on Thursday."

The next morning Sam broke bread, drank coffee and visited with a group of nine local black activists, businessmen, and preachers. After introduction formalities the conversation drifted toward the Fugitive

Slave Act, always a topic of conversation among abolitionists.

"...you take Mister Pennington for example," Reverend Logan said, "anyone looking upon Gabe sees a fine example of a handsome, successful white man, wouldn't you agree, Mr. Wood?"

"Yes, I would agree, Reverend," Sam was a bit confused by the statement.

In his baritone, slow, southern preacher's voice, Logan said, "Then I suppose you will be very surprised when I inform you that Gabe is a runaway slave."

Sam said with a smile and a sip of his coffee, "I would not only be surprised but I would be doubtful of the truth of that statement, no offense meant, sir."

"But it's true, Mr. Wood, I am a runaway slave, actually, the only slave in this room. A room full of Negroes, all free except for me. I am somewhere around one-eighth African heritage; my father is... or was my owner. Look here at Sylvester Rasmussen, a man anyone can see is descended from African parentage."

Rasmussen nodded to Sam, a very dark-skinned man with a broad nose, high forehead, intelligent dark eyes with a glint of good humor even in the serious conversation at hand. "I'm a printer, Mr. Wood. My company has been successful in the growth of St. Louis and I'm very grateful for it. As a third-generation free man, I don't have any knowledge of being a slave, any more than you do, sir. Yet, I am constantly harassed by slave catchers and bounty hunters who want to sell me south simply because I look like a slave. Mr. Pennington could walk up to the auctioneer over to Lynch's slave market on Locust Street, confess to be a runaway and those slave dealers would laugh him out of the building.

There's very little market for blond, blue-eyed, gentlemen in the slave trade."

Logan added, "That's the hypocrisy of the one-drop rule. Many people want to classify a slave as any person with one drop of black blood in their lineage. Why if that were the case, every man in the State Legislature would be bundled off to the cotton fields. I doubt that there is any person, after 250 years of inbreeding, that doesn't have some percentage of black blood, no matter how small it might be."

They sipped their coffee, discussed the situation in the territory, asked pertinent questions until a light went off in Sam's mind. They wanted something, but he couldn't put his finger on what it might be. What were these successful businessmen, religious leaders and community activists hinting at? Curiosity led to asking, "Gentlemen, is there something I can do for you. I feel that there is an unspoken agenda in our discussion today."

Reverend Logan, obviously the spokesman, nodded agreement with Sam's assessment, "Mr. Wood, as you know discretion is very important in certain matters involving the cause which we all support. Even among the Negroes we find turncoats, Judas, if you will, ready to sell his soul for thirty pieces of silver. We must be very careful."

"I'm aware of that, Reverend. I suffer from the same evils myself. My life is in constant danger in the territory."

"We know that you work with a young man by the name of John Thompson."

Sam sat up straight, sensing danger.

"Rest easy, Mr. Wood. We pose no threat to you or Mr. Thompson," Rasmussen comforted him. "We are interested in trying to be of help. You see, we've been blessed with success in St. Louis and we want to share that success with our less fortunate brothers and sisters. We are in a position to provide funds for Mr. Thompson's, shall we call it, enterprise; funds for clothes, shoes, food, transportation, those items needed when one... travels," he hesitated, thinking of the right word, then offered a smile of sincerity that convinced Sam of his good intentions.

Logan continued, "We have letters for Mr. Thompson that we hesitate to mail."

"And bank drafts," Rasmussen added.

"You are correct in that regard, Reverend. We fear our mail is being intercepted. I could carry the information for you, but I'm not returning to Kansas for at least six weeks. I'll be glad to meet with you when I get back to St. Louis on my way home. We could conclude our business at that time."

They shook hands, made plans for a future meeting and parted, each having made a new friend in the process. Sam was beginning to understand why Horace Greeley hired Gabe as the front man for the speaking tour. He seemed to know everyone of importance and was respected by all.

The Old Cathedral was packed to the walls with over 500 people when they finally arrived. The excitement of the gathered throng buzzed loudly even before they entered the gallery. Men, women and children, had all come to see the hero of the anti-slavery struggle in Kansas. Sam did not disappoint. First Gabe stirred the audience with a rousing introduction,

"A very strange phenomenon is taking place just to the west of us, my friends. An experiment in truth, justice and the American way of life. Our government passed a law, the Kansas-Nebraska Act and in that law, the powers that be said, 'Whatever the good citizens of Kansas Territory want, they shall have. If they vote for slavery, they shall have slavery and if they vote no

slavery, there shall be no slavery'; are you with me neighbors," and they cheered lustily, they were with him and way ahead of him.

"Then the good citizens of Kansas Territory voted, NO SLAVERY," he shouted at the top of his lungs. Then in almost a whisper, holding his hand up, *"But wait a minute, the powers that be said, 'we didn't think we would lose. We want Kansas to be a slave state, you have to vote again, there was something wrong with that vote, you cheated somehow'. So, they voted again and again they said, NO SLAVERY, and again the powers that be, President Pierce, all the southern politicians, they cried 'unfair, this can't be, arrest them, put them in jail', like a dictator not a democracy. But a few good men stood up to them and said, 'we won't allow it. We'll have a fair election or by all that is Holy we will go to war.' And now ladies and gentlemen, I bring you a man who has stood at the front of that battle, wielding his club like the sword of justice, denying those would-be dictators; a man who has been shot at, attacked with a knife, called every vile name in the book, the hero of the Kansas abolitionists, Mr. Sam Wood."*

The crowd cheered, the band played, then suddenly silence filled the hall. Sam marched up to the podium, shook hands with the much larger Gabe Pennington.

"I thought he would be bigger," one woman shouted from the front row. Laughter roared through the audience.

Sam pointed at her, *"They underestimate me at every turn. They underestimate me physically,"* he cracked his club on the podium, the audience began to stir. *"They underestimate me mentally,"* crack again went the club as the crowd began to cheer. *"And they underestimate the power of the Lord inside me screaming, 'destroy the slaveholders."* Pow! He slammed it down again. *"Destroy the wickedest sin that ever was,"* Boom, went the club and the audience screamed with delight.

Sam held them in his grasp for 90 minutes. Newspapers reported that "it seemed like nine". He shouted the details of the siege of Lawrence, the drunken Border Ruffians, the lying Sheriff Jones, the evil Senator Atchison. He wept shamelessly describing the death of his friend Felix Francis in the fall of 1854 at the hands of Border Ruffians; and cried with anger at the murder of Chuck Dow; begged them never forget Thomas Barber and his young wife left a widow on the frozen prairie. They booed and hissed at the mention of the villainous Bogus Sheriff Jones, and they roared with delight at the rescue of Jacob Branson. He ended by ordering them, *"pack your bags, load your wagons, take your wife, children, in-laws and grandparents, go to Kansas; vote it a free state and make the world a safe place for all God's children to live."*

The audience wouldn't let him off the stage, demanded to hear about deceiving the bounty hunters over the wagonload of slaves, revenge on LeCount; he answered honestly, disavowed the exaggeration of singlehandedly beating five Ruffians at the Kansas River crossing, a denial that caused the crowd to believe the story truer than ever.

Suddenly, a rowdy group of protesters stormed into the Cathedral, holding placards proclaiming, 'White Supremacy'; 'Slavery forever'; 'Nigger Lovers Go Home'. They screamed obscenities at Sam, disrupted the proceedings; but Pennington had foreseen the happening; they were unceremoniously ushered out by a well-organized crew of club wielding police. Sam stood on the stage brandishing his cane, "There are your cowardly slaveholders, those are the kind of men who keep our brothers and sisters in chains," he shouted. The band struck up 'Wait for the Wagon'; the chorus echoed through the Cathedral like thunder in a cave. Everyone sang and clapped together,

So wait for the wagon,
Oh! wait for the wagon,
Oh! wait for the wagon
and we'll all take a ride.
Oh! wait for the wagon
and we'll all take a ride.

The event was successful beyond Sam's most extravagant dream. Letters to Margaret were full of the news, including newspaper clippings from the St. Louis Republican and the New York Tribune; a drawing of Sam, his club held high, on the front pages. He was exhausted but overjoyed; if even one-third of the professed emigrants traveled to Kansas as they promised, the territory would be overrun with free-state voters.

Gabriel Pennington saw to the publicity; excitement was intense at each planned stop along the way, with the act repeated at Louisville, Cincinnati, Columbus, Cleveland, Chicago and all points East. Sam was dog-tired when they finally reached New York, but he couldn't rest until the convention documents were delivered to Washington.

He returned to New York, relaxed for a week at Horace Greeley's home before returning to Columbus. At the end of February, he attended the Republican Convention Planning Session in Pittsburg and chaired the resolutions committee that created the platform for the June convention.

Senator Atchison sent letters and telegrams to all the pro-slavery officials in the Territory and along the Missouri border, "Do something to stop Sam Wood. He's hurting us worse than if he were in Lawrence."

Make me a grave where'er you will,
In a lowly plain, or a lofty hill;
Make it among earth's humblest graves,
But not in a land where men are slaves.
I could not rest if around my grave
I heard the steps of a trembling slave;
His shadow above my silent tomb
Would make it a place of fearful gloom.
Francis Harper (1825-1911) From her Poem: Bury Me
in a Free Land

Sam was exhilarated, from the success of his speaking tour and the number of men and women committed to relocate to Kansas Territory. He spent the first week of March with his family and in-laws in Columbus. Bill and Elizabeth planned to return to the territory then send for the rest of their family as soon as it was safe. No one knew when that might be.

"I need you mother and father Lyon," as he handed Bill the list of emigrants signed up to go to Kansas. "We have a chance to make a real difference now. We'll have the votes necessary to carry the free-state candidates even with a little Missouri fraud."

Making the moment even sweeter, Beulah and Silas insisted on accompanying the family to Lawrence. "You white folk been tussling and carry'n on for two years and ain't no progress been made. Me and Silas get over there to Kansas, straight'n things out right quick. We can help John and Sally, we can look after Mrs. Wood, I know she workin' too hard; you out galivantin' round the country, Mr. Big Shot. We goin', so, no argument."

Sam certainly did not entertain the idea of an argument; the Wood family had coveted Beulah's help since the day they were married. She and Silas helped raise Margaret, had been a big part of their early married life in Ohio before traveling to Kansas. Her tears dropped like rain as they drove out of the yard two years earlier, leaving for Cincinnati and the riverboat. Punch claimed to still remember the sad moment.

Before too much celebration was in order, they had to get the emigrants transported to Lawrence. Sam traveled to Cincinnati along with Gabe to negotiate with the railroad and steamship lines to procure train cars at half price and reduced rates on the boats from Louisville to St. Louis. The group gathered strength at every stop from Cleveland to Cincinnati where a rally was held at the Buckeye Hotel on Pennsylvania Avenue with Gabriel Pennington stirring the crowd to a frenzy; a fact widely reported in the pro-slavery press creating a problem getting the settlers through Missouri.

Senator Atchison had been monitoring Sam's progress carefully from the first rally in St. Louis. He organized armed gangs to intercept the travelers, prohibit them from entering Kansas by river. The alternative would have been to go by train to Iowa then overland to Lawrence adding a month to the trip, making it a logistical nightmare.

Sam left the 150 settlers in the capable hands of Bill Lyon and Gabe Pennington with instructions to put them on the Louisville Packet leaving in two days. He hurried to St. Louis searching for a boat capable and willing to take the group on to Kansas City. The problem turned out to be significant because a boat of abolitionists had been stopped and ransacked in Lexington the week before. Several cases of Sharp's rifles, destined for the frontier had been stolen by pro-slavery roughs who found they couldn't use the weapons because the slides had been removed and shipped overland, they were already in Topeka waiting for the rifles themselves.

Much of this information Sam learned from his old friend Captain Johansen from the Sam Cloon, while taking on cargo for a trip to New Orleans. Johansen directed Sam to the Polar Star, a fast boat but one in disrespect because the Captain, Russell Wiley, had put a band of abolitionists ashore in February rather than risk having his boat damaged by the Border Ruffians in Lexington. Now he couldn't find passengers. Sam made him an offer, for $1,500 he would charter the entire boat. Only Sam's party would be allowed aboard with one additional prerequisite, if there were any problems from Ruffians along the way, Sam would be in charge of the response. The Captain reluctantly agreed; he needed the money. His only condition, they had to dock in Lexington to allow his wife to come aboard.

The arrangements made, Sam met with Reverend Logan, received the money and letters for John T and Sally's underground railroad enterprise. He promised that John or Sally would be in touch with reports of how the funds were put to use.

The Packet from Louisville arrived the next day. Passengers and their baggage transferred to the Polar Star along with 20 boxes of Model 1855, 58 caliber percussion rifle-muskets, donated by the Ohio State Militia; not Sharp's rifles but fine weapons that would be put to good use by the settlers. Sam supervised the boarding, met with the passengers in groups of fifty, explained the dangers that lie ahead, gave instructions on what to do if a situation did occur. He didn't hide the fact that it was a hazardous mission they were undertaking, but most of the men were ex-military and not afraid of a fight.

The wives were another matter. The excitement of leaving for the frontier clashed with the realization that the dangers were real. Bill and Elizabeth circulated among the families telling them of their first trip to Kansas in 1854, giving comfort where needed and hope where lacking. They didn't even get away from St. Louis before their worst fears came true. A commotion on the pier; Captain Riley summoned Sam to the Boiler Deck, "Here you go, Mr. Wood, you asked for it."

The scene was not comforting. A mob of knife and club wielding goons grew animated when they spotted him.

"We been waiting for you, Wood, saves us the trouble of going to Kansas City to kill some abolitionists, we can solve the problem right here."

"That is an excellent idea, Mr....sorry, I didn't catch your name."

"I didn't give it."

"Well, that's a strange name and I don't like it, so I'll just call you Jack."

The man furrowed his brow, "What in the hell you talking about Wood? I thought you was supposed to be smart; you don't make no sense. My names, Fredrich Reynolds, not Jack."

"Listen Jack, I don't have all day, what do you want?"

"It ain't what I want, it's what you're going to do. Turn this boat around and go back to Ohio. You ain't going west."

"Why?"

"Cause I say so."

"You want to kill us, good American citizens, just because you want to."

"Don't worry about the reason, just go on back where you came from."

"How many men you got?" Sam started counting, pointing at each one, walked down the gangplank poking them in the chest with his club."

"Hell, you're a runty little son-of-a-bitch."

"Watch your language, there are children on board," Sam poked him back away from the gangplank, really making the man angry, "Hey, watch it!"

"I count about 40, is that right?"

"About 40," he rubbed his chest, looking around at the men who were beginning to get a little nervous.

"Ok, I'll get 40 of my men. We'll meet here on the pier and have at killing each other, how does that sound? That way it'll save you the cost of the fare upriver and your bodies will be right here in your hometown, they won't have to be shipped back."

Reynolds contemplated this idea for a bit but gave no answer, just looked confused. His men were beginning to mutter, looking at each other. These abolitionists were supposed to be cowards, 'easy pickings' is what they were told.

Sam held up his hand for attention, "Jack, I want to make sure you understand one thing, if we should happen to lose this fight, those men stationed on the Hurricane Deck pointing their rifles will finish the job because we can't have fools like you harassing honest travelers on the river."

Arrayed around the upper deck were 20 or so men with rifles pointed at the hooligans. Gabe hollered down, "Step back a pace or two Sam, so we can open fire."

The gangsters in back immediately began to disperse. Finding himself alone, Reynolds followed suit. Sam called out, "Thank you for being reasonable, gentlemen. Let's cast off Captain, these men have graciously yielded the right of way."

The trip from St. Louis to Lexington was uneventful, yet a sense of calamity was in the air; word had reached the boat that a telegraph had been sent from St. Louis to

Lexington warning that the Polar Star was carrying a large number of Sharp's Rifles. The Captain wanted to know the truth of the matter. He didn't want to stop at all.

"We are well armed, Captain, but we have no Sharp's. All of our weapons are U.S. Rifles from the State Militia in Ohio. I will remind you of our agreement; if we are accosted in Lexington, let me handle the matter. You just be ready to cast off at a moment's notice."

As they approached Lexington, Sam could see the street thronged with men waiting for them. He ordered the women and children into the Salon; stationed 40 men with rifles at various strategic spots on all three decks, positions readily visible from shore.

"Where is Sam Wood?" they shouted as soon as the Polar Star touched the wharf.

"Right here," Sam announced at the head of the gangway, blocking entry to the boat. "What do you want?"

"We want the Sharp's Rifles you're carrying."

"We have no Sharp's Rifles; I don't know where that idea came from. However, we are well armed. Gentlemen," he shouted, "Show these men your rifles, show them that they are U.S. Rifles and not Sharp's."

The roughs were obviously uncomfortable with the arsenal of weapons pointed at them. Many simply turned and left. Those who remained were not nearly as boastful as when they arrived.

Captain Wiley continued docking the boat, securing the lines while Sam stood blocking the gangway. He shouted at the men remaining, "You bring me the Sharp's you stole last week, you can't use them anyway, can you? We sent the slides by freight and they're in Topeka. I'll buy back the stolen rifles but, of course, pennies on the dollar since they're useless now."

After much posturing on both sides, the Ruffians finally scattered. The Polar Star continued upriver without further incident. At the wharf in Kansas City, they were met by a large contingent of Lawrence and Topeka citizens with wagons ready to transport the settlers to their new claims. The Polar Star was the last boatload of abolitionists that made it upriver that Spring of 1856. The Ruffians were successful in blockading the River from further travel and all future Kansas settlers were forced to go north through Iowa and Nebraska to reach the Territory.

***

Sam arrived in Lawrence to a hero's welcome, a joyful reunion with his wife, family and friends. Margaret was overjoyed at seeing Beulah but most pleased were David and Punch who remembered her well from the earliest memories of their childhood. The festive mood was short lived as the harsh realities of life on the Kansas Frontier and the unchanging attitude of the pro-slavery Territorial Legislation destroyed the elation of a successful tour in the East.

Charlie Robinson was arrested and being held without bail, as were Wakefield and Brooks. James Lane escaped to the East and Tappan was hiding as best he could. Sam's life was in eminent danger and Sheriff Jones knew he was in town.

The abolitionists of Lawrence did not consider themselves anarchists, they all believed in Government, but only a just Government. No one advocated the overthrow of the Territorial Legislation, but they did insist that the Governor and Legislators listen to them and conduct fair and honest voting.

The situation he found himself in at that moment in history was a result of events that occurred randomly from the day he announced that he was going to Kansas Territory. Each incident happened in succession, from the murder of Felix Francis to the rescue of Jacob Branson and everything in between. These facts were not lost on the citizens of the rest of the Union who followed the events in Kansas religiously and took sides fervently. In May of 1856 the situation looked hopeless for the abolitionists many of whom were under indictment, including all of the city founders in Lawrence. Governor Shannon had turned nasty after the Peace Treaty in Lawrence. He wanted to show President Pierce that he was still firmly pro-slavery, in fact, he went to the opposite extreme and declared that anyone associated with the rescue of Branson and the resisting of Sheriff Jones would be imprisoned without bail. Northern citizens could not believe that rules of common law had been suspended in the Territory, in favor of retribution and revenge.

Sam was branded a criminal of the worst kind. But he didn't care.

During the last part of April, he received word from Washington that Senator Lewis Cass of Michigan had presented the Topeka Constitution to the Senate for consideration on the 24th of March. It was referred to the proper committee. On April seven it was presented to the House of Representatives by Daniel Mace of Indiana.

General Stringfellow, of the Leavenworth Herald, 1856: "We [pro-slavery forces] are determined to repel this Northern invasion, and make Kansas a Slave State; though our rivers should be covered with the blood of their victims, and the carcasses of the Abolitionists should be so numerous in the territory as to breed disease and sickness, we will not be deterred from our purpose"

April 1856

HIGH TREASON

Judge LeCompte's Territorial Grand Jury returned indictments of treason against all the leaders of the Lawrence 'rebellion', with additional charges against Sam Wood of resisting arrest, contempt of court and armed insurrection against duly authorized law enforcement officers. All of those charges detailed in a warrant delivered to the Wood home by Bogus Sheriff Jones prior to Sam's return. Margaret was horrified, incredulous, but most of all mad. Enraged at the very thought of this evil man, Jones, murderer of her friends, denier of citizens the right to vote; that he should threaten her husband with a jail cell. Everyone knew that capture by Jones was a death sentence for Sam. He would never reach the cell alive. She gazed at the document without speaking. Jones stood his ground as if expecting her to produce the criminal before he would leave. She looked at Jones, lips quivering, eyes back to the paper, "Treason," she spat the word as if it were an expletive. "You want to arrest Sam for treason," not a question but a statement, clarifying in her own mind the abhorrence of the thought.

"You... You evil man. You murdered my friends, Mr. Dow, Mr. Francis, Mr. Barber, murdered by you..."

"I never murdered nobody."

"Have you arrested Coleman? George Clark? Where is the warrant for their arrest? Sam Wood is the finest man that ever walked this earth, save one. You'll never arrest him as long as I've got breath in my body. Get off my property."

Jones stood fast. John T, as luck would have it, crouched in the kitchen repairing a hinge on the sideboard hutch that held Margaret's flatware. Curiosity got the best of him when Margaret's voice amplified as the conversation progressed. He stepped to the door, Jones took a step back, "What's the problem here?"

Margaret balled the warrant in her fist, threw it at Jones; he backed away and left. John picked up the paper, smoothed and read it then watched Jones disappear down the street.

****

The exhilaration of returning home from the east coast quickly turned sour with the charges hanging over his head, constant harassment by the bogus law officials and refusal of Governor Shannon or Judge LeCompte to meet with him to discuss the matter. Gone was Shannon's toleration of the citizens of Lawrence, replaced by a condemnation that bordered on hatred. Obviously, President Pierce got to Shannon and LeCompte, ordered them to toe the line or else. Word from William was that Pierce told Shannon to clear out Yankee Town or he, meaning Shannon, would be the next to face the rope. Jones posted spies around Sam's home and the homes of his friends. Sam was still a young man, only 31 years old, strong as an ox, but even he couldn't stand the constant pressure of eluding the bogus sheriff.

Sam and Margaret were finally able to share a quiet moment in their home during the evening of April 16, free from the worry of Jones and his men who were at a pro-slavery meeting in Atchison. A Federal Marshall by the name of Donaldson, sent by President Pierce, entered the hunt for the 'Lawrence Rebels'. Donaldson was being briefed by Senator Atchison, Governor Shannon and Sheriff Jones.

The weather turned mild, a beautiful spring day. Margaret had the windows open; she and Sam snuggled on the lounge in the upstairs of their home on Massachusetts Avenue. Intimate moments together had been few for the young lovers trapped in a battle they had anticipated but underestimated.

"It was difficult when you were gone but, in some ways, it was easier because we knew you were safe." Margaret cuddled into his arms.

He twined his fingers in her hair, rested his check against her head, "Maybe we should move to Council Grove or Cottonwood Falls. We wouldn't have to worry so much about Jones over there."

"We can't run away, Sam."

The door opened downstairs. "We're home Mom," David shouted.

"Next trip you and the boys are going with me, no more long separations."

That Friday Sam scheduled a meeting at the new law office of James Christianson on Vermont Street behind the Free State Hotel. The two attorneys were preparing documents for a transfer of city lots Sam had an ownership interest in. Christianson was a young lawyer recently arrived from Illinois with his wife and family.

Sitting in James's office after the usual greetings, Sam shared some of the details of the recent speaking tour in the east. Christianson reclined comfortably behind his desk, Sam in a straight-backed chair, his back to the door. Sheriff Jones burst in, put his hand on Sam's shoulder, "Wood, I've finally got you, you're under arrest, now come along peaceful."

Sam stood quickly, twisted to face him, surprised but unconcerned, "Well, hello Bogus. Didn't expect to see you today."

"You're under arrest. I'm taking you to Lecompton, right now."

"I don't think so, I doubt that Mrs. Wood would allow it. We can send over to the house and ask her, but I feel strongly that she will say no."

He turned away, went outside where several Lawrence citizens had gathered. Jones followed, "You think you're above the law, you bastard, but you aren't. You've caused more trouble in this Territory than anyone. I have a warrant for your arrest."

"Let me see the warrant," Sam frowned. "If it's legitimate, I'll consider turning myself in to Judge LeCompte. Otherwise, leave me alone. I'm getting mighty tired of you." He turned again to walk away. More Lawrence citizens had gathered. The street was full of buggies, horses, shopkeepers and neighbors.

Jones became incensed, "I left a copy at your house. Now come with me, Wood, the Grand Jury has found you guilty of crimes against the State..."

"Kansas isn't a State, this is a Territory and we..." Sam pointed at the gathering crowd, "...we have not yet established the laws. You say you're the sheriff, fine, take me to see your prisoners, Frank Coleman and George Clark. Both of them cold blooded murderers. If you have them in jail, I'll consent to your warrant."

The crowd was closing around the two men, growing hostile beginning to murmur, a low threatening hum. "Those men acted in self-defense," he glanced at the crowd.

Bill Speer interjected himself between the two, "Are you the judge and jury as well as the sheriff? Where was the trial you lying bag of wind?"

Jones pushed Speer aside, grabbed Sam by the collar, at the same time reached for his pistol. Sam beat him to it, snatched the gun away, handed it behind his back to someone who promptly disappeared, gun and all. Jones was incensed, took a swing at Sam who merely pushed him back, tapped him in the stomach knocking the wind out of him. Bill Speer and Christianson intervened, sending Sam on to his house then put Jones on his horse.

The sheriff returned on Sunday, charged Sam with an additional count of theft of a weapon; he tried to enlist passing townsmen to help him locate the arch criminal. The worshipers, who were on their way to church with their families, naturally refused making Jones even madder. He left Lawrence and went straight to Lecompton where he told Governor Shannon that the town of Lawrence was in open rebellion again; demanded warrants against the citizens who refused to help him. They were charged with contempt of court. It would have been funny, in a New York play, but in real life it was deadly serious, someone else was going to get killed. The people of Yankee Town continued the practice of tolerating Jones but refused to help him in any way.

***

John Brown was a problem of a different kind. Sam liked John personally and valued his friendship, but he worried constantly that Brown would do something rash and bring serious consequences to the Territory. The Federal troops were there under the command of the President and they would not be sympathetic in the case of Brown instigating violence regardless of the provocation.

Sam met with Brown on April 29 at the office of the Herald Tribune. Brown again registered his anger at the Lawrence abolitionists for their failure to attack the Missouri invaders, "Sam, I respect what you've done for the cause, I told you that, but we've got to convince Robinson and Lane that words will not carry the day. It'll take action and we have the weapons and the manpower to do so. This attitude of sitting and doing nothing while Jones and Shannon run roughshod over us has to end."

"I think, John, that Charlie is concerned the soldiers from Ft. Leavenworth will come down hard against us if we resort to violence. I can see his point, but I agree that we can do more in the way of resistance. My problem is that I can't let Jones take me into custody..."

Brown interrupted, "I agree with you, he'd shoot you down like a mad dog as soon as you were out of sight of Lawrence. He doesn't bother me much because he knows that I or one of my boys will shoot him on the spot if he tries anything with us. Maybe you should use that approach and he'll leave you alone."

"Believe me, John, that's my first inclination, but I'm trying to placate Charlie just like you say. It isn't working very well right now. Charlie and Wake are in jail, I'm constantly on the run. I may end up shooting the man after all."

***

Lecompton, April 20, 1856.
Major I. B. Donaldson;

My Dear Sir, — Samuel N. Wood is now in Lawrence, and I wish you to send me the writ against him. I arrested him yesterday and he was rescued from my hand by a mob.

The governor has called upon Col. Sumner for a company to assist me in the execution of the laws. I will have writs gotten out against Tappan and some twenty others.

In haste, your obedient servant,

S. J. Jones.

John T found Sam in the barn reading a newspaper account of an old speech by Fred Douglass. He often found solitude in the tack room where a comfortable chair, lamp and table had been placed for when he needed to be alone.

"I just heard from William over in Lecompton," John said, pulling up a stool, "Shannon authorized Jones to use Ft. Leavenworth soldiers to execute the warrants against those men who refused to help find you on Sunday. He's on his way with a posse, not sure of the exact number."

Sam nodded, "Listen to this, John, it's from a speech called 'The Church and Prejudice' Fred Douglass gave at the Plymouth Church Anti-Slavery Society some years back:"

"Another young (white) lady fell into a trance. When she awoke, she declared she had been to heaven. Her friends were all anxious to know what and whom she had seen there; so she told the whole story. But there was one good old lady whose curiosity went beyond that of all the others—and she inquired of the girl that had the vision, if she saw any black folks in heaven? After some hesitation, the reply was, "Oh! I didn't go into the kitchen!"

Sam laughed until tears rolled down his face, "Fred has a way with words, doesn't he John T?"

"Sam, did you hear what I said? Jones is on his way with a posse to arrest you. Best get out of town."

"I think I'll go over to Paul's house and watch from the attic window; I'm getting tired of running from Bogus. John Brown says I should just shoot him, anyway."

John T didn't find that to be funny.

Jones arrived about 2 PM with Lt. McIntosh and six regular soldiers who'd been deputized by the Territorial Government. They formed a line around Sam's house and Jones proceeded to the front porch where he was met by

Beulah. Sam couldn't hear what was said but he could just imagine when she crossed her ample arms and denied him entry.

"What are you laughing at, Sam?" Elvira asked as she bustled around doing her household chores while Sam sat in an alcove watching the proceedings.

"Beulah's giving him the business, come look."

Jones waved his arms, pointed at the soldiers, but Beulah didn't budge, in fact, took a step forward causing the sheriff to back up a step. Several citizens gathered around. Jones gestured wildly urging the soldiers to do something. They seemed to be laughing at him. Beulah took another step forward, Jones another back. That dance lasted a couple more steps until he stumbled backward off the porch and fell to the ground.

Beulah went back inside. Jones and the soldiers set up a tent south of the Free State Hotel and used it as a stockade for the heinous criminals who had failed to help in the search for Sam Wood. Sam strolled back to his house and sat down to supper with the family.

About 6:45, just before full sunset, with deepening shadows on the east sides of the buildings, as they ate their boiled beef and sweet potatoes, shots rang out in the street. They all scuttled under the table, including the hefty Beulah, thinking the shots were being fired at them. Finally, Sam crawled to the door, chanced a look outside where a crowd gathered at the hotel; he grabbed his pistol and cane, left to find out what happened. David and Punch followed, joined several of their friends trying to determine what the excitement was about. Paul Brooks spied Sam and hurried toward him as he crossed the street, "Sam, better stay hidden, someone shot Jones."

"What? Who shot him, is he dead?"

"Not sure, Stringfellow and Pomeroy are in there with him, so is Reeder, but the rumor is that you shot him."

"Me," Sam said incredulously, "If I shot him, there'd be no question if he was dead."

"That young guy, Lenhart, did it," Tappan answered, "he just rode out of town and told me what he'd done. He shot Jones with his own gun, the one you took from him last Wednesday."

"I don't know who that is," Sam said, "How did he get the gun?"

"I guess he was the one you handed it to; his name is Charley Lenhart, he came to work for the Herald of Freedom, he's a printer," Tap looked in the window, "he moved here while you were in Ohio."

"Well, he needs to come back and face the music or everyone will blame Sam for it," Paul said.

"They'll blame Sam no matter what," John T replied joining the crowd.

A military ambulance came rolling up, a soldier at the reins, the door to the hotel burst open; a stretcher carried by four soldiers emerged with Jones under a blanket, his eyes creased in pain. They put him in the back of the conveyance. General Stringfellow and Clarke Pomeroy climbed in with him; Ex-Governor Reeder came along leading his horse, "He's alive," he announced to the crowd. Then to Sam he warned, "The President sent a new Marshal. His name's Donaldson and he's bringing in a special deputy to serve the warrants against you, name of Salter. He may be worse than Jones."

***

Reeder's words were prophetic. Salter, a North Carolina pro-slavery fanatic had gained the confidence of the satanic faction. He was put in charge of a platoon of

United States Dragoon's, who, truth revealed, did not like their commanding officer at all. Salter was uncompromising; cruel to innocent and guilty alike. He terrorized any citizen of the territory that he considered to be anti-slavery, for whatever reason, whether abolitionist or free-soil; even the small-scale farmers who were neutral. He considered himself judge and jury. 'If you aren't for slavery you are my enemy', was his motto. Salters was assigned two tasks; first, bring slavery to Kansas Territory. Second, bring Sam Wood to justice for his crimes against 'the State'.

Sam was hounded day and night for a week; it was only the speed and endurance of Border Ruffian that kept him from the clutches of the relentless deputy; that and the sometimes sabotage of the Dragoons who were more on Sam's side than Salters.

Sam eluded the posse long enough to slip into the Free State Hotel and give testimony in front of the US congressional committee charged with determining the legality of the various votes and governments in Kansas Territory. The three-man committee, appointed by the United States Congress, was accompanied by four clerks, a reporter, and three sergeants-at-arms. They introduced themselves as John Sherman of Ohio, who Sam already knew, William A. Howard of Michigan and Mordecai Oliver of Missouri.

"Mr. Wood," Howard began, "We appreciate you meeting with us, your name has come up frequently in these proceedings and according to my notes, you are either the devil incarnates or the savior of Kansas Territory, which is it, sir?"

"Mr. Howard, I came to the Territory with one purpose in mind, to make Kansas a free-state. I will spare no effort in making that happen. If I felt that I could work within the framework of President Pierce's appointed pro-slavery administration, I would. But sir, that is impossible. They disregard our advice and invalidate our votes; they illegally imprison us without due process of law. Governor Robinson and Judge Wakefield are in jail at this moment. General Lane in exile and I would be in prison or dead, but they can't catch me. My only recourse is to oppose them with whatever means I can, short of violence, but rest assured, if it comes to that I will not temper my actions."

Sam spoke for 60 minutes describing voting irregularities, the Wakarusa War, the two-faced behavior of Governor Shannon, the treachery of Senator David Atchison. Mordecai Oliver was obviously pro-slavery and berated Sam for his anti-government activities.

"These warrants and indictments are legitimate actions by the United States Government," Oliver said, "how do you justify ignoring lawful orders being carried out by appointed officers?"

"I answer to the laws of God and not the bogus laws of man," Sam replied, "you and Atchison are cut from the same cloth."

"I hope you realize that I take that as a compliment," Oliver replied. "You demonize David Atchison, a fine United States Senator and glorify the Niggers, who are nothing but ignorant animals, below even the Indians, nothing more than property..."

The door to the meeting room hurled open; David Wood charged in, "Papa, they're coming up the road, I've got Ruffian at the back door. Go now."

Sam was out the door before the committee could respond, into the saddle and away. He rode in circles until he lost the posse, crept back to Charlie Robinson's house, where   Sara   received   him   with   graciousness, understanding the danger he was in. Her husband was still in custody in Lecompton.

"I'm going to send for Margaret, you have a fever, and you look terrible Sam. You're not benefiting anyone staying in Lawrence."

He sank quietly into a padded living room chair to wait for his wife.

"I guess I'll go north to Iowa and avoid the border for now," Sam sighed accepting a cup of water.

"I think Clarke Pomeroy is going to Iowa City to give a speech next week. You could join him."

"If I feel up to it I will."

Margaret arrived with clean clothes and a warm embrace. Sam thought to ask, "Is Major Abbott going as well?"

Margaret and Sara glanced at each other, "What's the matter with Abbot?"

Sara answered, "Evidently he's upset that you took all the credit for rescuing Jacob. The newspapers made it sound like you rescued him singlehanded."

"You've got to be kidding, I give Abbot credit every time I talk about it."

"He's in Osawatomie visiting with John Brown and Reverend Adair, when he gets back you should discuss it with him."

They had a good meal; Sam left through the back door. The soldiers were watching the streets and his home. He avoided Lecompton, riding south and west to a friend's home near Topeka, spent the night there, then crossed the river on the Topeka Ferry, rode north through the persistent cold rain.

Sam was as low in spirit and body as he could ever remember. His poor family watched day and night; John T and Sally's home under surveillance; the Territory about to become overrun with slaveholders and their slaves; the government in the hands of the pro-slavery party; and Charlie and Judge Wakefield in jail. The same fate, or worse, awaited him if Salter caught him. He almost missed his old adversary, bogus Sheriff Jones. At least, he knew what he was dealing with.

The rain increased to a torrent; the small streams became flooded. Crossing the Delaware River above Valley Falls about dusk that evening, he misjudged the danger and the current swept Border Ruffian off the sure footing of the crossing; they went under for a few frantic seconds until Ruff found traction, wallowed up the bank with Sam holding his tail. He sat, more dead than alive, then sprawled back on the bank too exhausted to move. Ruff nudged him, caressed his face until he managed to sit up, "Ok old friend, I won't let you down by dying on the bank of this river. I won't give the bastards the satisfaction. Don't tell Margaret I said that." He climbed into the saddle, clung to Ruffian's mane, thought of Margaret and the kids at home. They didn't know where he was, if dead or alive. He gave Ruff his head relying on him to follow the trail. Images of the boys, of Sarah, Margaret, John T, his in-laws, all come to Kansas because of him. Now they were all in danger, Sam drifting half-lost, half-drowned through the prairie.

They traveled on, crossed the Missouri at Iowa Point, stopped at the hotel in Oregon, Missouri where Sam, in his delirium, registered under his own name, S. N. Wood. He immediately regretted the mistake when in the lobby he spotted a St. Louis newspaper with news of the assassination of Sheriff Jones, Sam's name in large type as the murderer.

'Abolitionist Samuel N. Wood Murders Douglas County Sheriff', the headline screamed out at him, seemed to point at him, 'here's the murderer in this very lobby'.

Sam didn't even know Jones had died. He dropped into a hard-back chair in the dining room, scrutinized the crowd in stark fear of being recognized. He read the article twice glancing up after every sentence. The description of the event was accurate except the part naming him as the murderer.

He didn't recognize the names of the witnesses described as having seen *'the despicable abolitionist, Samuel N. Wood, fired three shots into the back of the sheriff. Wood was known to have threatened the sheriff earlier in the week when arrested outside his lawyer's office in Lawrence. Wood attacked the sheriff, stole his service weapon, then struck him with a club. The murderer's whereabouts are unknown at this time.'*

Disregarding fever and achy body, he remounted Border Ruffian, crossed the river back into Kansas to the village of Highland where he found the home of a friend, Martin Olguin, who offered him shelter and a bed. Olguin sent a letter by trusted messenger to Margaret letting her know the situation. Sam lay abed, in a bad way, sick with fever, fearing that he was being blamed for Jones' death; that the Territory was in worse hands than ever, and the southerner Salter looking high and low for him.

***

MAJORITY REPORT OF THE UNITED STATES CONGRESSIONAL INVESTIGATION:

Your committee report the following facts and conclusions as established by the testimony:

First - That each election in the Territory, held under the organic or alleged Territorial law, has been carried by organized invasion from the State of Missouri, by which the people of the Territory have been prevented from exercising the right secured to them by the organic law.

Second - That the alleged Territorial legislature was an illegally constituted body, and had no power to pass valid laws, and their enactments are therefore null and void.

Third - That those alleged laws have not, as a general thing, been used to protect persons and property, and to punish wrong, but for unlawful purposes.

Fourth - That the election under which the sitting Delegate, John W. Whitfield, holds his seat, was not held in pursuance of any valid law, and that it should only be regarded as the expression of the choice of those residents who voted for him.

Fifth - That the election under which the contesting Delegate, Andrew H. Reeder, claims his seat, was not held in pursuance of law, and that it should he regarded only as the expression of the resident citizens who voted for him.

Sixth - That Andrew H. Reeder received a greater number of votes of resident citizens than John W. Whitfield for Delegate.

Seventh - That in the present condition of the Territory a fair election cannot he held without a new census, a stringent and well-guarded election law, the selection of impartial Judges, and the presence of United States troops at every place of election.

Eighth - That the various elections held by the people of the Territory preliminary to the formation of the State Government, have been as regular as the disturbed condition of the Territory would allow; and that the constitution passed by the convention, held in pursuance of said elections, embodies the will of a majority of the people.

As it is not the province of your committee to suggest remedies for the existing troubles in the Territory of Kansas, they content themselves with the foregoing statement of facts.

All of which is respectfully submitted.

WM. A. HOWARD, JOHN SHERMAN

The Congressional Committee report created a crisis in the administration of President Pierce causing more damage to his re-election campaign than any other issue. Pierce had won election in 1853 guaranteeing that Kansas would be a slave state and Nebraska a free-state, thereby maintaining a delicate balance between the northern free-states and southern slave states.

He was furious with the testimony, which circulated far and wide, drowning out the feeble words of Mordecai Oliver's poorly written Minority Report; an obvious attempt to whitewash the truth. Pierce denounced the report, then labeled the Topeka Constitution invalid, and ordered the US Army to prevent the Free State Legislation from convening.

***

Sam began to recover on the third day of his confinement under the quality nursing of Mrs. Olguin. Margaret and the children arrived in a wagon driven by John T.

"You look like a drowned rat," John said.

"I kind of feel that way, my friend, thanks for bringing the family. Are you going on with us to Iowa?"

"No, I'll ride Ruff back to Lawrence, help Beulah and Silas guard the houses. The rumor is that Bogus Jones is going to burn Lawrence to the ground, again. Judge LeCompte and the Legislature classified the Hotel as a Fort so they're going to blow it up...."

Sam listened with a growing sense of confusion, "Wait, John T, what do you mean Jones is going to attack Lawrence, I thought he was dead?"

"Dead?" John frowned, "He's not dead, what made you think that?"

"I read a newspaper at the hotel in Missouri, it said the sheriff was dead and that I killed him. I know I had a fever, but I guarantee that's what it said. In fact, when I got here, I told Martin, first thing out of my mouth, I didn't kill Jones."

Martin laughed, "We heard you Sam, but thought you were delirious because we didn't have any idea what you were talking about. We didn't even know Jones had been shot."

Margaret brought a copy of the Independence Democrat to show them, "The border newspapers reported that Jones was murdered just to stir up the Missourians, and it worked. They spread the story that you murdered Jones, but he's fine and recovering in Lecompton. I'm scared to death they'll attack Lawrence, so I brought the kids and we're getting out of town for a few months. We can go to Iowa City first, but we're going back to Ohio after. I wrote a letter to Mr. Pomeroy and he's expecting us by Monday, so we need to get started, Stephan is going to meet us there and travel back to Ohio with us."

Sam was glad to leave the details to his lovely wife.

***

The Olguin's gave specific instructions and a map showing the best route to Iowa City where they had a son and daughter-in-law. The Woods set out in glorious sunshine, pleasant weather for easy traveling on the hills, but wallowing in mud in the bottom lands. The day was so enjoyable that they didn't mind the slow pace plodding through the meadows and dodging the mud holes, walking beside the wagon for the most part. Caleb and Missy joined David and Punch for the trip, partly to get them out of Lawrence in case of trouble and partly to visit family in Ohio. John and Sally preferred to stay and guard their belongings; surprisingly, the Border Ruffians didn't bother the free black community as much as they did the white abolitionists.

Margaret drove the first day while Sam rested in the back. David took the reins occasionally giving Margaret a break; by noon Sam was feeling well enough to drive, crossed the Missouri at Iowa Point then followed the

Nodaway River north. They stopped at a grove of cottonwood and elm near Burr Oak Creek, started a small cooking fire and prepared an evening meal of vegetables plus four perch the boys caught.

"Watch for snakes," Margaret called as the kids scattered to explore the new country. "It's probably too early and too cold for snakes," she said to Sam, "but you never know."

Missy limped along trying to keep up with the boys, her ankle and calf wrapped tightly. David and Caleb carried her over big obstacles as they climbed to the top of the hill above their camp. Sam was content to let Margaret take care of the cooking, a pleasure he seldom enjoyed traveling alone as he normally did. She came well prepared with food, a cask of water and bedding for the night. Sam usually slept on the ground, ate hard tack or dried fruit if anything. He planned to shoot a rabbit or antelope if they crossed paths with one the next day.

The evening turned chilly as the sun went down. They crowded around the fire drinking coffee, sharing the vegetable stew simmering in a pan on a flat rock; it was a moment of great contentment for Sam and Margaret, a glimpse of what their lives could have been had they not taken up the great fight against slavery; the innocence of children, carefree talk of their journey, how far they needed to go and how they would cross the stream and how beautiful the night sky was.

"Look Papa," Punch exclaimed, "a shooting star." They watched in awe as the light streaked across the northern sky and flamed out high above them.

Margaret said, "David, do you need to tell your father something?"

He took a deep breath, gave his mom a scowl that said, 'why can't we forget it?'.

"I got in a fight with Jimmy Pratt."

"Who won?" Sam replied.

"Sam, that's not the point. David, tell what it was about."

"Well, Jimmy says his Dad is in jail and it's your fault for rescuing Mr. Branson; plus you shot bogus Jones but you're trying to blame it on someone else. I told him that I was with you when we heard the shots so you couldn't have done it. Then he said I was a liar; so I hit him in the nose."

Sam watched Margaret, more concerned about her reaction than the quarrel of two young boys. She and Mrs. Pratt were good friends, as were Sam and Caleb, the indiscretions of youth would fade while the disputes of adults could turn into bitterness if left to fester. Margaret waited for Sam's reply which he carefully crafted, "Son, I thank you for taking up for me in my absence. I'm sorry that you had a fight with your best friend over something so unfortunate. Did he go tell his mother what happened?"

"I don't know, we left to come here before I saw him again."

"I didn't find out about it until we were halfway to Highland," Margaret answered.

"When you get back, I'll bet Jimmy will be happy to see you."

The fire crackled with a new branch added, sparks flew like tiny fireflies around the campsite. The horses were hobbled close to grass and water. The children gave each animal a handful of oats and a kind word as they all prepared to climb into the back of the wagon. Sam fell asleep instantly while Margaret visited with the children, answered their questions about what might lay ahead; a journey made even more frightful in their minds as they gazed into the eerie silence of the Iowa prairie. She was far more concerned about the fate of Kansas Territory; thoughts that she didn't share but were more frightening than the demons children imagine staring at them from the darkness.

"Not in any common lust for power did this uncommon tragedy have its origin. It is the rape of a virgin Territory, compelling it to the hateful embrace of slavery; and it may be clearly traced to a depraved desire for a new Slave State, hideous offspring of such a crime, in the hope of adding to the power of slavery in the National Government."

Massachusetts Senator **CHARLES SUMNER,** *Abolitionist Republican, in his 'Crimes Against Kansas' speech in the United States Senate, May 20, 1856.*

Iowa, the most progressive of the northern states, declared by law that any slave setting foot on Iowa soil was a freeman and removed barriers to inter-racial marriages as early as 1851. The new state capital building sat prominently on a bluff above the Iowa River visible from all vantage points entering Iowa City. Sam knew a good many of the State Legislators, foremost among them Samuel Kirkwood.

"Do you know how to get to Kirk's house," Sam asked Margaret.

"Jane's letter said they live west of town near Coralville; she said to ask anyone along the turnpike, they would know where the mill is."

Jane and Samuel Kirkwood provided a warm bed and meals for the Wood family while in Iowa City. 'Kirk' was a driving force for the Iowa Republican Party joining Sam in Philadelphia for the convention later in the year. The Kirkwood home, near their flour mill on Mill Pond, was a well-known landmark for the industrious and influential family.

Pomeroy and Gaius Jenkins met with them the evening before the presentation.

"Sam, let me begin by saying that we, in the Territory, are deeply indebted to you for all you've done for our cause," Pomeroy said, as an introduction.

"But you have some concern's, I take it, Clarke," Sam said smiling.

"Not necessarily concerns," Jenkins added. "More a discussion of strategy."

"Exactly," Pomeroy continued, "What if, instead of fighting the government, we work within their framework to make Kansas a free-state? We have enough voters that we can win at the polls, if the elections exclude the Missourians."

"The Congressional Report helps the Free State cause immensely," Kirkwood interjected, "they made it clear that the '54' and '55' elections were all fraudulent. It looks to me like you have the legitimate votes you need right now."

"I've already discussed that strategy with Andy Reeder. We're all in agreement about it. I think what you are getting at is resentment about my speaking tour last month," he preempted what he felt was the true agenda of the meeting. Pomeroy was noticeably uncomfortable at this sudden change in the conversation.

Jenkins extended his hand, halted Pomeroy from commenting, "You've done more for the cause than anyone, but sometimes you need to think about how your words impacts others, there are hundreds of men working to make Kansas free."

Sam leaned forward, spoke slowly making certain to prevent interruptions, "Gentlemen, you know me well enough that I don't care about the credit. But sometimes the message is beyond my ability to clarify. I deny something, that causes them to believe it even more. The words of others are creating this myth of who Sam Wood is. If you have a solution for that, I'll gladly listen. I just want to end slavery, no ulterior goal, no seeking higher office, no expectations of riches. I assure you, and the newspaper records will confirm what I say; I gave Major Abbott the credit for leading the rescue of Jacob Branson. I assume he is the one we are talking about."

Silence greeted the end of Sam's dialogue. The uncomfortable pause gave Kirk a chance to clear the air, "I was at the Republican planning meeting with Sam last February in Pittsburgh. He gave a magnificent speech, the star of the show, all the paper's agreed; he stated the situation accurately, gave Abbott credit, gave Jim Lane and Charlie Robinson credit, even your name was mentioned Clarke. This is an unfortunate topic that needs to be put to rest. Let history sort all that out. We have work to do, lets plan the agenda for tomorrow. Enough said on the matter."

They talked late into the evening; traveled together the next morning to the Capital Building where the Iowa Joint Session of Congress cheered every bit as loud as the audiences in Chicago and Baltimore. They asked pertinent questions, made excellent suggestions, offered to send election judges to help monitor the coming referendum.

Margaret had to stifle a laugh, as she sat in the audience gallery, when Gaius Jenkins described Sam's encounter with the Border Ruffians after delivering Babcock and Lowery to Lecompton. He used Tap's description, almost word for word only he inflated the number to five thugs; Sam disarmed them all with a couple of swings of his club; the audience cheered, gave him a standing ovation. He glanced up at Margaret, "My hero," she mouthed sarcastically, hands clasped to her heart.

The presentation complete, proclamations made and promises to stay in touch guaranteed, the Wood family took leave, selling the wagon and team to a local farmer.

They boarded a train heading east with the first stop Chicago. From the moment they climbed the steps into the cars, the children were wide-eyed with wonderment; their first ride on the railway. The steam engine began chugging, wheels screeched trying to gain traction, couplings clanged; the cars lurched forward, jerked slowly to a start, then began picking up speed. Trees and farmhouses rushed by, noise from the wind, roar of the engine, the steam whistle shrieking. The children with noses and palms pressed to the window stared astonished at the new world flashing past; never would they forget it.

"The senator from South Carolina has read many books of chivalry and believes himself a chivalrous knight with sentiments of honor and courage. Of course, he has chosen a mistress to whom he has made his vows, and who, though ugly to others, is always lovely to him; though polluted in the sight of the world, is chaste in his sight -- I mean the harlot, slavery. For her, his tongue is always profuse in words. Let her be impeached in character, or any proposition made to shut her out from the extension of her wantonness, and no extravagance of manner or hardihood of assertion is then too great for this senator."

Massachusetts Senator CHARLES SUMNER, an Abolitionist Republican, in his 'Crimes Against Kansas' speech in the United States Senate, May 20, 1856, Vilifying South Carolina Senator Andrew Butler.

They arrived in Columbus on May 1, 1856 to a homecoming fit for Royalty. Margaret hadn't seen Sam's family in three years, Esther, Toby, brothers and sisters, nieces and nephews, his old law partner, Robert Brumbaugh; family and friends, all together for what may be the last time, at least in Ohio. Stephan and his wife rode the train with them from Iowa City. It was like old times.

The next day Sam met with former Territorial Governor Andy Reeder and Ohio Governor Salmon Chase in the State Capitol building on 3rd street near Sam's old office. The State Capital was bustling with legislators, secretaries and Ohio constituents waiting an opportunity to meet with the Governor, all congregating in the anteroom and hallways. Reeder and Sam were ushered into a small meeting room to wait.

"The last time I saw you was outside the Free State Hotel," Reeder produced a cigar, offered one to Sam, he politely declined, "I thought you'd shot that asshole, Jones," said with a self-depreciating smile, blowing smoke toward the open window. Since being run out of Kansas as its first Territorial Governor, he had become a staunch abolitionist.

"Andy, you know me well enough to know I would never shoot from ambush. I was as surprised as everyone else. What happened that night anyway?"

"Long story short, Jones thought the shooter was a cuckolded husband of some woman he'd been seeing over in Lecompton. He never did think it was you, that story was put out there by Atchison and General Stringfellow to stir up the Border Ruffians. His wounds weren't severe; I hear he's back serving counterfeit warrants and stirring up the Ruffians again, even planning to burn down Lawrence."

"That's what John Thompson told me."

"Thompson always seems to know what's going on in the Territory before anyone else," Reeder said pensively. Sam did not mention the source, even to Reeder.

Andy continued, "Your tour of the east produced more benefit for the territory than anything you could have done at home. The fact you made Atchison so mad proves that."

Governor Chase came in with his personal secretary, shook hands as cups of coffee were procured and pleasantries exchanged. Chase was a bulky man with a high forehead and bushy brows bordering eyes that took in everything, a mischievous grin harbored a wonderful sense of humor in addition to a prodigious intellect.

"Look at this, Sammy," Chase handed Sam a letter on Kansas Territory letterhead from Governor Shannon stating that Sam Wood was known to be in Ohio and requesting Governor Chase to, "apprehend and extradite the aforementioned, Samuel Newitt Wood, to the Kansas

Territorial prison in Lecompton, K.T. He is under criminal indictment for High Treason against the United States; assault of a law officer, contempt of court, theft of government property, etc. etc." going on to say that he should be transported in chains under guard and that all costs of said extradition would be paid by the United States Government.

"You are a nefarious criminal, Sam, I never would have guessed it knowing you all these years. It doesn't look like Shannon realizes that we're family. I'll send him a nice letter politely declining, since you're not wanted for anything here, as far as I know. Except maybe setting those slaves free a couple of years ago. There are still some unhappy slaveholders running around cussing your name."

"We've got our work cut out for us, Governor. The Territory is being overrun with drunken Missourians come to kill abolitionists. Something bad is going to happen, just not sure what it'll be," Reeder pulled the ashtray close, set his cigar on the edge, "This year's presidential election will go a long way in deciding the fate of Kansas."

"Sal, I know you've declined seeking the nomination this year, but I want to nominate you at the convention, anyway, just so we've got a head start on the 1860 election. That'll be yours for the asking, I believe," Sam edged his chair away from the smoke.

"Let me think about it, Sammy, that might be a good strategy, but we need to talk to some of the others. What do you think Andy?"

"I'd love to see you win the presidency, but the south would secede immediately and that would be that as far as civil war goes."

"What does Charlie say," Chase looked at Sam.

"He'll give you his support. We're assuming that Charlie will be the first Governor when we become a state, Andy a Senator. But that could be a while," Sam said, "meanwhile, we've got to deal with Governor Shannon and President Pierce, although I doubt he gets the nomination this year after the mess he's made in Kansas."

"Who'll be the Democratic nominee if not Pierce?" Reeder asked.

"Surely not Stephen Douglas, most likely Buchanan. But I wouldn't count Pierce out yet," Chase answered. "What are your plans, Sam? Are you going back to Kansas with everyone wanting your head on a stake?"

"I've got some speaking engagements and then the convention before I go back; Margaret and the kids are returning to Kansas in a few days. Do you know the status of our memorandum of statehood?"

"Just that it's been submitted in both the House and Senate. I wouldn't hold my breath if I were you," Chase stood with his hand outstretched. He was a busy man; the meeting was over.

"Mr. Sumner, I have read your speech twice over carefully. It is a libel on South Carolina, and Mr. Butler, who is a relative of mine,"   South Carolina Representative Preston Brooks on May 22, 1856 just before savagely beating Senator Sumner with a heavy gold-headed cane.

Sam arrived in Rochester, New York on the afternoon of the 23rd. The station was in an uproar as travelers gathered around newsboys screaming the headlines, *"Senator Sumner in Critical Condition."*

"What in the world is going on?" Sam asked a businessman who shoved a paper in his hand, "Read for yourself, friend, all hell's broke lose in Washington."

Sam read the details of Preston Brooks beating the Senator with a heavy cane on the floor of the Senate because of an anti-slavery speech that Sumner had made, in which he ridiculed Brook's cousin, Senator Andrew Butler of South Carolina. Yet that wasn't what made Sam's heart stop, caused him to sit in a panic on a bench in front of the depot. The secondary front-page story, the headline in slightly smaller type, read, *"Lawrence, Kansas Territory, Burned to the Ground."*

He bolted for Frederick Douglass' house, he was expected for a meeting of abolitionists but changed his mind and ran to the post office to see if any letters had been forwarded to him. Finding none, he hurried to the meeting where Douglass, Gerrit Smith, Lysender Spooner, Susan B. Anthony, James and Lucretia Mott, several businessmen and activists, both black and white gathered to discuss the coming Republican convention. They could offer Sam no other information than what was in the newspaper. The meeting was in disorder with the news from Kansas coupled with the disaster in Washington.

William Still, Chairman of the Vigilance Committee for the Pennsylvania Anti-Slavery Society pulled him aside, "Sam, let's go to the telegraph office. See if we can get any news from St. Louis or Kansas City." They spent the rest of the morning waiting in the office for clarification of the situation. Everyone was in the dark as to the details of the disaster on the Kansas Frontier. They made small talk as best they could. Sam frantic with worry about his family, Still doing the best he could to keep his mind occupied.

"Sam, did you know that I'm writing a book about finding my long-lost brother after 40 years of separation? He was left in the south when my mother escaped from her master. A few years ago, a gentleman came into the office in Philadelphia looking for help in finding the family he was torn from those many years ago. He had escaped his cruel master only recently. It didn't take many minutes of discussion before I realized this was my brother, a most amazing coincidence."

"I have a good friend in Kansas writing a book about the same subject, Bill. She has been working on it for several years. Maybe you two would like to share notes about what you've seen."

"I'm afraid these matters are best kept close to the vest. If the slave's owner gets wind of the deception, lives will be placed at risk."

Sam nodded absently as the telegraph keys began rattling. They both jumped up, moved to the operator's side waiting anxiously for word from the west.

"I'm sorry Mr. Wood. No one knows anything."

Sam went through the motions, but his mind was occupied by the events in Lawrence; the Free State Hotel had been destroyed, Charlie Robinson's home burned along with 'other' homes of prominent Lawrence activists. The largely deserted city had been looted and pillaged by authority of the Territorial Government and local 'militia' which Sam knew to be Jones and his Missouri Ruffians.

Where were Margaret and the children? John T and Sally?

The next train west didn't leave until the following morning. Sam turned his thoughts to the problem at hand, answered questions his fellow activists had about the situation on the frontier. This new development made him heartsick, but Sam hoped and prayed the information was exaggerated as was often the case even in the best of times. It was the purpose of newspapers to sell their product and sensational headlines motivated the readers to buy.

The caning of Sumner hit Douglass and Smith hard, they were friends of the Massachusetts Senator; a terrible precedent in a country where respectful dialogue was the order of the day. Disagree all you want but it had to be verbal not physical. The entire nation was in a tumult by Saturday as the details of the brutal attack were reported. Proponents of slavery, from the southern states, lauded Representative Brooks as a hero of the cause, even sending him new canes, of which he received hundreds, to replace the one broken over the head of Senator Sumner. The *Richmond Enquirer* published an editorial that lionized Brooks stating that the attack was, "good in conception, better in execution, and best of all in consequences."

The north vilified the attack, William Cullen Bryant of *The New York Evening Post* wrote, *"Has it come to this, that we must speak with bated breath in the presence of our Southern masters?... Are we to be chastised as they chastise their slaves? Are we too, slaves, slaves for life, a target for their brutal blows, when we do not comport ourselves to please them?"*

Sam was driven to the train the following morning by Gerrit Smith who vowed to continue providing funds to the Kansas abolitionists as he had been doing since passage of the Kansas-Nebraska Act. Sam accepted his money with many thanks and guaranteed to use it to help rebuild Lawrence, regardless of the extent of the damage.

"Sam, this is a difficult time," he said. "I want you to know that my thoughts and prayers are with you and your family in Kansas. I pray that the news isn't as bad as it sounds in the newspaper."

"Gerry, I truly appreciate your words. Margaret and I knew this was coming and I have every confidence that she and the children are safe. I promise you that I will make Kansas a Free State and bring to justice those that have caused this outrage."

"Tear down their boasted Free State Hotel, and if those Hellish lying free-soilers have left no port holes in it, with your unerring cannon make some, Yes, riddle it till it shall fall to the ground. Throw into the Kansas their printing presses, & let's see if any more free speeches will be issued from them! Boys, do the Marshall's full bidding! - Do the sheriff's entire command! for today Mr. Jones is not only Sheriff, but deputy Marshall, so that whatever he commands will be right, and under the authority of the administration of the U.S.! - and for it you will be amply paid as U.S. troops, besides having an opportunity of benefitting your wardrobes from the private dwellings of those infernal nigger-stealers. Courage for a few hours & the victory is ours, falter & all is lost! - Are you determined? Will every one of you swear to bathe your steel in the black blood of some of those black sons of bitches? Yes, I know you will, the South has always proved itself ready for honorable fight, & you, who are noble sons of noble sires, I know you will never fail, but will burn, sack & destroy, until every vestige of these Northern Abolitionists is wiped out."

Portion of a Speech by Missouri Senator David Rice Atchison promising the Border Ruffians payment for attacking Lawrence, Kansas Territory, May 21, 1856.

Columbus, Ohio

Mr. Samuel N. Wood
c/o Governor Salmon P. Chase
State House
Columbus, Ohio
May 22, 1856

My Dearest Husband,

By now you've heard of the dreadful situation here in the Territory. I know you will be terribly worried about us, but, through the Grace of God, we are safe, though shaken by what we've witnessed. David and Punch are staying with John T and Sally, though their home is crowded with the weary and destitute, many of them slaves from Missouri seeking safety from all of this craziness. The children are scared, sick with fever and hungry because the enemy has blockaded the roads, just as they did in December. We've had no food deliveries for over a week. These men claim authority from the Federal Government, but they are nothing more than a drunken rabble.

We received word that Judge LeCompte and the Douglas County Grand Jury designated the Free State Hotel a 'fort' and the newspapers public nuisances. He ordered that they be demolished. News of Atchison's army reached us early that morning. Army, nonsense, they were nothing but a mob of drunken Border Ruffians. They took over Charlies house as their headquarters and sealed all the roads, then demanded that everyone turn over their weapons.

Mrs. Robinson, Mrs. Tappan and I ventured out to watch. The streets were full of men, women and children, at least until drunks began riding up and down the streets shooting their guns, herding the children and bothering the girls. We gathered all the younger people and sheltered them in Cherry Hollow. Those brave Negro men hid them in the woods where they guarded them all night.

My heart weeps at what I witnessed. The 'army' stopped just outside of town and speeches were made by Senator Atchison, Stringfellow, the Federal Marshal Donaldson and that disgusting Sheriff Jones, he makes me shudder just to think of him. They were all heavily into their drink, vowing to destroy every home and murder anyone who tried to stop them, and, Sam, they used the vilest, coarsest language and didn't care that there were women listening. They flew a blood red flag and banners proclaiming the supremacy of the White Race and other flags from South Carolina and Georgia; the south has invaded us under the protection of the United States government. We had no one to turn to.

Mr. Eldridge met with officers of this mob and invited them to a meal at the hotel, in hopes to placate them, and they accepted, proceeded to eat the meal then raided the larder in the cellar, stealing every bit of food they could lay hands on. Jones demanded a meeting with the City representatives, knowing that Mr. Robinson, Colonel Dietzler, Judge Wakefield and Mr. Branscomb were in jail in Lecompton; General Lane, Governor Reeder and you in exile, leaving only Clarke Pomeroy to meet with him, and Sam, please don't judge Mr. Pomeroy harshly but he gave up the cannon at Jones' demand, and they used it to bombard the City.

Senator Atchison was given the honor of firing the first shot, and the drunken fool aimed the cannon too high, the ball sailed over the hotel and destroyed the Guthrie's chicken coop. It might have been funny if not so tragic. The people lining the streets cheered at the spectacle which made the invaders even angrier. The women who remained began to leave at that point melting into the woods with the children. I took the opportunity to get John T and Silas to move your papers and our furniture to their house and thank the Good Lord that they were available to help.

The mob continued firing at the hotel only to have the balls carom off the stone walls and fly through the air scattering the crowd. Then Jones tried to blow up the hotel with kegs of powder, but he just succeeded in breaking windows, including the windows in our house. Finally, he torched the hotel and laughed while it burned. Someone reported they heard him say it was the 'happiest day of his life'. The Federal Marshall then dismissed the posse, but they didn't leave, they began looting and burning houses, including ours and the Robinsons. The fire lit up the night sky; along with the gunshots and screams, it was a nightmare. Thank God no one from Lawrence was killed. Just minor injuries and frightened children. One of the drunken 'soldiers' was killed when stones from the hotel fell on him. No one slept for two days waiting to make sure the invaders were gone. Then arrangements were made to accommodate everyone whose home was burned. They left the Pomeroy's alone and that is where I've been staying.

They destroyed the printing presses at the Herald of Freedom and Kansas Free State and threw the type into the river.

They burned all the papers and the libraries, destroying all the records. They looted the shops and most of the houses taking whatever they could find. Our men just stood in the street and watched, but don't judge them badly, had they resisted, it would have been a massacre, there were 800 Border Ruffians and only about 100 of us.

Now Sam, I come to the point of my letter, please stay in the east. We love and miss you beyond my ability to put in words, but I fear greatly for your life if you return now. The attack on Lawrence has motivated our friends from all the surrounding free-state communities to reform their militias and re-arm themselves. I believe Shannon and Atchison will find themselves in turmoil throughout the Territory because of this outrage. You can do more to further our cause by encouraging fellow abolitionists to come to Kansas and take up the fight. I sign off with love from your family and friends and my undying affection and belief that we will prevail and the many plans we have made for our family will come to pass with God's blessing and guidance.

Your loving wife,
Margaret

He finished reading Margaret's letter, handed it back to Governor Chase; sat quietly staring at the floor, so full of anger that he was afraid to say anything. Finally, Salmon broke the silence, "I've taken the liberty of having Margaret's letter sent to all of the newspapers in the north. Her words will do more than anything else to bring help to the Territory."

Sam nodded, "I feel like I should leave immediately for Kansas, Sal. Should I go or take Margaret's advice and wait until after the convention?"

"Wait! They'll be watching every port; you'd have to go overland through Iowa and Nebraska. Take her at her word; go east to recruit more money and men to go to Kansas and vote it a free state; freedom and statehood will be won at the ballot box, not with Sharps' Rifles... or clubs," he added, placing a calm hand on his good friend's shoulder.

"I have only a short time to live, only one death to die, and I will die fighting for this cause. There will be no peace in this land until slavery is done for."
                    John Brown, Kansas Territory

Sam took advantage of the three weeks before the start of the convention to travel across the north visiting with delegates, financial supporters and officials in each of the free states. He was accompanied by Mr. Pennington, in constant touch with Horace Greeley at the Tribune and the major newspapers in each city he visited. Gabe was an expert at media publicity; he made certain to promote Sam's Kansas exploits to the utmost.

Letters from Lawrence kept him appraised of the situation there and his letters back home provided input into Lawrence community affairs. On June 1, he was in Chicago visiting Allan Pinkerton when devastating news arrived in an article from the Chicago newspaper. John Brown and his sons killed five Pro-Slavery men in Pottawatomi in retaliation for the Sacking of Lawrence — he made good on his promise to quit sitting on his thumbs and take the fight to the Ruffians.

"What in God's name will happen now?" Allan asked.

Sam hesitated before answering because he feared the worst, "I'm afraid this is just the beginning. The whole area is a powder keg; the US troops are incapable of keeping order. I'll write Charlie and ask what he wants me to do. I have some influence with Brown. To tell you the truth, Allan, this was inevitable. We've let the Ruffians get away with murder; now they know we will no longer be passive. I won't discourage him from what he plans, he would disregard my advice anyway,"

"What do you mean?"

"Last time we talked he wanted me to rally Charlie and Jim Lane behind attacking the Ruffians rather than placate them. I agreed with him but felt it wasn't time. I should have realized that the sacking of Lawrence and the Caning of Sumner would set him off. He knew Sumner pretty well from his time in Massachusetts."

"Sam, there's nothing you can do about it right now, your place is here working for the Republican cause. The more people you motivate to go to Kansas the quicker it'll become a Free State.

The very flag of freedom that waves over our heads is formed from material cultivated by slaves, on soil moistened with their blood drawn from them by the whip of a....taskmaster!
Elijah Parish Lovejoy

June 17, 1856
Philadelphia, Pennsylvania

The Republican Party was born in the horror of the Fugitive Slave Act and nurtured through the chaos of the battles in Kansas where the war against slavery was being waged by a few men and women, supported by money and arms from friends in the north. This, the inaugural convention, was held in Philadelphia's Musical Fund Hall on Locust Street between South 8th and 9th, about a block from Washington Square. The Kansas delegates, Sam Wood, Charles Branscombe, Martin Conway and Clarke Pomeroy were housed at the Harbor Hotel on South 4th and Spruce.

The men met in caucus in the dining room of the hotel on the afternoon of the 16th. Excitement saturated the smoke-filled room full of delegates from the northern states, all moving from group to group, greeting old friends, meeting new ones. At some point in the evening each delegate gravitated toward the Kansas table to discuss the tenuous situation on the frontier.

Sam and Pomeroy spent part of that morning in private discussion of the Sack of Lawrence, as the attack was now being called, and the embarrassing gift of the 'Old Sacramento Cannon' to Jones and Atchison. He made peace with Pomeroy preferring not to pass judgement on a matter where a decision had to be made on the spot with no advice from other city officials. The problem was not the cannon, it was the corrupt Territorial Government, the men who represented special interests in Washington, D.C., especially the slave states. Pomeroy vowed to get the cannon back and hinted that plans were being made for that mission.

Unable to sleep that night, Sam, Abe Lincoln of Illinois, Charles Adams of Massachusetts and Salmon Chase of Ohio sat talking until early in the morning.

"Sam, Philadelphia has changed, hasn't it? The Irish and Germans have turned this into a Catholic town, the Quaker's are the minority now," Adams said, lighting a cigar, his glass of wine close at hand.

"Changed dramatically, Charles. We drove through the new row houses on the south side yesterday. Somebody is making a lot of money off those," Sam moved his chair out of the billowing smoke. "By the way, I've been meaning to read the biography about your father, just haven't had time."

"Not my father, Sam. It's about John Adams, my grandfather."

Salmon fanned the smoke away from his face, noting that Adams didn't seem to care where he blew it, "Charles, you've got so many illustrious ancestors, it's hard to keep track."

"What do you know about the latest John Brown incident?" Lincoln asked, stretching his long legs, eyes half closed under his thick brows.

Sam shook his head in frustration, "The newspapers have been fairly accurate. I know the Brown family is on the rampage. I got a letter from Owen day before yesterday. Evidently Henry Pate was part of the group that sacked Lawrence, in fact, he said that Pate is the one who burned my house, personally. I don't doubt it, he hates me. He's been harassing me since the rescue of Branson. I understand that Atchison or Jones got him appointed a U.S. Marshall, then when the Browns killed the Pottawattamie men, he took it on himself to capture Brown."

Chase interrupted, "The paper's made it sound like Brown turned the tables on Pate. He was just rescuing his son's, wasn't he?"

"Pate had captured two of Brown's sons," Abe confirmed.

"Yes, John, Jr. and Jason," Sam clarified.

"Was anyone killed in that skirmish?" Adams asked taking a large drink of wine, holding his glass up for a refill. The waiter scurried off for the bottle.

"No one was killed but a few of Pate's men were injured. Brown is a master tactician," Sam explained, "he only had eight or nine men while Pate had twenty-five. Someone called it the Battle of Blackjack but they were in Palmyra not BlackJack, not that it matters."

"Where is that in relation to Lawrence," Abe questioned.

"About twelve miles south and east. Not far. Here, listen to this, I got a letter from Fred Douglass, he has a man among Brown's troops that keeps him informed. This kind of sums it up,

With only eight men he met, fought, whipped, and captured Henry Pate who had twenty-five well-armed and well-mounted men. In this battle he selected his ground so wisely, handled his men so skillfully, and attacked his enemies so vigorously, that they could neither run nor fight, and were therefore compelled to surrender to a force less than one-third their own."

"I take it Mr. Douglass condones Brown's actions," Abe made it a statement rather than a question.

"He does," Sam nodded, "Brown is a fanatic, but he gets things done. I worry that he is going to do something that goes beyond the battles in Kansas. He believes that we will never end slavery through politics and negotiation. I agree with him. I don't necessarily like his tactics, but I won't try to make him stop."

"I don't believe we've heard the last of Mr. Brown," Abe said stretching his arms, drawing his legs up, knees almost to his chin.

"Nor do I," Salmon sighed, "I guess we'd better turn in, busy day tomorrow."

"Sal," Sam signaled them to wait a moment, "I'm scheduled to address the general assembly at 2. I'll nominate you; you immediately rise and decline the nomination. I assume that Sumner will do the same. Abe, I understand that you'll be the vice-president elect, is that true."

"I won't turn it down if nominated," he yawned.

Chase added, "Sam, the convention is going to want to hear you fellows from Kansas give the low down on what's happening out there."

"We discussed it at length earlier this evening. Pomeroy and I will give our usual summary of what's happened so far, Branscombe will summarize the Emigrant Aide Society situation and Martin will make the pitch for financial support. Some good news, I just heard that Mr. Eldridge is going to rebuild the hotel."

"If Fremont wins the nomination, which I expect," Lincoln said, "the South will scream sectionalism and we'll have a difficult time getting any votes from down there. I believe we're setting the stage for 1860; Salmon, the nomination will be yours for the asking."

"A lot can happen in four years, Abe."

Sam retired at four in the morning, slept a few hours, washed his face, put on the new blue shirt that Sally made for the occasion; was on his way to the Hall by eight for the nine AM meeting. He walked through Washington

Square, took notice that there was still not a monument of any kind for General Washington.

Someone hailed him from the other end of the park; Henry Lane, a delegate from Indiana, President of the convention. They strolled together, deep in discussion about various issues expected to become a part of the platform. They stopped on 9th street to allow a couple of carriages to pass, observed, for the first time, a large crowd gathered outside the Hall with guards checking credentials of the delegates. A shout went up from a rowdy gang on the north side of Locust Street; several rough looking characters began bellowing that they had found Sam Wood.

"Henry, this doesn't look good, you might want to walk over and see if the security detail can come help me, it looks like I'm outnumbered."

Lane eyeing the Ruffians, began edging away, "Discretion being the better part of valor, I'll take that advice, Sam." He hurried toward the police.

Sam stood his ground as the gang of five confronted him from the street, "Gentlemen," he said calmly, "to what do I owe the pleasure of your company?"

"You don't recognize me, you son-of-a bitch?" A tall, mustachioed man with a black bowler advanced with teeth gritted, his fists doubled, "I won't let you take me by surprise this time, Wood. I've been waiting for a chance to kill you for a long time."

It suddenly dawned on Sam who he faced. In the fall of 1854 this rough looking fellow had assaulted David in the Westport post office with the intention of drawing Sam into a fight. Sam had killed this man's buddy, Roland LeCount, the very man who had murdered Sam's good friend, Felix Francis. "Why, hello Moose, how in the world are you? I see that you chose the east route from the options I gave you, after I beat you senseless."

"You cheated, you asshole, anyway, that had nothin' to do with it. I knew you'd be back to Philadelphia. I missed you when you were here last month, but I read that you'd be here for this. Too bad you ain't gonna' be able to participate."

"I plan on addressing the convention on two occasions, but I doubt I can get you an invitation, Moose, they have certain intelligence requirements, you can see those gentlemen checking credentials at the door," Sam glanced toward the security detail.

"You bastard," Moose roared, "No wonder everyone hates you, you smart mouthed son-of-a-bitch. You never even got arrested for killing Roland."

"He murdered a fine young man, a friend of mine. I wanted him alive, just so I could see him hang for what he did."

"I'm done talking," Moose took a step forward as did his gang.

Sam tried to stall a bit longer, a crowd had gathered including some of the delegates, but no sign of security, "Very eloquently spoken, Moose, but wait a minute, you need to draw your gun, who has the pistol? I know this coward wouldn't be without one because I already whipped him once."

One of the gang, with a heavy Irish brogue said, "Jasus, man, you're outnumber five to one, why would we need a gun?"

Had the gang stayed in a tight group they probably would have overpowered him, but they began to spread out, intent on a surrounding tactic, which was a mistake. Moose took a step forward, lashed out with the leaded, butt end of a snake whip and slashed Sam on the neck; He recoiled in surprise, dropped down, feinted the same move he'd used in Westport, reversed course and struck Moose on the side of the head dropping him in his tracks. He spun left, broke the next man's arm, cracked the Irishman in the ribs and by then the others were having second thoughts about their strategy. Suddenly, whistles, shouts; officers in uniform came charging into the fight causing the able-bodied Ruffians to abandon the scene, billy-club officers hot in pursuit.

Pomeroy and Martin rushed up hoping to be of help, but the festivities were over by the time they arrived, "Sam, did you stage this for the benefit of the delegates?" Martin laughed.

Pomeroy added, "Good way to drum up sympathy for the cause."

Sam picked up his valise, "Not the way I wanted to start the convention. I hope this doesn't get back to Margaret," he checked the extent of his wound, "Oh no," when he noticed the blood on his new shirt.

"You'll elicit more sympathy with that," Martin said.

"That's a good visual of the bloodshed we've faced," Pomeroy used a handkerchief to blot the blood.

The commander of the Security detachment asked Sam for a report of what had happened, "Three men are seriously injured here."

Henry Lane took the official aside explained that Sam's actions were self-defense. All Sam wanted was to find a wash basin to clean the blood. At the door he began to remove his documentation from the valise; the Sergeant-at-Arms waved him through, "That club is identification enough for me, Mr. Wood," with a flourish of his hat and a slight bow.

"I can never acknowledge the right of slavery. I will bow down to no deity however worshipped by professing Christians - however dignified by the name of the Goddess of Liberty, whose footstool is the crushed necks of the groaning millions, and who rejoices in the resoundings of the tyrant's lash, and the cries of his tortured victims."
THADDEUS STEVENS, House of Representatives from Pennsylvania and Delegate to 1856 Republican National Convention

Rumor quickly spread that the confrontation was an organized protest by South Carolina Representative Preston Brooks, the man who beat Sumner with his cane. No matter how often Sam explained the truth of the matter, that the man had a personal grudge against him, the newspapers spun the story as a southern disruption against the anti-slavery plank of the Republican Platform. He confided in a letter to Margaret that Atchison or Jones was behind the attack. The idea that Moose had the forethought or harbored that big a grudge seemed a bit far-fetched; without proof, he preferred to explain it as a personal matter.

The convention agenda advanced without incident. Few surprises resulted from the various committees and nominations as they progressed through the busy day. Sam nominated Salmon Chase for the Presidential nomination; Chase immediately rose to give an inspiring speech that helped solidify his position as one of the primary movers and shakers in the Republican Party, but he was obliged to decline the nomination in favor of 'his good friend and fellow abolitionist, John Fremont.' The same tactic was used by the supporters of William Seward, Governor from New York, and Charles Sumner, Senator from Massachusetts, recent National media sensation from the caning by Representative Brooks.

Several cynical Senators claimed that Sumner's ascendancy was due to the caning notoriety rather than his contributions to the anti-slavery cause. His injuries were still apparent and Sam, for one, sympathized with the man, stating that he had done more for the cause by taking the beating than his speech in the Senate Chamber.

Sam mounted the podium, next day, wearing the same bloodied shirt, his jaw and neck covered in white bandages, holding the cane high in defiance, shouting that Kansas abolitionists would never back down. He kept the delegates on the edge of their seats for more than two hours describing the situation in the Territory and what plans they had for using the ballot box to make Kansas a free state. The recent violent events made John Brown a household word throughout the Union. Sam attempted to sugarcoat the impact he had on the events in Kansas explaining, as much as possible, that Brown was acting on his own and not with the permission of the Free State Legislature. On the 19th the *New-York Daily Times* carried a story picked up by all the newspapers reporting that "Samuel Newitt Wood, was the Lion of the Evening." Clarke Pomeroy reinforced that idea in his 30-minute follow-up speech.

John Fremont won the Presidential Nomination on the first ballot. The battle for Vice-President was a bit longer with William Dayton of New Jersey gaining the nod over Abraham Lincoln of Illinois. The Kansas Delegation pledged their support for 'Pathfinder' Fremont whose slogan, 'Free Soil, Free Men and Fremont' best described the tenants of the Republican cause and their platform summarized as: No slavery in any state or territory in the Union; Free land for farmers on the frontier; No plural marriages in the Mormon Religion; Accept Kansas as a State and drop all bogus indictments against the leaders of the Free State movement; And restore the action of the Federal Government to the principles of Washington and Jefferson.

***

On the afternoon of the 19th, the Kansas delegation met with Fremont, his wife, Jessie, and John Bigelow, campaign manager, in one of the antechambers of the Fund Hall. Bigelow was ostensibly Fremont's manager, but everyone knew that Jessie was the de facto power behind the throne. She was much more proficient in politics than her husband, considering that she had grown up in the middle of some of the most important political intrigues of the time, her father was Missouri Senator, Thomas Hart Benton.

"Lion of the Evening, eh Sam," Fremont said straddling a chair, resting his arms on the backrest preserving his image as a rugged man of the outdoors.

"Sam deserves all the praise he gets," Branscombe said.

"Mr. Wood, I've heard so much about your wife, Margaret, I wish she could have joined us here so that I could meet her," Jessie Fremont strode into the group with a poise born of many meetings where she was the only lady in the room.

"I miss her greatly, Mrs. Fremont, but someone has to run things in the territory while I'm gone," Sam laughed.

"Mrs. Wood is a very capable woman and a blessing to all of us in Kansas," Pomeroy added, "I suppose you heard about her exploits during the siege, dashing through the enemy lines for kegs of powder."

"That and her wonderful letter in the paper about the sheriff burning down the hotel. I hear they burned your home as well," Fremont added.

"They did, but we're in the process of rebuilding in a different location."

An assistant interrupted to take drink orders. Sam and Jessie drank water, the rest whiskey.

"We want to do everything in our power to get you elected, John," Martin said with agreement from the other delegates, "So we've devised a strategy that we'd like to discuss with you..."

"And, of course, your lovely wife and campaign manager," Branscombe added awkwardly.

Pomeroy took the initiative, outlined the crux of the Kansas strategy, "Mr. Branscombe, Mr. Martin and I will return to Lawrence. We're not under an indictment of any kind..."

"At least that we're aware of," Martin laughed.

"Precisely," Pomeroy continued, "we'll resume sending dispatches and working toward a legitimate vote for a Territorial Government. Meanwhile, Sam will stay here and conduct the Fremont campaign on behalf of all Kansas supporters. It would be disastrous for him to return now with the hostility of the sheriff, Senator Atchison and Governor Shannon."

"Not to mention President Pierce," Fremont added.

"He's the worst of all," Pomeroy agreed.

Branscomb continued, "We've tentatively set a date of July 4 for the Topeka Legislature to meet. Charlie Robinson has been elected Governor."

"Let's get through that test and see how Shannon and Pierce respond," Fremont said.

Sam added, "I believe there will be problems at the Topeka meeting, probably best that I'm not there," then looking at Jessie Fremont, "I plan on having Margaret and the kids join me in a few weeks. I assume you'll be staying at your home in New York." Sam waited for her acknowledgment before continuing carefully, "Will your illustrious father be supporting John's campaign?"

Fremont answered for his wife, "Father Benton has been a Jacksonian Democrat all his life and we don't expect him to change his feathers now; no, Sam, my father-in-law will vote straight Democratic ticket and he'll campaign for James Buchanan."

Jessie stood, placed her hand on Fremont's shoulder, "It's a difficult situation, Dad has completely changed his position on slavery. He wants to end it as badly as we do, but he won't forsake his party this late in life."

Sam understood, "I will be working full time on your campaign, I'd like to have Gabe Pennington as my assistant," he addressed Jessie.

"You can use whoever you want, we'll coordinate the dates, the venues and you handle your own logistics for getting there plus accommodations, work with Mr. Bigelow on the expense reimbursement."

Bigelow added, "Sam, we think that you should focus on the states from Ohio west, but there will be times when we'll need your Kansas perspective in the east. You'll work with Abe in Illinois, Oliver Morton in Indiana and, of course, Kirkwood in Iowa."

"I met Mr. Morton yesterday, I look forward to working with him," Sam replied.

The convention ended on that positive note. Sam felt especially confident about working with the Fremont's although they would not be actively campaigning themselves.

He spent the evening writing letters, the first to Margaret instructing her to bring the children and leave for Ohio as soon as possible. He wrote to Tap and John T, outlined the Fremont Strategy and made arrangements to deposit the Gerrit Smith funds into the Lawrence bank account. Sam had mixed feelings about what he was doing, missing the action in Kansas, but he took Salmon's words to heart, the battle would be won at the ballot box, not by gun and club.

***

I am a member of this body (republican party). Therefore, sir, I shall neither fawn nor cringe before any party, nor stoop to beg I am here to demand my rights, and to hurl thunderbolts at the men who would dare to cross the threshold of my manhood.

HENRY MCNEAL TURNER (1834-1915), Bishop of the African Methodist Episcopal Church and member of the Republican Party.

No one, within the Republican Party, threw themselves into the campaign more than Sam, knowing as he did the devastating effect Democratic President Franklin Pierce had on the crusade to prevent slavery in Kansas. Northern abolitionists were somewhat naïve after passage of the Kansas-Nebraska Act believing that the concept of Popular Sovereignty was real. The Washington power brokers assumed that slaveholders would dominate Kansas voting and once it became apparent that the abolitionists meant to make a fight of it, President Pierce removed the kid gloves, used all the resources of the Federal Government to stymie the Free State agenda. The new Democratic Presidential Nominee, James Buchannan, would be just as bad, if not worse.

Sam dedicated the summer and fall of 1856 to the campaign trail. Fremont left the campaigning to Republican celebrities; staying, for the most part, at his picturesque home on Staten Island near the Clifton Ferry, at the mouth of the Hudson River; entertaining lavishly, personally paying for everything with the gold money from his California ranch, Las Mariposas.

He confided to Sam, in one of their strategy meetings that Las Mariposas wasn't the property he had intended to buy. In 1848, he sent $3,000 to an intermediary, Thomas Larkin, who was US consul to the California Territory, with instructions to purchase a ranch near San Francisco. Larkin, for some unknown reason, purchased former California Governor, Juan B. Alvarado's 10,000-acre land grant near Yosemite. It was part of the Miwok Indian tribal land and they were a hostile crowd, not disposed toward any intruders. Fremont wanted to void the sale, buy a ranch closer to San Francisco; but before he could act, the California Gold Rush took hold and his ranch became one of the wealthiest holdings in the state. Fremont was born with a good luck charm around his neck; he and his wife became fantastically wealthy.

"Sometimes it's better to be lucky than smart," Sam chuckled at the story, "my good luck comes in dodging bullets, knives and fists. I wouldn't mind a little money luck someday."

"I may be able to help in that regard, Sam. You'll meet some pretty wealthy people next month when we have the rally at my house."

***

August 16 was a hot and humid day at the Fremont home where Sam, Margaret and the children were staying for a week of meetings and parties with various politicians, businessmen and donors. That Saturday evening the air cooled as the sun moved toward the horizon, tables were set on the beautiful lawn slopping from the large Victorian house to the water. Jessie invited a number of New York luminaries to meet the hero of the Bleeding Kansas battle against slavery. Horace Greeley,

Cornelius and Billy Vanderbilt, even John Cisco, who was a Democrat, on President Pierce's cabinet in the Treasury Department.

It was a landmark evening for Sam as he met and became a friend of Commodore Vanderbilt who considered him a man's man, living the life that he would have liked had things been different. Several of the Vanderbilt daughters were in attendance, doted on by eight-year-old David Wood who had become somewhat of a celebrity himself attending the political rallies with his father, carrying a miniature club. He would stroll on stage flourishing it at appropriate moments causing the audience to go wild with enthusiasm for the pint-sized abolitionist. Margaret was a hit with all the ladies telling and re-telling her adventure through the enemy lines in the Wakarusa War and watching the danger firsthand at the Sacking of Lawrence.

By the end of the evening, the Wood Family was exhausted. They retired to their rooms occupying a full wing of the Fremont home; a luxury that was hard to ignore when contrasted with the rough life they lived on the Kansas frontier. After putting the boys to bed in an adjoining bedroom, Sam and Margaret snuggled into a big, soft feather bed in a room with a window looking out on the bay.

"You really hit it off with Mr. Vanderbilt, didn't you?" Margaret said.

"He's going to help us with some funds for Kansas and for the campaign. I didn't ask, he volunteered. I'll ask John, tomorrow if he had already said something to him or if it was spontaneous. Either way, we need the money. The campaign is costing a fortune and the funds aren't coming in as fast as we'd like."

"Times are difficult for most people. The country is suffering tough times, not like the people who were at the party tonight. Did you see the necklace Mrs. Cisco was wearing? I'll bet it cost two hundred and fifty dollars."

"Meg, I didn't know you wanted an expensive necklace. Are you disappointed I can't afford one for you?" he tickled her.

She squirmed, laughed; held his hands, "Not for a second. You're all I need to make me happy, you and the boys; Oh, and the new daughter I'm carrying."

Sam was still laughing, "David was a big hit with the Vanderbilt girls. I hope one of them has a daughter he can marry and get rich quick."

"Did you hear me, Sam?"

"What did you say?'

She took his hand, placed it on her stomach, "Your daughter will be here about Christmas."

"Oh my," he gripped both her hands, lay his head on her stomach, "the boys will be so excited about a new sister."   He offered a silent prayer, 'please don't disappoint her with a son'.

"Does anyone else know?"

"Just your mother."

"We'll tell the boys in the morning."

"And John and Jessie, I really like them, darling, I hope we can always be friends."

For the first time, in their married life, Margaret fell asleep first. Sam lay staring blankly out the window thinking about a new mouth to feed, the danger in Kansas, the uphill battle to get Fremont elected, plus he needed to make more money. The news from Charlie and Pomeroy was not good. The July 4th Topeka meeting had been disrupted by Federal Troops let by Colonel Sumner of Ft. Leavenworth. The troops shut down the meeting, ordered the delegates to disperse under threat of arrest. The newspaper reports resulted in a resounding protest from both the north and south decrying the use of Federal Troops to disrupt a legitimate meeting of United States citizens.

The Fremont campaign issued a press release condemning the action in the harshest of terms. President Pierce replied that he would declare martial law in Kansas if the free-state men should persist in pursuing their anti-slavery agenda. Sam felt that he should return to Kansas and support his friends, but Charlie, Tap, Judge Wakefield, Clarke Pomeroy, all insisted that he was more effective working to bring new voters to Kansas than he would be dodging Bogus Jones and his posse.

He turned from the window, watched Margaret sleep, a delicate smile brightened by a beam of moonlight. He brushed a wisp of hair from her forehead and closed his eyes.

***

A long letter from Clarke Pomeroy reached the Woods on the 15th of August. With the lamp turned low, the children in bed, Sam read portions of it to Margaret.

Sam, much of the following you probably know. I won't detail the rampages of John Brown, that has been well reported in the papers. Troops from Ft. Leavenworth continue to 'enforce' the laws of the bogus legislature, terrorizing everyone in Lawrence and Topeka. Jones is worse than ever holding open meetings vowing to wipe out all abolitionists in Kansas. We fully expect him to try and make good on his promise. Sentries are posted every night, but we are not well organized without you, Jim Lane and Charlie Robinson. Don't take this as a suggestion that you return. Stay in the east. You are a marvelous thorn in the side of Atchison and Jones, but don't let your guard down. Your whereabouts are reported constantly. Jones and Atchison have agents everywhere.

Here is a summary of The Topeka constitution which was presented to Congress asking admission as a State under its no-slavery provisions, early in March. On the 24th of that month it was presented in the Senate in due form by Lewis Cass, of Michigan, and referred to the proper committee. On April 7, it was presented to the House by Daniel Mace, of Indiana.

The House passed the bill but, of course, the Senate defeated it. That bastard (excuse my language), Stephen Douglas tried several different approaches. Basically, he created a new bill for the complete reorganization of the Territory requiring a new census. The Senate passed it but, of course, the House rejected it.

The army appropriation bill failed to pass, except with a proviso that the United States Army should not be used for the enforcement of the Territorial laws in Kansas. That failed to pass, as we've already seen with the Army running amuck in Kansas.

In summary, we will receive no direction from Washington. We are on our own. We will continue to fight for our rights in the courtroom, the voting rooms and the battlefield.

Your progress is easy to follow in the newspapers. Send news of your family. Mrs. Pomeroy asks about Margaret's health.

Clarke

The campaign kept Sam and Gabe crossing the northern states at a whirlwind pace, often accompanied by the entire Wood family. Margaret became a favorite at book clubs and coffee klatches. David and Punch were tremendous assets to the Free State cause describing life on the frontier from a child's perspective. Large crowds greeted them in all the larger cities, sometimes two rallies in one day, but they didn't neglect the whistle-stop depots, well aware of the happenings in Kansas through the rapidly growing newspaper reports and the expansion of the telegraph.

Former Whig President Millard Filmore was running as a third-party candidate for the American Party. Sam was concerned that Filmore would steal votes benefitting Fremont. He met several times with Filmore, in Springfield, with Abe Lincoln, in Indianapolis with Oliver Morton, all to no avail as Fillmore was in favor of slavery in the southern states; felt that the election of Fremont would cause the south to secede. He was probably right.

Events in Kansas continued to dominate the news. Sam's neighbor and good friend, Samuel Walker led a large force of Kansas Calvary against Henry Titus' well-fortified home on August 16 using the 'old Sacramento Cannon' which had been recaptured from the Border Ruffians. The Free State men killed several of the pro-slavery forces and captured others. The newspapers had a field day with the information that the cannonballs used in the bombardment of Ft. Titus had been made from the type from the newspaper offices destroyed during the Sacking of Lawrence.

Sam read the following article aloud to Gabe.

"Col. Titus was wounded in the head and shoulder, another of his men was wounded, and two others killed. There were six wounded on the Free-State side. Col. Titus had taken an active part in the Sack of Lawrence, and on that day publicly declared, That if he ever came into that place again he would kill every Abolitionist in it. Some of the prisoners taken with him participated in this sack and assisted in destroying the presses of the Herald of Freedom and throwing the type in the river. The cannon balls used in firing at the cabin of Col. Titus were made of the lead melted down from the type of those presses, dug from the sand on the bank of the river; and as they plowed their way through the walls of Titus's cabin, they shrieked, Surrender to Freedom! as they sped on their way. Capt. Bickerton, when he pointed his cannon at the walls of the cabin, calmly announced that he should give them a new edition of the Herald of Freedom. Col. Titus, instead of coming to kill Abolitionists, came whiningly begging of the Abolitionists to save his miserable life. He was supplied with comfortable quarters, and

a physician to attend him. The other prisoners were confined in the Herald of Freedom building, where, on the 21st of May, some of them thought they had struck a deathblow to the freedom of speech, with the blood-red banner of South Carolina disunion waving over them. How strange the contrast! Yet such is the fortune of war."

New York Times correspondent, 1856

The first week of September, Sam, Gabe and David arrived in Chicago for a rally and meetings with several Republican dignitaries. Abe Lincoln, Allan Pinkerton, Amos Alcott, David Anthony, among others attended the events. The evening of the seventh found them sitting in Pinkerton's comfortable home discussing the news from the Territory.

"Amos, so good to see you again," Sam said to Alcott, "How is your lovely wife and daughters, what do you have, three, four?"

"I'm blessed with four, Mr. Wood, I call them my Little Women and they are a blessing, headstrong though they are. Thankfully Mrs. Alcott has a strong mother's control over them, or I would be overwhelmed," he smiled weakly, suffering from fatigue caused by the journey from the east.

"We're about to have our third and it better be a girl or I'll never hear the end of it," Sam looked at David, "Will we son?"

"Mother has her heart set."

"I've followed your adventures in Kansas pretty closely," Alcott continued.

"I'm afraid that I'm a bit too close to those adventures, right Sam," David Anthony said.

"What are you doing in Chicago, Dave?"

"Susan's having a rally here next week and I promised to handle the publicity for her," meaning his famous sister, Susan B. Anthony.

"When did you leave Leavenworth?"

"Two days ago. Things are still in an uproar in Lawrence and Topeka over Col. Sumner disrupting the Free State meeting."

"I'm sure the Ruffians are ecstatic," Sam answered.

Lincoln said, "Do you miss being in the action, Sam?"

"I miss the fact that I'm not helping my friends. I don't necessarily miss the violence because I think so much of it is unnecessary. As Margaret said, if this isn't Civil War, I don't know what is. My heart goes out to Brown..."

Pinkerton interrupted, "The rumor is that two of his sons were killed. Have you heard anything different?"

"The last letter I received from Tappan said that two of the boys had been captured and were being held at Ft. Sacket, the same place Charlie Robinson is a prisoner. The youngest son, Frederick Brown was killed in Osawatomie. John didn't save the community from being pillaged; he lost a son, but he killed quite a few of the enemy and enhanced his reputation. As far as I'm concerned, this is war, gentlemen."

"John wrote me last week asking for more money," Pinkerton said.

"We're all short of money," Sam replied, "Especially when compared to the Ruffians. The Slaveholders don't seem to be hurting."

"Well, you made a good friend in Vanderbilt," Pinkerton laughed.

"I see where the Ruffians burned Judge Wakefield's house last week," Lincoln said.

"Wake lost everything. He's staying in our new house on Henry Street while they build a new one. Daniel Woodson's the acting Governor. I think Pierce has panicked and is urging the pro-slavery forces to do anything they can to kill abolitionists before the election. He fired Shannon; Woodson won't do any better."

Pinkerton said, "You'd think that Pierce would see the handwriting on the wall, he keeps appointing pro-slavery Governors and they fail because there are more free-state votes than pro-slavery. They'll have to give in at some point."

"After the Presidential election and I get back there, we'll hold a free and valid Territorial vote and verify every voter as being a Kansas resident. That will be the turning point."

***

Sam arrived in Columbus in November to await the election results with his family. Buchannan won the popular referendum with over 1,800,000 votes to Fremont's 1,300,000. Filmore received 873,000 most of which would have gone to Fremont if Filmore would have bowed out of the race. Buchannan received 174 electoral votes to Filmore's 114. The consensus being that Fremont did better than anyone expected, and most of the credit went to Sam. It was strange that Fremont didn't even carry his home state of California where he was either loved or hated and it looked like more people hated him than he thought.

***

November 1, 1856
Lawrence, Kansas Territory
Sam,

I hope this finds you and your family of good health. The Mrs. and I are well. I continue to have the stomach problems that have plagued me for some time. I have taken to a blander diet and that seems to be helping although I don't enjoy eating any more. I suppose that is a good thing. I've been following the campaign in the papers and hope that Fremont can make a strong showing, but I have my doubts. The south will vote in a bloc and Buchannan is well entrenched there. Filmore's involvement will hurt the Republican cause. It is going to be four more years of turmoil here in the Territory. I will be mighty glad when you get back. We miss your steady hand. Charlie is out of jail thanks to Governor Geary. General Lane is working to bring more citizens through Iowa and Nebraska. The Border Ruffians burned my house, but we are rebuilding.

Our little experiment drew fruit. Bogus Jones showed up at Abbotts house at the time designated in the letter you sent to Margaret. I had a postal inspector with me by the name of Howser. He was brought up to speed about our little trick; he, Tap, Major Abbott and I waited patiently to see what would happen. About 15 minutes after the appointed time, Jones and his deputies surrounded the house and called for "the criminal Sam Wood to surrender." We all stepped outside to a reception of pistols and rifles. Jones searched the house. Mr. Howser asked him point blank, "Why did you expect to find Sam Wood here?"

He hemmed and hawed, "Someone told us." "Who?" Howser asked, and he refused to answer. Howser said that he was going to Federal Deputy Donaldson and file a complaint against Jones for tampering with the US mail.

I wish you could have seen the look on Jones' face. He would have murdered us all if other witnesses hadn't gathered by that time. Of course, nothing has come of it because I would imagine that Shannon and Donaldson were in on the little scheme, but the Federal government has been put on notice and I don't think they'll be reading our mail anymore. Jones is losing his popular support around here. He's becoming more of a liability than an asset.

We'll deal with it further when you get back. Hurry home, Sam.

Your friend,
John. A. Wakefield

As soon as the election was over, Sam, David and Punch traveled to Cincinnati; booked a berth on the Lexington bound for St. Louis. Margaret stayed in

Columbus with her mother and mother-in-law to await the birth of the baby. The travelers hoped to arrive in Kansas by December 10. Letters were written to John T asking him to meet them in Westport on that date.

Lawrence had grown in the six months they were gone. A new butcher shop, restaurant and even a saloon had sprung up since Sam fled north to avoid the sheriff waving his warrants for treason. As far as he knew, he was still under indictment.

After the destruction of their house during the Sack of Lawrence, Margaret had contracted to build a new home on Henry Street in West Lawrence. Also living on the property were Margaret's parents, Bill and Elizabeth Lyon, John, Sally, Caleb, Missy, Beulah and Silas.

The week of December 12 turned off bitterly cold. Sam worked around the property gathering firewood, caulking the windows and doors, trying to make the house cozy for when Margaret returned with the new baby. He wrote every day, she answered just as loyally. The inhabitants of the Wood property gathered each evening in one or the other of the houses to sit around the fire talking, knitting, reading or sometimes playing cards. They were good friends as well as close neighbors. Sam missed Margaret terribly as did David and Punch. Heavy snow began falling on the 15th and didn't stop until the 18th. Getting to and from the barn to feed the animals required digging tunnels. Everyone had to pitch in just to survive. It looks like they were going to be snowed in for Christmas.

David and Punch loved their new home where everyone lived close by. They spent a lot of time with their grandfather, Bill Lyon and partner, Silas. Both men were excellent farmers, had worked together for many years back in Ohio. The claims they held, Bill and Sam, were each 160 acres with timbered land along the river bottom, farmland into the hills located between Lecompton and Lawrence.

Margaret was anxious to get back home but there was no sign of the baby by early January. The thought of a Christmas present bundle of joy was set aside, as time passed, with worry of Margaret's health growing more every day. Sam gave serious thought to returning to Ohio, but her letters persuaded him otherwise. One positive side effect of the snowstorm was that Sam didn't have to worry about Sheriff Jones.

***

On January 10 Sam was finally able to make his way to Lecompton and meet with Governor John Geary, appointed in August by President Pierce to replace Shannon. Geary was assumed to be pro-slavery, but he quickly assessed the serious problems in the territory and became passionate about creating a safe environment for the true Kansas citizens. A state of affairs that was far from true when he arrived, and one that did not agree with his superiors in Washington. He greeted Sam as a long-lost friend even though they had never met. Charlie joined them to discuss making another attempt to ratify the Topeka Constitution in the U.S. Congress.

"I doubt that will happen with Buchannan as President," Geary said. "I sure wish you would have been successful in getting Fremont elected, Sam, even though it would have meant Civil War." Geary towered over his visitors; six feet six inches heavily bearded with deep-set dark eyes that conveyed a seriousness not to be argued with. He served well in the Mexican American War rising to the rank of Colonel. After the war he was appointed Postmaster of San Francisco by President Polk, then elected Mayor of that city prior to replacing Shannon in Kansas Territory.

"War is inevitable, Governor, it's not a matter of if, it's a matter of when. In fact, as far as I'm concerned, the events in Kansas are the opening shots."

"I'm beginning to believe war will be the only way to end slavery," Charlie shook his head.

"I've heard wonderful reports of how you've calmed the situation here, Governor," Sam got up and put his coat back on; the cold wind was seeping through the windows, "but it sounds like Judge LeCompte has gone totally over to the pro-slavery side."

"Charlie has heard this story, Sam, but I'll repeat it for you. On my way here the boat stopped in Glasgow, Missouri to board a squadron of Missouri volunteers going to Kansas. Without revealing who I was I asked them, 'Why are you going to Kansas'. All they seemed to understand about the matter, was, that they were to receive a per diem from the state for going to Kansas to hunt and kill Abolitionists. They had been told that Abolitionists killed a number of Missouri citizens, and they were hired to revenge their deaths."

"Who told them that," Sam frowned, "Atchison?"

"I guess so. I'm not sure, more than that they neither knew nor seemed to care to know. Then I asked them what they knew about these Abolitionists, who were they? Because I was getting the distinct impression they didn't know. And they didn't. They had an ambiguous notion that, whatever an Abolitionist was, it was a virtue to kill him and take possession of his property. There was no danger to themselves, they were told, because Abolitionists would not fight. They would run away, leaving behind their land, horses, clothing, guns, everything they owned, all of which was to be divided among the Missouri boys."

Geary paused to take a sip of water. Sam threw his head back in frustration, "My God, Charlie, the politicians are lying to those men for political gain. They're using them as tools to eliminate the free-state vote."

Geary continued, "While we were in Glasgow a downstream boat docked next to us and guess who was on board?"

Sam shrugged, "Don't know, who?"

"Ex-Governor Wilson Shannon, and he was a fright running for his life, literally. I've never seen such an unnerved man. The Border Ruffians, Atchison, Jones all threatened to kill him, and they meant it. He briefed me as best he could under the circumstances and his words conveyed a situation much worse than what I expected. He told me the whole Territory was in a state of insurrection, and a civil war was devastating the country. Murder ran rampant, and the roads were everywhere strewn with the bodies of slaughtered men. No language can overstate the awful picture that he drew. I doubted the truth of the matter. He was distraught, exaggerating... had to be. I just couldn't imagine it being that bad."

Geary leaned back, put his long legs comfortably on the desk, something Governor Shannon never would have done. He pointed his finger out the window, "It didn't take long, just the trip from Leavenworth City to here in Lecompton and I knew he was right. There were roaming gangs of men looking for someone to rob, but there were no prospects except for me. Thank God for my military escort. Every farmhouse was burned or burning, no settlers in sight; they had all gathered for safety in the villages. It looked like a battlefield. I called the leaders of these so-called militia groups together and told them to disband immediately. That was in September. It took until November to get any kind of compliance."

Geary stood to pour himself another glass of water, offered the same to Sam and Charlie. William materialized to take the pitcher for a refill. He nodded to Sam with just a hint of an approving smile.

Charlie added, "We've been in constant turmoil. Families like Harold Barnett have been able to hold off the looters because they have the weapons and manpower, but most families just up and left. Sam, they murdered David Buffam."

"No! Why?"

Geary scowled, "Stole his mule from him right out of the field. He protested, so they shot him. We just happened to be passing that way, he was still alive when we got there."

Sam shook his head, "David was a good friend. He was one of the men who smuggled the canon into Lawrence."

Geary shook his head, "I didn't know that. I've never been so disgusted with human beings in my life. Killed him for a mule. I've issued a writ for the arrest of the murderer, Charles Hays from Atchison, but no one has found him yet; if anyone is really looking. We've also issued a warrant for George Clarke, the man who murdered Tom Barber."

"Finally! What about Frank Colman, the fool who murdered Chuck Dow?"

"No sign of him. Rumor is he left for California."

Sam stood and paced, "I can't tell you how much I appreciate your actions. What can we do to help?"

"By the way, gentlemen, did you know that Sheriff Jones retired last month?"

Sam stopped walking, looked at Charlie, "Not a clue."

"I had no idea," Charlie echoed.

"I actually fired the fool, but we gave him the chance to submit his letter of resignation."

"What in the world happened?" Charlie asked.

Geary laughed, "I didn't like the man the first time I set eyes on him. He was obsessed with bringing all the outlaws to justice."

"Meaning me, I guess?"

"You and Jim Lane. Charlie was still in jail at the time. Plus, there was the tampering with the mail situation. When you came back, Sam, he came to me with a requisition to purchase... here, let me read the requisition to you."

The Governor took a paper from his desk, "He makes the usual salutation and so on and so forth... Ah, here it is, 'I have it on good authority that Sam Wood is back in the Territory. I can also put my hands-on Charlie Robinson who was illegally released from jail by Governor Shannon before his term was up, and I can arrest J. B. Tappan in Lawrence. Therefore, I request funds in the amount of... and he left it blank, 'to purchase sets of ball and chain in order to secure the said criminals, all guilty of Treason'."

"Ball and chain? Does he think this is 1700?" Charlie laughed.

"Well, I hate to say it but I'm going miss him. He made life pretty exciting the past few years," Sam sat back down, slapped Charlie on the knee, "how about them apples?"

Geary held his hand up to protest, "Don't get too excited, gentlemen. The man the Douglas County Council wants me to approve as the new sheriff, a fellow by the name of William T. Sherrard, is a worse villain than Jones.

He already threatened to kill me if I don't approve his appointment. He is going to cause this territory a great deal of trouble. He should be in prison instead of up for public office. But the pro-slavery men want him as sheriff."

"What can we do to help you, John?" Sam leaned forward, he liked Geary. Liked everything about him.

"I want to have a meeting here in Lecompton to discuss the entire situation as soon as the weather permits. I want all your free-state delegates to join us."

Charlie stood, grabbed his heavy coat, "We'll do whatever you ask."

"I understand you have another child on the way, Sam," Geary said.

"Yes, any day now. It better be a girl or I'll never hear the end of it." They shook hands, wishing each other a better new year than the last.

A new sign adorned the wall next to the door, "To make God laugh, tell him your plans". Sam chuckled, "Appropriate for Kansas isn't it, Governor."

Geary touched the stitching fondly, "My wife. She embroidered it when I left for the War."

They agreed to convene the Free-State legislature as soon as the snow cleared enough to get a quorum of delegates together for the next step in making Kansas a free state, at least from a legal standpoint. The battle with the Ruffians had no end in sight.

Charlie and Sam rode back to Lawrence, bundled to the eyes, muffled so that conversation was difficult in the howling wind. Sam turned off to his house. Charlie continued on the short distance to his new home, rebuilt on the same spot as the one Jones burned. He turned slightly, encumbered by his heavy coat, "Let us know when you hear about the baby. Sara and I have a bet on boy or girl," his words evaporated in the wind.

Sam shouted, "Which side did you take?" Charlie's answer disappeared along with Charlie into the blinding whiteness of the snow shrouded prairie.

About the Author

Henry E. Peavler

The author has a home in Texas, near his five children. Against all odds, he continues to write.

www.ingramcontent.com/pod-product-compliance
Lightning Source LLC
Chambersburg PA
CBHW070819190726
48292CB00006B/2051